Phenomenal Praise for
STEPHEN CANNELL and his Thrillers

"Cannell's brand of thriller is served straight up . . . and he knows how to cut to the chase."

—*The New York Times*

"A pro at the top of his game."

—Stephen Coonts

"Cannell leaves 'em begging for more."

—*Booklist*

WHITE SISTER

"Cannell dishes out the action in forklift-sized servings."
—*Publishers Weekly*

"[A] very satisfying thriller written by a born entertainer."
—*New York Post*

"A strong piece of fiction that leads readers . . . through the harrowing underbelly of L.A."

—*Daily News*

"One of the hallmarks of Cannell's writing is his ability to have characters who speak as real people would."
—*Sunday Journal* (Albuquerque, New Mexico)

"A terrific read."

—*New York Sun*

MORE . . .

COLD HIT

"As the case spirals outward from local crime to international espionage dating back to the 1980s, the action rarely lets up. When it does, we're reintroduced to the back story that is one of the pleasures of reading the Scully series."

—*Los Angeles Times*

"The action rarely lets up."

—*Chicago Tribune*

"A thriller, a procedural, and an indictment of the Patriot Act in the wrong hands. Scully, the plots, and the characters get better with each book."

—The Sunday *Oklahoman*

"If you are hungry for a great police procedural, look no further. Cannell knows what he's doing . . . this mystery works on every level."

—*Tulsa World*

"An intriguing, torn-from-today's-headlines premise on his fifth Shane Scully outing."

—*The News-Press* (Fort Myers, Florida)

VERTICAL COFFIN

"Readers will enjoy watching [Scully] puzzle out the twists and turns of the plot and watch breathlessly as he undertakes a climactic high-speed chase."

—*Publishers Weekly*

"Cannell certainly knows how to tell a story . . . You'll probably read the entire book with a smile on your face."

—*Cleveland Plain Dealer*

HOLLYWOOD TOUGH

"Cannell, creator of such TV shows as *The A-Team*, clearly knows the ins and outs of the entertainment industry, and the detective story, with its wry, subtle humor, doubles as Hollywood satire . . . the cops-and-robbers sequences hit the mark as well. Well-drawn characters and keen observations on the similarities between Hollywood and the mafia make this a winner."

—*Publishers Weekly*

"Scully has ample opportunity to prove how 'Hollywood tough' he is . . . veteran writer/TV producer Cannell has concocted his special brand of reader candy."

—*Kirkus Reviews*

RUNAWAY HEART

"A cop thriller with a futuristic, sci-fi twist . . . Cannell has a genius for creating memorable characters and quirky, gripping plots . . . this is a fun read."

—*Publishers Weekly*

THE VIKING FUNERAL

"Stephen J. Cannell is an accomplished novelist."

—*New York Daily News*

"Stephen J. Cannell's *The Viking Funeral* is the sort of fast and furious read you might expect from one of television's most successful and inventive writer-producers."

—*Los Angeles Times*

"Solid plotting with nail-biting suspense and multiple surprises keep the reader guessing and sweating right up to the cinematic ending . . . Cannell has a knack for characterization and a bent for drama that will satisfy even the most jaded thrill lover."

—*Publishers Weekly*

THE TIN COLLECTORS

"I've been a Stephen Cannell fan since his remarkable *King Con*, and he keeps getting better. *The Tin Collectors* is an LAPD story that possesses both heart and soul; a fresh and different look at the men and women who, even more than the NYPD, are the most media-covered police force in the world. Stephen Cannell has the screenwriter's fine ear for dialogue and great sense of timing and pacing as well as the novelist's gift of substance and subtlety. Cannell likes to write, and it shows."

—Nelson DeMille

"Cannell turns out another winding, suspenseful thriller."

—*New York Daily News*

"Readers who enjoy cop novels by Robert Daley or William Caunitz will find Cannell right up their dark, dangerous alley."

—*Booklist*

"Cannell has created a reputation for top-rate suspense in four novels . . . his latest, *The Tin Collectors*, is his best . . . Cannell . . . knows how to tell a good story."

—*Wisconsin State Journal*

"Cannell conjures up images of McBain, Wambaugh, and Heller; only tougher, grittier, more underhanded, with plenty of street-smart savvy, and a frightening and wholly believable plot and characters . . . crackles with high energy and suspense . . . Cannell is in top form."

—*Charleston Post & Courier*

"Compelling, frightening, and . . . very moving. Don't miss it. Cannell is a first-rate storyteller and *The Tin Collectors* never stops."

—Janet Evanovich

"Stephen Cannell has a chilling thought: What if the guys who police the police went bad? As in crooked? Then what? Then chaos, a message that comes through with decibels to spare in *The Tin Collectors*. This is classic Cannell: fast, full of action."

—*The Cincinnati Enquirer*

"In Shane Scully, Cannell brings the reader a dynamic new hero with promise of new adventures in the field of law and order."

—*Abilene Reporter-News*

"A sure winner . . . Cannell keeps the tension and pace at high levels."

—*St. Paul Star Tribune*

"Cannell is a great storyteller . . . a fresh and edgy story."

—*Buffalo News*

"Exciting . . . a fast-action tale that continues to build up momentum until the story line exceeds the speed of light."

—*The Midwest Book Review*

"Cannell's . . . best novel . . . begins with a bang and closes with one . . . a fast-paced well-told story."

—*The Osceola Magnifier*

WHITE SISTER

STEPHEN J. CANNELL

St. Martin's Paperbacks

This is a work of fiction. All of the characters, organizations, and events portrayed in this novel are either products of the author's imagination or are used fictitiously.

WHITE SISTER

Copyright © 2006 by Stephen J. Cannell.

Cover photo of woman © Josh Sheldon
Cover photo of palm trees © Stewart Cohen

Library of Congress Catalog Card Number: 2006043898

ISBN: 0-312-34736-7
EAN: 978-0-312-34736-9

Printed in the United States of America

St. Martin's Press hardcover edition / August 2006
St. Martin's Paperbacks edition / July 2007

St. Martin's Paperbacks are published by St. Martin's Press, 175 Fifth Avenue, New York, NY 10010.

10 9 8 7 6 5 4 3 2 1

*Shane is lucky to have Alexa
But I'm blessed to have Marcia
This one's for you, babe*

CHAPTER ONE

It was early evening on Thursday the first week of July and Alexa and I were walking through San Julian Park in Skid Row, on our way back from the LAPD Central Division Jail. Homeless men in tattered coats swung blood-shot eyes in our direction, tracking us like government radar. We were returning from a training day in jail transport procedures.

The retraining had been mandated after a Mara Salvatrucha gang-banger named Hector Morales got bludgeoned to death while shuffling on a drag line through the underground tunnel that connects the jail to the Fifth Street courthouse. A rival Hispanic gang-banger had done the work by somehow slipping out of his waist restraints and hitting Hector in the head with a cut-down chair leg from the jail cafeteria. He'd been hiding the weapon inside the leg of his orange jumpsuit.

The Professional Standards Bureau, our new, media-friendly name for the Internal Affairs Division, investigated. All supervisors and detectives above grade two were ordered to undergo a refresher day on incarceration and transfer tactics. Alexa and I were dressed in grubbies—jeans and old sweatshirts—but before we were twenty feet into the park, everybody there had made us for cops anyway.

"Tony says this surgery is no sweat, but you can tell he's

scared," Alexa was saying as we stepped carefully around some dog shit, a pile of trash, and a sleeping homeless couple. She was talking about the upcoming heart surgery our Chief of Police was scheduled to have tomorrow morning.

"Bypass surgery is getting to be pretty common," I offered. "It's natural to be scared, but he'll be okay."

Hollow words, considering Tony Filosiani was getting a complete coronary makeover. The surgeons were cutting his chest open, taking both mammary arteries, and grafting them around the four blocked arteries in his heart. Any way you looked at it, he was in for a tough ten days and wasn't scheduled back on the job for a couple of months.

"Is it me, or does this park smell worse than ever?" Alexa said, changing the subject. "Like a big outdoor latrine."

"July heat," I answered. "It always smells worse in the summer."

We walked past a line of portable toilets, which were called Alices by the people on the Row, because Alice Callahan of the Las Familias del Pueblo Community Center had badgered the city council until they finally funded their installation. In a vengeful act of municipal retaliation, the toilets were rarely cleaned out but nonetheless served both physical and commercial needs. A lot of drug and prostitution deals were consummated within the smelly three-foot confines of those portable johns.

"I'm gonna check my messages, see if I have a meeting that was supposed to be set up tonight," Alexa said. "Then if there's time, I'd like to run over to the hospital and see Tony on the way home." She stepped over a well-known park character named Horizontal Joe. He was huddled under a blanket stenciled with a W—a sure sign it was stolen from the Weingart Center on South San Pedro Street.

"Watch where you're goin'," Joe growled, without bothering to look up.

Parker Center loomed before us like a drifting glass iceberg; a huge box of a building with absolutely no architectural significance. One of the strange anomalies of Los Angeles was that the Central Division Jail and the Police Administration Building were contiguous to the city's fifty-square-block section of blight known as Skid Row. Some Parker Center cops felt it was easier to take the seven-block walk if you were headed toward the lock-up, rather than move your car out of the Glass House garage and look for nonexistent parking by the jail. As a result, the cops and homeless spent countless hours in mutual distrust as we shared the urine-soaked walkways and broken drinking fountains in San Julian Park.

Alexa and I stepped off the curb where an ageless man wearing tennis shoes with no laces and a greasy brown poncho was ranching quarters out of a parking meter, a practice known as spanging. He didn't even bother to stop. Most of these people had discovered by now that no cop worth his wage would waste two hours booking a guy at the jail over a twenty-five-cent misdemeanor.

"I hope Tony gets back on the job before two months," I groused. "I can't stand the thought of Great White Mike being in charge of the department." I had a recent and unrewarding history with Deputy Chief Michael Ramsey, who I viewed as little more than an ambitious power junkie in a braided hat.

"Mike's okay. Just a little jacked up," Alexa said, smiling slightly.

My wife is the head of the Detective Services Group. I'm a Detective III assigned to Homicide Special, so technically she's my boss. She's about to make captain and is three layers above me on the department flow chart. All of which means I get to put out the garbage on the job, as well as at home. Just kidding.

We finally left the squalor of Fifth Street, known as the Nickel, and headed toward the air-conditioned sanctuary of the Glass House. Brown burlap slowly gave way to starched blue as we entered the marble lobby. We got on the elevator, and since it was empty, I gave my beautiful wife a kiss. She has long black hair, high cheekbones, and is one of the most striking women I have ever come across. She could easily have made her living doing fashion shoots. I, on the other hand, look like I got emptied out of a vacuum cleaner. I'm five-eleven and a half, lean, and gristly. Topping this unholy collection of scars and medical mistakes is a hammered flat nose and short black hair that never quite lies down. All of this makes me resemble a club fighter who's stayed in the ring too long. It's a miracle Alexa ever agreed to marry me. But then, if Julia Roberts could once marry Lyle Lovett, I guess anything is possible.

The door opened on four and two young patrolmen got on, so we cut the funny stuff and I said good-bye.

"See you at home in about an hour and a half," Alexa said as I got off on that random floor and pushed the Down button for the parking garage.

Five minutes later I was in my freshly leased, silver Acura MDX, enjoying the new car smell as I headed out of the administration-building parking garage on my way home. A bleak landscape of urban blight and human misery passed by outside, but I was oblivious with the windows up and the AC on. I was in my sweet-smelling automotive capsule, immune to the reek and cries of the Row, thinking about Tony Filosiani.

In the last decade or so, the LAPD had experienced a run of disasters, from the Rodney King case to the Rampart scandal. Recently, we had been cleaning up the mess, and that was mostly because of Tony. Our chief arrived from Brooklyn four years ago and was known by the troops as the Day-Glo Dago because of his colorful, somewhat out-there personality and management style. I was worried about him and would have liked to go over to USC Medical Center where he was being prepped for surgery to let him know he was in my thoughts. But I'm just a Detective III, and somewhere deep in the reptilian part of my brain that processes police protocol, it felt like an ass-kiss, so I didn't go. It was different for Alexa. She was a division commander.

I was in a silent argument with myself over this dilemma when I took my eyes off the road to reach in my glove box and turn on my police scanner, which is mandated off-duty protocol.

As I switched to Tac One, I heard a loud crash and a thump. I jerked my eyes up just in time to see a Safeway shopping cart full of junk skitter across the street in front of me, spilling empty Evian bottles and useless debris everywhere. I stood on the brake pedal as I heard screaming.

I'd hit someone.

I piled out of the Acura and started to look for the pedestrian. Nothing in front. Nothing in back. Where the hell was he?

"Under here, you stupid muthafucka!" a man shrieked.

I kneeled down and looked. Wedged under my oil pan was one of the scrawniest, scruffiest men I have ever seen. Dusty black skin, dreadlocks, and a greasy, brown coat that looked like it had been used as the drop cloth under a lube rack.

"Look what you've done, you asshole!" the man screamed, holding his wrist. "Can't you watch where you're going?"

"You okay?" I stammered.

I reached under the car and tried to grab him by the shoulder to drag him out, but when I touched him, he started screaming louder.

"Whatta you want me to do?" I asked helplessly, wondering how to get him out from under there.

"Just get away from me, ya dumb muthafucka."

Then he slowly started to worm his way out from beneath my car. It was hard to guess his age under the tangled beard and layer of grime, but if I had to, I'd say around thirty-five. He had a cut on his head and scrapes all over the side of his face. His right wrist looked broken. How I had not killed him was a miracle.

Once he got out, he spent several moments moaning and cradling his wrist before he stumbled over, sat on the curb and glared malevolently. It took him about ten more seconds to figure me out. "Cop," he finally growled.

CHAPTER TWO

His name was Jonathan Bodine, and he was a sidewalk sleeper from Julian Street where the hard-core homeless lived in cardboard condos—old shipping crates covered with Saran wrap to keep the rain out. He smelled worse than a tuna boat, had tobacco-stained teeth and a colorful vocabulary.

"You just another drives-too-fast-don't-give-a-shit-half-stepper," he growled at me, cradling his broken right wrist with his left hand, glaring with enough hatred to start a race riot.

I felt guilty and offered up my excuse: "I didn't see you." The defense rests.

"Jus' 'cause you a cop, don't mean you can go an' plow poor folks down."

"You were jaywalking. You're supposed to cross in the crosswalks. Section P-dash-one-oh-six of the motor vehicle code. Look it up." The last thing I needed was a frivolous lawsuit from this guy.

"You just an A-train hard-ass out here gorillin' and Godzillin'. But you ain't helpin' nobody. Hit my black ass and now *I'm* the damn problem?"

He tried to stand up, but he was half lit and fell to his right, instinctively putting his bad wrist down to break his fall. He shrieked when his hand touched the ground, falling awkwardly onto his shoulder. Again, I tried to help him, but he knocked me back with the sleeve of his good arm, then whined and moaned for about two more minutes.

"I'll take you to the hospital."

"They ain't gonna do nothin'. One look at me and I get the nigga chute."

"I'll pay for it. We'll get your wrist set. It looks broken."

"Damn right, it's broken." And now a crafty look crept up onto his face, filling his dark eyes like bilge water. "Think you can just plow folks down, then back over twice to finish the job. But this here kinda brutality got big economic consequences."

"I didn't back over you twice. And you were breaking the law. You can't cross in the middle of the block, buddy."

"Who cares what you say? You jus' talkin' shit an' swallowin' spit."

Quality discourse. Next, we had an extensive discussion over what to do with his Safeway cart.

"I leave it out here it gets jack-rolled by them Quality-of-Life criminals from the Nickel," he whined.

"I'm not putting all that junk in the back of my clean car," I defended.

He got to his feet without answering and started to wander across the street toward the shopping cart, which was tipped over at the far curb. A yellow cab with its roof light on was speeding down Sixth and didn't see him either. The cabbie hit the binders and went sideways in a desperate slide, accompanied by the squeal of tortured rubber.

"Watch where you're goin' you blind-ass-piece-a-shit!" Jonathan Bodine screamed drunkenly at the cabbie, who had missed him by scant inches before straightening up and powering on.

I crossed the street and reluctantly helped him load his grubby possessions back into the shopping cart, thinking I was going to need a tetanus shot when this was over. We pushed the cart back across the street, and after another argument, which I lost, loaded it all into my car, filling my brand-new Acura SUV like a Skid Row dumpster.

"Stick the schooner in the back," Jonathan ordered.

"Unless your name is John *Safeway,* we're not stealing this shopping cart," I declared.

Five minutes later, with the Safeway cart wedged in behind the front seat, we took off toward the hospital. Along the way, I was forced to endure my first Jonathan Bodine hard-luck rant.

"You think it's tough on the Row, you should try it in the Bassaland. Your lily-white ass wouldn't last ten seconds in that African rainforest," he rambled.

I tried to tune him out by focusing on the steady stream of social mistakes bubbling from my police radio. But I couldn't do it. He was relentless.

"I hadda survive almost a year in that jungle. Couldn't a lasted 'cept I was wearin' the purple robes a the royal house, an' I got the Third Eye of tribal wisdom." He rattled like a tambourine, delusional, craziness spewing out of him. "I got people in my head talkin' to me—dead people from all the way back to the Black Holocaust. These half-steppers is all the time tellin' me how slaves from the Bassaland got exiled from the tribe and sold to do all kinda mystical work and what all. When I was growin' up in Cameroon, 'fore I got my commission in the Royal Navy, these voices was tellin' me desperate stories about how tribal brothers was being sold to slavers in the *Kon* where their souls got sucked out by the walking dead who live there. Walking dead make all these assholes on the Nickel look like prissy faggots with their twenty-eight-day shuffle hotels an' shopping cart elections for a dumb-ass seat on the neighborhood council. All a that ain't nothin' up against a rainforest where you got dead people suckin' out your soul an' shit."

I decided to take him to County-USC instead of the closer Queen of Angels Hospital. I made my decision mostly because Tony was at USC Medical Center. I glanced over at Bodine. He seemed totally unplugged from reality.

A few months ago, I'd read a flyer about the homeless passed out by Administrative Affairs. The one-sheet was supposed to better acclimate us so that we as law enforcement officers would understand the problems faced by our neighbors on the Row. It said that half the people there were alcoholics and one-third were mentally ill. The rest were just holding on to the bottom rung of society, hoping to survive one day at a time. I looked over at my passenger. Jonathan Bodine's eyes flashed in the dimly lit car possessed by ideas as he listened to voices only he could hear.

We pulled up to the emergency room entrance and I parked my car in a red zone, left the flashers on, and hung my cuffs over the steering wheel, a universal cop signal identifying a plain-clothes car. Then I led him inside.

ER admitting rooms in gang areas serviced by hospitals like County-USC are quickly becoming L.A.'s strange new nightmare. More and more, these facilities are degenerating into desperate war zones where rival bangers bring their wounded homies, frequently resuming hostilities in the pastel waiting rooms. MAC-10s would suddenly begin chattering, chewing up plaster divides and vinyl sofas. As a result, bulletproof glass and lead wall security were being installed on a priority basis.

With the help of my badge, Bodine was processed quickly. I really wanted to get him patched up and out of my life. I talked to Admitting and signed a payment voucher. After he was signed in, a pretty African-American nurse escorted the disheveled Mr. Bodine into one of the small observation cubicles. I could hear him complaining through the curtained wall, em-effing his way through a preliminary orthopedic exam.

I decided since I was here, what the hell, might as well go up and wish Tony luck. Maybe I'd run into Alexa. I needed advice about what to do with Bodine. I wasn't sure how far my responsibility to him extended. I had run him over. No argument there. But he *was* jaywalking. I didn't want to get wrapped up in a lawsuit, but I felt guilty. Mostly, I just wanted to mail the package to somebody else. I hoped Alexa would advise me that after his wrist was set, my obligation to him was over.

When I arrived in the coronary care unit, the floor nurse informed me that they had just given Tony a sedative and he was already asleep. Surgery was scheduled for seven A.M. tomorrow.

"Did Lieutenant Scully show up, by any chance?" I asked.

The nurse checked her clipboard and shook her head.

"It would probably have been less than thirty minutes ago."

"Nobody by that name has been here."

I had a momentary inkling that something was wrong. I called Alexa's office and got her assistant Ellen.

"She left here almost an hour ago," Ellen said. "She was going to see Tony at the hospital. You could try there."

"That's where I am. She didn't show up. Tony is already sedated and asleep."

"Maybe that's it," Ellen said. "Alexa said something about trying to fit in a short appointment. She could've called from the car, found out he was asleep, and gone to the meeting instead."

"You're probably right."

I hung up and dialed our house. The phone rang ten times before the machine picked up.

I tried her cell. It went straight to voice mail.

I wondered where she was.

CHAPTER THREE

He changed all the admittance forms," the pretty nurse said. She was tall with a lean body and glossy black hair. Her nametag identified her as Sheala Whitman, RN. We were standing by the check-in desk and the admitting clerk reached across the counter and handed me the forms I'd filled out twenty minutes earlier identifying the patient as Jonathan Bodine, address unknown. That name had been erased on the top of the page and something illegible was now smudged there in pencil.

"Can't read this," I said, squinting at the writing. "He told me his name was Jonathan Bodine."

"Now he's Samik Mampuna, Crown Prince of the Bassa-land," the nurse said. "He says he's from the Bassa Tribe that lives in the Central African rainforest."

"Prince Mampuna," I said, trying to sound impressed. "We should all be sure and get our pictures taken with him before he jumps on the royal jet back to Africa."

She didn't think it was funny. "We need his real name on the admitting form."

"Look, Nurse Whitman, the guy's not quite there. He stepped in front of my car and I'm trying to do the right thing and get him fixed up. If he wants to be Crown Prince Mampuna,

I'm all for it. He's just a homeless guy who hears voices and needs medical help. The city will pay for this. What's the problem?"

"And you're Shane Scully of the LAPD," she said.

"Mostly I'm Shane Scully of the LAPD, except when I'm Lord Bullwinkle, the Vicar of Kent." I gave her a loony smile and she finally relented, stifling a laugh.

"Okay. He's all yours, Lord Bullwinkle. Get him outta here. None of us down here can take much more."

What happened next was right out of a Steve Martin movie. I bundled him into my car and drove from the ER back to the Nickel. My theory was, when trying to return something, it's usually a good idea to put it back exactly where you found it.

"I'm just gonna drop you on the corner of Alameda and Sixth," I said casually. I was in a hurry to get all his junk out of my car and go home to Alexa.

"Ain't no good squat spots on Sixth. Assholes all whizzin' by like there ain't no tomorrow. All a buncha reckless-don't-give-a-damn-hit-and-run half-steppers, like you."

"Right. Okay." I choked down a few more confrontational responses. "So, where do you want to go?"

"Anywhere but the VOA," he said, referring to the Volunteers of America drop-in center. "Them Bible-beaters all hump yer leg fer Jesus. Maybe the Southern . . ."

The Southern is a recently remodeled single-room-occupancy hotel on Fifth Street across from San Julian Park. For years it had been a hellhole where street people would pay for their drugs at the front desk and then go stand behind the hotel and wait for the dealer to drop the cut down from the roof in baggies. A developer took it over, cleaned it up, and renovated. Single rooms went to homeless people for about one hundred ninety dollars a month. For SRO housing, that was considered pricey.

"Pretty expensive over there," I said. "You got the cash?" I asked.

"No. But you do," he said.

"I'm not gonna buy you a month in a hotel!"

"Lookit this!" he said, holding up his plastered wrist. "This be my green and gold lifetime pass. Green for da money, gold for da honey. This here's gonna cost you. I can't be scuffling for quarters with no broken wrist."

"You were jaywalking, stop trying to shake me down!" I was running out of patience.

"I'm going to the Legal Aid!" he shrieked. "Gonna hire me a kick-ass-get-some-money street lawyer. Got some big-time payback comin'."

I needed this guy out of my life without a lawsuit, and I figured if a hundred and ninety bucks did it, then it was probably a good buy. "Okay. I'll give you the money," I finally said. "But that's it between us. After that, we're done."

"Righteous." He grinned.

The Southern was an old, five-story hotel. The brick front, which had not yet been sand-blasted, was still stained brown from eighty years of L.A. smog. But the interior was renovated, the marble in the lobby and the open balconies that ran down the long hallways had been repaired. Fifty-five rooms overlooked a large square atrium. I'd been inside a few times in the past, to make drug arrests. Now, with the renovation and the new management, it was a favored spot on the Row.

When I pulled up in front, five homeless men were sitting on the steps. As Jonathan got out of my car, they all popped up like they were shot from air rams.

"It's Long Gone John," a big red-faced guy with a beard yelled. "He stole my radio! Get him!"

Bodine turned to face them. "You leave me be, Tuck. This here's the po-lice." He waved an arm at me, but one of the men threw a beer bottle in our direction. It broke on the pavement behind us.

"Get outta here, you jack-rollin' piece of shit!" a third man yelled.

Then they all started advancing on us.

"Git this pile a bolts moving," the Crown Prince of Bassa-land commanded as he ducked back into the car.

They were throwing bottles, and since I didn't want to get hit or scratch the paint on my new silver Acura, I ignored my required police response to a felony 415, jumped back behind the wheel and sped off up the street.

The same thing happened at the Simone and the Union Rescue Mission. The minute anybody saw Jonathan Bodine, they started throwing stuff. In five minutes, he got two death threats and several promises of permanent injury.

"They really love you down here, John," I said, wondering how I was going to unload him. "You also a typhoid carrier or something?"

"I'm having some temporary problems with these lie-like-a-crack-whore half-steppers," he grumbled. "Get over it."

"Everybody's calling you a jack-roller. Does that mean my trunk's full of other people's property?"

"I ain't gettin' outta this car till you find me a squat spot with windas," he said, crossing his arms and slumping defiantly in the seat.

I tried twice more to unload him, once at the Weingart Center and once in the park. Both times it was like the last reel of a zombie movie. Guys in rotting overcoats lurched toward us growling. Throughout this miserable experience, I continued to call Alexa on her cell and at home, but voice mail kept picking up.

I don't know what moved me to take him home with me. Probably guilt for running him down, or maybe a deep-seated feeling that I was still legally responsible, but mostly, I think it was because I was tired of screwing around with him and wanted to get home because of a growing concern over Alexa.

"I hate Venice," he said, as we drove down Abbot Kinney Boulevard. "Nothing but panhandlers and such on that beach."

He sort of had a point. The current wisdom on L.A.'s homeless was that panhandlers went to the beach, either Santa Monica or Venice. Teenage runaways ended up in Hollywood, and only the most desperate down-and-outers like John lived in boxes, Alices, or doorways on the Row.

"I'm gonna take you home with me," I finally admitted. "You get one night in my garage, then we'll figure out what to do with you in the morning."

"I ain't sleepin' in no garage," he complained, pulling at his shirt. "This here look like a Texaco uniform?"

"It's okay. I'll put a cardboard box in there so you'll be more comfortable."

"You run a man down, don't say shit, or I'm sorry. Then you insults me and makes me sleep in some cold-ass garage 'stead a one a them sweet SROs."

I took him home, thinking this may be the dumbest move in my entire police career. As we pulled into the driveway in front of my Venice Canal house I immediately saw that Alexa's car wasn't there. It was now almost nine-thirty. I wondered if maybe she had gone to the market and had left me a note inside.

As we got out of the car, Jonathan Bodine looked around despairingly. "I spent a month down here once. It sucks. Got rats by this canal big as fuckin' meat loafs."

I let it go, went to the front door, unlocked it, and walked into the entry hall. There was no note from Alexa on the floor by the door where we always left them. All the lights were out. I started flipping switches.

Jonathan Bodine wandered in behind me. "Man, talk about four walls and a chair."

Here was this guy who lived in a cardboard box, standing in my living room, dissing my classic canal house. I swallowed my irritation and said, "There's a shower in my son's room. Come on." I led him through the summer heat of the house and turned on the central air. I could already smell him and didn't want that stink to get caught in the curtains.

I turned on the lights in Chooch's bedroom. It was empty because my son was beginning his freshman year at USC on a football scholarship. His girlfriend, Delfina, who had come to live with us after her cousin died, was visiting relatives in Mexico and wasn't due back till the end of the summer. The house felt empty. Jonathan Bodine moved up and stood in the doorway behind me.

"You'll sleep in here," I told him.

"Thought you said it was a garage."

"It was. We converted it into a room for my son. The shower's in there. Take off those clothes. I'll wash them and send that coat to the cleaners."

"Now you finally talkin'," he grinned.

He peeled off the coat and started to unbutton his shirt, kicked off his soiled boots, then dropped his trousers and stood there in his skivvies. Without his clothes, he seemed even skinnier than before. He had light coffee-colored skin peeking out from under a layer of street grime. Some kind of African tribal tattoo wrapped his small bicep. He walked toward the bathroom wearing only his boxers, which were yellowed with age, or urine. God knows what.

"Kick the boxers out through the door. There's shampoo and soap in the shower."

He nodded and started inside.

"And Bodine . . . if you think you're gonna steal anything out of this house, remember I'm a cop and I make my living shooting people."

"Already run me down. Might as well shoot me, too."

He slammed the door. A minute later I heard the shower running.

I turned around and saw Franco, our adopted marmalade cat, standing behind me sniffing the air like somebody had farted. His yellow eyes were packed with distrust and his ears were back, giving me attitude. His look said, "Why on earth did you bring that home?" Good question.

I went through Chooch's dresser and found a red Harvard-Westlake sweatshirt, jeans, a belt, some clean underwear, and socks. I put them on the floor outside the bathroom door, picked up Bodine's dirty clothes, and carried them out to the laundry porch. I loaded the washer and turned it on, all the while wondering where the hell Alexa was.

I tried calling her cell, but again it went straight to voice mail. I gave Franco fresh water and filled his dish with dried food.

Then the phone in the living room rang.

CHAPTER FOUR

I t's Tommy Sepulveda," a voice crackled through the telephone.
"What's up, Tom?" I said.

Tommy Sepulveda and Raphael Figueroa were a detective team that worked with me at Homicide Special. Since Sepulveda Boulevard and Figueroa Street are two main drags in Los Angeles, it was inevitable that some wise guy in personnel would find a way to put them together. Sepulveda was Italian; Figueroa, a second-generation Mexican-American. They were good dicks and had a cubicle two over from me and Sally Quinn, my incoming partner. I remembered seeing that Sepulveda and Figueroa were next up on the roll-out board when I had left the office for the jail at ten this morning.

"Listen, Shane, you need to get up to the top of Mulholland Drive right now," Tommy said.

"I'm not back in rotation yet. I'm breaking in a new partner next week."

"We just got an APE case. You need to get up here now!" He sounded tense and all of my alarms started flashing. An APE case was sixth-floor speak for Acute Political Emergency.

"What's going on?"

"I'm calling you on a radio hook-up. My cell doesn't work up here. I don't want this out on an open channel. Just move it."

"On my way." I hung up and wondered what the hell to do with Jonathan Bodine. If I left him here alone, there wouldn't be anything left in the house when I got back. The shower had stopped running in Chooch's bathroom, so I went looking for him. He was in the kitchen foraging in my refrigerator, his hair still wet, wearing a towel wrapped around his skinny hips. He was holding a leg of lamb in his right hand, gnawing it right off the bone. In his left hand he had an open bottle of table wine.

"We gotta go."

"I'm having dinner."

"No, you're not."

I rushed into Chooch's room and grabbed the clothes I'd laid out for him, snatched his grimy boots off the floor, and hurried back into the kitchen, throwing the bundle on the dinette table.

"Put 'em on. We're leaving." My stomach was balled up in a knot. There was only one reason I could come up with why Sepulveda would call me out on an APE case. It had something to do with my missing wife.

"Let's go!" I yelled, and grabbed him. The towel came off his hips and fell to the floor. He dropped the bottle of wine and it rolled under a chair and started emptying on the floor. I threw a pair of Chooch's undies at him, still holding his skinny arm.

"Leggo a me!"

"Bodine, I can take you out of here naked in cuffs if that's the way you want it. You got six seconds or less to get dressed."

"I got rights, asshole. I got a broken wrist courtesy a your shitty driving."

I pulled out my Beretta and aimed it at him in an elaborate bluff. "How 'bout I just drop you and throw you in the canal?"

"Okay, okay. Calm down," he shrieked. Then he put down the leg of lamb and started jumping on one leg, trying to poke his left foot into the shorts. His plaster cast made it difficult to grasp the undies, but he finally made it. Then he put on the sweatshirt and shimmied into the jeans, which were two times too big because Chooch is six-three, two-thirty, and Bodine was a runt. Five-foot-nothing and a hundred and fifteen. There was room for two of him in there, but we weren't going to a fashion show, so I could care less. I handed him his boots and a belt, grabbed him by the collar of the sweatshirt and yanked him out of the kitchen.

He made a grab for the leg of lamb but missed, and the bone skidded across the floor and stopped under the table. I left it there, a few feet away from the emptying bottle of wine.

I have a Kojak light in my glove box and a siren under the hood. You can't go Code 3 in L.A. without permission from the communications division, which I wouldn't get because I wasn't on call. But I grabbed the magnetized bubble light anyway and slammed it up on the roof. I used it intermittently and growled the siren to bust through red lights at intersections. Technically a no-no, but I didn't care. I had the pedal down, passing cars on the right as I sped north on Abbot Kinney Boulevard.

"This be some more-a-that crazy nickel-slick driving," was about all that Jonathan Bodine kept saying. He had his boots on and both feet stretched out in fear, planted on the floor mats in front of him. He was gripping the door pull with white knuckles.

It took me almost ten minutes to get out of Venice to the 10 Freeway. Then after another quarter hour, I transitioned to the 405 North, growling my siren and flashing my headlights at slower moving traffic until they moved over.

I got off the 405 at Mulholland and headed east, climbing up into the Hollywood Hills past Beverly Glen. The houses were sparse up here, but the ones I passed were big. This was prime L.A. real estate. Pine trees and elms hugged the slopes on both sides of the road. The Valley lights twinkled below as my headlights sawed holes in the dark.

"Slow down, motherfucker," Bodine said. It seemed like usable advice. I was close to the summit, so I took my foot off the gas.

Then I saw a police circus up ahead. Half a dozen patrol cars and a coroner's van. Sitting in the middle of yards of yellow crime-scene tape, was Alexa's black BMW. I hit the brakes and skidded to a stop, getting out of the car almost before it had stopped, running toward the twenty cops and techies who were milling around beyond the tape in front of Alexa's car.

Raphael Figueroa saw me coming and broke off, intercepting me. He was six feet tall with a weight lifter's build and a tea-brown, Indio face.

"Hold it, Scully! Slow down!" he barked.

"Where is she?"

"Not here. We haven't got a line on her yet."

I could see a black male slumped over in the front passenger seat of the car.

"Who's that?"

"The guest of honor," cop-talk for a body. "Looks like he's been dead about an hour. No lividity yet or rigor."

I tried to push past Figueroa, but his left hand was holding my arm in a strong grip. Then he put two fingers of his right hand under his tongue and let out a shrill whistle.

"Tommy, get over here," he yelled.

Tom Sepulveda broke away from the coroner's van, where he'd been talking to Ray Tsu from the ME's office. Ray was a narrow-shouldered Asian man with such a quiet manner and voice he was known by most homicide cops as Fey Ray. Sepulveda was his exact physical opposite, an Italian stallion. Short, bull-necked, aggressive. Like his partner, he was in his mid-thirties and they both knew their stuff. Tommy grabbed my other arm, then he and Figueroa led me about twenty yards away to their maroon Crown Vic, opened the back door, and pushed me inside.

"Let go of me," I said, and they released me.

"I called you because if that was my wife's car, I'd want a call, too. But you're not on this case," Sepulveda started by saying. "That's protocol, and me and Rafie are holding you to it."

"Don't quote the rule book to me. Where is she?"

"We've done a preliminary search of the surrounding areas," Figueroa answered. "It's pretty dark and it's dense foliage up here, but so far no sign of her."

"Who's the stiff?"

"Unknown," Rafie said. "No wallet but he's got gang ink all over him and expensive, chunky, diamond jewelry so he's probably some street G. Whoever capped him wasn't interested in bad-taste jewelry. There's a big ABC tattoo on his right bicep."

"Crip?" I asked. ABC usually stood for Arcadia Block Crips, a dangerous gang from the Piru Street area in Compton.

"ABC also stands for American Broadcasting Company," Tommy said. "Let's not get ahead of ourselves."

"I need to look in the car."

"No way!" they said in unison.

"I'm a material witness. I know what was in that car this morning when she left for work. You don't want me to even take a look and inventory that for you? See if anything's missing?"

Raphael and Sepulveda looked at each other. They both suspected this was bull. But technically, I had a point.

"Okay, Scully. You can go over there with us," Sepulveda said. "But that's it. No touching, no asking questions. I don't want a bunch of grief from the rat squad about this later. We square on that?"

"It's my wife's car."

"We know, man." Rafie took a breath. "I'm sorry, but if you get into this, the Professional Standards Bureau is gonna fall on all of us."

"I get it," I said. "I'm not gonna get in your way.

They took a moment and studied me. I have a little bit of a reputation in the department as a walk-alone, and I could see they were slightly skeptical. But operationally, they had no choice, so finally they exchanged a silent nod and led me over to the car. As we ducked under the yellow tape, Ray Tsu looked up at me.

"Sorry, man," he whispered. Ray and I had worked at least twenty homicides together and had established a good on-the-job relationship. I nodded at him, then we walked over and I looked into the car.

The front seat was drenched in blood. Fear swept over me, almost blinding my vision. I took a deep breath and tried to calm down. I told myself that I was a trained homicide detective and I needed to treat this car as just another murder scene. I willed myself to look at it dispassionately. I already knew this was going to be the most important investigation of my career. Regardless of what I'd told Sepulveda and Figueroa, there was no way I was going home to wait for these guys to call and fill me in. Until Alexa was located, I was going to be all over this. I took another deep breath and began to form a careful mental picture of the crime scene.

The guy in the passenger seat was a middle-aged African-American. His wrists were cuffed behind him and he'd been shot behind the left ear, execution style. The bullet's trajectory looked to be downward and the exit wound had taken out half his right cheek. He was slumped forward with his forehead resting on the dash, still dripping blood and cerebral spinal fluid all over Alexa's right floor mat. He had long, black hair, which was straightened in a Marcel. The impact of the bullet had knocked the Marcel loose and strands of the shiny, straightened do now hung over his ears. He was muscular, dressed in a sleeveless leather vest and pants with gang tats all over his arms. The big ABC tattoo decorated his large left bicep. He also had BTK on his arm—Born to Kill. There was blow-back and blood spatter everywhere, except for where the driver had been sitting. If the driver was the shooter, and the bullet was fired from the driver's seat, it seemed to me that the trajectory was slightly wrong. Alexa is five-eight and for the bullet to have a downward trajectory, the doer had to either be taller or standing outside, shooting across her. The passenger side window had not been broken by the exiting bullet, so the slug was probably buried in the lower door panel. Alexa's backseat held several old case boxes and a green sweater. All of it had been there this morning. The backseat seemed untouched.

"Looks like someone was sitting here when the shot was fired," Figueroa said, pointing to the clean spot where the driver would have been.

I didn't respond.

"See anything we can use?" Sepulveda asked, looking hard at me.

"We were doing that retraining day at the jail this morning," I said. "She was in jeans, tennies, and a gray, unmarked sweatshirt."

"Better put that on the air," Rafie said, and Sepulveda crossed to their car to make the broadcast.

"All that stuff in the backseat was there, but her briefcase is missing. And her purse."

"Okay," Rafie said. "Describe those."

"Purse was canvas and black. One of those designer deals with pockets all over it. Briefcase was brown alligator. Small. Wafer-sized."

Rafie said, "You know the vic?"

"No."

"Never seen him?"

"Nope."

"If those turn out to be her cuffs, we're gonna have us a situation here."

"She didn't drive up here and pop this guy," I said hotly.

"Let's move back. Give the C.S. guys some room to work," Rafie said. He led me away from the BMW and back to their Crown Vic where Sepulveda was just hanging up the mike.

"Anything else?" Rafie asked.

"I left her at Parker Center around six. She said she was going to go visit the chief in the hospital before his surgery tomorrow. I was over at USC Medical on an unrelated matter but she never showed up. Her secretary said she was maybe going to try and fit in an appointment."

"You know with who?" Tommy asked.

"No. But you could ask Ellen in her office. Maybe she does."

"Okay, what next?" Tommy said.

"I went home. She wasn't there. Then you guys called."

"Who's the rat-bag sitting in your car?" Rafie was looking over at my Acura.

Bodine was still in the front seat. He had his head back, his dreads hanging over the headrest, eyes closed, zoning out. I'd stupidly left the keys in the car. Probably the only thing that was keeping Long Gone John from clouting my ride was he would have had to do it in front of ten cops.

"That's Jonathan Bodine. He's a homeless guy. He has nothing to do with this."

"Okay, Shane. That's it, then. If you think of anything else, write it down and leave it on my desk."

"Right."

"And if you try and work this, me and Tommy will break your back."

"Right."

"I'm serious, man. Mess with this and we're all headed for the zoo."

"Gimme a little credit here. I'm not going near it."

They exchanged looks, nodded, and then both moved slowly away from the car, treading on that questionable promise like thin October ice.

Once they had stopped looking back at me, I got into my car and pulled away.

"What we doin' now?" Bodine asked. I ignored him and drove past the commotion and found a spot around the bend where I pulled the car off the road and down into some trees. Then I killed the lights and turned off the engine.

"We on some kinda dumb-ass camping trip here? What's this about, douche bag?" Bodine complained.

"Shut up and stay in the car."

I got out, taking the keys, grabbed my black Maglite from behind the seat and began to walk down the hill through dense foliage, making my way back toward the crime scene, using the underbrush for cover. I didn't know what the hell I was doing, or what I was hoping to find. I guess my plan was to look in the bushes below the site where the car was parked, hoping I wouldn't find my dead wife down there. My stomach was full of acid and I was fighting back waves of nausea.

I kept the light on, but as I got nearer to the cops at the crime scene above, I took out my handkerchief and wrapped it over the lens, cutting the light down by two-thirds. Then I swung the dull beam right and left looking in the underbrush, praying I wouldn't find her. I don't know how long I walked around. Ten minutes, maybe thirty. I could hear cops talking above me on the road.

Then, I shined my light to the right, and something glinted. I moved over and found myself looking down at a small, nickel-plated, 9mm foreign automatic.

There was little doubt in my mind that it was the murder weapon. I also recognized the pistol. It was Alexa's purse gun. Her 9mm Spanish Astra.

CHAPTER FIVE

I stood looking at the gun, forcing myself to deconstruct the situation, analyze its components. I knew that if Alexa didn't turn up soon with a good explanation why there was a dead gang-banger handcuffed and executed with her weapon in her car, then she was going to be the number one suspect in the case.

My first inclination was to scoop up the gun and suppress the evidence. I actually bent down and started to retrieve the weapon but as I reached for it, I knew I couldn't do it. My reasons were not very complicated. First, it violated everything I now tried to stand for. Second, it seemed to be an admission that deep down I actually thought she might be guilty of this, and I knew she wasn't. I hesitated with my fingers inches from the gun, then withdrew my hand.

I also had practical evidentiary concerns. If someone had forced Alexa over, abducted her, then shot the Crip in her car using her gun, there might be fingerprints or DNA on the weapon that could be traced and eventually lead to my missing wife.

I retraced my steps and found John Bodine standing beside the car looking down at me as I came up the slope.

"I'm freezin' my ass off. Where you been?"

"Hey John, if your busy schedule can't accommodate this and you wanta take off, it's okay with me."

"You still owe me. Got me some payback comin'."

"That's what I thought."

I turned and walked back up the road toward the crime scene. When I rounded the bend, I could see Tommy Sepulveda standing next to the coroner's van talking to a crime scene photographer. I couldn't spot Rafie.

"I thought you left," Sepulveda said as I approached.

"Come here. I need to talk to you."

Tommy Sepulveda moved away from the CSI and followed me down the road, around the bend. "Where're we going?"

"Wanta show you something."

I stayed a few yards ahead of him, moving fast enough so he couldn't catch up and pepper me with questions. I didn't want to talk about this with him because I didn't trust what I might say. Emotionally, I was too close to the edge. We approached my car where Bodine was now leaning against the front fender, watching us with disinterested, bloodshot eyes.

"Howdy," Sepulveda said.

Bodine just grunted as I led Sepulveda past and started down the slope through the underbrush, shining my flashlight, trying to follow my exact path from earlier. I didn't want to contaminate the drop site in case the killer had walked down here from the road above. A minute or two later, we were standing over the Spanish Astra, both shining our flashlights on it.

"Bingo," Tommy said softly.

"I think it's Alexa's," I admitted. "She packs a nickel-plated Astra nine."

Sepulveda let out a long sigh, which more or less said it all. He didn't like where this was going any more than I did.

"She didn't kill that guy, Tommy."

"I'm not saying she did."

"That's what you were thinking."

"Yeah." He stood there for a long moment and then turned to me. "I told you that you were not part of this investigation. So what the hell were you doing down here?"

"Wanta just leave it here?"

"Don't be a cowboy, Shane. Me and Rafie told you to stay away from this. You know how much shit we're all gonna take if I.A. thinks we let you investigate your own wife's disappearance and potential involvement in a homicide."

"I came down here to take a leak—happened to see it. Is it against the law to piss, now?"

"Forty yards through sticker bushes and brambles. Now I'm supposed to be an idiot, too?"

"Book the gun, Tommy. Look for prints. She didn't pop that guy, somebody else did. If that's the murder weapon, then somebody else fired it."

"Get out of here, Shane. I'm not gonna tell anybody you found this. Believe me, I'm doing you a big favor, but so help me, if I see you anywhere near this case again, I'm gonna write up a one-eighty-one." A Professional Standards Bureau complaint.

"She didn't do it. How about extending her a little loyalty? How about you and Figueroa keeping an open mind till all the facts are in?"

"I never should've called you. I should've seen this coming. It's my fault, but you've been warned, Shane. From here on, it's a book play. Turn up on this again and I'll have you arrested for obstruction of justice."

He turned and walked back up to the road to get the crime techs. I followed, then got into my car with Bodine and backed out of the trees and onto the road. I drove over Mulholland to Coldwater Canyon and headed down the hill into the Valley.

"I'm hungry," Bodine said.

I didn't answer.

"Man's gotta eat."

I still didn't answer.

"Gonna go get me a fire-breathing hard-on from the Legal Aid. You gonna curse the day you ran down the Crown Prince of Cameroon. The prince ain't some sleep-in-the-park half-stepper you can scrape off yer shoe. You about to explode in the oven, asshole."

He never stopped. He just kept filling the car with nonsense and complaints. So I pulled over and parked about a block from the 101 Freeway. Then I reached across Bodine and pushed open the passenger door.

"Get outta my car." I had no more time for this. My life had just taken a horrible turn and I had too much on my mind to deal with him.

"You can't just throw me out!"

"Watch me."

I got out of the car, came around, and threw Bodine's door wide. I yanked him out of the seat by the collar of Chooch's sweatshirt and slung him away from me. He stumbled into the trunk of an elm tree, but managed to keep from going down.

"That's assault! Police brutality!"

"Leave me alone!" I was totally over the edge, out of control and screaming at him.

"This is the Valley. I don't wanna be in the Valley. I hate the Valley. Wanta go back to Sixth Street."

I shoved a handful of bills at him and yelled, "Take a cab!"

I got back in the car and put it in gear. Bodine started banging on the window, but I locked the doors before he could get inside. I pressed the accelerator down and pulled away. He ran alongside, banging on the glass until I finally left him standing in the middle of Coldwater, screaming after me.

It wasn't until I got off the freeway on Mission Street that I remembered I still had his shopping cart and all of his rubbish in the back of my car.

CHAPTER SIX

Fifteen minutes later I was parked across from the Medical Examiner's Facility on North Mission Road in a spot with a good view of the lighted parking lot. The coroner's van would be arriving in the next half hour with Ray Tsu and the dead Crip G aboard.

I knew I had to call Chooch. I didn't want him to hear about this on the news in the morning, but I dreaded making the call. Reluctantly, I pulled out my cell phone and dialed the number for USC summer football housing. The team was staying at an apartment complex near Howard Jones Field to facilitate training table, curfews, and six A.M. wake-ups. After ten rings, an assistant coach finally answered and after I told him who I was, said he'd go and get Chooch out of bed.

Ten minutes later, Chooch came on the line.

"Yeah?"

"It's me, Chooch. I've got bad news."

He sounded sleepy, but that brought him out of it fast. "What bad news?"

"Your mom is missing. They found her car up on Mulholland an hour ago. There was a dead gang-banger in the front seat. She's not there. Nobody knows what happened to her."

"What?" he shouted.

"I know . . . look, there could be a lot of explanations. Unfortunately, some of them are bad. I don't have anything else, but I'm working on it. I'll let you know as soon as I come up with something."

"I'm coming home."

"No, you're not!"

"Dad, if Alexa—"

I cut him off. "Listen to me, son. I'm not supposed to work on this because she's my wife and I'm emotionally involved, but screw that, because nobody will work it harder than me. And there're some problems I need to address. An issue with her gun."

"Dad, I'm not staying here."

"You're not coming home, either."

"Why not?"

"Right now, I've got a chance to run free for a short time, but that won't last long. I might get a jump on this if I kick ass right now, but when the two homicide cops who got the squeal catch up with me, I'm gonna be in a world of hurt. I can't put you in the equation. I don't have time."

"She's my mom!"

"I know. But son, what are you gonna be able to do, really?"

"I'll . . . we'll talk it over. I'll . . . I don't know. I can't just stay here and hit a blocking sled."

"Tell the coaches. I'm sure they'll let you take some time off. But you've gotta stay where you are. Let me do this my way."

There was a long pause. I could hear him breathing.

"Dad, what do you mean there're issues with her gun?"

"It might be the murder weapon."

"And they think Mom shot this banger dude?"

"They're cops. They'll follow the evidence wherever it leads. But whatever you hear on TV, remember who your mom is. I'm not letting this get sideways. Wherever she is, I'll find her."

"What if . . . what if . . ."

"She's not dead, son. She can't be. I won't allow it."

After that, we didn't know what to say to each other.

"I'll call you in the morning," I said.

"Okay."

"Love you," I said. There was silence. "Say it back, Chooch. I need to hear it."

"I love you, too, Dad." He sounded devastated.

I hung up the phone and looked out the window again at the North Mission Road building. It was a new, plain-looking structure that housed the morgue and all of our forensic science units. Like most municipal buildings, budget considerations had deprived it of any architectural extras. It was a shoebox with windows.

I'd worked enough homicides to know pretty much how the next hour would play out. Ray Tsu would bring the corpse here, and do the preliminary death photos, prints, and dental work. Sepulveda and Figueroa would finish up at the crime scene, impound the car, and then head back to stand over the body while Ray, or the chief ME did the autopsy. Because Alexa was missing, it was an APE case and ticking PR bomb. For that reason, there wouldn't be the standard two-week wait for an autopsy, which had been a growing problem for homicide cops in L.A. They would do the cut tonight. That meant if I moved fast, I might have half an hour to forty minutes alone to work on Ray Tsu before Tommy and Rafie arrived. I had to make that forty minutes count, and find out who this dead Crip was. Then I had to work that angle fast. It was the best thread in the case.

I sat in the front seat of the Acura, running the other permutations. I couldn't come up with a theory that accommodated what appeared to have happened. If you took Alexa out of the equation, it was easier to understand. A dead banger in cuffs, executed up on Mulholland, could fit a lot of scenarios. He could have been kidnapped, driven up to that lonely spot, popped, and left there for somebody to find in the morning. Handcuffs were easy to get. I'd seen dozens of hits that more or less went down like that.

It was adding Alexa to the picture that skewed everything. What series of events, what missing facts, made Alexa's involvement and subsequent disappearance add up? I couldn't think of anything.

Half an hour later, the coroner's van swept into the lot. I waited while Ray Tsu and the driver pulled the gurney out of the back. They popped the wheels down and rolled the dead Crip inside. On their way, they hit a button to close the electric parking lot gate.

I jumped out of the Acura, locked it with a chirp, and sprinted across the street, making it through the gates just as they were closing. I rang the bell at the back door of the building, held up my badge for the security camera, and was buzzed in.

Nobody was sitting behind the downstairs admitting desk. The midnight-to-six shift had been pared in half during the last round of budget cuts. Usually there were two guards back here—a lucky breach of security because I had no business to conduct. There was a camera in the entry hall taping the room, so I crossed to the security desk and signed in for the benefit of the guard up on three, writing Samik Mampuna on the entry log. Then I took the elevator to the fourth floor where autopsies and body preps were done.

Under most circumstances, the morgue is a crowded place full of sheet-covered corpses waiting for their final desecration. Every time I'm up here, I wonder if one day my own precious remains will be parked in these over-wide corridors, waiting for this last indignity. Strange chemical smells mixed with some disinfectant pine scent wafted through the halls. I'd been up here when there were over twenty bodies parked on metal gurneys, most of them too young to be dead, each tray with its own special tale of woe and unfulfilled ambitions. Tonight, for some reason, the corridor was almost empty. Two lonely corpses under green sheets haunted the hallway. The building was unusually quiet. I saw a lighted doorway halfway down the hall and headed toward it.

Ray Tsu was leaning over the dead Crip when I entered. He had just finished rolling a ten card, imprinting all of the man's fingerprints. He looked up as I entered.

"You aren't supposed to be here."

"How the hell can I not be here?"

Ray was a good guy, even though it was always slightly annoying that he rarely spoke above a whisper.

"You're gonna get your ass cooked unless you get out now," he warned.

"I need to know who this guy is."

"Not from me tonight. Get it from Figueroa and Sepulveda tomorrow."

"Ray, I won't burn you. Please, help me."

He shook his head.

"She's my wife. She's the only person who ever gave—"

I stopped, because there were suddenly tears in my eyes.

"Shane, look at you," he said softly. "You're a mess. How're you gonna do anybody any good like this? Go home. Let Tommy and Rafie handle this."

"We could put that print card through AFIS instead of NCIC," I said. AFIS was the Automatic Fingerprint Identification System, which we'd just installed downstairs. It had a much bigger and faster database than the National Crime Identification Computer. "If this gangster's prints are in the system, AFIS will spit an ID back on a ten-finger roll in less than two minutes."

"Come on, Shane. Really. Let those guys handle it."

"I've seen this vic before," I lied. "His name's right on the tip of my tongue, but I can't quite get it. If AFIS gives us an ID, I know I can remember what his connection to Alexa is. That's gonna be a huge help here."

I watched as Ray processed this nonsense and rejected it with a frown. "Wait for Tommy and Rafie," he said. "It's their call."

So I just reached over and snatched the drying card out of his delicate fingers.

"This could end your career, Shane!" he said, as I walked out of the room with it.

I didn't wait for him to follow. I was already sprinting toward a bank of freight-size elevators, each one large enough to carry three gurneys. I took the first one down to the basement where the electronic identification unit was housed. I exited just as the phone started ringing at reception. Had to be Ray. There was no one at this desk either. My luck was holding. For the first time since the cutbacks happened, I applauded the city's budget crisis. I jumped over the vacant counter and picked up the receiver hitting the Hold button. Then I put all of the remaining five lines on hold as well. When I left, the desk telephone was blinking like a Vegas slot.

I found the AFIS machine in a small room at the end of a long corridor. A young bored-looking blond girl was running a stack of print cards.

"Hi. I need this run immediately," I said, offering her the ten card.

"ID number?"

I pulled out my CREDS and showed her. After she wrote down the number, she took the print card from me and scanned it into the machine.

"If it's in the system, this should only take a few minutes," she said.

I tried to make small talk, but frankly, I couldn't think of anything to say. I was an emotional wreck. Suddenly, her eyes went down to the flashing phone on the table across from us.

"I wonder why the lines are all on hold," she said. "There's almost nobody down here."

"There was a phone guy out front. Maybe he's working on the system." Total B.S., but it must have worked because she nodded her head and smiled.

Then I heard Ray coming down the hall. "Shane! Dammit, Shane! You down here?!" It was the first time I could remember hearing him shout.

"He's with me, Mr. Tsu," the girl called out.

Seconds later Ray Tsu planted his skinny body in the doorway, acting as if he could actually use his pipe-cleaner build to physically restrain me from leaving with his print card.

"Shane, come on," he said. "Don't make this any worse."

Then the AFIS machine started buzzing and a printout shot into the catch tray. We had a match. Ray made a move toward the tray, but I beat him to it and grabbed the printout along with the ten card and folded them both in half. I knew, of course, that he would just run it again, but he'd have to reprint the body first. That would buy me at least a ten-minute head start.

"I'm reporting this, Shane."

"I know." I turned and ran out the door, taking the stairs two at a time, exploding back into the rear lobby. The security guard had returned from the toilet, or wherever he'd been when I first arrived, but they aren't there to stop you from leaving, only from getting in.

"Have a good night," the guard called, as I speed-walked past him out the door and into the parking lot. I pushed the button to open the parking gate from the inside, then sprinted out of the lot and across the street to my car. I jumped in and powered away.

I still hadn't looked at the printout. My heart was slamming inside my chest. My hands were shaking as I gripped the wheel tightly with sweating palms. When I was ten blocks away and felt safe, I pulled over, turned on the dome light, and unfolded the AFIS printout.

The DMV photo I was looking at was of a clean-cut man with short hair. But despite the different haircut, I recognized him as the dead guy from Alexa's car. He was handsome in a rakish way. A slightly skewed smile said he knew he was hot. His driver's license identified him as David Morris Slade, six-one, one hundred ninety-five pounds. He lived at 420 Cypress Street, Compton. Following that, the AFIS printout had added other pertinent information, and that was the surprise.

There was a police identification number, with a notation. David M. Slade was a member of the LAPD Academy class of 1982. He was currently a sergeant assigned to a special gang in-tel unit. I folded the paper and looked at the empty street in front of me while I tried to process all this. Of course, it was the missing piece.

The reason he was in Alexa's car.

CHAPTER SEVEN

Compton is bordered on the south by Long Beach and on the north by Watts. The city has a bloody gang history.

In the late sixties a new form of Jamaican music caught hold in New York, then quickly spread to Compton. Rap music was fueled by rock cocaine and violent street gangs. In the late eighties, N.W.A cut their first incendiary rap album, titled *Straight Outta Compton*, which featured the hit single "F—Tha Police." With that album, gangsta rap was born. While Crips and Bloods competed for drug turf around Piru Street in Compton, rap impresarios with serious gang affiliations were recording street artists and making millions. But there were downsides. The average lifespan of a Compton drug dealer was twenty-five years and gang violence at hip-hop awards shows had become common.

Rappers like Easy-E, Dr. Dre, and DJ Quik were just kids growing up in Compton in the eighties. Snoop Dogg was a few miles away in Long Beach. Rap and crack made stars and millionaires out of some and corpses out of others. In recent years the black gangs in Compton were in a struggle to control their turf, losing street corners one by one to the new, violent Hispanic gangs like the Ninos Surenos and Mara Salvatruchas.

As I made my way down toward the Long Beach Freeway, I

tried to fit David Slade into the equation. Slade had that big ABC on his arm, and I knew you didn't put Crip ink on yourself unless you were in the gang. There was only one way I could reconcile a cop with that tattoo. After the Watts Riots, the LAPD was having trouble recruiting minorities. In a desperate attempt to get more "color" on the job, some nitwit in administration had suggested we drop the juvenile felony restriction, opening the department up to people who had committed serious crimes as long as they'd done them under the age of eighteen. The result of this change allowed ex-gang-bangers of all ethnic backgrounds onto the police force. Cops like Raphael Perez had joined up, later becoming involved in the Rampart scandal and disgracing the department. Was David Slade just another example of this failed policy? Once you were jumped into a set, you rarely got out. If he'd joined the LAPD in the early 1980s, it explained why he still lived in Compton.

Most black cops felt disenfranchised by the hood, and were called out for being on the job. The majority of them moved, preferring places like Stevenson Ranch or the Marina. I wondered if Slade stayed in Compton because he was still Crippin'—working both sides of the street. I needed to access his I.A. file and his current caseload. His gang drapes told me he was probably working undercover. All this left me back where I started: What was he doing shot to death in Alexa's car?

I had a dozen questions and no answers. I was also running out of time. I was pretty sure by now Ray Tsu had alerted Sepulveda and Figueroa to my commando raid on North Mission Road, and fed them the info from the print card. Those two cops would be on their way to Compton to head me off. Coming from Mulholland gave them a geographical advantage, but I had a big time jump. I was probably still a few minutes ahead. I was navigating with the Acura's GPS and stayed on main streets, which at this time of night were faster. I was busting lights, dangerously.

I got into Compton a little past midnight and turned onto Cypress Avenue. It was an old, residential street lined with rundown bungalows and duplexes. Chain-link fences fronted lawns where the grass was mostly brown. The paint on everything seemed faded and chipped.

As I sped along, I was surprised to see a young boy about five or six riding a tricycle on the sidewalk. It was past midnight. Where the hell were his parents? Fifteen years from now, would I be chasing this kid down these same streets and end up in some desperate shoot-out because when he was five, nobody cared enough about him to tuck him in at night?

Slade's residence was a tan Spanish bungalow with brown shutters and wrought-iron security bars across the front windows. It was one of the rare houses on the street that had been freshly painted. I parked about twenty yards away, behind an old gray Chevy Caprice, and left my door ajar in case I needed to make a quick exit. Then I sprinted back to Slade's house. I didn't bother with the front door, because I didn't have a search warrant and a white guy jimmying a front door might not go unnoticed in this neighborhood. I had already decided to break in from the rear where I would be less visible. I went directly around back and looked in the porch window. Then I tried the back screen door. Everything was locked. I pulled out my gun and crept silently along the side of the house looking for a good window to break. I found one in the middle where the security bars were loose. I pulled one away, bending the old screws until the bar came off in my hand. Then I reached through the remaining two bars and broke the glass with my gun, found the latch, and slid the window open.

I stood quietly for a minute, listening for trouble: an alarm or a drooling Rottweiler. The house remained quiet. A strange truth is a lot of police officers don't install electronic security because they think that no street burglar would be stupid or brave enough to try and rip them off. I jumped up and shinnied through the window, squeezing between the two remaining security bars, and dropped inside.

I landed in a guest bedroom. Cardboard boxes full of junk were all over the floor. I didn't bother with them, but instead moved out into the hall. The smart thing to do was to clear the house first, to make sure there wasn't some armed homie crashing on the front couch. I knew I didn't have much time, but even so, I decided to do a quick shake to be safe. It wouldn't do Alexa much good for me to get shot as an intruder.

The house was so small that it only took a few minutes.
There were three bedrooms; one had been converted into an office for Slade. The front area consisted of a dining room, living
room, kitchen, and guest bath. The whole place wasn't 1,200
square feet. The furniture was old. Nothing matched. It was the
kind of look you end up with after a relationship fails and you
divide everything up. Before Alexa, I'd had half a dozen apart-
ments furnished exactly like this.

Most shakes start in the bedroom because that's where people tend to hide their secrets. The master was a third larger
than the two guest bedrooms. The walls were painted blue.
LAPD blue or Crip blue? I wondered. The space was dominated by an unmade king-sized bed. A large Spanish dresser
sat opposite it against the wall. There was a closet full of Fila
running suits, known in law enforcement as 211 suits because
for some reason hold-up specialists from the hood seemed to
favor them.

I went quickly through the hanging clothes, checking pockets for notes, cards, or other personal debris. Nothing. I then
turned to three cardboard boxes stacked on the floor and found
that each one was packed with old clothes. At the back of the
closet, my eye fell on a large, rectangular, black case about
three feet long by one foot high. I pulled it out, broke the lock
with a metal hanger, and pried the lid open. Lying on the bottom in black cut Styrofoam was a fully automatic Beretta AR-
70 with two thirty-round clips. I looked down at the illegal
firearm and wondered what David Slade used it for. I closed the
box and pushed it back into the recesses of the closet.

Next, I searched the dresser. In with his socks, Slade had
some thong underwear, some condoms, and in the bottom
drawer, half a dozen hand-laundered, five-hundred-dollar silk
shirts. It seemed extravagant for a guy on a sergeant's salary.
There were half a dozen pictures in silver frames on top of the
dresser. In all of them, Slade was dressed in silk or satin, wearing tasteless, chunky, diamond-encrusted jewelry. His straightened Marcelled hair glistened. In several shots, he had his arm
around some very hot-looking ladies. Some were white, some
African-American. In one picture he was with a prominent, up-

and-coming rapper whose name I couldn't remember, but had seen on TV. Both were grinning and throwing Crip gang signs.

Then, I heard two car doors slam out front. I flipped off the bedroom light and sprinted back to the guest room just as I heard knocking on the front door.

"This is the police. Open up!" I heard Rafie yell. Then the door was being pounded on again and Sepulveda shouted, "Shane, if you're in there, open up or we'll break it down!"

I was halfway out the window when I heard the front door smash open. I landed on the grass, did a shoulder roll and came up running. I was just passing the garage when I noticed a brand-new, white Cadillac Escalade parked inside. Most cops drive midline Japanese iron. Not that a cop can't get financing on a ninety-thousand-dollar sled, but it seemed a little out of place sitting in Slade's ghetto garage. He had really pimped out the ride with twenty-inch, custom chrome wheels, known in the hood as blades or dubs. The car was talking to me. Something, some instinct, told me I had to check it out. I veered into the garage and tried to open the driver's side door. Locked. I could see the alarm light flashing. No alarm in the house, but a dude always wires his snap. Go figure.

I glanced over my shoulder at the back porch and saw lights going on inside. I heard Rafie and Tommy calling my name. It wouldn't be long before they'd be out here. I started frantically looking around for a hide-a-key under the bumpers. I found it in the right front wheel well, stashed high up behind the headlight—a small metal box attached by a magnet. I pulled it off, opened it, and slipped the key out. There was a small alarm remote on the key, so I chirped it and opened the door.

The car was loaded with expensive extras: leopard seats, color TV in the back, fifty-channel satellite dish on the roof. It had the latest GPS and telephone, and a sound system with enough muscle to blow all the fur off a pimp's collar. I opened the glove compartment and pulled out the registration. In the dim light from the open glove box, I could just read the DMV info. The car was owned by somebody named Stacy Maluga. The name sounded vaguely familiar. The address was 223 Oceanridge Drive, Malibu, California.

Then I heard the back porch door open and I got out of the car.

"Hey, Tommy, there's an Escalade out here. He might be in the garage," Figueroa yelled.

I was trapped. No way to get past him. I rolled up the registration slip and held it in my right hand like a baton. Then I edged toward the open garage door and looked out. Rafie was standing about twenty yards away on the porch, looking in my direction. He hadn't spotted me yet.

Here goes nothing, I thought, and sprinted out of the garage past where he was standing, and down the drive.

"Hey! Who is that?" Rafie yelled, startled. "Come back here, Shane!"

I heard footsteps behind me. I was pretty sure I could outrun him. He spent way too much time in the gym, and guys with lifter's thighs are usually slow as hell.

I rounded the corner at the end of the drive and pumped like crazy, heading for the Acura.

"Come back! Dammit, Shane! Stop!"

I made it to the car, jumped in and put it in gear. I could see Rafie clearly now, about five yards away, closing fast.

"Scully! You son of a bitch! Come back here!"

I floored it and shot away, speeding off the mean streets of Compton on my way to the mansions of Malibu.

CHAPTER EIGHT

Below me, on the left side of the road, the Pacific coast stretched in a lazy horseshoe defined by the lighted curve of the Malibu Shoreline. Off to the northeast was Pepperdine University. I was driving along twisting Oceanridge Drive, looking for 223. Finally, I pulled up and parked in front of a huge, multi-million-dollar mansion that sat by itself on a point that overlooked Malibu far below. A gold M adorned the center of an ornate design on the double-hinged, wrought-iron gates.

I put aside my fear over Alexa's fate. I had to play this carefully, and I knew I wouldn't do it right unless I had complete control of my emotions. I walled off my panic as I looked through the gates at the estate. Whoever Stacy Maluga was, he or she had a much better appreciation for security than David Slade. Floodlights blasted the grounds and signs promising armed guards and killer dogs were posted everywhere. I looked across two acres of rolling lawns toward a gorgeous neoclassical house. White columns, a flat roof, marble steps—all displayed in carefully placed uplights. It looked like the U.S. Supreme Court. Hard to guess how much land was involved, but it had to be at least five or six acres.

I got out of the Acura and approached a state-of-the-art communication system on a post near the gate. The unit had two cameras: one up high for a wide shot, another set at face level to catch my close-up when I used the intercom. I pushed the buzzer and waited. Nothing. I pushed it again. About a minute later, a man spoke. He had a deep bass voice with a homeboy lilt.

"Whatchu want?"

"Is this the Maluga residence?" I asked, using my stern, no-kidding-around cop voice.

"Who be wantin' ta know?"

"Shane Scully, LAPD." Then I heard some muffled sounds, like he'd put his hand over the mike to talk to someone.

Seconds later, the man said, "Nobody here called the po-lice."

"It's about a white Cadillac Escalade," I said, playing out a little more line.

"Say what?"

"A new, white Cadillac Escalade, belonging to Stacy Maluga was involved in a fatal accident tonight," I lied. "The deceased isn't the owner and I'm trying to determine if the car was borrowed or stolen."

"Mrs. Maluga's Escalade?"

"Yes, *Mrs.* Maluga."

"What be happ'ning to that ride again?"

"It was involved in a fatal accident. I need to speak with Mrs. Maluga."

"Damn!"

And then, our little communication ended and the intercom went dead. I started to turn around, but the man was obviously watching me on the security screen, because as soon as I turned, he said, "You got some po-lice credentials and such?"

"Yeah."

"Hold 'em up t'the lens there, so I can see 'em."

I pulled out my badge and held it up.

"Jus' a minute, 'kay? Gotta lock up the dogs."

The intercom went dead again. I knew that it wouldn't take Rafie and Tommy long to run the plate on the Escalade. They'd be here soon. I prayed that I had enough time to run some kind of a bluff. I wasn't limited by the truth like Sepulveda and

Figueroa. I had so much personally at stake, the rules of the criminal justice system had no consequences for me anymore. However, once these people found out what was really going on, they'd clam up and we'd be doing our talking through lawyers, which wouldn't help me find Alexa.

A few minutes later, I heard a humming noise and looked off across the grass. A four-seater, fire-engine-red golf cart with a corny Rolls-Royce hood and a fringed canvas top was zipping across the lawn toward me with two African-Americans aboard. It slowed and bounced over the low curb, rolled down the drive, and parked on the other side of the ornate gate. The larger of the two men got out. He was six-foot-three, two-twenty, and wore a Lakers tank and baggy jeans. He had one of those lean, cut bodies that looked like the anatomy chart in a doctor's office. He also had the shaved and shined bullet head that fighters and tough guys favor.

He never smiled but said, "Where the Escalade at?"

"There was a fatality. I need to speak with Mrs. Maluga."

"You best tell me, Cochise. She ain't seein' no visitors."

"'Cept I ain't gonna tell you. I'm telling the owner of the car. I can put out a call and get the Malibu substation up here to help me with this. You want, in ten minutes I can fill this drive-way with cops."

"Mrs. Maluga ain't home."

"Fine! Have it your way." I turned, walked back to my car and pulled out the dash radio mike. An elaborate bluff, but it worked.

"What fatality?" he said. "Who be deuced out?"

"I need to talk to the owner of the vehicle," I repeated.

"If they be rock or bags a cut or some such shit in that snap, it ain't ours."

"Would you open the gate, sir? I'm about through fussing with you."

We glared at each other through gold-initialed wrought iron, until finally he nodded to the second man, another steroid experiment in basketball togs. The number two hit a remote and opened the huge gates.

"Get in the back," Baldy ordered.

I climbed into the back of the silly Rolls-Royce golf cart and off we zipped toward the house, the little electric engine humming happily while my stomach rolled and roiled.

I had been to some expensive homes in Los Angeles, but never one quite like this. Acres of manicured lawns were punctuated with several beautifully sculpted fountains, all tastefully lit from below. Flowerbeds with colorful red and white impatiens fronted trellises overhanging with purple bougainvillea, framing the edges of the garden.

They took me around to the side of the house. All this wealth helped jog my memory. I recalled where I'd heard the name Maluga before. There was some kind of big-time rap producer named Maluga. Not Stacy, but Louis. I remembered now that he had recently done a nickel in San Quentin for assault with intent to commit. He'd gotten out about a year ago. He was legendary for his violent temper, which had earned him the nickname "Luna" Maluga. Stacy had to be his wife.

After the cart stopped, my two escorts got out and led me through a back door into a large, empty kitchen pantry.

"KZ, wait with this buster while I go see if Stacy wanna give the man some play."

I guess she was home after all.

He left me standing with the other guy, KZ, who kept glowering at me like I'd just bitch-slapped his sister.

"This Lou Maluga's place?" I asked, trying to sound nonthreatening and friendly.

No response. But he had his hands on his hips and I could see the wood-checked grip on a big automatic peeking out from under his basketball jersey.

"Nice spread. How much does a place like this go for?"

Not expecting an answer and not getting one.

A few minutes later, Baldly returned. "You strapped?" he asked.

"Yeah."

"Gimme it."

"Hey, Mister whoever you are. In my line of work, letting go of your gun is a career felony. I don't give up this piece unless you pry it outta my cold, dead hand."

He studied me for a long moment, then he pulled up his Lakers shirt and showed me a mean-looking automatic that looked like a big 9mm Glock or some equally brutal, hard-case piece of iron.

"I work security here," he informed me. "You go off on me and your ass gets served. We straight on that?"

"Very impressive." I smiled and pointed at his piece. "Hope you're permitted for that thing."

He didn't smile back. "KZ, walk this motherfucker's six," he said, and we headed out of the kitchen single-file. Baldy was leading the way, with me following. KZ was trailing at six o'clock.

Two doorways and a short, narrow hallway took us into an expansive living room. The place was overdecorated, but reeked of money. Some Melrose designer had made a killing here. Inch-thick glass coffee tables with sculpted chrome legs squatted over large, white area rugs. Lots of leopard- and tiger-print sofas were placed around the room like sleeping jungle cats. The ceiling was at least fifteen feet high and adorned with expensive, carved beams. A built-in bookcase ran along one wall and was full of pictures in silver frames and expensive knickknacks, but not many books. There was a line of what looked like leather-bound photo albums on the bottom shelf. Gold records hung on every wall.

Standing in the center of all this eclectic expense, wearing a pink terrycloth robe, was a woman about thirty years old, with white-blond hair and a strong jaw. She was pretty in a hard, strip-club kind of way. You could tell that under that fuzzy pink robe she had very nice equipment. She dissected me with angry ice-blue eyes.

"Mrs. Maluga?"

"Hey, Wayne? This fool be packin'?" she asked, the words accented by the street. She was looking over at Baldy, who was now revealed to me as Wayne. He didn't look like a Wayne; he looked like a Sluggo or a Spike.

"Man wouldn't give up his strap, Stacy."

She glowered at me. "I don't allow no chrome in here." I

guess she wasn't counting all the chunky ordnance Wayne and KZ were packing.

"I'm a police officer. It's against regulations for me to surrender my weapon."

"'Cept it's my crib," she answered. Her voice still full of flat vowels and the colorful lilt of the hood. She was Caucasian, but talked ghetto . . . a white sister.

I wasn't about to do another round on whether or not I could keep my gun, so I didn't respond, and just moved on. "Do you own a white Escalade?"

"So what if I do?" she finally said. "Zat against the law now?"

"The vehicle was involved in a fatal accident tonight. A man named David Slade died at the scene." I watched her carefully as I said Slade's name.

Nothing. Her expression remained cold and steady. Then she said, "Don't know no David Slade. That Cad got vicked last week when I was shopping on Beverly. Slade must be the busta who jacked it."

She glanced at Wayne, who nodded.

"You report it stolen?" I pressed.

"I got a lotta cars, sugar. Didn't get around to it just yet. Wayne gonna do it Monday."

"David Slade was a police officer, so I don't think he stole your car," I said, dropping it on her and watching to see how she handled it.

"Wayne," she said softly. It must have been some sort of pre-arranged signal because Wayne and KZ suddenly turned and walked out of the room, leaving Mrs. Maluga and me alone.

"Lou Maluga is your husband?" I was out of time and already down to fly-casting. Flicking an empty hook across the water, hoping to snag something.

She watched me for a long moment. Then she said, "If that be all, I got things need tending," pulling the belt on her pink robe tighter.

"I'm trying to find out what a dead police officer was doing in your stolen car. I'm afraid this is going to take a little longer, Mrs. Maluga."

"Then make a damn appointment with my attorney. He inna book. Name a Nathan Red," lobbing that name at me like incoming mortar fire.

Nathan Red was L.A.'s new Johnnie Cochran, an African-American lawyer who handled high-profile media cases for wealthy minorities. When Nathan Red was behind the bar, somebody was usually about to be accused of racism.

"And you're sure you've never heard of LAPD Sergeant David Slade?" I continued on.

"What I be doin' scrillin' with some five-oh? I don't kick it with no po-lice. You go now, 'fore I have them put you out."

Stacy looked toward the kitchen, but Wayne and KZ were still gone, probably making me a glass of arsenic lemonade. She was angry that they were taking so long and sighed theatrically, then went to look for them, leaving me alone for a minute. For a street-smart, tough lady, this was a major error in field tactics. As soon as she was out of the room, I quickly moved to the sliding glass doors and opened them wide. Then I hurried to hide behind the bar. Just before I ducked down, I saw her pager sitting on the green marble top. I had already broken enough regs to end my career, so I thought *what the hell* and snatched it up, turned it off, dropped it in my coat pocket, and crouched low with my gun drawn.

A minute later, Wayne and KZ returned. "Where he be at?" KZ blurted.

They did a quick sweep of the living room, completely missed me, but then saw the open glass door and ran into the backyard. Adios, g-sters.

I waited until they were clear, then sprinted across the white area rugs and closed and locked the slider. Next I walked over to the bookcase, kneeled, and looked at the picture albums. I found one labeled for this year, pulled it out, and started paging through it. I was looking for a shot of David Slade like the ones I'd seen in his bedroom. Stacy Maluga was the star of most of the pictures. She had a tight gym-trained butt and long stripper's legs, which she dressed to show. There were shots of her at different private parties and rap music events, always the center of attention, often with her arms around well-known celebrities. On every page, there were pictures of her looking hot and trashy.

Then, sure enough, in one of the photos, there he was: Sgt. David Slade of the good old LAPD. All decked out in his black 211 suit partying his heart out with a bunch of guys in Crip head wraps, looking as out of place as a cockroach in a Waldorf salad. The picture also made a liar out of Stacy Maluga because in the shot, she was sitting on Slade's lap with her hand between his legs, groping him like a Tijuana hooker. He had his tongue halfway down her throat.

I pulled the picture out of the album just as Stacy came back in from the kitchen.

"Where's Wayne and KZ at?" she snapped.

"Stepped outside for a breath of fresh air," I said. Then I handed her the picture. "Tell me again how you never heard of David Slade."

CHAPTER NINE

She was frozen, holding the picture, looking for a suitable response.

"I want to know about that photograph," I pressed.

She looked up at me. Blue ice turning to hard steel.

Just then, I heard a car pull up out front. Seconds later, the front door was thrown open. I couldn't see the entry from the living room, but the door slammed so hard against the wall that the crystal chandelier shook, rattling the glass teardrops like wind chimes.

"Stacy!" a man roared.

"In here, Lou."

Then the biggest man I have ever seen lunged into the living room. He was carrying a .50 caliber, chrome-plated Israeli Desert Eagle Mark XIX, which is a huge gun, but despite its size, it still looked like a toy in Maluga's giant hand.

I'd seen pictures of him in the Calendar section of the *L.A. Times*, usually at some music awards banquet. The press shots didn't begin to capture the essence of him. He was a monster. From what I'd read, he was half-black, half-Samoan. His head was basketball-sized. Round black eyes glinted maniacally from under hooded brows; his mouth an ugly tear in a steroid user's pock-marked face. The rest of him was right out of a Marvel comic—muscles on muscles. He was maybe six-feet-seven or -eight, and four hundred pounds, but I usually stop estimating height and weight after six-three, two-fifty, because beyond that, it's a SWAT exercise anyway. Maluga was dressed in a loose-fitting tan and yellow dashiki. There wasn't much else funny about him.

"How'd he get in here? Where's Wayne and KZ at?" he snarled. "What I pay them bustas for if dey can't keep shit like this from happenin'?"

"He's a cop," Stacy said, glowering at me. "They left the room to call you and he was going through my stuff, no warrant or nothin'."

Then Lou Maluga started toward me. There was little doubt how he'd earned the nickname "Luna." Roid rage flared in his eyes, sparking maniacally as he advanced. I felt like a wuss, but I knew I couldn't take him, so I yanked out the Beretta.

He saw it, then stopped, raised his gun, and said, "Go ahead, but I'll fuck you up, homes. One shot never gonna do it. You be dead 'fore you get off two."

"David Slade died tonight. It wasn't a car accident. He was shot behind the ear. Let's talk about that." I was trying not to look down the barrel of the huge Israeli cannon cradled in his right hand.

"Slade was a cheese-eater. . . . If he's dead, we all better for it."

I took the photograph out of Stacy's hand and tossed it across the room to him. He plucked it out of the air. Then I said, "That looks like a motive for murder to me, Lou."

He glanced at the shot and threw it aside. "I don't kill nobody over pussy, asshole." Then he pushed the gun forward at me. "Let's get this done." He was actually up for it, willing to stand there and shoot it out with me at point-blank range right in his own overdecorated, African-themed living room.

Then, breaking the moment, KZ and Wayne exploded into the den through the side door. Both had their guns drawn. The odds, lousy before, were suddenly impossible. I heard KZ trombone the slide on his auto-mag and I knew I was probably seconds from going down in a brutal crossfire. We stood there, John Wayne–style, faced off over gun barrels.

That's when the front gate buzzer sounded and Tommy Sepulveda's voice crackled over the intercom.

"LAPD. Open up," he said. Everybody in the room tensed.

"Open up!" Figueroa shouted next. "Open up or we're breaking it down!"

"I know Nathan Red is a good lawyer," I said to Stacy, "but in his absence, let me advise you that shooting it out with a cop in your house when the LAPD is standing at your front gate is a terrible idea."

KZ and Wayne started swinging their eyes back and forth from Stacy to Lou, looking like spectators at a tennis match, clearly hoping for further instructions.

"I got a better idea," Stacy finally sneered. "Why don't we just let five-oh handle this shitbird?"

CHAPTER TEN

Five minutes later, Tommy Sepulveda and Raphael Figueroa were in the living room. Two sets of angry cop eyes pinned me. While they glared, Stacy Maluga shouted accusations through porcelain-capped teeth.

"He was going through our stuff," she brayed. "I leave the room to see where Wayne and KZ be at, an' when I come back this motherfucker's searching through my picture albums. Stuff in books that ain't open an' in direct line of sight is protected from illegal searches without warrants or probable cause. And you ain't got no warrant. This here's an illegal search." She sure knew her Fourth Amendment.

"You want my side of it?" I said.

"No," Tommy said.

Lou Maluga was under control now, standing by the bar, uncapping a beer. His brown eyes looked sleepy, the craziness tucked safely out of sight.

"Let's go," Rafie said to me. "Tommy will take their statements. You and I are going to talk about this outside."

Rafie crossed the room and took my arm. What is it about bodybuilders that makes them think it's okay to put their hands on you and yank you around?

"Rafie, you need to hear me out. These people are directly

involved in Alexa's disappearance and Slade's murder and I
think I can prove it."

"Let's go. We're doing this out front."

Sepulveda stayed with the Malugas, while Rafie and I made
the long walk down the drive to the car. No cart this time, but
Wayne and KZ followed us, driving the miniature Rolls-Royce
fifty feet behind, making sure we left the grounds.

When we got through the front gate, Wayne closed it on us
and turned the cart around, heading back to the house. Rafie led
me over to his maroon Crown Vic. The car was still warm from
their drive up here. Rafie opened the back door and shoved me
inside.

"Stop pushing me around, will you? Next time you grab me
and yank on me like that, get your hands up, 'cause I'm tired a
your shit," taking my frustration out on him, even though he'd
done nothing but play by the rules. I was the one who was way
out of line, but I was stressed and not thinking straight.

"Don't you think I get it, man?" Rafie said. "If my wife was
missing like this, I'd probably be running around doing the
same things you are. But what are me and Tom supposed to do?
Should we just stand back and watch while you rip up and flush
half the criminal code? This is a high-profile murder case. Tomorrow we're gonna be up to our necks in media. If there *is* evidence in that house, you just blew it with an illegal search. You
know who that guy in there is?"

"Yeah. Lou Maluga. Some ex-con rap producer. I've read
about him. He's not a player anymore. Since he got out of
prison, he can't even get a CD distributed."

"Lou Maluga is CEO of Lethal Force, Inc. It's a huge rap label. And you're wrong, this guy is not out of it. He's got a pile
of money and throws big fund-raisers for charity. He's put a lot
of dough into politics. Real tight with U.S. Congresswoman
Roxanne Sharp. I've run six cases on this guy. I know what the
score is with this crowd. When people mess with the Malugas,
people tend to disappear."

"So because they've got dough, they get to kill David Slade,
maybe kidnap or kill my wife, and we can't say anything?"

"If you keep violating their rights and threatening them,

you're gonna get hit by so much paper, you're gonna think it's raining affidavits. So calm down."

"Okay, okay. I'm calming down." I took a deep breath. "Since you've worked this bunch, tell me about KZ and Wayne. Who are those two guys?"

"KZ is a Crip drug dealer turned bodyguard from Compton. He's a hitter. His yellow sheet is impressive because every witness to ever point him out didn't live to testify. The other guy, I don't know much about. Wayne Watkins. They call him Insane Wayne. He's new. The bimbo in the pink terrycloth robe is Stacy Maluga. She's Lou's estranged wife and the president of his record label. They're still married, but two months back, she filed for separation. Lou got himself some fresh trim, a hot-looking woman named Sable Miller. Before I had to pull my bugs out of his beach house, it sounded like they were thinking about getting married soon. Lou lives behind the gates in the Malibu colony. Stacy's got this place, which will give you an idea of what a tough, hard-nosed piece of work she is."

"She was having an affair with David Slade," I said.

"Prove it."

"There's a picture in there of the two of them, all wrapped around each other, swappin' spit."

"And your theory is what? That Lou Maluga shot David Slade because Slade was messin' around with his estranged wife who he doesn't even live with anymore?"

"It's been known to happen," I said, wondering if I had such a good theory here after all.

"These people don't play by the same rules you do, Shane."

I didn't say it, but I knew there were no rules for me anymore.

"Just try and answer two questions if you can," Rafie finally said.

"Okay."

"How did this all end up in Alexa's car and, assuming that Astra nine is Alexa's, why was Slade shot with her gun?"

"I don't know yet. But you tell me what an LAPD sergeant was doing screwing around with a gangsta rap producer's estranged wife. There's something here."

"Yeah, and a third-year law student could suppress everything you've turned up so far."

"Alexa didn't kill David Slade. And before I'm through, I'll prove it."

"You're not going anywhere. Put your hands out. I'm cuffing you to this floor ring back here."

"You and Sepulveda can play around with these Gs all night for all I care. I'm out!"

I pushed my way out of the backseat, stood, and Rafie rose up with me. We were now facing each other outside the Crown Vic. He was big and fit and obviously trusted his moves. For a moment, I saw something in his eyes that told me this was about to go physical.

"Don't do it, Raf," I said. "You and I have known each other ten years. I need some slack here. I'm asking for some understanding."

His hand moved, then fell to his side. He didn't want this any more than I did.

"I'm filing that one-eighty-one," he finally said.

"You know what? I think that's a good idea. It will cover you and Tommy with the dick squad at PSB."

Then I turned and walked to my car and got in. He watched me go. As I drove off, he shook his head and said something. I'm not much of a lip reader, but it looked like, "Good luck, man."

CHAPTER ELEVEN

By the time I was six, I had life pretty well figured out. I was sure nobody really cared about anything . . . especially me. Shuffled back and forth between group homes and foster families, I spent every other Saturday morning in some County Health facility, sitting for endless psych evaluations administered by bored civil servants. They usually turned up troubling results.

"He seems to have a dissociative personality, Mr. Jones."

Of course he does. He has nobody to associate with.

"His lack of concentration indicates severe emotional distress, Mrs. Smith."

Of course he lacks concentration. He's got nothing to care about.

Into the van, off to the group home, back to the dorm. Kick a ball on a dirt field behind the Huntington House for Boys. Watch an endless parade of fake smiles and furrowed brows, all of them telling me I was just another problem that had been laid off on society and would never be solved.

So you internalize. You get tough. You build calluses that will defend you from the darkness that has defined your life. When it starts so early, these dark spells can become who you are, but the people who run the meat machine always know where the soft spots are. They know where to poke and prod. To stay alive, you get tougher. Hard skin and a hard mind-set. They become your calluses. But calluses only go an eighth of an inch down. To survive, you know you have to make yourself harder, so you do. You work to protect what's left of your soft center. But over time, these emotional calluses can get so thick they become who you are. When that happens, there is very little left to fight for.

That was me by the time I was ten. I had little I really cared about, nothing that interested me. When I joined the LAPD, it was after a stint in the Marines and it was just an easy next step. The police department, like the Corps, was a way to trick myself into believing that I knew who I was. *The man in the green uniform is a Marine. The man in the blue uniform is a police officer.* On the door of my black-and-white patrol car it said, "To protect and serve." That was my new identity, my new code. But it wasn't me.

When I looked in the mirror I saw a uniform. A man of authority. But I didn't feel like one. I was good at being a cop, mostly because I didn't care what happened to me. *Go ahead, shoot me, you dirtbag. There's nothing here but hard skin and a heartbeat anyway.*

And then came Alexa and Chooch.

They flooded into my life, slowly softening my protective calluses like oil on dried leather. Little things, at first—pensive moments where new personal thoughts seeped into me, filled hollow spots in my infected psyche. And these thoughts and feelings started slowly curing me like antibiotics pumped into a throbbing abscess.

The idea that people were actually important came next, along with the notion that there really was such a thing as an unselfish act. I began to realize that love was an actual condition, and not just something faked—a manipulative ploy.

Little by little, I was pulled back from the darkness, reclaimed like a submerged, barnacle-encrusted hulk. It seemed like I would never fully come alive again, but I did.

The last four years had been a rebirth, with Alexa and

Chooch performing emotional CPR. They taught me there was strength in vulnerability, and wisdom in restraint.

Driving back to Venice from Malibu, I tried to make sense of what was happening. Selfish as it seemed, I knew that losing Alexa would probably cost me more than I could deal with. I had Chooch, but he was an adult now, off at college. I couldn't live my life for him much longer. Without Alexa, I was afraid I would slip back into the same, murky, alcohol-infested swamp I had just managed to crawl out of.

I wasn't sure if Alexa was alive, wasn't sure why there was a dead cop in handcuffs in her car. I had absolutely no idea how Stacy and Lou Maluga figured in, but there was one common denominator in all this, and that was the late Sgt. David Slade. I knew that Rafie and Tommy had no choice but to hang me out with the dicks in the Professional Standards Bureau. Their careers were at stake if they tried to give me cover. I wasn't going to back off and by now they knew it.

The problem was that nothing was anything without Alexa. I love her with a power so pure it sometimes frightens me. Without her, my life has no meaning.

I had been in some life-threatening situations, but I had never been in such jeopardy before.

I got home to Venice and parked in the drive. When I opened the front door, I realized that I had left without turning the alarm on. Like David Slade, deep down I knew I was tougher than anybody dumb enough to come after me. All the lights were still on, just as I'd left them. It was past one A.M. but I knew instantly the house was empty. It had that empty house feel, like a murder scene where everyone was dead.

I walked into the den and checked the answering machine. It was an old machine and the remote access system had become temperamental, so I couldn't retrieve calls. But it didn't matter because there were only the same three messages I'd left for Alexa earlier. I sat in the half dark, thinking about what my next move would be. I probably shouldn't stay here because if Rafie and Tommy followed through and filed a 181 complaint on me, by morning the Professional Standards Bureau could go to the D.A. and get an arrest warrant for obstructing justice. I could be picked up, booked, and taken to the courthouse for arraignment. It would take me half a day to get through all that. I didn't have half a day.

I figured I'd better clear out and come back here only to shower or change. They would try to serve the damn warrant two or three times, but they wouldn't make a career of it. After a couple of tries, it would go on the computer along with a BOLO to pick me up. I'd broken some internal department policies, some search and seizure regs, and a criminal obstruction of justice statute, but it was all Class-C stuff. I hadn't shot anyone—yet.

I stood and moved slowly out of the den. I was halfway across the partially darkened living room when I saw something move in the backyard.

I froze in my tracks and looked out. It was hard to see too much of the backyard through the room reflection on the glass, but someone was definitely sitting in one of the metal chairs back there, looking at the canal.

Had Luna Maluga already sent some energy in my direction, or was it Alexa? Taking no chances, I pulled my gun, moved to the side of the room, and edged to the glass slider. It was locked. I silently unhooked the latch and using my foot, slowly slid it open. I knelt down to nonfatal shooting height and looked outside.

There was someone stretched out on the lawn chair. It looked like Chooch. He had ignored my instructions and come home. In that instant, I was glad he had. He'd been right, I needed someone to talk this over with.

"Chooch!" I stepped outside and crossed toward him.

A man screamed in terror and jumped up, dreads and skinny elbows flying. Then John Bodine stumbled and went down, managing to catch himself with his good wrist, balancing himself precariously. "Like to scare a motherfucker to death," he whined.

I put my gun away. "What are you doing here?"

"Got no place else," he said. "And you still got all my what-alls in the car. 'Sides alla that, I got . . ."

"I know. Payback coming."

"Finally got that right, half-stepper."

CHAPTER TWELVE

I grabbed his skinny arm and pulled him into the house.

"I ain't no sack a shit you just yank here and about!" Bodine whined.

Once we were in the entry hall, I turned to him. "I can't deal with you right now. I'm in trouble—maybe about to be arrested. I've gotta get movin', so you're outta here." I went into the laundry room to get his stuff. He trailed after me, lost in one of his rants.

"You about to get arrested, are ya? In Cameroon, during the workers' strike, I got my black ass arrested six times. Got put on trial—no legal representation or any such shit. Weren't nobody there for me, but I was on a royal pilgrimage. A prince leading a people's rebellion against tyranny. In his manuscript, *Tonio Kröger*, Thomas Mann calls a killer one who permanently kills the ills of his people by piercing them with the arrows of the true word. That was me. Prince Samik Mampuna, killer of ills. Know what I'm sayin'?"

"No." I grabbed his clothes out of the dryer and rolled them up in his old coat, which had not yet made its trip to the cleaners. I was definitely through with this joker.

"I grew up watching hungry folks," he rambled on, trailing

after me, blabbering nonsense as I gathered up his things. "Watchin' them grab their swelled-up bellies; so far gone they couldn't even keep nothin' down. My daddy was a king—a tribal chief. He said the act of true sacrifice is giving even when you got nothin' left to give. And that be exactly what I'm talking about here."

"Don't move. I'll be right back." I left him standing on the laundry porch rambling about Africa, and headed to the bedroom to get my extra gun, a small .44 special Bulldog Pug. It's only accurate for a few feet, but it weighed less than two pounds and was an easy carry piece. I wasn't too worried about its accuracy, because I figured if Maluga came for me it would be close combat.

As I was pulling the piece out of the dresser drawer, something started vibrating in my pocket. I reached in and retrieved Stacy Maluga's pager. I'd completely forgotten about it. The number on the screen read: 310-555-6768. I jotted it down on a piece of paper and put the pager back in my pocket. As this was happening, I got the germ of an idea on how I might put that stolen gadget to work. I took a stack of cash out of a lockbox under the bed and stuffed it in my pocket. Then I grabbed Alexa's spare office key from the coin dish on our dresser, fitted the Bulldog into a small belt-clip holster and tucked it inside the waistband of my pants at the small of my back. My Beretta was still riding a holster on my hip. I grabbed a box of shells for each gun and left.

When I returned to the living room, true to his name, John was long gone. I found him in the den near the side window, looking out at the canal.

"Let's go."

He jerked up, shrieked in terror, then spun around. He was sure jumpy. It took him a minute to reclaim himself. Then he was back at it. "This ain't right. You run a man down, a prince of all things. Then you just give him a roll-up, and push him out the door with no howdy-do here's some cash."

I pulled out my wallet, extracted four hundred dollars, and handed it to him.

"I'll drop you back on the Nickel. How you deal with all that

anger down there is up to you. As of now, you and I are done,
friend."

He wouldn't move, so I grabbed his skinny arm Rafie-style,
and hustled him out of the house. Ten minutes later we were in
the Acura heading east on the 10 Freeway.

"Can't go to the Nickel. Ain't got no friends on the Row."

"Okay, I'll drop you in Hollywood then." I wasn't paying
much attention to him anymore. I was trying to get my thoughts
sorted out, make a list of investigative priorities. The order of
my next few moves could mean everything.

"Hollywood is like Tibet on acid," Bodine whined. "It's all
prayer rugs and hoop earrings down there. Buncha crackheads
and trapdoor Johnnies. My voices be tellin' me Hollywood ain't
no place for a straight Christian man to be."

"Come on, John. I'm through. I told ya I got my own problems."

"Hey, who run me over, huh? Was it you? I fuckin' think it
was."

We exited the freeway at Main, heading toward Parker Center.

"This ain't where I want to be at," Bodine whined.

I had stopped answering him. I finally pulled up across the
street from where I first hit him. "Door-to-door service.
Doesn't get much better than that."

I set the brake, got out, and pulled his shopping cart out from
the back of the SUV. I heard the sound of leather ripping as it
snagged the upholstery. I jerked it out angrily. Pissed me off,
but a torn backseat was way down on tonight's list of problems.
As I started to load Bodine's junk back into the cart, I could see
him in the front seat. He wasn't about to move. He just sat
there, rocking back and forth, moaning slightly.

When I finished with the cart I went around to the passenger
side, opened the door and glared down at him. "Let's go."

"Half-steppers at the sperm clinic won't even take my jizz
anymore," he said, looking up. His desperate eyes blazed.
"Muthafuckas won't even pay me to jerk off into a bottle. Say
my count is low. I tole 'em you eat outta garbage cans, your
sperm goes all ta hell. No vitamins in a grapefruit rind, know
what I'm sayin'?"

"Get out."

"Can't sell my blood, can't sell my jizz, what am I supposed to do?"

"I gave you four hundred. Don't make me drag you outta there."

He sat still and looked up at me. "Officer Scully, I'm kinda at my wits' end right now. I ain't brilliant or even that smart really, but you know what I am?"

"Stubborn."

"I'm worthwhile. Underneath all these problems is a very worthwhile person."

"John . . . please." I reached in and pulled him out of the car.

"I could be dead in the morning," he said.

"Me too."

We stood looking at each other in the dim light of the street lamp.

"No man is an island," Bodine finally said. "Some people help me along, but some, like you, just push me away. Ain't easy being an African prince in a cold-ass place like L.A. I keep sending out my resume, but I'm not hearing back."

I got behind the wheel. As I pulled out, I looked in my rearview mirror and saw him standing on the curb with his shopping cart full of junk. There was a moment, sucker that I am, when I almost went back and got him.

As things turned out, I would have been way ahead if I had.

CHAPTER THIRTEEN

There are more videotapes running in Parker Center than at NBC Burbank. Five security cameras photograph the lobby and multiple cameras cover all the main hallways of each floor. Everything is fed down to a tape room in the sub-basement. I knew that there was very little I could do to defeat all that high tech security. After what happened up on Mulholland, the Deputy Chief wouldn't have to think very hard to figure out what I was doing in my wife's office on the command floor at three A.M. I was disobeying direct orders and the tapes would confirm it.

I didn't care.

I pulled out Alexa's spare office key and used it to open the door, moving through Ellen's neat outer office, past a stack of crime manuals and new forensic journals that the chief made mandatory reading for all command rank officers.

I sat behind Alexa's desk and turned on her computer. While it booted I looked at a photograph of us taken in Nevis last year. In the shot, Alexa's black hair was lustrous in bright sunlight, blowing in a tropical breeze. Her dark tan and bright smile made my heart clutch. In the picture, two glasses of Planter's Punch with colorful umbrellas rested between us on the wooden plank table of the beach bar where we'd stopped. She wore her beauty like a casual gift, I wore a Hawaiian shirt and a jackass smile. It was as good as it gets. A roving photographer had taken the picture. Twenty bucks to memorialize a romantic moment that now broke my heart.

As I studied the photo, the knot in my stomach tightened. Memories of those five romantic days flooded over me, underlining my loss. That time spent on a Caribbean island had been a glimpse into our future. In a few more years we'd both have twenty-five years on the job and be out with full pensions, able to travel the world. I hadn't told her, but lately I had started to look past the daily uncertainty and harsh realities of police work, contemplating a more tranquil existence.

We had made love in the sweet-smelling garden suite at our hotel. We made love in the ocean at midnight. We talked about secrets and shared our fears. I'd told her about parts of me that nobody else knew. Instead of being repelled, she had caressed my shortcomings. She told me that fear is at the heart of the human condition, that it's one of the two basic reasons that anyone does anything. The other reason, she said, was love. I knew she was right. In a few short years she had changed what motivated me.

Now she was missing—maybe gone forever. Would I ever see her again? Would I even recover her remains? Desperate thoughts arced around inside my head—murderous plans of violence and revenge. I thought about what I'd do to Maluga if he had hurt her.

The computer had loaded and I turned toward it. Her password was "lacey." The TV show *Cagney & Lacey* was what had motivated her to be a cop when she was a girl. I typed it in and started opening windows.

I found a file on undercover assignments. I could find nothing in the file on David Slade.

Next I accessed the e-mails. All communications from yesterday and today had been purged. I wondered if Ellen had come back in to do that after Alexa's car was found or if Alexa had done it before she left for that mysterious appointment. When we'd walked back from the jail, did she know she was in danger? I sat there for a moment, turning that over in my mind.

Then I went back to the document files. I opened half-a-dozen with coded names like "Operation Rhinestone," which turned out to be an undercover op on a ring of jewelry store burgs. "Walking Tiger" was a sting on Chinese gangs. The last one I opened was called "Dark Angel." It contained one short sentence.

FILE TRANSFERRED TO AHC

I had no idea what AHC stood for.

Then I heard footsteps in the hall. I turned off the computer and crossed to the door where I met Tommy Sepulveda.

"Scully," he said, looking at me with tired eyes.

I was so busted, it was pathetic.

We stood there, each not knowing what to say.

"What're you doing here?" he finally managed.

"Thought maybe Alexa might be . . ." I didn't finish the sentence because the frown on Sepulveda's face was so deep it was almost comical.

"This isn't working," he said.

"For me either."

"I'm not gonna try and take you down, Shane. But I'm putting it all in the report. Me and Rafie look like morons letting you run around gumming this up."

"Right. When I get the PSB charge sheet, I'll tell them you gave me the word and I wouldn't listen."

He heaved a disappointed sigh before he said, "As long as you already shook this place, you find anything worthwhile?"

"There's a purged file on Alexa's computer, code named 'Dark Angel.' That seems a little strange. Says it's been transferred to AHC. Whatever that is."

I still wasn't convinced that Sepulveda wouldn't try something. If it were me, I'd have gone for it, so I kept my eyes on him as I slipped past and out the door. He watched me walk down the corridor and get in the elevator. As the doors closed, he was still staring.

It was three-thirty A.M. when I left Parker Center. I was pretty sure Sepulveda and Figueroa wouldn't be able to get a warrant to search my house until at least eight A.M., so I decided to risk it and headed home. Something was buzzing in my head. It felt as if there was some piece of this that linked up, but because of all the adrenaline and emotion, I had walked right past it. It wasn't until I pulled up in front of my garage that I suddenly knew what it was. I scrambled out of the car and ran to the front door. Once I got into the entry, I was immediately struck by the fact that it was cold inside. We usually keep the temperature at seventy-five. It was well below that. Then I saw the reason. The window in the den was half open, cold marine air was blowing in. I closed and latched it. Bodine must have opened it when I found him standing in here two hours ago, looking out.

I walked into the bedroom. I was looking for a blue book that was about an inch thick. It was not in the bookcase or in Alexa's bedroom chest of drawers. I finally found it in the bottom of her closet in a cardboard box that had been in the garage when we'd redone the space for Chooch after Delfina came to live with us last year. I pulled out the book and took it to the front room, sat down by the light, and opened it up. It was Alexa's LAPD Cadet Academy class book. I felt something brush my leg, looked down and saw Franco rubbing against me. He looked up, knew something was wrong, and let out a pitiful cry. I patted him but didn't speak. I opened the blue Police Academy yearbook.

The thing I had just remembered was that both Alexa and David Slade had joined the department in 1982. There were only two Academy classes a year. That meant there was a fifty-fifty chance they'd gone through police training together.

I leafed through the book, looking at the graduating cadet pictures. They were all standing straight, hats off, looking sternly into the camera. There were several people I knew in this class. William Rosencamp. His picture showed a tall, handsome African-American officer whom I hadn't seen in about a year, but I thought was now a patrol sergeant in Devonshire Division. The caption under his picture said he was tenth in a class of fifty-six. He had won a cadet street combat tactics competition and had a long-gun shooting classification of Marksman. His Academy nickname had been "Rosey." Still was.

I found Alexa's picture. Even though she had her game face on, she looked breathtaking as usual. I skimmed through her cadet accomplishments. Alexa Hamilton was second in her class. She had won the Distinguished Marksman shooting medal and held a dozen other cadet honors including obstacle course champion in the one-hundred-fifteen-pound division. Her academy nickname was "Hambone."

And then, toward the back of the graduation shots, I found David M. Slade. He was rakishly handsome and clean cut, smiling through perfect teeth. His coffee-colored skin glowed against his crisp blue Academy uniform. His moustache was clipped and perfect. Slade had graduated forty-fourth. He had a sharpshooter's medal and came in third in an academy martial arts competition.

His nickname was "Dark Angel."

CHAPTER FOURTEEN

"Come on out. Don't be afraid," Alexa shouted through the bolted iron door. "You've been afraid since you were born. It's time to put all that behind you."

"That's ridiculous," I called back. "The only fears we're born with are fear of falling and fear of loud noises. All other fears are learned." Sweat was dripping out of my hair, into my eyes.

"I won't hurt you, I promise," she said. "Open the door."

My heart was beating fast, my eyes strained to see in the dark enclosed space. "Fear is what lets you grow," I shouted through the door. "I've had my head shrunk by the best. I know the drill. You can't just live in a comfort zone. You have to take chances if you want to improve." I could barely make out the walls. Dim light seeped in through a few holes in the rafters.

"Come out, Shane. I promise I won't hurt you."

"But you already have." I was crying. I never cry, but I was crying. Tears ran. Hot tracks of salt and self-pity.

"But I don't mean to hurt you," she called to me.

"I know. But I can't take this. I can't live like this. Not knowing is killing me."

"But I'm right here. Right outside this door. All you have to do is come out."

I woke up without opening my eyes. I had departed from

one darkness and was suddenly in another. I remembered lying down on the bed with the police graduation book on my chest, trying to sort out what it meant that Slade and Alexa's relationship dated back to the Police Academy. I had not intended to fall asleep, but fatigue had overtaken me. Then I dreamed, and my dreams were torture.

I opened my eyes, sat up, and looked at the clock in our bedroom. It was eight in the morning. *Damn.* I jumped out of bed, went into the bathroom, slapped water on my face, and looked into reddened eyes. I looked different. Everything was the same, but somehow it wasn't. There was less here than there was yesterday.

Then the front doorbell rang.

I grabbed my jacket and moved to the side window and looked out at the street.

Parked by the side of my house was the maroon Crown Vic. It was empty. Tommy and Rafie were at the front door.

Decision time. What do I do? Do I open up and risk taking an arrest? Or do I slip out the back door and beat feet down the canal walk to the side street? I was still half-asleep, but then a thought hit me. Maybe these guys knew something. Maybe they'd found Alexa.

I opened the door.

"Thank God you finally went home," Tommy said. There was a piece of yellow paper in his left hand that looked like some kind of internal department document.

"Yeah," I answered. "Finally came to my senses. Whatta you doing here? I was expecting the I.A. rat squad."

"Takes a little time for a shit soufflé to rise," Rafie said. "They gotta get a deputy chief to sign their warrant and DCs don't get in till ten. We got our paper from the division commander who gets in at seven."

"What paper is that?"

Tommy handed me the yellow sheet. It was an internal demand served on Alexa's computer.

"You want her computer?"

"Police property. We're reclaiming it as part of the investigation."

"I see," I said, cussing myself. I hadn't even thought to look at her personal computer. I didn't want these two guys in my house going through her files so I centered myself in the doorway.

"Don't be a schmuck," Rafie said.

"Look, I'm . . ."

"You gonna step aside or is this going to turn into a police incident?" Rafie said. Both of them looked like they were a heartbeat from thumping the crap out of me. Actually, scanning her computer was a good idea. I should have beat them to it, but with the two of them standing there, I knew that race was pretty much over.

"Okay," I finally said, and stood aside.

"Where is it?" Tommy asked.

"Her office." I led them through the house into a small storage room off the hall that we'd converted into a place for Alexa to work. No windows, a small workspace, everything stacked and organized neatly, Alexa-style. I turned on the lights and motioned to the desk. Her computer was gone.

"Where is it?" Rafie said. The tension in his voice was hard to miss.

"I don't know." And I didn't.

"Starting last night you were a problem, but me and Tommy were trying to look past it because the Lieutenant is your wife. Now, however, we're talking criminal malfeasance. Obstructing justice, withholding evidence, interfering in a homicide investigation, accessory after the fact. You're stacking up felonies faster than an E-Street gangster."

"I don't know where the computer is," I said. But in the next instant, I figured it out. John Bodine stole it. He hadn't been looking out my side window earlier, when I'd caught him, he'd been unlatching it. That's why he jumped. Then after I dumped him on the Nickel, he must have rented a cab using my money, come back here, shimmied through the window, and stole the computer. My guess was when I checked the house I'd find he'd liberated a lot of other stuff as well.

"I'm going to ask the Professional Standards Bureau to pick you up, Shane. You won't stay out of this, so I'm gonna have you held," Tommy said.

"We all do what we have to do," I answered.

They turned and walked out of my house, leaving me standing in Alexa's office looking at her empty desk.

After they were gone, I took a quick tour. Bodine had stolen two TVs, Chooch's stereo, and a microwave, along with Alexa's computer.

He'd clouted our stuff and true to his rep, was long gone.

CHAPTER FIFTEEN

Howard Jones Field on the USC campus is where the Trojans football team holds summer two-a-days. Pete Carroll has open practices during July, so I parked behind an athletic equipment building and walked past the track to the field. It was nine-thirty in the morning and players in shoulder pads, practice jerseys, and shorts were huddled in separate groups working with their position coaches.

I spotted Chooch with the quarterbacks. Steve Sarkisian was leading them through a footwork drill, teaching both three- and five-step step drops. As I approached I couldn't help a flash of pride. My son was handsome. He was the result of a one-time fling I'd had with a beautiful Hispanic call girl who had given up being an escort to become a confidential informant for the department. Five years ago, before she died in my arms, she told me that he was a son I never knew I had. Now I watched him across the football field and marveled at how perfect he seemed. Six-three with his mother's dark good looks, he was even more beautiful on the inside where it counted. Chooch saw me coming, said something to the coach, and then sprinted in my direction carrying his helmet. He met me on the thirty yard line. Tension was etched on his face.

"Did they find her?"

"Not yet."

His shoulders slumped.

"Look, son, I promise I'll get to the bottom of this."

"Dad, let me help you."

"I can't. Since this happened, I've broken a lot of department regs along with a few low-grade criminal statutes. The acting chief is probably pissed, so there's a good chance the District Attorney could press charges. I can't have you mixed up in this."

"Dad, how can I just—"

"I know. I know, it's tough," I interrupted. "But you've gotta trust me, Chooch. If I have something for you to do, I'll call. Until then I need to know you're safely out of this."

"One of the guys had a radio on this morning. They're saying an LAPD undercover officer was found dead inside of a high-ranking female police commander's car. They made it sound like she's at fault sorta."

I was surprised that the media had the story already. Usually the department tried to keep a police shooting under wraps until they had all the facts. Somehow, it had leaked.

"There're some very tough characters on the edge of this. The press is going to blow it up into something it's not."

"Whatta you mean?"

"I have a bad feeling about the way they're going to spin it. In the meantime, I'm going to find your mom. That's my focus. If this goes the way I think it will, it may get a little uncomfortable for you, even here."

"They're gonna say she killed him? That's ridiculous," he said.

"In a high-profile deal like this, speculation often gets played like fact. The uglier it seems, the more the press likes it. I don't know what they're gonna say, but we've gotta believe in Alexa."

"Dad, how can you say that to me? I know Alexa. I know who she is. I'll always believe in her." He had tears in his dark eyes.

"I'll call you at least once a day."

"No cell phones on the practice field. You've gotta wait until after eight, when we're out of the film room. Or send somebody out to get me."

"Okay. Hang tough. I'll call you at eight unless it's urgent."

I didn't hug him in front of his teammates, even though I wanted to. Instead, we shook hands. It felt awkward and forced. I turned and walked back to the equipment building where my car was parked. As I drove away and made the turn at the end of the field, I looked back and saw Chooch still standing there, holding his helmet, all alone, watching me leave.

Driving out of USC I tried to get a number for William Rosencamp. I called a friend in Personnel and found out that he had moved from Devonshire to the old Newton Division. Newton used to be its own division, but was now reorganized as part of the Central Bureau. The area was bordered by the Harbor Freeway on the west and Florence Avenue on the south. The reorganized Central Bureau was a hot zone that now included South Central L.A. The streets around the Newton stationhouse were still notorious. As a result, it had retained its old moniker, Shootin' Newton.

I needed more information on David Slade. On the surface he just seemed like a bad apple. I knew from reading *The Blue Line,* an LAPD magazine, that Rosey Rosencamp was the recently elected head of the Oscar Joel Bryant Association for black police officers. I was pretty sure that a wrong number like David Slade would be a special topic of interest for those guys. Since Rosey was an old friend of mine and had been in the Academy with Alexa and Slade, I was also hoping he might be able to shed some light on this guy and maybe point me in a fresh direction.

I reached him on the first try. He was just heading out to get breakfast. With Slade's murder all over the news, he didn't have to ask why I was calling. We agreed to meet at a pancake house near the station.

Driving through Newton, I realized that not much had changed here since I first pinned on a badge. Some areas are so infected with urban blight that there is no reclaiming them. As I drove down surface streets, I saw three guys in silver-and-black Raider jackets huddled in a doorway. They glared as I passed. A crack deal went down right under my nose when I stopped at a light on Fifty-fourth Street.

Like everything in this neighborhood, the pancake house had seen better days. I parked in the lot, chirped my alarm, and walked into the half-empty dining room. Rosey was seated by the window, where he could keep an eye on his black-and-white parked on the other side of the plate glass. He was wearing his blue uniform with sergeant's stripes. Rosencamp was a big man and had put on a few pounds since the last time I saw him, but he was still a long way from fat. He had one of those stocky builds that made him a tough commodity on the street; hard to push around or move in a fight. He was well liked but had been stalled at sergeant for six years. He should have made lieutenant by now. I wondered if his membership in OJB had marked him as a troublemaker. The LAPD liked to pretend we were colorblind—no white, brown, yellow, or black . . . just blue. Despite this carefully orchestrated fiction, nightmare incidents from Rodney King and the now-famous "Gorillas in the Mist" mobile computer transmission, to the more recent Rampart scandal and the OJ trial, had kept racial strife inside the department simmering. Nobody wanted it, but it was there just the same. Everybody on the job already knew that this thing with Alexa and David Slade wasn't going to help.

"How're you holding up?" Rosey said, even before I sat down.

"It's tough."

"Gonna get tougher," he said. Then he filled me in on how the story had leaked. "The planets musta been lined up wrong after they found Alexa's car," he said. "Some still camera stringer jumped the first patrol car radio transmission, snuck up in the trees above Mulholland, and got pictures of the body and your wife's license. Sold his shots to the *L.A. Times*." He grabbed a paper off the seat beside him and dropped it on the table in front of me. It was all there: the BMW surrounded by cops and crime scene tape, David Slade slumped forward with his head resting on the dash. "They got Roxanne Sharp on the TV already," Rosey continued. "She's cutting up the department. Great White Mike's in full vapor lock. For a guy who loves being on the tube, he was stuttering and muttering worse than Elmer Fudd. We're about to get our big blue asses kicked. The real chief came through surgery okay, but he's gonna be out of it for weeks. We could sure use him on this 'cause Great White Mike's gonna get pasted."

"Yep," I said, angry at myself that I hadn't even given one thought to Tony's surgery. I'd been too consumed with worry over Alexa. I knew that Rosey was right. Mike Ramsey was no match for the media sharks and political whores that were already circling.

"You got any clue what Slade was doin' dead in her car?" Rosey asked, bringing me back.

"I'm just getting started."

"Yeah, and the way I hear it, PSB is lookin' to slow you down. Also heard the D.A. is studying it. Your best bet is to go right to the chief before he issues you a two-six."

A two-six was a forthwith. Go to the chief's office on the sixth floor, Code Two, which was with all possible dispatch. Ignore a two-six and your badge goes into Lucite.

"Rosey, I need your help."

"Puts me in the dumper, I help you, Shane."

"You guys at OJB must have a case file on David Slade."

"You bet we do. I know this guy's one-eighty-one file by heart. He's the kind of police makes a nightmare for all of us. We talk about Slade least once a month."

"I need some background."

He hesitated, but then finally nodded. "Okay, but you didn't get it here."

I nodded.

"A lot of this goes back a ways, to when Chief Brewer was on the job. Back then, Slade picked up seven or eight road-rage incidents in his PSB file. The way it would go down was some civilian would cut him off on the freeway and Slade would go postal, pull out his nine and wave it through the window at the guy. Start yelling how he's gonna cap the poor schlub. Trouble is, once the civilian made a complaint, it kinda just never got completely dealt with."

"You're saying he's got juice down at the Professional Standards Bureau. That doesn't sound right."

"Who the hell knows? This was under Chief Brewer. You know more than anyone what a corrupt bastard he was. Back then the chief had the power to reach down at will and adjust any Board of Rights finding. Couldn't make a penalty worse, but he could lighten it if he wanted to, and that's exactly what Chief Brewer did for Slade. All eight times. Cut two flat-out dismissals down to thirty days off without pay. If you or I went and pulled a gun on some civilian over a lane change, we'd be working at Wal-Mart."

"You think he had something on the department?"

Rosey shrugged.

"Anything else?"

"All kinda stuff. You know he got in on that juvenile felony waiver."

"I kind of figured that."

"Slade grew up in Compton. By the time he was thirteen he was already a baby G doin' lookouts on dope deals. Cripped all through high school, gets popped on two righteous felonies— an ag-assault and an attempted murder. He does two years at the County Youth Offenders camp, gets out when he's eighteen. He was lookin' for new windows to break, sees our recruiting ad saying all is forgiven, and joins the department."

"You knew Alexa in the Academy. In your opinion, is there any way she'd ever use Slade on an undercover assignment?"

His brow furrowed. Something was going on, but he wasn't sure if he wanted to share it.

"You got something?" I asked.

"It'll keep," he finally said, and changed the subject.

"Last scam Slade pulled should a got him bounced for sure, but again, he gets out from under it. It was just before Filosiani became chief."

"Let's hear."

"The story is that he was partying in Lou Maluga's house, way up on top of Malibu. Big place—fountains, lawns—all they don't have is a polo field. One night, about three years

back, a guy calls nine-one-one and says he was just up there de-
livering pizza, and some black dude jumped the fence and is
running around waving a gun on the property. The caller says
the intruder is six-one, two hundred pounds, and is wearing a
maroon two-eleven suit. The Malibu sheriff rolls a car and
when they get out there, sure enough, here's this black dude
running around in maroon Fila acting all crazy. The cops don't
see a gun, so they tackle the suspect, put him down hard. He
motherfucks them up one side and down the other, takes a
swing, and it gets nasty. Batons come out and these two cops
start doin' a marimba on the homeboy's skull. 'Bout then the
man identifies himself as David Slade, an LAPD sergeant."

"I don't get it."

"It'll make sense in a second. Next, he hires Nathan Red and
sues the Sheriff's Department for a hate crime in civil court. He
wants a million bucks. Stacy Maluga, who he's screwin', backs
him in a statement and pays the attorney fees. She says she saw
the whole thing."

"Got it."

"He set them up. It looks like a good beef that's gonna stick.
The D.A. is circling and the press is all kneeled down in the
blocks waiting for a starter's gun, and the city is talking about a
big settlement to keep it out of court. Then somebody in our Internal Affairs who is familiar with this dirtbag's package calls
the sheriff's investigator and suggests that they make a voice
print on David Slade and check it against the nine-one-one call.
Just like that, the fool is busted. Slade is the phony pizza deliv-
ery guy who phoned it in."

"What happened?"

"Sixty days off without pay. I'm telling you, if the rest of us
had this kind of cover, we'd all start holding up banks for a living."

"I might, but you wouldn't," I said.

"Probably right," he said. "Got this dumb white hat all stuck
down on my nappy head." Rosey grinned at me and then while
we were looking at each other, the grin disappeared and the
frown came back.

"What is it, man?" I asked. "Something's bothering you."

"I can't, Shane. We're friends. You got enough to deal with. I don't want to go and make it worse."

"Alexa's missing. She may be dead. I've got the rat squad and maybe the D.A. chasing me with warrants. I don't have any time. How can it get worse?"

He took a deep breath and then let it out slowly. "Back when we were all in the Academy, there was a rumor about David and Alexa."

My heart was beginning to beat harder in my chest. "What kind of rumor?"

"You know what kind of rumor. *That* kind of rumor."

"You mean they were seeing each other?"

"Lotta testosterone and estrogen flowing back then. Slade was definitely a ladies' man. A mac daddy from Compton. We were all real young. Hard to keep your arithmetic in one column."

"I don't think Alexa would get involved with some Crip gang-banger," I said hotly.

"Maybe not. Like I said, it was just a rumor."

The waitress came to take our order, but I had no appetite. I thanked Rosey, shook his hand, and walked out into the parking lot. I stood outside by my car for a minute, looking at the interior through the windshield. My face was reflected in the curved glass window, distorted and ugly. I didn't look like me. I didn't feel like me. And Rosey was right.

He'd made it worse.

CHAPTER SIXTEEN

It was a lot to process. Pieces didn't fit.

How could somebody like Alexa find herself attracted to a tattooed Crip criminal with a juvenile felony package? I looked hard inside myself, trying to see if there was a racial component guiding my skepticism. I had started so low on the ladder as a kid, I didn't usually think in terms of race. For me, there were just assholes and mega-assholes. They came in all colors. But still, is anybody completely immune? I'd had Chooch with a Hispanic woman, but did that indemnify me? Sex without commitment is just a party. As I turned this over in my mind, I knew that I didn't have a problem with the idea that Alexa might have had a black lover as long as he was a quality person, but from what Rosey had told me, David Slade was a dirtbag. The road rage incidents, the crazy attempt to shake down the Sheriff's Department with that 911 call. That kind of character flaw didn't just suddenly pop up in your early twenties. This guy had been dirt from the beginning. So what was Alexa doing messing with him? She should have sensed who he was under that fake smile and carefully clipped moustache.

I was pretty sure he had never left his Crip gang, despite being on the LAPD. That was probably why he still lived in Compton. It was his hood. His old crew was kicking it there. He

looked to be about the same age as Louis Maluga. I wondered if
Slade knew Maluga back when he was a baby G doing corners.

I picked up my radio mike and called communications.
When they answered, I identified myself and said, "Wants, warrants and background on a Louis Maluga and Stacy Maluga."

"Roger," the RTO came back. "Stand by."

I was almost out of Newton, driving on Washington Boulevard, heading toward the Harbor Freeway.

While I waited, I turned my thoughts to our Chief Filosiani's
predecessor, Burl Brewer. Rosey was right, I had experienced
firsthand the full extent of his corruption. I was the cop who finally had him arrested for conspiracy and murder back in the
late 1990s. Had Chief Brewer somehow been involved with
Lou Maluga and Lethal Force, Inc.? I knew I would never get
an answer to that question, so I moved on.

As I drove, I kept wondering why Slade had been found
dead in Alexa's car. Was that old Academy relationship important? Did it affect everything that was happening now?

They were not easy thoughts. They swung carelessly around
in my brain like dangerous wrecking balls, knocking into emotional barriers, punching holes in my value system. If she could
betray me like this, what was anything in my life worth?

"One-L-Forty. On your wants, warrants, and background.
Stand by."

I keyed my mike. "Go."

"Louis Maluga. Born March sixth, nineteen sixty-five to
Rita Maluga, father unknown. He did five years in Soledad
from ninety-nine to oh-five for aggravated assault and attempted murder. His first arrest was in Compton in nineteen
eighty: assault with intent. Juvie never filed. Second arrest in
April: attempted murder. Witness died same result. Third arrest, June of ninety-nine: attempted rape, attempted murder.
Witness disappeared. Never filed."

"Okay, I get it. What about Stacy?"

"Stacy Maluga, nee Stacy Adams. Born in Norway in
seventy-two at a naval hospital. Moved to the states in seventy-
three when her father was discharged. He was killed in nineteen
seventy-five. DUI. Family moved to E Street in Compton. Her

booking sheet is mostly drugs. She was also arrested in July of ninety-five for indecent exposure and lewd acts. She had sex on stage at a strip club."

"Okay. Can you download both yellow sheets and fax them to my office at Homicide Special?"

"Roger that."

I gave her the number, then disconnected. I didn't ask for David Slade's yellow sheet because I knew there wouldn't be one. All his prior crimes had been sealed juvie busts, or he wouldn't have qualified for the felony waiver. Everything he'd done wrong once he was on the LAPD would be in his PSB package, if I could find a way to access it. With all the heat coming down after his murder, it was going to be hard to get my hands on it. But I have friends and I'm devious, so I intended to try.

Without really planning it, I realized I was heading back to my house in Venice. It was probably stupid to keep going home, but I was drawn there. That house was my only connection with Alexa. I kept thinking I'd walk in and find her with a perfectly plausible explanation. Or I'd find a message on our answering machine. If she was alive, I knew she would get in touch with me.

I parked half a block away and moved down the street looking for department-issue, four-door sedans with black tires. Nothing. I kept in the shadows of a line of elm trees and worked my way past the house. If detectives from the Professional Standards Bureau were here to question me, they were pretty damn good at blending in. I couldn't see any sign of them but decided to enter my house from the canal side anyway, just to be safe.

I moved quickly along, hoping none of my neighbors would see me. I entered the backyard, took out my key, unlocked the sliding glass door, and carefully pushed it open.

The minute I stepped inside and smelled the stale air, I knew she was still missing. Nobody was there. The house was lifeless and still. It was just after ten-thirty A.M. I turned on the kitchen television as I walked through, but was stopped in my tracks by what I heard.

"Speculation is running rampant. What was a dead under-cover police officer doing murdered in the front seat of the head of the LAPD Detective Bureau's personal car?"

One of the anchors from Channel Four was leaning for-ward, looking stern, but you could see the excitement in his eyes. I turned away from the TV and checked on the answering machine hooked to our kitchen telephone as the newscast con-tinued.

"This morning, in a brief statement, Deputy Chief Ramsey confirmed that Sergeant David Slade was killed while in police handcuffs, but refused any comment on the guilt, innocence, or whereabouts of Lieutenant Alexa Scully. He also wouldn't say if she was a suspect in the execution-style shooting."

I froze with my hand on the telephone, watching this asshole engage in rampant speculation. *Suspect in the execution-style shooting?* How could he even imply that? The video package played behind him, complete with separate shots of Alexa and David Slade. They had used Slade's Academy photo. He looked handsome and clean cut. It would not have helped this media hatchet-job to show him like he really was, in his Mar-cel do with an armload of badass Crip ink. The shot switched to a pleasant-looking, middle-aged African-American woman in a TV-friendly, dark blue suit and pale blue blouse. She wore a small gold angel pin prominently on her lapel, attesting to her purity and faith. The on-screen graphic identified her as Con-gresswoman Roxanne Sharp. She had a long record as a media whore who always weighed in on racially charged situations.

"If this is what it appears to be, I can assure you that I will personally take the LAPD to task," the congresswoman prom-ised. "This fine, African-American officer was gunned down in his prime, left dead in his bureau commander's car. I can prom-ise the people of Los Angeles, this will not become the latest example of LAPD arrogance or investigatory incompetence."

Nathan Red was up next. Handsome, with gray flecks in his black hair, he looked like Billy Dee Williams in a tailored Ar-mani with a silk tie.

"David Slade's family is considering legal redress against the LAPD and the city. At this time, we will withhold further comment, except to say that it certainly raises questions that Lieutenant Scully is suspiciously missing."

My heart sank. I knew this was only the beginning.

I played my messages as the newscast continued spewing speculation and misinformation. My three calls to Alexa were still on the machine. A call from the Professional Standards Bureau came in at nine A.M., issuing me the dreaded two-six to report to Mike Ramsey's office. Then Alexa's voice was on the machine.

"Shane, it's me." She sounded small and tired. "I'm so sorry about this, darling. I can't bear to think what this is doing to you and Chooch, but I had no other choice." Then there was a long pause before she said, "I killed David Slade. An argument over something personal. I'm confessing to his murder. Please turn this tape over to the department." Then, another long pause, before she said, "I can't go on. Things have been too difficult. I'm too far gone to save myself. I love you, darling. Kiss Chooch and tell him I love him, too. Try not to hate me too much."

Then I heard a gunshot.

CHAPTER SEVENTEEN

A lexa would not *commit suicide!*

But her words and the gunshot were still ringing in my ear. After a few seconds, I shook out of it and dialed the communication section at LAPD. I got a watch commander, who identified himself as Captain Doug Chang.

"Captain, I have a police emergency," I shouted. "I need an immediate phone check on this line." I then gave him my badge and home phone number.

"What is this regarding?" He seemed hesitant to run the trace.

"A possible police shooting. The call came in on this line. Officer down. I need an immediate trace on this number with the time the call was placed!" I shouted. "I'm heading out, so when you get it, call me on my mobile phone."

I gave him that number and hung up. Then I sprinted to my car, threw it in reverse and squealed away from the curb, hitting my neighbors' trash cans and knocking them over. I punched the shift into Drive and powered up the alley toward Abbot Kinney Boulevard. I had a vague hunch where Alexa was, so I took a chance and hit the 405 South.

Somebody inside the car was saying, "No. No. No." In a second, I realized it was me.

My cell rang and Doug Chang was back on the line. "Last call at ten-thirty this morning, only a few minutes ago, from area code three-one-oh. Five, five, five, six, seven, eight, four."

"Where is that?" I screamed.

"Compton," he answered.

"Okay. Get me a trace on that number from the reverse directory. I need to confirm the address. Call me back."

I was pretty sure I knew where she was. I transitioned onto the 105 East and put the pedal down. In seconds I was doing over a hundred miles an hour. I passed people like they were parked, putting my life and everybody else's on the line.

I was on Long Beach Boulevard when Doug Chang got back to me. "The number traces back to Four-twenty Cypress Street," he said.

"Roll an ambulance to that address right now."

"It's rolling."

I was going almost seventy. I couldn't get the monstrous idea that Alexa had committed suicide out of my head. I was going so fast, I overshot the house and hit the brakes half a block past, squealing rubber as I brodied to a stop. Then I hit reverse and fishtailed backward, slamming into the curb in front of David Slade's house. I opened my car door and ran for the backyard. The front door was double locked and the quickest way in was through the broken back window. I reached the spot, jumped up, and shimmied into the guest bedroom, landing awkwardly on the floor. I gathered my feet under me and ran through the house.

"Alexa! Alexa!" I shouted, as I ran.

I found her in Slade's bedroom, covered in a spray of blood and cerebral spinal fluid. She was shot in the head and splayed backwards on Slade's big, unmade, king-sized bed. I ran to her.

Ragged pulse, shallow breathing, irregular heartbeat. And then, while my fingers were on her carotid artery, I felt her heart stop.

"Oh shit," I moaned as I grabbed her nose, pinched it shut, and leaned down, blowing two breaths of air into her lifeless body. After that, I rose up and did fifteen chest compressions. Blood, CSF, and little shattered pieces from her skull were all over the bed. The gun was her backup piece. A blue steel Spanish Astra, which had flown out of her hand and was lying against the headboard. *Why had she packed two guns yesterday morning? We were on a training day. Had she known this was coming all along?* I was in anguish as I kept up the CPR.

"Please," I mumbled and blew more air into her mouth and did more chest compressions. The Lord's Prayer became a silent mantra in my head.

And then, the distant wail of a siren. Seconds later, I heard the ambulance pull up in front. I had to leave her for a minute to let them in. I blew air hard into her lungs one more time and then sprinted for the front door, threw the latch, and screamed: "In here! Hurry, damn it! I'm doing CPR!"

Two EMTs ran up the steps carrying a medical kit and a light metal stretcher with folding wheels. As they charged past me I shouted, "Back bedroom!" then followed. They had already resumed CPR when I arrived in the room a second behind.

"AVPU unresponsive," the lead man shouted to his partner.

"Please, please don't let her die," I pleaded.

The EMT continued yelling instructions. "Gimme some four by fours," he commanded. "Gotta cover this hole. This is gonna be a scoop and run."

The other medic had just finished snapping on rubber gloves. He grabbed a large piece of cut gauze and a bottle of saline solution. He put the gauze pad over the exit wound in the back top of Alexa's head, then poured saline onto the pad.

Then he shouted, "Gimme the EPI, start an IV. We gotta get her to the truck fast."

The second EMT opened his case and retrieved a syringe of epinephrine. The paramedic shot it into a bottle of saline and started an IV.

"Will she make it?" I croaked as they got the IV started and continued CPR, using an oxygen bottle.

"Shut up and let us do this," the lead man snapped. Then he laid the stretcher on the floor and brought it up to bed height, and they made the transfer as he said to his partner, "Call trauma at Big County and tell them to have a neurosurgeon and a crash cart ready. Tell 'em we have a full arrest coming in."

The second man triggered a shoulder mike and made the request.

"We can't intubate her," the lead said. "We gotta try and get some vitals going." They started out with her on the gurney.

"She's my wife," I said, trailing in their wake. They were working furiously and had dialed me out.

Then we were outside. I'd seen the drill half a dozen times before. She needed to be revived instantly or it was over.

I ran behind them and tried to follow her into the ambulance.

"You can't go," the lead man commanded.

I snatched my badge out of my pocket, shoving it into his face as I pushed past him into the back.

All the way to the hospital, the inside of the ambulance was a turmoil of medical procedures and shouted instructions from the radio emergency medical officer at the trauma ward. The EMTs told the REMO there was no pulse or respiration. The REMO said give her this, give her that. Take lactated ringers. Put the paddles on. Shock her. The second man yelled, "CLEAR." A zap, and Alexa arched her spine up to meet the charge. The EKG remained flat.

"She's flat-lining. No help from the defib," the paramedic shouted.

"Dial up the charge," the REMO instructed. "Try again."

All the way there, I was pleading, "Please don't let this be happening."

We got to County-USC in less than fifteen minutes. The EMTs ran her out of the back of the ambulance, pushing the rolling gurney into the trauma ward. I climbed out to follow, but my legs gave out underneath me. I went down on the hard concrete and couldn't get back up. Emotional shock? Traumatic paralysis? Whatever it was, for a moment I couldn't move. I just lay behind the ambulance, moaning.

CHAPTER EIGHTEEN

I finally got my legs to work and made it into the ER, where I took a swing at a hospital attendant who was only trying to keep me out of the trauma area. I knew I was being an asshole, but I couldn't stop myself. Two cops, who were there writing a report on a DUI who'd gone through his windshield, sat me down forcibly. I cursed them out.

"Just leave me alone!" I finally shouted and tried to get up. The one nearest me pushed me back hard. I hit the wall and a picture of two horses in a wheat field fell and landed beside me.

For the moment, I guess I wasn't going anywhere.

Detectives started to roll in. Word had spread fast that Alexa was in the trauma unit, a possible DOA from a gunshot wound to the head. A fallen officer rates a big turnout. Every unassigned detective or Code Seven car was on the way. By noon, there were thirty plain-clothed detectives, both men and women, and again half as many uniforms sitting with me in the waiting room. I tried calling Chooch but couldn't get through. Somebody handed me a Consent for Surgery form, which I signed.

Then Raphael Figueroa and Tommy Sepulveda arrived, walking down the hall toward me, resolute looks carved on their tired faces. I knew they'd been working this straight for almost fifteen hours. Tommy stopped at a coffee machine and got three cups while Rafie came over. He nodded at the two blues who were still standing close, keeping a wary eye on me.

"I got it," Rafie said, and they took a few steps back but continued to watch me from a distance. "How bad is it?"

"Horrible," I said. Tommy came over with the coffee and handed me a cup.

"I don't want that," I snapped, so he put it on the vinyl-topped lamp table beside me.

"We heard she was all the way down in Compton. What was she doing in that ghetto?"

"She was at Slade's house," I said, as I reached out and took the coffee, drank some, and set it back down. Bad idea. It was coming right back up. I swallowed hard three times and barely kept it down.

"What the hell was she doing there?" Rafie asked, surprised.

"I don't know," I flared. "Why don't you guys back off?"

"Listen, Shane. You're real lucky me and Tommy got this squeal. There's guys up at Homicide Special who would've wrapped you in canvas by now."

"So whatta you want? A thank-you note?"

"I want you to stop attacking us. I want you to give us a little help. We're on the same side," Tommy said.

"Right." I still felt like I was about to throw up. Nausea was coming in waves.

Then Rafie's cell phone rang.

"Figueroa," he said, then: "We're there now. Yeah sure, he's sitting here with us." Rafie handed me the phone. "Captain Calloway." Cal was our boss at Homicide Special.

"Hello?" My voice sounded dead even to me.

"Shane? Jeb." I've known this guy for six years and nobody ever called him Jeb, especially him. It was always Cal. The Jeb thing sat wrong. Something was going on downtown. Twenty years of dealing with Glass House politics had my alarm lights flashing. Then he said, "How is she?"

"She's . . . she's . . ." I felt tears coming. So far I'd managed to hold them back. I didn't want to cry in front of these guys, so I took a moment to center myself. "Not so hot," I finally said.

"She's in good hands, Shane. The trauma guys at USC are the best."

"They're okay, but I want to move her," I said. "I have a friend who's a brain surgeon at UCLA. This slug . . . it . . ." Again, I couldn't finish the sentence. This time coffee-flavored bile rushed up my esophagus and filled my mouth. I spat into the paper cup and set it down. "Slug did a lot of damage, Captain."

"Sometimes this stuff looks worse than it is," he said.

"Yeah." I decided not to tell him there were bone chips from her brainpan all over the bed, or that her hair looked like a mop dipped in red paint. That I'd felt her heart stop while my fingers were touching her neck.

Then he said softly, "Listen, Shane. I've got to bring you in."

"I'm sorry, you have to what?"

"Chief Ramsey wants you in his office forthwith. He's got some issues."

"He's got issues? *I'm* the one with issues! Everybody's pissing on Alexa on TV and he has almost no comment. He owes her some fucking cover."

"Shane, he sent you a two-six hours ago. You can't ignore that. You're gonna have to deal with it."

"I've got a little situation going here, in case you haven't noticed. I'm not taking time out to deal with that moron." He said nothing, so I added, "I need to be here to make medical decisions if necessary."

"That's your call, but Rafie and Tommy can stay with her. They'll have your cell number and can keep you posted. The chief's office is only ten minutes away. It's probably gonna be a while till you get any word. Be smart about this, Shane."

"I'm not leaving her!" My voice was raised in frustration.

"Okay. Fair enough. Put Rafie back on."

I handed the phone to Figueroa. He put it to his ear and nodded. "Yep. Can do," he said, then closed the cell and glanced at Sepulveda. There must have been a lot of hidden meaning in that look, because suddenly they both dove at me.

Rafie got my hands pinned. Tommy got his cuffs out. The two blues from across the room joined in and held me down.

I'm good and I'm fast, but I was operating at half-capacity. My nerves were fried. It took them about thirty seconds to get the bracelets on while I struggled and hurled insults. Then they dragged me out of the hospital and shoved me into the back of their Ford.

"Why are you doing this?" I asked. They wouldn't look at me, neither willing to engage my eyes. We all knew it was wrong, but the order had come from the acting chief, so it wasn't up for discussion. I was going to this meeting.

Seven minutes later we were sweeping into the underground parking garage next to the Glass House.

We took the elevator ride to the sixth floor in silence. I stopped struggling and decided that if I wanted to leave this meeting without making a side trip to the Central Division Jail, then I would have to look like I wasn't carrying my shit around in a sock. Nobody wanted me raving insults on TV or feeding smug Roxanne Sharp her little gold angel pin.

I'd broken enough laws to merit a criminal arrest. The fact that Alexa was in critical condition or maybe already dead just didn't weigh very much compared to the media tornado that was threatening to blow careers up into the air before dropping them like twisted Chevy trucks. If I was looking for cool heads, loyalty, or a commitment to a fallen comrade, I wasn't going to find it on the sixth floor of the Glass House today.

Great White Mike hadn't wasted any time moving into Tony Filosiani's office for his interim stay as acting chief.

We paused in the outer part of the chief's suite and looked at a young female operations lieutenant from Ramsey's regular support staff who was sitting to the right of the double mahogany doors. She motioned us to a sofa, picked up the phone, and started talking softly, announcing our arrival.

"I can't face this turd in handcuffs," I said softly.

"If you go nuts in there, we're all gonna get it," Rafie said.

"I won't. I'm solid."

Rafie and Tommy glanced at each other. They weren't sure what to do. I had played these guys badly. They had been trying to deal with me for close to a day, and I had lied, screwed them over, and physically threatened them. But they were good cops.

Deep down they had sympathy for my plight. Beyond that, most of Alexa's detectives liked her. She was an evenhanded, fairminded bureau chief. Nobody quite understood how all this made sense yet, but everybody knew she was getting a bum deal on TV.

So after exchanging a look, Tommy leaned over and unhooked me just as the door opened and a fifty-year-old Commander of Operations, named Keith Summers, looked out at us.

"Good," was all he said, then motioned us inside.

Great White Mike was standing by a large picture window that looked out over Olvera Street, which was the first street in Los Angeles and located in the most historical section of the city. The roof of Union Station was visible off to the north. Under most circumstances, Mike Ramsey looked like we got him out of Central Casting. He was pale-skinned, thin, and handsome in a forties movie star kind of way. He had slicked black hair and a trimmed moustache that rode below a patrician nose like a delicate afterthought. His sculpted chin was heroic. Deputy Chief Ramsey was the kind of cop who had spent the minimal amount of time on the streets before making a headlong dash toward administration. He liked being on TV and kept makeup in his briefcase for those unexpected prime-time appearances. But right now all of his swagger was gone. He looked tired. Tired and overmatched.

One of the things most media-relations officers will tell you is the press is like a furry little puppy that looks like it would be loads of fun to play with. And most of the time it is. You do an interview and then go home and tell your wife or girlfriend that you were on *Greta* or *Geraldo*, or that Ken and Barbie on Channel Seven were kissing your ass and couldn't get enough of you. The press would ask respectfully for your opinions. You quickly learned how to scratch the furry little pup under the chin, and how to kiss his damp whiskers without getting any drool on your lips. But then, sometimes without any warning, the little beast would snarl and bite you on the nose. That was what Great White Mike was just now discovering. The TV in his office was on and he was taking the brunt of a full media onslaught. Roxanne Sharp, Nathan Red, and a black activist named Reverend Leland Vespars, just in from New York, were all piling on. They felt that Deputy Chief Mike Ramsey was criminally mishandling the investigation. Police pundits were also weighing in. As I came through the door, I could hear the Deputy Chief screaming at one of his administrative assistants, a lieutenant from Press Relations.

"Who the hell *is* this guy?" Mike was pointing at the TV screen, where Fox News—fair and balanced—was peeling strips off Chief Ramsey in particular and the LAPD in general. "When was this antique on our dick squad?" He shouted at the screen.

I looked over at the TV and saw a gray-haired, retired, homicide detective who used to work for our old Special Crimes unit. I remembered him from the late eighties. I think his name was Merle, or Mel something. He'd pulled the pin over a decade ago and was now a Fox News analyst. He was just opinionating that due to the obvious racial component in this murder, the department owed the public a much more detailed description of events.

"I'm sure when this popcorn fart was on the job he was sharing all his case facts with these ghouls," Ramsey whined.

Then somebody motioned toward me and they all turned. The media relations guy crossed the room and turned down the volume on the TV.

"I need answers, Scully," the Deputy Chief said without preamble. "This department is getting the shit kicked out of it. I gave a direct order yesterday that you were to desist in this investigation. Then I gave you a forthwith to this office three hours ago! You ignored my two-six, just like you've ignored all my wishes for almost a day."

He crossed the room and took up a position directly in front of me, then rocked forward until he was at least a foot into my personal space. Some kind of lavender cologne was wafting off of him.

"I'm waiting for a response," he said coldly.

"Chief Ramsey, my wife is critical. She's in the gunshot trauma ward. I'm only here because of the two-six, but sir, I really need to get back to the hospital." I was trying my best to look and sound calm, but my voice was shaking.

He looked over at Figueroa and Sepulveda. "We got people down there covering her progress, right?" Both detectives nodded, but neither of them seemed too happy about the way this was being handled. "Okay, so if something changes, they'll call you, right?"

I didn't answer, but Ramsey seemed satisfied that base was covered and went on. "You're a Level Three detective assigned to Homicide Special. You're supposed to know what you're doing. But instead, because of you, I've got a rap producer named Maluga all over my phone sheet. He's hired this Nathan Red character who's halfway up my asshole wearing golf cleats. He's laying groundwork for a wrongful death suit on behalf of Sergeant Slade's family and he's also complaining about the illegal search you did at Maluga's house. On the criminal front, I got the District Attorney looking to charge you with two or three low-weight felonies and PSB wants you picked up and held for internal questioning on this bad search. Have I missed anything?" Operations Commander Summers shook his head, so Ramsey continued. "But despite all this reckless behavior, I've delayed these actions against you, and do you know why?"

"No, sir."

"Two reasons. The PR blowback from arresting you will get all over us and just make this look like a bigger scandal than it already is. The second reason is I want something from you. You gimme what I want and we'll see what we can do about holding the line on this internal investigation and all the criminal stuff."

"What do you need, sir?"

"Lieutenant Scully's computer."

"I don't have it."

"What you don't have is a career if you give me any grief on this."

"Hook me up to a poly," I said. "I don't know where that computer is." Which was technically true, if somewhat disingenuous and inaccurate.

He stood there, rocking back and forth, leaning in and out of my space, the cologne drifting around us, sweet and cloying. He was panicking and I could see it in the tightness around his eyes. He was no Tony Filosiani. Just a big, overdressed palooka with plucked eyebrows, who was on the edge of a meltdown.

"I may have an idea where that computer is," I said. "But I'll need a little time to run it down."

"You don't have time. This shit storm we're all in erased our time."

"The computer was stolen from our house. But I may have a way to get it back."

Great White Mike's tweezered brows shot up into the middle of his forehead and hovered there uncertainly. "Stolen?" He didn't believe me.

"Yes, sir. It's a long story, but a homeless guy I let into my house took it."

"You let a homeless guy into your house?" He glanced over at Commander Summers with a "do you believe this?" look.

All I wanted to do was get the hell out of there and back to the trauma ward, but there was no leaving without cutting some kind of deal. The handcuffs were still dangling from Rafie's right hand, reminding me of how perilous my freedom had become.

"He's a wit on one of my open homicides. I was giving him a hot meal, working him for information." Complete B.S.

"What's this homeless guy's name?" Ramsey asked, still suspicious.

"He's got lots of names," I dodged. "He's a delusional schizophrenic. Right now he's calling himself Samik Mampuna. He thinks he's a Crown Prince from Cameroon."

I saw Mike struggling with this. He didn't know how to handle me. Then something happened, and his frown disappeared. He was suddenly on a different track.

"Look, Shane. Nobody says you shouldn't be upset over your wife, but you don't just throw the rule book away," he said with more compassion.

"Exactly, sir. And you should know, I'm in much better control of myself now." In a moment, we'd both have to start rolling up our pant cuffs.

Then from out of nowhere he said, "You know with all this media scrutiny, we're going to have to examine the idea that Lieutenant Scully shot this police officer for some unknown reason. There's no way to ignore that possibility, given the circumstances of his death."

"Sir, he was a dirtbag. A practicing Crip who got in on the felony waiver policy. He was dirty, hanging out with this ex-con gangster Maluga's estranged wife."

"I will not let this turn into some kind of cooked-up racial incident," he shot back. "The way we keep that from happening is we will look at all possibilities including the one I just mentioned. Despite Sergeant Slade's rather questionable record, we will also not defame the memory of this dead African-American police officer. All that will do is make us look insensitive and will fan the flames higher. But so help me, if it comes out your wife is involved in this murder, she is not going to get any cover from me or this department. A lot of this looks real suspicious. She had a prior relationship with Sergeant Slade. It's even written up in her Academy instructor's review."

"She didn't kill him!" My voice was shrill and dangerous. "You think she's so stupid she'd kill one of her own detectives and leave him in the front seat of her own car?"

"Ah, yes. The good old Robert Blake defense. Too smart to be that dumb. You never heard of heat-of-the-moment killings?"

"She didn't kill him!" I repeated.

Ramsey began ticking off points on his fingers. "Slade was found dead in her car, wearing her handcuffs. When ballistics is through, my bet is the murder weapon will be her gun. They used to be intimate, making this your classic relationship gone bad. Motive, method, and opportunity. The prosecutor's trifecta."

I know how cops think. I couldn't explain any of it. Besides all that, I couldn't get Alexa's phone message out of my head. *"I killed David Slade. An argument over something personal."* I was so confused and twisted up, I didn't know if I was fighting for her life, her career, or her memory. Whatever it was, I was determined that Great White Mike would never get his hands on that answering-machine tape.

"If she did it, then I agree she should go down for it," I said disingenuously. I had to get out of there.

"Okay, then I'm going to give you till end of the day tomorrow, that's eight o'clock P.M.," Ramsey said. "You have that computer in this office by then or I'm gonna fall on you."

"Thank you, sir. That ought to be enough time."

After some more rocking back and forth and some very theatrical stink-eye, Great White Mike finally let me walk out of Tony Filosiani's office. Figueroa and Sepulveda left with me. As we got silently in the elevator, Rafie looked over at Tommy and me.

"That guy's a purebred asshole," he muttered softly.

CHAPTER NINETEEN

When I got back to the trauma ward it was two P.M. and there were twice as many cops as when I left.

Pagers kept going off and people would get up and leave the room. Some didn't come back, but more kept arriving.

When a police officer is shot, it's standard for the chief to make an appearance. The one time I can remember when that didn't happen was when one of our guys got hit and then Chief Willie Williams was in Vegas on a junket and elected not to come home. The other time was now. Mike Ramsey stayed conspicuously absent.

Two network news teams were hovering in the corridor outside, drinking machine coffee. I pushed past their shouted questions and checked with the trauma desk. Still no word on Alexa.

I had been trying to get through to Chooch, but the Trojans were having afternoon practice and nobody had been picking up the phone at the football dorm. I sat down and tried again. This time I reached him.

"What's going on?" he asked quickly.

"I found her. It isn't good. She's been shot in the head. She's in the trauma ward at County-USC.

"No!" he said softly.

"Listen, Chooch, you should stay there."

"I'm coming!" he said, and hung up.

My head was throbbing, my palms sweating. I had a heavy feeling in my chest and I couldn't breathe. If Alexa died, I would never find my way out of this.

The next hour dragged by. My mind kept wandering off in search of some ray of hope—any slight sign that Alexa would be okay. I heard laughter from behind the glass. *Would they laugh if someone were about to die?* I wondered. *People died every day in this place, so it might mean nothing.*

I heard someone say, "She's not . . ." I couldn't hear the rest of the sentence so I moved closer to the bulletproof window dividing us. *She's not what?* I thought. *Talking? Breathing? Alive?* It was torture.

At that moment, the door opened and a tall, slender doctor with glasses and curly red hair came into the room. He looked way too young to be involved with my wife's near-fatal trauma, so I turned my gaze away.

"Scully?" he called out.

"Here!"

"Come on back."

"Is she . . . ?"

"Tell you in a minute." He led me through the door and down a trauma ward hallway.

"Is she in one of these rooms?"

"Just follow me," he said.

We entered a small, windowless office that had three desks jammed together and clipboards hanging on the walls.

He closed the door and introduced himself. "I'm Doctor John Romer, Chief Resident of Neurosurgery here."

"Is my wife okay?"

"Sit down," he said.

"Just tell me, damn it!" I almost shouted. "I've been waiting out there for hours!"

"No, she's not okay. When she arrived here she was technically dead. We managed to get her heart started. The good news is that the bullet missed the brain stem, which governs breathing, swallowing, and heartbeat. If it'd hit that, it would have been over. Her heartbeat is ragged and we had to give her electroshock to even it out. I've put her in a drug-induced coma to help reduce intracranial pressure and we're keeping her body temperature at thirty-three degrees Centigrade for the same reason. That's the good news. Here's the bad. She's probably not going to make it."

His words fell on me like slabs of concrete. "But her heart is beating, she's got a pulse, so she's alive," I said.

He nodded.

"Then what do you mean she's not going to make it? If she's alive, she has a chance."

"Are you familiar with the Glasgow Coma Scale?"

"The what?"

"We use GCS to measure head injuries. It goes from three to fifteen—three being worst. The prevailing judgment says anyone at four or below is a lost cause."

"What's hers?"

"Between four and five."

"That doesn't mean she can't survive," I pleaded.

"In that numeric range, something like under four percent make it, and if they do, their quality of life is usually pretty gruesome. We're talking about persistent vegetative states. Total life comas. People who never wake up and live out their days on life support."

"That's not Alexa," I said hotly.

He heaved a deep sigh. This was tough duty. As a cop, I'd offered up this kind of devastating information to family members and I knew he was desperately trying to get through it. He needed to communicate the rest of Alexa's condition, and plowed ahead.

"The bullet entered her skull at the right temporal lobe. It angled upward, and barely managed to stay to the right of the midline. It's what we call a marginal multi-lobar wound, which means it came close to crossing the midline, or midcoronal tract in her cranium. Fortunately, it didn't. It exited at the parietal lobe at the lower right side of her head. Had it crossed the midcoronal plane, both sides of her brain would have been affected and she'd already be dead. Even so, wounds of this nature have generally been associated with poor outcomes." He took a deep breath before continuing. "The temporal lobe deals with memory, hearing, language, organization, sequencing—that sort of thing. Your wife's functions in those areas have undoubtedly been traumatically affected by the path of the bullet. The parietal lobe deals with touch and visual senses, as well as spatial perception. These are her two main problem areas."

I was trying to take it in, but in truth, it was just a jumble. I was hearing what he said, but panic and loss were scrambling his words, making it impossible for me to comprehend very much.

"The bullet fragmented, resulting in some collateral damage. We tried to get as much of that out as we could. The MRI showed there are still little pieces all over the place. Those might need to be dealt with later to repair normal blood flow. She's not responding to stimuli. Her motor reflexes are nil. There are several other poor prognostic neurological indicators, including fixed and dilated pupils and hypotension, which is low blood pressure. We've given her plasma in an attempt to bring her BP up and she seems to be responding." He took another breath, then added, "The bullet was a nine millimeter, which, as you know, is a pretty high velocity load. All in all, not a good prognosis. I don't foresee a favorable outcome. I'm sorry, but you need to know the truth."

"Damn it, you can't just give up on her," I said. Then I started to cry. I put my head down and tears ran. The young doctor finally put a hand on my shoulder.

"I suggest you get a second opinion from another neurosurgeon," he said.

"Can I stay here for a minute?" I pleaded.

"Yeah, sure . . . I'm sorry."

He walked out of the room.

Then, without asking permission, I walked down the hall looking for Alexa. I passed open doorways where trauma patients were leaking precious fluids onto sterile surfaces. Medical assistants stared at me as I passed. I obviously didn't belong. I didn't have a knowing frown. I wasn't wearing green scrubs and paper slippers.

Somewhere halfway down the hall I found the neuro-ICU.

The only way I knew it was Alexa was that I recognized her blue-trimmed running shoes sitting on a table across from her. Her head was completely wrapped in gauze. Tubes ran out of her mouth and from behind her ear. Some sort of metal cone was placed over her head. Machines gurgled and hissed; the heart monitor beeped in a soft uneven rhythm.

This really has happened, I thought as I looked in horror at Alexa's gauze-wrapped head.

I felt a hand on my arm. "Sir?" a woman's voice said.

"I'm her husband," I offered numbly as I turned and looked at the woman. She was slender and in her fifties, with tight gray curls escaping from her hair cap. "What's all that stuff on her?" I asked.

"We're performing hypothermia," she said softly. "It lowers her brain temperature from thirty-seven to thirty-three degrees Centigrade."

"Oh . . . yes . . . hypothermia."

"It reduces the chance of swelling or of a secondary brain insult like a stroke or subdural hemotoma. The next forty-eight hours are critical. I think it would be better if you waited in the waiting room."

"Sure . . . okay . . . if you think that's better."

I turned and walked with her back down the hall.

"She's my wife," I repeated numbly. "She isn't going to die."

"Yes, I know," the nurse said softly.

CHAPTER TWENTY

"Is she going to make it?" Chooch asked. It was a few minutes after three in the afternoon, just four hours past when I'd found Alexa at Slade's house in Compton. Chooch's dark features were pinched. The fingers on his right hand were crossed as he waited for my answer.

"She's stable. The next forty-eight hours will tell."

"But . . . is she? She got shot in the head. Is that . . . ?"

"Serious," I said. "I won't lie to you, son. It's bad, but she's alive. Beyond that, I just don't know."

We sat on the vinyl sofa and played eye tag with the thirty or more cops waiting with us. As before, they kept getting calls and leaving, new officers taking their place. I opened my cell and scanned the contact numbers looking for Luther Lexington, a neurosurgeon at UCLA. I had worked on his daughter Levonda's murder two years earlier.

Levonda had been visiting her grandmother in South Central when she accidentally became an innocent victim in a senseless drive-by. I'd worked the case for almost two months before getting a ballistics match on a liquor store shooting. I finally put the case down, busting two members of the Grape Street Crips in Watts. Luther said he'd never be able to pay me back. We were friends, but whenever we talked, I could feel sadness

coming off of him in waves. Levonda's ghost was standing between us. No matter how hard we tried, I was a reminder of that
tragic day.

I dialed his office in Westwood and his receptionist put me
right through. "Luther, it's Shane Scully," I said after he
picked up.

"I saw it on TV. I tried to call you at the office and at home,"
he said. "Your Lieutenant took a message. How's she doing?"

"She's in an induced coma. You know what the Glasgow
Coma Scale is?" I asked, knowing he must.

"What's her number?"

"Between four and five," I said. "She's stable, kind of, and
her brain stem is functioning."

I got up and moved away from Chooch. I didn't want him to
overhear any of this. I walked into the corridor, heading toward
a small patio at the end of the hall. But some news crews were
waiting there, so I turned and headed the other way.

"Did they also give you a GOS?" Luther asked.

"What the hell's that?"

"Glasgow Outcome Scale. It's determined by a lot of diag-
nostic stuff. If she's in an induced coma, it may still be too early
to get an estimate. GOS measures ICP, pupil dilation, motor activity recovery. Regeneration of reflexes, stuff like that. It attempts to predict survival rates."

"They didn't say," I muttered. "The trauma ward doc is a
neurosurgeon named Romer. He told me it's a right side transverse injury, temporal lobe to parietal lobe, but that it didn't
cross some plane."

"The midcoronal plane," Luther said. "If the bullet didn't
cross from the right side into the left, that's good. They'll probably line up a team. Neurologists, otolaryngologists, a vascular
surgeon, some head and neck people."

"Luther, I want you to take the case. I want to transfer her to
UCLA where you are."

"Let's not talk about that yet. Give me the doc's name again.
I didn't have a pencil before. But you need to know she's in a
good place. USC is a level-one trauma center and an excellent
neurosurgical facility."

After I gave him John Romer's name, there was a long pause. I filled the space and said, "He made it sound pretty bad, Luther."

"I won't kid you, Shane. A four or five GCS is hairy."

"The doc here said I shouldn't hope for too much. That I should start preparing for the worst."

"Okay, Shane. One thing you need to understand is the Glasgow Coma Scale is just a scale. It's not carved on stone tablets."

"Yeah, but—"

"Doctors use it to try and predict who will make it and who won't. If a case is deemed hopeless, then generally, treatment isn't advised. Obviously, if you don't treat a four or a five, you're gonna get a pretty shitty outcome. In other words, the scale itself can skew the results. You understand what I'm saying?"

"Yeah, I guess."

"A couple more things to remember. When it comes to head injuries, nobody knows anything. The brain is a damned complicated organ and we don't understand exactly how it works. We have to remember that a person with a brain injury is a person first, and a patient second. Alexa is precious, so we're never gonna quit on her, okay? And that could affect her survival and recovery rate."

"I understand. Thanks."

"I'm not through. The next thing I want you to remember is, no two brain injuries are exactly the same. The effects vary greatly from person to person."

I hoped he wasn't just trying to make me feel better.

"The effects of a brain injury depend on a zillion factors," he continued, "including location, track of the bullet, severity of the injury, as well as the age and health of the person involved. I had a patient last year who was a gunshot victim with a transverse injury. He was twenty-eight and in great shape. He was a four GOS when I got him. Thirty-two days later I shipped him home. Yesterday he was shooting baskets behind his garage."

"Please make her better, Luther. I can't live without her."

"Yes you can, Shane. Just like I learned to live without Levonda."

"What do I do?"

"You hit your knees, babe. Get the Boss working on it."

So Chooch and I went down to the little chapel on the first floor, and prayed.

CHAPTER TWENTY-ONE

omer is a good doc." Luther Lexington was standing in the hall outside the trauma ward speaking with Chooch and me. It was four-thirty that same afternoon. He was tall, with a muscular build, and had played halfback at Cal State in the eighties. Now he was the chief of neurosurgery at UCLA and, according to the Internet search I'd done two years earlier while investigating his daughter's case, was regarded as one of the foremost neurosurgeons in Los Angeles. A perfect inner-city success story, until his only daughter was killed by that stray bullet.

"Can she come back from this, Doctor Lexington?" Chooch asked.

"You and your dad have some tough decisions to make. I just completed a preliminary exam and checked her chart. She's not in good shape, but there is some positive stuff. As I already told you, we're lucky the bullet didn't cross the midline. But right now she's not responding to stimuli and her brain waves are not good."

I was confused. "But you said—"

"I know what I said, Shane. I also said nobody knows anything. We can make all the skill moves and treat her with the best procedures—and we will—but the outcome is in God's hands."

"I want to transfer her to UCLA," I said. "I want you to take over the case."

"The only difference between this hospital and mine is I'm more familiar with the doctors I would put on the team at UCLA. But that has to be weighed against the risk of moving her. If we medivac Alexa by ambulance or even helicopter, there's an hour, maybe more, where if she suffers a secondary brain insult, she'll be between ICUs and very vulnerable. But in the end, it's your call."

"I want home field advantage. I want her with you in a place you're familiar with, with doctors you choose."

"Okay, but I can't move her for a day or so, until she's more stable. For now we'll monitor her, keep her intracranial pressure down, watch for infection. In a day or so we can make another evaluation and see where that leads us."

"Luther, thank you for being here."

"Hey, Shane, you didn't have to keep working Levonda's case. You never quit until you found those guys. That's worth a lot to me."

"It was my job."

"And now, Alexa is mine."

I shook his hand with both of mine.

"You two need to take turns sleeping here for the next day or two," he said. Then he wrote a number on the back of his card and handed it to me. "Here's my cell. I have it on me all the time. Anything changes, you call, no matter what time it is. I'll visit her three times a day and check in with you."

Then he tried to get the worried look off Chooch's face by talking football. But Chooch was still frowning when Luther left.

"You got the first shift, son," I said.

I needed to get my hands on that answering machine tape before somebody wrote a warrant for our house and I lost it to Mike Ramsey's investigation. Then I had to drop off Stacy Maluga's pager at the Electronic Services Division.

As I drove across town toward Venice, the afternoon sun was blazing, pushing July temperatures into the mid-nineties. I parked the Acura in the alley behind my garage. I entered the house, checked the answering machine, and retrieved the old message from Luther, as well as several new ones from friends offering condolences. There was one from my incoming partner, Sally Quinn, expressing support and concern. I listened to Alexa's inexplicable confession and that horrible gunshot. Then I rewound the tape and removed it, replacing it with a fresh one.

I grabbed a plastic container out of the kitchen cabinet, put the tape inside, snapped on the rubber lid and carried it outside where my barbeque sat. I dug a hole in the ashes, buried the container, smoothed it over, then replaced the grate. After that I locked up the house, set the alarm and got back into the Acura. It was five o'clock.

My drive across town was now impeded by Friday rush hour traffic. As I drove, I dealt with priorities and tactics. I needed to get Stacy Maluga's pager worked on, but the sound techs in the electronics division at Mission Street would be unlikely to help me, especially after I stole that fingerprint card and the AFIS printout. By now everyone in the LAPD knew I was off the reservation. That meant, to get what I wanted, I'd need some help from one of my close group of department buddies.

I ran the list and finally settled on Sally Quinn. I had supported her transfer into the Homicide Special Division two months ago and we were scheduled to become partners in a week. I knew she was grateful to me for championing her transfer into the elite murder squad, but she would be damaging her career if anybody found out she had cooperated with what I was going to ask of her. Still, she was my best bet. I dialed her at Valley Homicide where she was busy cleaning up the last details on her old caseload before moving over to join me at the Glass House.

"Sally, it's Shane."

"Jeez, I left a message on your machine. I'm so sorry, man."

"Yeah. Yeah, I got it. Thanks."

"Is she . . . ?"

"Not good. The next forty-eight hours will tell us a lot." I cleared my throat and moved on. "Listen, Sally, I need your help on something."

"Name it."

"I need you to take a pager I have and hook it to one of your open cases, one where a judge wrote you a broad search warrant. I need the warrant so the guys in ESD will wire this thing up with a bug. I can't do it myself 'cause I'm not too popular down there right now."

There was silence on the other end of the line.

"Listen, Sal. I wouldn't ask you, but this has to do with who shot Slade and Alexa. It's really important."

"You've gotta drop this, Shane. You've gotta let the primaries handle it. It's all over the department what you've been doing."

"Sally, I didn't call to get a lecture. You're either down for this or you're not."

There was a long pause while she considered it. "Where are you?" she finally said.

"I'm heading to Mission Road right now. I'll be there in ten minutes."

"It's gonna take me three quarters of an hour to write the paper and get over there."

"God bless you, Sally."

"If He was blessing me, I wouldn't have gotten this call," she said softly, and then hung up.

I used the time to scroll through the numbers logged on Stacy Maluga's pager, pulling them up on the little LCD screen. There were forty numbers with no names or messages— suspicious, since the pager had both voice mail and text messaging features. Most of the drug dealers I'd busted had pager screens that looked like this. People involved in crimes didn't want to leave electronic trails. That meant most of these people who had left numbers for Mrs. Maluga were probably up to no good.

Forty minutes later, a tan detective's car pulled into the lot and Sally Quinn got out. She had red-blond hair and was stocky, with short legs, a compact torso, and a freckled face that made her look younger than she was. She was frowning as she walked over to my car.

"Thanks, Sally."

"Hey, Shane, I'm only here because we're about to be partners, and I feel bad about Alexa. But it's a gonzo move. If this is the way our partnership is gonna go, then maybe I'm gonna have to revisit it."

"You need to know something else before you get involved," I said. "This pager was obtained during an illegal search, which Chief Ramsey is aware of. I'm going to plant it without a warrant, so it's gonna be an illegal tap."

"Will we be able to get adjoining cells? Can I pick out the wallpaper?"

"If you wanta back off, I'll understand."

"Gimme it." She held out her hand and I dropped the little gadget into her palm. Then she turned angrily and walked across the street, disappearing into the building through a side door.

While I waited, I called Rosey. He wasn't in, but I left a message that I needed to see him and that it was important. He called back ten minutes later. We picked a bar we both knew, called Miserable Harry's, that was a dive but geographically handy, halfway between us on Main Street. We agreed to meet in an hour.

Sally Quinn reappeared at six-fifteen and crossed to my car. The July sun had started to sink behind the buildings to the west. "It will be done in five hours," she said, as she reached the Acura. "I told them to send it over to our new digs at the Glass House."

"Thanks."

"Right," she said angrily. Then she turned and walked across the street with short, choppy strides, got in her car, and drove away.

CHAPTER TWENTY-TWO

Miserable Harry's had sawdust on the floor and angel dust in the bathroom. Guys who didn't shave stopped talking as I entered. There were three active billiards tables, all with cash on the rails. The serious pool shooters were leaning over polished mahogany, lining up their cushion shots. The serious heroin shooters were in the men's room toilets, slapping up their veins. I found Rosey in a back booth with another huge black police officer. Since both were in sergeant's uniforms, they had flushed the dope dealers into the bars up the street.

I slid into the open seat and Rosey introduced me to the cop with him.

"This is Dario Chikaleckio," he said. "He's vice-president at Oscar Joel Bryant."

I knew about this guy. There'd been a story about him in our police department news magazine, *The Blue Line*. The article said he'd been adopted at birth by an Italian family from Pasadena. The Chikaleckios were social activists who had taken in and raised a rainbow family of over twenty kids, often having ten or twelve at a time in their big house in South Pasadena. When he was eighteen, Dario had changed his name from Washington to Chikaleckio out of love for his adopted family, thus becoming the LAPD's only black cop with an Italian name. Dario was one of those wide muscle guys. His traps were so big, his arms wouldn't hang straight at his sides. He bulged and flexed as he sat next to Rosey, looking at me through rimless glasses.

"I need some help," I said.

"What you need is to stop running around screwing up a high-profile murder investigation," Dario butted in.

"Do we really need this guy?" I said, staring hard at Rosey.

Rosey then said, "Ballistics just matched Alexa's gun to the shooting. It's all over the Glass House, and you can bet somebody will leak it to the news in a matter of hours. These media activists are cranking up the pressure. It's already affecting the rank and file." Then he looked over at Chikaleckio. "Tell him about the morning roll call in Devonshire."

"I had a regular Mason-Dixon line in there," Chikaleckio said. "Black cops all huddled up on one side of the room, white guys on the other. The old wounds over Rodney King are tender. We don't need no more 'Gorillas in the Mist' B.S. Assholes like Reverend Leland Vespars will try and make this about race to raise money for his Harmony Coalition. He'll be on us like a quart of blue paint. And you're just makin' it worse, Scully. You need to go home."

"Alexa's computer was stolen out of my house yesterday. The chief has directed me to get it back."

Rosey leaned forward, looking at me carefully.

"I swear, Rosey. I'm under Ramsey's orders."

"This man is playing you, Rosencamp," Chikaleckio said.

"I've known Shane for twenty years," Rosey replied. "He's not a liar. Hear him out."

"They're already calling Alexa a racist on TV," I said. "Rosey, you've known her since the Academy. You know she's not a racist. Whatever's going on here, she didn't kill Slade execution-style and then try to commit suicide. There's another explanation."

"Why did he come to you, Rosey?" Dario asked.

My friend didn't answer.

"I'll tell ya why," Chikaleckio continued. "If he gets the president of the Oscar Joel Bryant Association working with him to prove Alexa's innocence, it's like we're endorsing him. We'll be saying the black cops on the department don't believe she killed Slade. It's a media play. He's using you, man."

"Shut up and let me think," Rosey said. It was quiet for a moment before Rosey said, "If there's one thing this town doesn't need, it's allegations that the head of the Detective Bureau is a race hater when she's not."

Dario sat quietly, staring at me before saying, "It ain't about you or your wife, Shane. It's about cops of color not getting a square shake in the field, with the promotion board, or down at PSB. There's not a police force in America where you don't have this same double standard."

"If OJB is gonna stand for anything, we gotta be who we say we are or none of it matters," Rosey argued. "All these black activists want is more strife 'cause it gets them airtime, money, and votes. They want us to all be victims because if we aren't, what the hell do we need them for?"

Dario leaned forward. His gun leather creaked as he put his muscled forearms on the table. "Who stole Alexa's computer? Tell us what happened." I could hear the skepticism in his voice.

I told them about Jonathan Bodine. How I hit him with my car and ended up taking him home with me. After I was finished, they both just sat there, staring.

"We're supposed to risk lookin' like assholes 'cause a this homeless guy and a computer, which may have nothing on it?" Chikaleckio said.

"Last night, right after they found Slade in her car, I dropped by Alexa's office. I went into her computer. All of her e-mails had been purged. But in her Special Ops files, one had been transferred. It was labeled 'Operation Dark Angel.' "

Rosey perked up. "Dark Angel . . . that was David Slade's nickname in the Academy."

I nodded.

"That doesn't mean that file's on her computer," Dario said.

"Her office computer said: File transferred to AHC. There's no AHC acronym in the department directory, but I've been thinking about it, and I believe it stands for Alexa's Home Computer."

We all sat in silence.

"One crazy homeless guy in a city of ten million?" Rosey finally said.

"I was hoping you could make it an off-duty project. Get some of the guys at OJB to help. I need to sweep the cardboard condos on the Nickel, from Alameda to Main. Check the parks and SRO hotels. This guy doesn't leave a forwarding address. His street handle is Long Gone John 'cause he's a thief and moves around a lot. I'd do it myself, but I'm just one person and I also need to stay close to Alexa right now."

I told them what he looked like, and described Chooch's Harvard-Westlake sweatshirt. After I'd finished, Rosey looked at the muscle-bound sergeant sitting next to him.

"We gotta do this, Dario," he said.

It took a while, but after several minutes, Chikaleckio finally agreed.

CHAPTER TWENTY-THREE

I relieved Chooch at ten o'clock. Nothing new on Alexa, but I made arrangements with him to return the following morning. He told me that Luther had called the ER and planned to move Alexa to UCLA tomorrow if she remained stable. Then he hugged me and headed back to the USC football dorm.

I stretched out on the sofa in the trauma ward and watched the story of Slade's murder evolve on TV. My wife had graduated from a victim to a person of interest. As Rosey and Dario feared, the ballistics match from her gun had all but sealed a guilty verdict in the media.

"Questions keep coming back to one fact," a concerned CNN news anchor said. "Why would the head of the Detective Bureau's gun and handcuffs be used as instruments in the death of her own detective?" This was followed by a shot of David Slade at fifteen, looking angry, all decked out in gang colors, scowling under a blue head wrap.

"David Slade grew up on the mean streets of Compton, California," the anchor continued. "Despite poverty and numerous brushes with the law, he had aspirations for a better life. Early gang affiliations threatened his future, but he tore himself out of that downward spiral and at age twenty-one, joined the LAPD."

Now Slade's handsome, clean-cut Academy shot replaced

the scowling, angry one to demonstrate his magnificent transformation.

"Slade became a force for good, maintaining a residence in Compton where he gave back to the community and served as a role model for other gang-influenced children. All of this was tragically snatched away yesterday in one dreadful moment of violence."

Shots now appeared of Slade slumped forward in Alexa's car on Mulholland.

". . . dead in the front seat of his commanding officer's personal car. Shot with her gun, restrained with her handcuffs."

Now a shot of Alexa appeared. They'd chosen one of those macho firing range photos the department takes. In the picture Alexa was wearing a black flack vest and plastic shooting goggles; her hair was pulled back under an LAPD ball cap. She was crouched low in a Weaver shooting stance, her 9mm clutched in both hands, looking mean and determined.

"On the other side of this senseless tragedy is Lieutenant Alexa Scully," the anchor said. "Privileged, beautiful, and the youngest bureau commander in LAPD history. She was only a thirty-five-year-old lieutenant when promoted to acting head of the Detective Bureau by the LAPD's then incoming Chief of Police Tony Filosiani. Lieutenant Scully's career was highlighted by postings in Internal Affairs, followed by a transfer to L.A.'s hottest division, the old South Central Bureau, where she also saw action on the same mean streets where David Slade once flirted with crime as a child. What angry forces led these two officers to that place where one now lies dead and the other dying? For more on this, CNN Special Correspondent Ann Richardson Brown has a story of passion and civil unrest."

An African-American correspondent took over. She was standing outside the gates of the police academy at Elysian Park. "Against a backdrop of racial strife in L.A., it appears that much more was going on between these two police officers than just a command relationship."

Still shots of Alexa and Slade at the Academy appeared on screen, followed by candid photos of a police graduation party, where Alexa and Slade, both in their early twenties, were pictured together.

I couldn't take any more. I could see they were leading up to a relationship-gone-bad story followed by a murder-suicide.

The trauma unit was beginning to fill with the first-round losers in Friday Night's Gunshot Lottery. As the first victim was rushed in on a gurney, I got up and went to the elevator.

A few minutes later I had found my way to the coronary care unit on the ninth floor. I asked a nurse what room Chief Filosiani was in. She gave me the number but told me I shouldn't stay long, adding that he'd just been cleared for visitors that afternoon and was still very weak. When I found his room and looked in on him, he was sleeping, so I turned to leave.

"What took you so long?" His voice sounded like sandpaper from two days with tubes down his throat. He was pale and tired.

"How're you feeling?" I said, turning back.

"Like I got a pasta machine grinding in my chest." He beckoned me into the room. "Siddown."

I walked in and sat beside his bed. "Alexa's been shot. . . . She's . . ."

Tony held up his hand and stopped me. "I'm getting hourly reports."

"They won't tell me much," I said bitterly.

"She's stable but not yet responding. They put her in an induced coma with barbiturates. Pheno-something or other. Some guy from UCLA is making arrangements to medivac her out of here and over there."

All stuff I already knew, but I was glad he'd been checking on her.

"You stay pretty close to things for a guy just out of a quadruple bypass."

"She's one of mine," he said softly. "She's getting a raw deal." His face was now shiny with sweat. He needed a shave.

"David Slade was dirt, and they're acting like he was some reclaimed ghetto hero," I said. "He pulled guns on civilians over bad lane changes."

"Yeah, I read his PSB file," he said. "But the mayor doesn't want us to hit this guy. Slade's already dead. Kicking dirt on him will only make it worse."

"But it's okay to kick dirt on Alexa?"

"It's all gonna come out eventually. It'll get straightened out. This is too big to push down."

"And what am I supposed to do, Tony? You're over here. Mike Ramsey won't deal with it. The press is dying to hang this all on Alexa. She's in a coma and can't defend herself. How do I stop this?"

"She's your wife, son. Go find the piece that's missing."

"Lou Maluga is involved," I said. "I think he may have even pulled the trigger because Slade was having an affair with his wife, Stacy. But I've been so busy with Alexa, I haven't been able to do much to prove it yet."

He reached out and took my hand. "I want you to remember two things." He paused and looked right at me. "There are times when you must risk everything to achieve your goal. And life's defining moments are usually played under the shadow of doubt."

CHAPTER TWENTY-FOUR

It was after eleven P.M. and the trauma ward was still filling up. The sobbing mothers of gang-bangers held the hands of slack-faced relatives as their half-dead teenage sons were wheeled past.

My head was throbbing. I left my mobile number with the trauma nurses telling them I was going to sleep on a sofa in the hall.

The rest of the night was fitful. Nobody called me, but I kept dreaming that my cell phone was ringing. In the dream someone was trying to give me critical information about Alexa's condition over a bad line. I strained to hear a transmission that was always garbled and unclear.

The next morning at seven A.M. after checking on Alexa and getting the usual guarded description of her condition, I treated myself to a sponge bath in the hospital men's room. While I was in the middle of this, my cell phone actually did ring. Luther Lexington was on the line.

"We're moving her at ten A.M. I'm going to use a helicopter because it will cut the transport time and limit her exposure to only fifteen minutes or so. I'll ride over with her in the chopper. I want you at UCLA Neurosurgery on the fourth floor when we arrive around ten-thirty."

"How is she? They still aren't telling me much, Lex."

"There's really nothing to tell. That's the way these things often go, Shane. She's stable and in an induced coma. Until we try and wake her up, we won't know much. I've been studying her brain CTs. There's quite a bit of foreign matter still in there. Some of the bullet fragments look like they might be restricting blood flow to her temporal and occipital lobes. If those areas don't get sufficient blood supply, then brain cells will die. We may need to consider another surgery soon. I'll make that evaluation along with my vascular guy later today. But you need to know, I wouldn't move her if I didn't think I could pull it off."

Next, I called Chooch and gave him the news. After I finished, he said, "I'm coming over there now."

"I'm gonna need you over at UCLA to stay with her, so go there. I've got to get working on who really killed Slade. I need to disprove all this nonsense they're spreading about her on TV."

The problem was, I was unsure of exactly how to do that. The Academy photos proved Alexa and Slade had certainly been friends. But that didn't mean their relationship was more complicated. I believed in Alexa. She had saved me more than once. Now it was my turn to save her.

The medivac flight went off as scheduled. I caught a glimpse of Alexa as her stretcher was wheeled into the elevator for the quick trip up to the helipad. She was covered with green hospital sheets, her head wrapped in gauze. A drip trolley rode a bed rail above her, feeding fluids. She looked vulnerable and small. Moments later, I heard the blades of the chopper rev up, whining loudly on the roof above. I watched through the window as it headed west, flying low across the skyline carrying Alexa's unconscious body away from me.

I made it to UCLA in less than forty minutes. I parked in a red zone, leaving my handcuffs on the dash, and ran inside, taking the elevator up to neurosurgery.

Luther met me thirty minutes later and reported that Alexa was stable. Everything had gone as he had hoped. He asked me to be back here at seven that evening to meet the team of doctors he'd picked to be on her surgical and treatment teams.

It was a long morning until Chooch arrived. I told him he

would need to stay all day, and about the meeting at seven.
Then I gave him a hug.

"Dad, I don't know what to tell some of these guys at practice.
With everything on TV, they're starting to look at me funny."

"Tell them Alexa's your mom and that you love and believe
in her."

As I said this, my mind flipped back to the plastic container
buried in my barbeque, with Alexa's taped confession inside. I
didn't know why I was so sure it was false. I just was. I left
Chooch and headed back to the main entrance.

As I was coming out of the hospital, I ran into a cluster of
news camera crews and field correspondents who had been
alerted that Alexa had been moved to UCLA.

"Detective Scully, CNN. Can we have a word with you?"
one of them shouted.

"No."

"Detective Scully? Channel Four. Would you talk to us,
please?"

"No."

I pushed past them as they turned on their cameras and
chased after me. I knew I looked like one of those creeps they
ambush on *60 Minutes*. I ran past the cameras to my car, trailing
a flurry of No comments. *Husband of Lieutenant Scully flees
reporters' questions.*

My next stop was the Glass House. I needed to pick up Stacy
Maluga's pager, which I hoped was back from ESD and on
Sally Quinn's new desk. As I drove into the underground
garage I noticed at least ten news vans parked out in front of the
police administration building. I took the elevator to five.

I was hoping to just pick up the pager and get out. But coming off the elevator, I ran straight into Captain Calloway.

"What are you doing here?" he asked, startled to see me.

Cal was about five feet four with a shaved, black, bullet
head, and Mighty Mouse muscles. He was not a guy anybody
took lightly.

When I didn't answer, he said, "Hey, Shane, I want you out
of here, now. Did you see that circus out front? You need to be
invisible."

"Lemme pick up my briefcase and I'll get lost."

I pushed past him and got to my cubicle. There was a message slip in Cal's scrawled handwriting in the center of my desk saying that Dr. Lexington had called yesterday, along with the yellow sheets on Stacy and Lou Maluga that I'd requested. There was also a sealed envelope from ESD waiting in Sally's In-basket. My desk was a clutter. She hadn't used hers yet, so it was without a scrap of personal paraphernalia. I snatched up the ESD package without opening it and turned to leave. As I did, my cell phone rang and with it, my heart froze. *Something new on Alexa?*

But it wasn't the hospital. It was Rosey.

"Hey, Shane, I think we may have a line on this Bodine character."

"Where are you?"

"Meet us at Pepi's Mexican Diner on the corner of Lucas Avenue and Emerald Street in Echo Park?"

"Now?"

"This place is a grease pit. You wait too long, we'll all be in the can, fighting for toilets."

I ran to my car and sped out of the underground garage. All the way there I wondered what they'd found in Echo Park. Suddenly it hit me. If you were so down and out that you had no options left, if you were willing to sleep in a cave with rats the size of house cats, if you could endure the damp reek of the ungodly, then you would go to the old Belmont Tunnel near the corner of Lucas Avenue and Emerald Street.

That abandoned subway tunnel was the lowest rung on the human ladder. The last stop for lost souls in L.A.

CHAPTER TWENTY-FIVE

They were sitting out front of a small taco stand under a Cinzano umbrella which was liberally dappled with pigeon droppings. Four tough-looking black guys in Polo shirts, windbreakers, and jeans. I spotted Dario and Rosey. The other two, I didn't know. I pulled up to the curb and got out. They were all eating tacos and drinking Cokes out of paper cups.

"Shane, this is Lawrence Fischer from West Bureau Vice," Rosey said as I approached and all four stood. I shook hands with Fischer, a skinny undercover cop who was obviously working street strays and dope mokes because he wore long, braided hair, beads, and had arm tats. "And this monster with bolts through his neck is Adrian Young. Known in South Central as Young Frankenstein."

Adrian Young shook my hand, popping two knuckles in the process. He was tall and square, and looked hard as a hickory.

"These guys are also in Oscar Joel Bryant," Rosey said.

"Thanks for helping," I replied. "You think Bodine's in the Belmont Tunnel?"

"Yeah, maybe," Dario said. "Some of his housing associates finally copped to assaulting him. They caught him stealing a bicycle and dusted him up. That was yesterday. Afterwards, they think he might a crawled in there."

I sighed. "If we're going into that sink hole, we're gonna need flashlights."

"And oxygen tanks," Adrian Young said. "It stinks in there."

"It ain't gonna get any sweeter smellin' while we're standin' around talking about it," Rosey said.

Everyone got a black Maglite out of their car and joined me in front of the taco stand. Then we walked five abreast down Lucas Avenue toward the decommissioned tunnel.

The old, boarded-up Pacific Electric Station sat in front of the concrete-faced tunnel entrance. The abandoned terminal was a big, two-story, concrete box with plywood-covered windows and a cathedral-sized metal door. Over the decades, the building had become a living canvas. There was almost no tagging on the big facade. Most of the decoration had been done by aerosol artists. Dragons adorned the walls in bright colors. Some guy with a lot of leftover turquoise paint had rollered the top third of the building all the way across, creating a cornice effect, giving the structure a strange art nuevo look. A few hundred yards beyond this colorful concrete box loomed the tunnel entrance itself: a large gaping arch cut into the Echo Park hillside.

The electric Red Car had been an early attempt at rapid transit in Los Angeles that had lasted from the mid-twenties to the mid-fifties. The Pacific Electric subway tunnel had originally been dug as a shortcut for trolleys going from downtown L.A. to Hollywood or the San Fernando Valley. It had become a victim of the gradual dismantling of the 1,100-mile rail system as freeways took over. Eventually, the electric Red Cars went the way of the snap-brim fedora. The tunnel was used temporarily for city storage, until 1967 when the section between Figueroa and Flower Streets was filled in to pour the massive foundation for the Bonaventure Hotel. The existing tunnel and tracks now went into the hills only for about a mile before they abruptly ended at a concrete wall. Over the years I'd fished several dead bodies out of that miserable hole in the hill. It was the most dismal place I'd ever been. Once a year the County would come out and plow the reeking gunk and human refuse out of the cave and repair the broken-down chain-link fence that attempted to block the entrance. Twenty minutes after they were gone somebody would cut it open again and the cycle would begin anew.

As we neared the mouth of the tunnel, I began to pick up the sour sweet stench coming from inside. Wounded men and animals crawled in here for refuge and often to die. Homeless people cooked food or drugs over newspaper fires, slept in the tunnel's dank confines, and defecated in the slight indentations where the red car tracks used to be. Their old cooking fires had blackened the walls while the spirits of the long dead seemed to hover in every crack and crevice.

"Welcome to Paradise," Rosey said, as we switched on Maglites and began the gruesome trek down the bleak corridor.

Before we were a hundred yards in, a pair of feral eyes reflected in the light of my flashlight beam. Huge rats, known by tunnel dwellers as track rabbits, scurried away from us in the dark. They were ugly rodents that hunted in the dark. Anything they could digest, they tried to eat, even crouching in packs to nibble the fingertips of blitzed-out bums in a drug haze. But in this desperate place the tables could quickly turn. The tormented men and women would sometimes trap the rats and spear their rodent carcasses on sticks so they could be eaten, roasted over smoldering sections of the *L.A. Times.*

We found our first cardboard condo about four hundred yards in. The resident was a woman with stringy black hair and oozing track marks on both arms. She peered out of her crate like a ghoul in a horror flick.

"You know John Bodine?" I asked.

She had a different kind of deal in mind.

"You got five bucks I'll suck off all a you," she whispered, her voice rasping.

It was hard to understand her because somebody had knocked out most of her teeth.

"We're looking for John Bodine," I repeated.

"You don't want a blow job, then get the fuck away," she said, slinking back into her box.

We shined our lights on down the tunnel and kept moving. The beams only penetrated fifty feet ahead. From beyond the reach of our flashlights, something growled at us. Man or beast,

I couldn't tell. We were flushing people and animals up the tunnel ahead of us. They would sometimes hide in the cutbacks and then try to sneak back around. We shined our lights on them as they scurried past. Nobody looked like Long Gone John.

A half a mile in, we encountered a larger cardboard condo complex: six shipping crates huddled together where people lived. Most were currently empty, but two appeared occupied. I went over and shined my light into a box where there was a man lying inside. I reached in to wake him.

"Shit," I said, as my hand touched his cold, stiff body.

"What is it?" Dario asked from behind me.

"This guy's dead."

I could smell his rotting flesh. God only knew how long he'd been there. His next-door neighbor was snoring, so I woke him.

"Whatta you want?" he groaned at me.

"Your buddy here is dead."

"Not my buddy." He sat up. "Fucking guy," the man said, leaning out and looking over at his dead neighbor who was now illuminated in the narrow beam of my Maglite. "Thought he was just sleeping off a powder fix."

"You know John Bodine?" I asked. He looked at me through tangled hair. "They call him Long Gone John," I added.

"I can know lots about him. You got some cash?"

"Describe him. If you get it right, then we'll talk money."

"Fat guy. No teeth."

"Nice try." I turned back to Rosey. "Better radio this DB in."

Lawrence Fischer triggered his walkie-talkie and tried to put out the call, but he only got static. "We're in too deep," he said. "Gotta wait till we're outside."

We moved on. The smell was horrific. The few people we encountered who hadn't slipped past us turned away, trying to hide from our flashlight beams. They looked like grotesque Salvador Dalí sketches. The ones we did talk to claimed not to know anything. I pinned each one with my flashlight, asked about Bodine, got nothing and moved on.

"I can't take much more," Adrian Young said. "This stench is gonna make me yak up those tacos."

Half an hour later I was beginning to feel like we were wasting our time. The end of the tunnel was coming up. The opening stopped at a dirty concrete wall, which was the foundation of the Bonaventure. It seemed a striking contrast. On the other side of that wall, just a few floors above, was a luxury hotel with people eating steaks while down here they were lined up waiting to get into hell. The paradoxes in this town can drive you nuts.

The smell was not quite as bad at the end of the tunnel because very few homeless people came this far in. The walls were damp and sweating with moisture, the air cool and moist. Something large scuttled past me, and I swung my light at a possum-sized rat scurrying toward the mouth of the tunnel a mile away.

Then I saw him, all the way back at the very end at the corner of the wall, as deep in as you could go. John Bodine had finally found the end of the line. I spotted the white plaster cast first, then Chooch's red Harvard-Westlake sweatshirt. I moved quickly toward him. As I got closer I could see the information Rosey had received was correct. Bodine had been badly beaten. Blood ran down the side of his face. His lip was split and he was clutching his stomach with both hands. Dried blood caked his fingers and stained much of Chooch's sweatshirt. I knelt in front of him and looked into his dusty brown eyes. Then I raised the sweatshirt and saw a deep knife wound in his left side.

"Ain't gonna put up with no more a your half-steppin', Scully," Bodine whispered. "See what you gone and done? I'm dying here and it's all your fault."

"What the hell happened to you?" I said, shining the light on his knife wound. It looked deep but had stopped bleeding.

"Ohhhh, man. This ain't no way to treat no prince," he moaned.

"How long you been in here?" I asked.

He looked at a watch on his wrist and whispered, " 'Bout six hours, I guess."

It seemed strange that he would even own a wristwatch. I didn't remember him having one before. Then I took a second look. Of course it was mine—the good one from the top drawer of my bedroom dresser.

"This guy's been stabbed. Let's not wait for the EMTs and a stretcher. They hate coming in here; it's always a hassle," I said. "We gotta get him out now!"

The four cops behind me moved up. I lifted John to his feet and Rosey and Dario made a seat for him on their forearms. "It's almost a mile, so we'll take turns carrying him," I said.

Then we carted the Crown Prince of Bassaland out of the most miserable spot in L.A.

CHAPTER TWENTY-SIX

The first thing I noticed when we brought Bodine out into the sunlight was that somebody had hacked off his dreadlocks. What hair he had left was now unbraided and sticking out at strange angles, chopped and uneven. It made him look even crazier than he probably was. Lawrence Fischer and I were carrying him. As we hurried up Lucas Avenue toward my car, I asked him, "Who cut off your hair?"

"I did. African prince don't be needin' no fancy man hair. It's a tribal thing," he ranted. "In Africa, you see a brotha with no hair, says he's a revolutionary, 'cause first thing a freedom fighter in the Bassaland goes an' does is breaks his mutha-fuckin' hair pick, 'cause a hair pick look just like a field tool, like for pickin' cotton. Be like a rake or some such. I say to hell with the rake and the pick and the whole exploitation of my African brothers." Naturally, I was sorry I had asked.

We set his feet down so that I could unlock the car door. When we did that, he stopped talking about hair combs as a symbol of slavery and started screaming in pain.

"What you bust-out-muthafuckas doing to me?" he shrieked.

Gary and I loaded him into the front seat of the Acura. We must have opened the wound carrying him a mile out of the tunnel, because when he slid in, he left a streak of fresh blood on the gray leather. I slammed the door shut while he was still braying insults at me and looked at Rosey, Dario, Adrian, and Lawrence, who were all now shaking their heads in disbelief.

"That's the sorriest human being I've ever seen," Adrian Young said.

"This is as far as we're gonna take it," Dario added. "We'll stay here and call in the tunnel DB. Wait for the coroner. But we aren't gonna get involved. Gonna have nothing more to say on it."

"Thanks for finding him," I said.

"Shane, you want some advice from a friend?" Rosey said.

"Sure."

"I wouldn't lone wolf this thing. You're gonna get caught in the net."

"I'll be careful."

Then I got into the car and pulled away from the taco stand.

"Ohhh . . . OHHH! Watch them bumps. Got myself gizmoed here. Got guts an' shit hanging all out."

"I'm taking you back to the hospital."

"That be our thing, ain't it? First you downs me, then you clowns me."

"How'd I down you? You stole my wife's computer. I need it back."

"How'd you down me? Is that the question? 'Cause a you, I end up with four hundred in Benjies I shouldn't never have, plus what I got for selling all your dumb-ass junk. Bunch a no-good quality-of-life criminals put me down with a hobo's birthday, take all the money. 'Cept for you, I never would a had all that coin in the first place."

Tortured logic, but I pushed on. "What's a hobo's birthday?"

"Put a blanket over your head and start hitting ya with a pipe till it blow out your candle."

"Where's the computer, John? I need it. It's got important stuff on it."

"It be G-O-N-E."

"Where to?"

"Man, I'm dying here. Why I gotta be constantly in da mix? Do we got to talk about this now?"

"Yes!"

"I pawned it at Jungle Jack's on Alvarado at Seventh. Next to the produce market."

"You got the pawn ticket?" A crafty look came across his face. "Gimme the ticket, John. I'm not screwing around here."

He fumbled deep in Chooch's loose jean pockets and finally pulled it out and handed it to me.

Fifteen minutes later, I parked under the porte cochere at County-USC. I went inside the ER, found a wheelchair, got John out of my car, loaded him into the chair and pushed him into the waiting room. He was slumped over, bitching and moaning. His wound was still bleeding. Fresh blood was again seeping through Chooch's sweatshirt and beginning to puddle under the wheelchair. I tapped on the glass and got the nurse's attention. It was early afternoon and the ER wasn't busy yet.

"I need some help here. This guy has a knife wound in the gut."

She looked through the glass, saw blood was leaking all over her clean ER floor and quickly buzzed a male nurse through the door. He grabbed the wheelchair and started to push John into the back. Before he left, I got my watch back.

I waited while they gave John a preliminary exam. I wanted to rush right over to Alameda and Seventh and retrieve Alexa's computer, but I also needed to make sure Bodine was okay. Thirty minutes later a pleasant-looking female doctor came out of the back and found me. She had some of John's blood on her ER smock.

"That's one lucky dude," she said. "The blade missed his stomach by a fraction. Missed his large intestine by even less. It went in clean, nicked his bottom rib, and hit nothing but muscle and bone. If I was trying for that same track with a laproscope I doubt I could do it."

"What are you going to do with him?"

"We'll keep him overnight. He'll need some whole blood transfusions. He's lost a lot. From the smell of him, he doesn't have insurance, so he's gonna be a charity ward case."

"He's a material witness in a murder. I want him to have good care. If he needs anything beyond just normal M.T., the

City of Los Angeles will cover it." I showed her my badge. "He should have an admittance form from earlier yesterday when his wrist was broken and you guys set it. Put any charges with that and I'll make sure it gets covered."

"Sure cusses a lot," the doctor said.

"He's an African prince. That gives him verbal immunity."

The doctor raised her eyebrows. "A prince? Really. Last royalty I got to treat was the Count of Crisco, but he was just a transvestite porn star."

"Not the same thing," I told her. Then I wrote my new cell number on a business card and handed it to her. "I don't want him to leave here until I get back. If he tries, have somebody sit on him."

As I was walking out of the ER waiting room, Alexa's story was on TV again. This tragedy had not only taken over our lives, but it was now becoming entertainment for the entire country.

MYSTERY AT THE LAPD was the graphic scrawled across the TV screen. It displayed a collage of shots, including Alexa's shooting range still. A handsome news anchor with blond-tipped hair came on with a fresh angle.

"A new break on the David Slade LAPD killing," he announced gravely. "Police are speculating that there may be yet another explanation for the murder."

"Finally," I whispered. Then I watched as my own picture hit the screen.

"In a new scenario floated this afternoon by sources close to law enforcement officials, Lieutenant Scully's husband, Detective Shane Scully, is now being called a person of interest in the execution-style murder of LAPD Sergeant David Slade. Shane Scully, a member of the LAPD's elite Homicide Special unit, has reportedly been picked up by detectives working on the Slade murder and whisked off to Parker Center in handcuffs, where he underwent a prolonged and intense interrogation conducted by acting Police Chief Michael Ramsey."

The shot switched to a gray-haired man whose on-screen graphic identified him as retired LAPD homicide detective Chuck Bowman.

"If reports are true, and Lieutenant Alexa Scully was roman-
tically involved with Sergeant Slade, then her husband should
certainly be considered a suspect in both acts of violence," the
retired cop said.

I didn't stick around to hear the rest. I sprinted to my car and
pulled out. How could I have missed it? Of course, I was going
to be a prime suspect. If I'd been working the case as a homicide dick instead of a grieving husband, I would have put that
together in a heartbeat. Rosey's warning had been right. I was
caught in the net.

I decided as I drove away from the emergency room that I'd
rather have the story be about me than Alexa. If they started focusing on me, maybe they'd stop pounding her. However, if I
was a suspect, my movements were soon going to become seriously limited. I had to work fast. I decided to see how much
trouble I was really in, so I picked up my cell and called Captain Calloway's direct line at Homicide Special.

"Calloway," he said, coming right on.

"Cal, it's Shane."

"Hey." His voice sounded cool, but friendly. "Where are
you?"

"You hearing what these jerks on TV are saying about me?"

"You need to come in, Shane. We need to talk."

"Captain, you can't believe I did this any more than Alexa
did. Slade and Alexa weren't having an affair. There's some
other reason he was in her car."

"Rafie, Tommy, and I don't buy any of this either, but now
that it's come up, we gotta deal with it. We'll get it straightened
out, but you gotta come in."

Yeah, right, I thought.

Then he said, "We need your time line for yesterday, and if
you have an alibi for your whereabouts when Slade got killed,
we're gonna need that, too."

"I can't come in yet. I'm trying to get Alexa's computer," I
hedged. "I made a deal with Great White Mike to get it for
him."

"That can wait," Cal said. "Your alibi, if there is one, can't."

"Don't worry, I have an alibi," I promised.

"It better be solid."

I didn't answer. I just hung up. The guy who could vouch for my whereabouts was lying in a hospital bed at County-USC with a knife wound in his gut, and all of his hair chopped off. He looked like he'd just been hit by a thousand volts of electricity. My alibi was raving like a lunatic, crazy as a shithouse rat.

CHAPTER TWENTY-SEVEN

Jungle Jack's Pawn Shop was in an old wood-sided house, tucked between two large vegetable stands in the produce market near Seventh. The fly-specked front windows displayed canteens, army knives, and other people's dusty clothes hanging on chipped mannequins. When I walked inside, a bell over the door rang, and after a moment, a rail-thin elderly man wearing his glasses up on his forehead came out from the back. He had Einstein hair and skin so white that it appeared almost purple in the overhead fluorescents.

"Don't break the circle, brother," he said listlessly, as he shuffled around behind the counter. On the street, the circle was your group of tights—your buddies. The circle was supposed to protect you. But it was a worthless concept because on the Row, you couldn't count on support from anybody who wasn't pushing free meals, Bibles, or a campaign agenda. The old man stood looking me carefully up and down.

"Cop," he finally announced.

I pulled out my badge and showed him. He leaned down behind the counter and pulled out several sheets of paper.

"I'm running a business here, least I'm trying to, but you guys in property crime never get tired a putting me through these inventory checks, do ya? I gotta bring in part-time labor to compile all this stuff. Here's the list you bozos had me do yesterday. Ain't my fault an occasional serial number gets filed. If you take my paid-for inventory and store it over at the PAB, how'm I supposed to stay in business?" The PAB was the Police Administration Building—Parker Center.

"I'm not with property crimes." I fished John's pawn ticket out of my pocket and handed it to him.

He pulled his glasses down off his forehead and looked at it. "Says here, Samik Mampuna." Then he looked up at me. "You don't look like no Samik Mampuna."

"Sure I do. Use your imagination." I reached into my pocket and handed him a fifty. "Why don't we stop screwing around and you go get that computer out of the back?"

"Gotta stay here twenty days. State law. Only guy who can pick it up 'fore then is the guy who pawned it. After twenty days it goes up for general sale. That's the rule. This ticket was bought yesterday, so you got yourself a few weeks to wait."

He smiled, happy to finally be getting some payback on the LAPD.

"But you're gonna make an exception in this case, Jack, or I'm gonna get a desk and set it up on the sidewalk right in front of your place and check the serial numbers on every toaster and TV that walks in here."

He frowned at me. "Cops. All you people wanna do is mow my grass. Ain't nothing else you care about."

"Right. That's us, the Jungle Jack detail. Now, let's go. I want the computer."

He took a minute before moving toward the back of the shop. The laptop was my stolen property, but I knew this was going to be much quicker. To retrieve it on a fencing beef, I would need the numbers on the warranties, which were back in my desk in Venice Beach, not to mention a pound of LAPD paperwork and grief I didn't have time for.

After another minute Jungle Jack returned carrying Alexa's laptop and charger. He set it on the counter and I turned it on. It was working, but the LOW BATT was flashing so I shut it down, closed it, and turned to leave.

He stopped me and said, "That's three hundred fifty."

He was a crafty bastard who sensed that I had reasons for not wanting to go through the department. I didn't have time to argue, and I didn't want him to file a complaint against me downtown, so I pulled some more fifties off the wad of cash I had taken from home and dropped them on the counter.

"Don't break the circle, brother," he said as he picked up the cash.

"Then don't break my balls," I replied and walked out the door onto the street with the computer.

I needed a quiet place where I could work and didn't want to sit in my car parked at the curb. I drove a few blocks down Seventh to the old Ford Hotel. I parked in a side lot under a dusty palm tree, went inside, and paid the indifferent desk clerk twenty bucks. He handed me a key to a first-floor room that was at the end of a narrow, paint-deprived corridor. I let myself into a dingy rectangle with a window that faced a brick wall. I closed the door, set the laptop on the bed, and plugged it into the wall socket. Then I sat on the stained red bedspread and waited for it to boot.

Most of what was on the computer was case-related, and contained a lot of correspondence from Alexa to her division commanders at the four bureaus. For the past month, she had been working on crime stats for all the detective divisions, attempting to evaluate the crime complaint to clearance rate percentages for each section she supervised. It was a tough problem, because some bureaus, like Central and South, had a lot of gang activity, which included stranger shootings, carjackings, and payback homicides. These cases were notoriously hard to put down and the detectives in those divisions usually had a higher open unsolved percentage. The Valley Bureau, on the other hand, encompassed a lot of bedroom communities like Foothill and Devonshire, where detectives generally had a much easier go of it. When some jealous husband catches his wife with the golf pro and bludgeons her to death with his nine iron, it's pretty much bing-bang-boom! Gotcha.

Alexa was attempting to balance all this for performance evaluations. She had the stats for each detective division that she supervised, divided into different criminal categories:

Rape, Robbery, ag-assaults, Child or Spousal Abuse, Property
Crime, and Homicides. The clearance rates for each division
were broken down by both arrests and by how many of the
cases the D.A. had agreed to file. On another page, there was a
running total of cases tried and their eventual outcomes, how
many busts resulted in convictions. She was tabulating not only
the arrests, but also the the quality of the arrests. It was extremely comprehensive and I marveled at her thoroughness.

As I scanned file after file, nothing seemed out of the ordi-
nary. I found a Special Ops file and used her password to open
it. DARK ANGEL wasn't listed. I kept opening and closing windows like mad, my fingers flying over the keyboard. By mistake, I opened an unsecured folder marked 2005 OVERTIME
DEPLOYMENT PROJECTIONS. It was hardly the place to store sen-
sitive documents, but since it was already open in front of me, I
scanned it. The first few files were statistics, spreadsheets,
archived correspondence, and e-mails. All of it, as expected,
dealt with manpower deployment and overtime projections. I
was scrolling and scanning, not paying too much attention,
when all of a sudden there it was, hiding in plain sight: the
DARK ANGEL file. It contained twenty or more e-mails from
Alexa to David Slade and from Slade to her. All were sent
within the last two months. As I began to read, my heart went
cold.

> *Dark Angel . . .*
> *My thoughts are always on you. We must meet tomorrow night.*
> *I can't go another day without holding you. You need to give me*
> *another floor score. I ache to see you. How 'bout Cryto 457?*
> *   Love—Hambone*

Hambone—Alexa's Academy nickname. I scrolled down
further and read one from Slade to her.

> *Dear Hambone,*
> *Time away from you is agony. This time Watts is the key. I can't*
> *be away from my Queen. It's all about lost performance and*

royalty. Don't make me wait, darling. I've got WYD and plenty
of ammo. I'm in the cut, waiting.

Love—Dark Angel

They were all like that. Twenty of them. Hers more straight-
forward. His full of hip-hop sex references, always signed Dark
Angel.

Toward the end, I read one posted where the tone was different. It sounded ominous. Actually, it read like a blackmail
threat.

Hambone,
You better come with everything I asked for—NOW. I'm losing
patience. You know I'm not kidding. This isn't much fun. You
don't come through I'll go to the Old Man. Those are my
conditions. You have 24 hours to deliver.

Dark Angel

I couldn't read any further.

As I looked at the e-mails, my vision blurred. All I kept
thinking was, *Why?* How could she betray me like this?

I didn't know what to do. If this file ever fell into the wrong
hands, it would become the motive for Slade's murder.

CHAPTER TWENTY-EIGHT

I lay back on the stained red bedspread in the Skid Row hotel and tried to come to grips with it. All of the e-mails had been written over the last few months. Had I been too busy with my caseload to give Alexa what she needed? The enormity of her betrayal swept in on me like a black tide, washing pieces of my well-being away with each violent surge.

I tried to examine the past two months, going back to late May, when the e-mails started. Had I sensed anything different between us? Had there been a distance there that might have hinted at this affair with David Slade? And why him? Why some bad seed cop, some unstable psycho who pulled guns on people over lane changes? It just didn't add up.

But one of the things I'd learned as a homicide cop was that human behavior often didn't add up and that the hardest condition to understand is the human condition. I'd seen murders committed over gardening tools; children shaken to death because they wouldn't eat their vegetables. The unpredictability of human behavior was a tragic constant in the criminal justice system.

But despite this, there were some things that I had come to take for granted. Areas where I had finally let my guard down and been at peace. My relationship with Chooch was one, my marriage to Alexa another. I never dreamed of something like this happening. I continued to search for a framework that made sense. I couldn't find one.

But one of the hard lessons all young cops quickly learn is that truth is always subjective. It is colored by point of view and the way we choose to see things. At the bottom line, truth is just opinion and can be viewed differently depending on bias. I was a big loser here, and I didn't know how to deal with that. Worse still, I couldn't scream my anger or disappointment at Alexa. I couldn't demand an explanation or grant forgiveness. She was lying in a coma that she might never come back from.

Time ticked slowly on the old-style digital clock that was bolted to the bedside table in the dingy hotel room. I could hear the little metal numbers flipping over every sixty seconds, changing the readout on the display.

What should I do about this? How do I handle it? How does it change me?

Then I remembered something that had happened when I was twelve and living at the Huntington House group home. I was a point guard on our elementary school basketball team, a ragtag group of orphans in mismatched uniforms. One afternoon, we were playing a game against a rich, private school. We were way behind, getting our asses kicked, and being fouled like crazy under the basket. We were on their home court, with their fathers refereeing, and none of the fouls under the basket were getting called. At halftime, our dejected Huntington House team was sitting on benches in the guest locker room of this expensive private school gym, complaining about how unfair it was and how we'd never win with them cheating like that. Our coach was a tough old duck, and he used to scream a lot when the team was losing. But that afternoon he taught me a great lesson.

"All you guys are doing is bitching about stuff you can't change," our crusty old coach said. "Bitching how this guy's fouling you, or how the refs aren't making the calls. Well, welcome to the real world, boys. If you fret about stuff you can't control, I guarantee you'll always lose."

Then he'd told us that we could only play our game, not the

other guys'. It was such a simple concept that it was often over-looked. We went out in the second half and played our game on their court and won.

Alexa was who she was, and whatever choices in her life led her to this, they were hers, not mine. It was out of my hands. It wasn't my game. Despite the overpowering evidence to the contrary, some part of me still prayed it was wrong. Some inkling deep inside still told me that it was. All of it—the murder, the attempted suicide, the answering machine confession, and now the e-mails with the damning blackmail note. But it really didn't matter, because I knew I still loved her. The thought that she was lying in a coma and might never recover still devastated me. I knew in that instant that whatever the reasons for all of this, I couldn't let them beat me. I was getting fouled, but if I didn't want to lose, I had to ignore the bad calls and play my own game.

I sat up and looked at the computer. The damning e-mails were still up on the screen. David Slade was dead. Alexa was in a desperate fight for her life. She might have had an affair with him, but I just couldn't believe she would put him in her cuffs and execute him gangland-style. Not Alexa. Not the woman who turned my life around and taught me how to love. In accounting, they teach if your balance is off by only a few cents, those few cents might be hiding a much larger error. This balance was off, and that's what I was hoping for.

Broken-hearted, I packed up Alexa's computer. I took one last look back at the faded decor before closing the door. I knew I would carry this ugliness to my grave. I walked out of the hotel and back to the parking lot. As I unlocked my car door, I was sure of only one thing.

This wasn't over.

CHAPTER TWENTY-NINE

H ere was my predicament:

It was five o'clock and the grace period Mike Ramsey had given me was almost over. I had Alexa's computer, but given the content, there was no way I was turning it over. Going to UCLA at seven-thirty would be risky because if Deputy Chief Ramsey made good on his promise, the PSB dicks could be there waiting for me. That meant I should stay away from that hospital at all costs. At least that was my excuse. But I suspected the real reason I didn't go was because, deep down, I wanted to run from this. I couldn't face Alexa, even in a coma.

Instead, I decided to fall back on police work and see if I could run a surveillance on the white sister. I tried to convince myself that right now that was more important; but it was just cowardice.

At ten to six, I parked a few hundred yards up the road from Stacy Maluga's Malibu estate. I got out of the Acura and walked slowly back to a spot where I could see the hedge-lined, wrought-iron fence that framed the property. I was close enough to the front gate to see the manicured gardens through the big, gold-scripted M, but at the same time was out of range of the driveway cameras. I was pretty sure that KZ and Insane Wayne weren't in the security lounge looking at a wall of video

monitors. Those two ace-cool busters were probably drinking
Mai-Tais out by the pool with Stacy. But why take a chance?

I found a protected place out of the late afternoon sun and
sat on the ground. From this vantage point, I could just barely
see the driveway. I opened the little package from ESD and removed Stacy's pager and a small hand-held monitor. There was
a short memo attached from the ESD technician who had installed the bug. It contained an inventory list and brief instructions, which I read carefully.

> *This two-way listening device is a VXT voice-activated room*
> *transmitter and is inside a Motorola pager with the number*
> *(800) 765-3333. The device has an output power of 20 MW at*
> *100–120 MHz. Range is 1,000 meters. Batt life is*
> *approximately twenty-five hours.*
> *Inventory List:*
> > *1 Motorola Pager (VXT device installed)*
> > *1 VXT Radio Receiver with earplug*
> > *1 extra 9V battery pack*
>
> FOR QUESTIONS: CALL EARL FELLOWS ESD (310) 555-5770

I turned on the receiver unit and set it to the correct fre-
quency, then clipped it on my belt and put the earplug in my
jacket pocket.

Since the pager had been stolen off Stacy's home bar, my
problem was how to get it back into her purse without causing
suspicion. I had a plan for that, which I thought might work.

It entailed following her when she left the mansion. But
since I had no idea what her social plans for the evening were,
all I could do was sit here and wait.

I tried to keep my mind off what had just happened with
Alexa by concentrating on Stacy and Lou Maluga, looking for a
possible motive. I began examining Stacy's relationship with
David Slade and her estranged marriage with Lou. That, of
course, put me right back on Alexa's relationship with Slade
and my own marriage. I finally forced myself to stop thinking
about it because in the end, my thoughts all came painfully
back to Alexa.

At six-fifteen I heard a loud squeaking sound followed by a rattling of metal chain as the huge wrought-iron gate was cranked wide.

I ran back to the Acura and put on a baseball cap and some dark glasses I keep in my glove box. Then I started the engine. I needed to time this just right. I didn't know if the gate had been opened from the house or with a remote while the vehicle was heading down the long drive. I didn't know if it was Stacy or just one of the steroid twins leaving the mansion. That meant I had to get a passing look inside the car as it was leaving the estate. I sort of played the timing by ear and after what seemed like the right span, put the Acura in drive, and pulled away from my parking spot. The idea was to pass the gate just as the car was coming out of the drive and the occupants were looking for cross-traffic. If they were concerned about oncoming cars, hopefully they wouldn't recognize me.

But I blew the timing. I got there thirty seconds too early. A tan Rolls-Royce Phantom with personalized plates that said WHT SUGR was parked in the drive with the engine idling. Had to be her. I couldn't see the drive because the low afternoon sun had blown out the windshield with reflected light. I had no choice but to keep driving right on past.

About a quarter mile down the road, I spotted a switchback driveway and hung a right, pulling off the road to a spot where I was out of sight of cars passing on Oceanridge Drive. I shifted into park and took my foot off the brake to douse my taillights and waited. If the Rolls was headed to Malibu, it would quickly pass the place where I was waiting. If it was going to L.A. via the Ventura Freeway, it was already headed down the other side of the mountain, away from me.

I waited for three minutes. The car didn't pass. I'd guessed wrong.

"Damn," I muttered, then backed down the drive onto Oceanridge, right into the path of the oncoming Rolls. Whoever was driving honked the horn angrily, swerved out of my way, and continued on toward Malibu. It was low comedy. I couldn't have screwed it up worse if I'd been wearing clown makeup and a rubber nose.

My car had been spotted, but I was out of time and options, so I hung a U and followed. One of the good things about running a tail in a silver Acura is that the car looks like half the iron on the road. It blends in. A Rolls-Royce Phantom, on the other hand, is so wide and tall, it's hard to lose. You can tail one of those parade floats from three or four cars back and still keep visual contact.

The big, elegant car hummed out of Malibu down the Coast Highway. It turned left on Sunset Boulevard, and twenty minutes later I was six car-lengths back, negotiating the twisting turns near Mandeville Canyon. We continued on Sunset past UCLA, into Westwood. Expensive real estate slipped by on both sides of my windows; long rolling lawns fronted big Colonial and French Regency houses. Everybody had a nice gold initial on their wrought-iron gate.

The Rolls turned right off Sunset at Doheny and went down the hill to Santa Monica Boulevard where it pulled into a valet stand in front of a famous L.A. nightclub and old-time music biz watering hole called The Troubadour. The front of the club was painted completely black. It had been a trendy spot for new bands to perform in the eighties but recently the place had gone retro. However, over the last two decades a lot of music acts had been broken on that stage.

I pulled up half a block back and watched Stacy Maluga get out of the Rolls. She was dressed to stop traffic in a sequined dress that ended just below her ass and was cut so low in front it almost exposed her navel. She was wearing four-inch hooker heels and crossed the sidewalk using long stripper strides, the short hem of her dress flipping seductively around shapely legs. She handed her keys to the appreciative valet and disappeared into the nightclub.

The first problem I encountered was the valet decided to leave the expensive Rolls right out front to show everybody who drove by on Santa Monica what a classy joint The Troubadour still was.

I parked the Acura a block away and moved up the street on foot. Even though it looked busy, The Troubadour was not a place you went for dinner. I also figured this early in the evening, Stacy wasn't here scouting music acts because the marquee said the first show didn't start until eight. She was probably meeting someone for drinks. I had made such a memorable first splash at her house, I figured even in my baseball cap and glasses, I couldn't chance going in for a look around. I decided to stick to my original plan and not get greedy.

I waited until the valet stand in front of the nightclub was overloaded. Guys in red jackets were jumping into waiting cars and wheeling them around the corner up the hill on Doheny to the nightclub's parking lot, then running back and jumping into the next idling car.

Once I got the rhythm of it, I figured I would have maybe thirty seconds if I was lucky. When all three valets were away from the stand, I made my move. I speed-walked to the passenger side of the Rolls-Royce, opened the door, leaned in, and jammed Stacy's pager down into the crack between the front seats, pushing it far enough in so it would look like it had fallen from her purse and become accidentally squashed down and hidden. As I was doing this, I heard the slap of tennis shoes on pavement as one of the red-jacketed track stars came running back down the side street. I almost got my head out of the Rolls before he appeared at the corner and saw me still half inside the glitzy tan car.

"Hey, whatta you doing?" he shouted at me.

"Man, would you look at this thing?" I gushed. "Look at that leather, like butter."

"Leave the car alone," he ordered, approaching me angrily.

I needed to give him something else to think about so I said, "Boy, Cadillac really knows how to build 'em, huh?"

"It's a Rolls-Royce, dipshit."

"This is a Rolls?" I said incredulously. "You sure?"

"It says right on the steering wheel. RR—that's Rolls-Royce. Whatta you, some kinda moron?"

We were now talking about how stupid I was and not about what my head was doing inside somebody else's car.

"Get away from it," he commanded, so I turned and walked away.

I got in my Acura and found a new parking spot heading the

same direction as the Rolls. Then I scooted down in my seat and waited.

At seven o'clock Stacy came out of the club. It had been a short meeting. I watched as she tipped the smiling valet, got into the Phantom and sped away from the curb. I followed.

Halfway down Santa Monica Boulevard, I pulled up directly behind the Rolls at a red light. I could see her clearly through the back window, so I dialed her pager with my cell phone and waited. The light changed, but the pager must have been ringing because Stacy didn't move. The Rolls was still parked at the green light while she began digging around in the seat cushion with her head down looking for it. When she finally raised her head, she held the pager up triumphantly in her right hand. She'd found it.

Then she dropped my bug in her purse, right where I wanted it and powered away, taking a right, heading north back up the hill toward Sunset.

CHAPTER THIRTY

It was seven-fifteen. Instead of fulfilling my responsibility to Alexa and meeting with Luther, I continued following the tan Rolls into Hollywood.

The car turned onto Sunset Boulevard and headed toward the Strip, then pulled into a parking lot behind the old Whiskey A Go Go. Stacy was hitting her share of retro clubs. She exited the car and chirped the alarm, but didn't go inside the Whiskey. Instead, she did her runway strut down Sunset toward a two-story office building in the middle of the next block.

Two exposed upstairs dormer windows relieved the non-descript brown stucco facade and elevated the architecture from boxy to eclectic. Maintenance was slipshod and the building seemed to crouch low in the middle of the block as if trying to hide its faded paint and chipped trim. Tattered and old, the place was a reminder of better days when the Sunset Strip was the place to be.

I parked in the same lot behind the Whiskey and followed her down the street. I was still wearing the baseball cap and glasses as I entered the run-down building, but in a clever shift of disguise, I swung the bill of my ball cap to the back, gangsta-style, and took off my coat, draping it across my arm. I arrived inside the building only two minutes behind her, but the lobby was already empty. She had disappeared.

There was a building registry behind a plate of smudged glass identifying the lucky businesses that officed here. The place had a sweet, acrid smell, like Lysol mixed with pot, and the list of tenants appeared to be mostly music companies. One on the second floor was named Chronic Inc. On the street, chronic is potent, homegrown-style bud favored by marijuana users. Chronic Inc. A rap label? Maybe.

I pulled the earpiece out of my pocket and again looked at my watch. Seven-thirty. Alexa's medical meeting would just now be starting at UCLA with only Chooch in attendance. I pictured Luther frowning, and had a mental flash of my son not understanding why I hadn't called. Because it was all over the TV, both had to know by now that I was a suspect in Slade's murder.

I shook off these thoughts, inserted the earpiece and plugged the jack into the VXT receiver hooked to my belt. A sudden rush of shame flooded over me. I needed to be at that hospital. I was better than this. But just as I turned to leave, I heard Stacy's voice loud and clear, coming through the earpiece.

"Chicken head bitch be lyin' in a coma." Stacy was talking about Alexa. It froze me. I hit record on the VXT receiver.

"Slade couldn't never keep it in his pants," she continued. "All the time messing with new bitches, floatin' his game."

"You sound like that still be a problem, Stacy. Push off. The man's dead." It was a male voice. Deep, soft, and lyrical. "Come here, baby. I can get your mind offa that chump. Lemme give ya my flava."

"Hey, Curtis, we ain't got time. You got more Lou problems." Stacy said. "It's why I come down here."

"This just gonna be bidness?" he teased. "My gun needs cleanin', Mama."

"You need to hear me out," she said. "I been checkin' expense sheets. Lou got all kinda janky shit goin' on with your concerts. Stuff even I didn't know about. He's also been skimmin' your performance royalties. It's time for you ta use that escape clause I told you about. Go over to WYD."

"When's that man gonna give me a day off?" Curtis moaned.

"You want a day off, you shoulda been a secretary," Stacy said. "This just be the way the man thinks."

"You're right," Curtis said. "He's stealin', not takin' care of business. It's all kryptonite. Ain't just my *Savage Bitch* CD gettin' shelved, or no Wall Street backing. Now my new side, "Nigga Got Game," ain't even getting no radio play. All Lou does about it when I complain is threaten my ass—walkin' around with some ball bat, bustin' chops like the old days. Them East Coast–West Coast Beat Downs. You the only one over there gets it. Don't he know the Jew suits at Sony and Warner Records won't put up with his gangsta vibe?"

"You need t'have your new accountants check the last four royalty statements," Stacy said. "The shortfalls are mostly in event fees and expenses. You got a good civil suit here, baby."

"Man," he said. "Thank God you and me got our swerve on. Weren't for you, I wouldn't even know about any a this. If you hadn't found that escape clause Dante put in my contract, I'd be stuck." A chair scraped, somebody moved, and then Curtis said, "Lou finds out you been helpin' me, Mama, he gonna buck down hard."

"He ain't gonna find out 'less you start slippin', sugar. Since he got outta San Quentin, Lou lost his skills. He gonna end up goin' right back in the joint for fraud. I'm doin' this to teach him a lesson, so you gotta make sure it stays between us and the attorneys. Far as Lou knows, your accountants found this."

"You can count on me, baby. Now come here an' gimme some play."

Then I heard a chair scrape again, followed by heavy breathing. It went on for almost two minutes.

"Damn, that be fine," Curtis said, followed by a moan coming over the VXT. He was getting a hummer.

As I hid in the corridor listening, I tried to figure out Stacy's game. At her house, when I showed up, she called Lou. She obviously looked to him for protection. Everything I'd learned about Lethal Force, Inc. suggested that she was the brains behind the label, so why was she pushing this guy Curtis out the door, giving him insider information so he could break his contract and even possibly sue them? She said it was to teach Louis a lesson, but it seemed an expensive way to do it. Like everything else in this case, it was hard to understand.

"I'm out," I finally heard Stacy say.

The door at the end of the hall opened and she exited the room. I dove into a little alcove in the hall. Stacy strode up the corridor, straightening her blouse, right past the alcove where I was hiding. She was momentarily focused on the elevator and I didn't think she would see me. Then her eyes snapped to the side and she stared right at me. Her expression didn't change, and she showed no sign of recognizing me in my hat and glasses. But one thing chilled me as she hurried on by. Stacy Maluga's eyes were hard and cold and showed no emotion or humanity. Those eyes said she would stop at nothing to get what she wanted.

In that moment, I wondered if I'd been worried about the wrong Maluga. I suddenly wondered if it was Stacy, not Lou, who I should be afraid of.

CHAPTER THIRTY-ONE

Where the hell are you, Dad?" Chooch sounded angry over the speaker on my cell phone.

"Son, is Lex still there?"

"Yeah, but the other doctors all had to go."

"Put him on."

"Where are you?"

"Put him on, Chooch. Stop arguing with me." Anger flashed. *Why was I taking it out on him?*

After a few seconds, Luther came on the line. "Shane?"

"Luther, I'm sorry I missed the meeting."

"There were two cops here. They had a warrant for your arrest." His voice was guarded now.

"I think that was just an Internal Affairs charge sheet, not a warrant," I said. "It's an interdepartmental document. They have to serve you with a notice of the I.A. complaint. It's just their way of trying to get me to stop looking into this. But I can't stop, Luther, and you wouldn't, either."

He didn't say anything, so I asked, "Are the cops still there?"

"No."

It wasn't easy for him, given all the pressure coming from the chorus of black activists. I knew what they were accusing us of on TV.

"I didn't kill David Slade," I finally said. "Neither did Alexa."

"It's not my job to judge you, Shane. My job is to bring Alexa out of this coma."

"Will you still meet with me?"

"You mean become an accessory after the fact in a murder?" he said coldly.

"Luther, I know this isn't fair. I know what I'm asking is tough."

"I owe you for Levonda, but let's be straight. Even though you went way beyond what was normal there, you were still only doing your job. I didn't ask you to put your life's work in jeopardy by harboring a murder suspect."

I wasn't technically a murder suspect. Last time I checked, I was just a Person of Interest, but that was quibbling.

"Alexa needs surgery," Luther said. "The blood flow to parts of her cerebral cortex is low. In time, brain cells will die. I've scheduled her for Monday at ten A.M. This is a risky one, Shane. She's not too strong, and she's not responding to stimuli. Frankly, I have my doubts, but if we're going to have any chance at all of bringing her out of this, I need to go in and fix some things. As her next of kin, I need your signature on a surgical consent form. I had it with me and was going to get you to sign it at our seven-thirty meeting, but you didn't show."

"Luther, I can meet with you now. I can set this up so it will be clean, so nobody will know. Put Chooch back on."

A moment later, Chooch was on the line. "Yeah?" he said.

"You know that place where we had dinner after the Servite football game last year?"

"Yeah."

"I'm worried about the department putting a cell phone track on this number, so don't say the name of the restaurant. Meet me there in forty-five minutes. Try to make sure you're not followed and bring Luther."

After I hung up, I headed toward the Valley. I knew there was a BOLO out on me, and any patrol car that spotted my plate could pick me up. To avoid that, I drove on residential side streets across the Valley, and forty minutes later, pulled into the parking lot at Dupar's on Thousand Oaks Boulevard. I locked my car and went through the back door of the restaurant into a flurry of activity inside the busy kitchen.

"Is the manager here?" I asked a harried waitress who was retrieving orders.

"That guy," she said, pointing out a bald man in his forties, wearing dark slacks and a company shirt with DUPAR'S inscribed over his heart.

I walked up and tapped him on the shoulder. He turned and I showed him my badge.

"I'm a police detective," I said, not giving him my name. "I'm working a case undercover and I need to borrow an apron and one of those paper hats. My guy is coming in here in a few minutes."

"This better not turn into some San Diego Denny's-style shootout," he said, warily.

"It's a tax case, all very nonviolent and boring," I assured him.

He crossed the room and grabbed a Dupar's apron off a hook on the wall. Then he handed it to me along with a paper hat. I put them on and looked at myself in the shiny refrigerator door. My theory is that anybody in a restaurant wearing a paper hat and apron, standing next to a tub of dirty dishes, instantly becomes invisible.

"What's your name?" I asked the manager.

"Howie Lent."

"Okay, Howie. Just act normal, don't call attention to me. Everything's gonna be fine."

I pushed through the swinging door of the kitchen, and entered the busy restaurant. It was around nine o'clock Saturday night. The Cineplex up the street had just let out, and there were a lot of kids eating and clowning around in the dining area. I'd chosen Dupar's because there were high partitions, which created difficult sight lines. The din from the customers permeated everything. I took a position beside a serving station and stood there in my paper hat and apron, watching. Nobody paid any attention to me. I knew if the PSB dicks were serious about picking me up, they would have a tail on Luther and Chooch. But I had a way to defeat that.

Ten minutes later Chooch's Cherokee pulled into the parking lot followed by a midnight blue Chrysler PT Cruiser, which I knew was Luther's.

I watched Chooch and Luther enter the crowded restaurant and look around, trying to find me. Like everybody else, they looked right past the guy in the apron and paper hat standing by the bus tray. They found a table, sat down, and waited. If there was a tail, it would come inside soon. I continued to watch the parking lot through the window. After five minutes, I was pretty sure they hadn't been followed. But I still didn't want to take a chance and be wrong. I turned and walked out of the dining area without talking to Luther or Chooch. Once back in the kitchen, I stripped off the apron and handed it to a very relieved Howie Lent and left.

Out in the parking lot, I pulled out a spiral pad, wrote Chooch a note, and put it on his dash. Then I went to the far side of Luther's PT Cruiser and knelt down behind his passenger side rear fender.

Twenty minutes later, Luther and Chooch came out of the restaurant. Both looked at their watches and frowned. This was two meetings in a row I'd missed. Then Luther shook Chooch's hand, they said good-bye, and each headed to his separate car.

As Luther chirped the lock on his PT Cruiser, I stood up.

"Open the back door."

Luther jumped in fright. "Shit!" he said. Then he regained his composure, glared at me, and chirped the key lock again. I opened the door and slid into the backseat while he got behind the wheel.

"Let's go," I said. "Turn right and park anywhere in the middle of the street, on Moorpark. It's right up the hill."

"This ain't workin' for me, Shane."

I didn't answer because, of course, he was right.

Luther pulled out and I saw Chooch's headlights following us. We climbed the hill to Moorpark and pulled to the curb. My son parked behind us, then got out of his Cherokee and climbed into the front seat of the Chrysler. His face was strained as he looked back at me.

"Hi," he said.

"Hi back at ya." I tried to grin, but he wasn't having any.

"I'm gonna make this quick," Luther said. There wasn't any sympathy in his voice. He started right in. "The skull acts as a protective covering or helmet for the soft cells of the brain, which are made of neurons. These neurons form tracts that route through the brain, and those tracts carry messages to the various parts of the brain."

"Luther, I don't need a course in Neurology One-Oh-One. I need to know what her prognosis is."

"Shut up." He was angry and almost took my head off with those two words. "You don't know the first thing about any of this, okay? You think the brain is just a big bowl of gray jelly that we only use like ten percent of. You think since we only use a fraction of it, if Alexa loses a few neurons, what's the big problem? She'll just compensate with what she has left."

"I didn't say that."

"I've been talking to people like you for ten years, man. You don't have to say it. Since she's breathing and has a heartbeat, you think time is gonna heal this."

"And it's not?"

"She's in bad shape, okay?"

"Calm down."

"Right, of course. Calm down. What's got into me here? I'm only sneaking around in the middle of the night, having clandestine medical meetings with the prime suspect in a racially charged cop murder. What am I so upset about?"

"Hey, Luther, Dad didn't do it," Chooch said softly.

"You don't know that," Luther said. "It's bad enough what's going on here medically, but now we've got this other angle— this race thing. I'm talking a load of incoming fire in my community. I'm trying to pay my debt to you, Shane, but do you have any idea how far it is from One Hundred and Sixth Street to the Neurosurgery OR at UCLA?"

"A long way," I said.

"He didn't kill that guy, Luther. I know my dad. He didn't do it." Chooch's voice was shaking with passion or anger, I couldn't tell which.

It suddenly got very quiet in the car.

Chooch went on. "That means this is an injustice. It doesn't matter what all those people on TV say. Mom didn't shoot that guy and neither did Dad. Is it always just science for you? Don't doctors ever have to deal with what's right and wrong?"

Luther looked over angrily. "I don't need a lecture on ethics from you, Chooch."

"You told me in the restaurant, just a minute ago, that my dad solved Levonda's murder for you and your wife. But you're wrong. He didn't solve it for you. He did it for Levonda. He always says that he's the last one to speak for the dead. That's why he never quits. He was doing it for Levonda, and he kept speaking for her until he caught the guys who killed her. Don't do this for me or for Dad, because it's not about us. It's your turn to step up, man. You need to speak for Alexa."

Luther put his head in his hands and sat very still for a long moment. When he finally looked up, something had changed.

"I'm gonna try," he said. "I'm going to do everything in my power, but I'm not God."

"If anybody can save her, you can," I said.

He shook his head sadly, then handed me the consent form. I signed it and handed it back to him. When I saw his face, I knew I had pushed him too far. Our friendship was close to over.

CHAPTER THIRTY-TWO

I left the Acura at Dupar's and drove Chooch's Jeep Cherokee back to the hospital. My eyes stayed on the road, but I could feel the sadness and loss coming off my son in waves as he leaned against the passenger window. I stole a look as we passed under the street light on Ventura Boulevard. His expression reminded me of the bleak looks on the faces of the forgotten boys I'd grown up with at Huntington House.

In all of this, I'd been so consumed with Alexa's betrayal and my own grief over her injury that *I'd* forgotten Chooch in the process. I'd been giving him orders—be here, do that—counting on his support, but not thinking enough about how this was affecting him. I had been dealing with my pain and ignoring his.

"I'm sorry," I finally said. "I apologize, son."

"You didn't do anything. You don't need to apologize to me, Dad."

"Yes, I do. You know, Chooch, you're so tall and strong now that I forget you're still only a teenager—just eighteen. I think I rely on you too much, and I'm sorry."

He sat quietly.

"Sometimes in life, you get dealt bad cards," I went on. "And when you get a bad hand, that's when you get to find out who you really are, because that's when it starts to make sense to compromise your principles and take shortcuts. These last few days, I've been doing some of that. I don't like myself for it, and I especially don't like that it's been falling on you to deal with the backlash. I've been asking you to pick up after me, and that's not right, especially now. So I'm apologizing."

Still, he said nothing and seemed to be guarding his thoughts.

"I want you to know I understand how much there is at stake here for you. It's bad enough what's happening to Alexa, without also losing your respect for me." Again, he said nothing, so I went on. "These last two days, I've been thinking about Sandy. You lost one mom, and now you're having to go through it a second time. We never talk much about Sandy, but it's there, and I know it haunts you."

Then Chooch finally turned to face me. "We didn't talk about her because I never really knew her—two weeks here, a month there. She was so worried I'd find out who she was and what she did for a living, that she never let me see inside her. We never communicated. The best thing she ever did was getting you to take me for those two weeks, five years ago. She knew that I needed your strength and values. I love her for that and I certainly owe her. But I don't really have any fond memories. She was never there." He paused, then said, "Dad, nothing can ever diminish what I feel for you and Alexa. You gave me a real family. You guys are everything to me, and as far as cutting corners? Nobody gets it right all the time. I know that. But even when you're wrong, you know what makes it alright?"

I shook my head, not trusting my voice.

"You never stop worrying about it. You never stop questioning yourself. You taught me how to be a man by being someone I can believe in. So now that I am a man, it's only right for you to lean on me a little."

After a moment, I looked over at him. "We'll get through this together," I whispered.

"I know," he said softly.

We arrived at UCLA Medical Center and I parked in the lot

and shut off the engine. We sat in silence for a minute before I finally spoke again.

"Listen, Chooch. I've got to keep on this. Could you help me with something?"

"Sure, Dad. Anything."

"You're always reading *Street Beat* and those other music magazines, so you know the rap scene pretty well, right?"

"Yeah."

"You ever hear of a record company called Chronic Inc.?"

"It's not a record company. It's a management company like Rush Management, or one of those."

"They have any hot acts? Somebody named Curtis?"

"Curtis Clark. He's big. Does mostly West Coast rap, but years ago he started out doing some very badass street underground. He records for Lethal Force."

"Maluga's company."

"Yeah, but according to the music mags, they're having a feud. Nobody knows what it's about. They got in a screaming match at the Source Awards in Miami when Floor Score won Best New Artist."

I turned to face him. "Floor Score is a band?"

This hit me out of nowhere. I must have looked stunned or my mouth had fallen open, because Chooch said:

"You okay?"

"Yeah. . . . Tell me about Floor Score. I thought it was a sex act."

"Technically, it's street slang for drugs you find on the ground," he said. "Curtis Clark is the lead guy—the front man."

"What's WYD?"

"WYD stands for Who's Your Daddy. They're a huge label. Lionel Wright owns it. He's also their biggest star. Lionel records under the name Bust A Cap."

My excitement was growing. This was a whole new direction.

"Lionel Wright is the brains behind WYD and he's a marketing genius," Chooch continued. "Besides his rap songs, he's got a Bust A Cap clothing line and Bust A Cap hair products. He's kinda like Sean 'Puffy' Combs. Used to be that Lionel was only in magazines like *Rap World* and *Street Beat*. Now he's in every other issue of *People*. He and WYD have been pirating acts away from Lethal Force."

"Acts like Curtis Clark and Floor Score," I muttered, remembering the conversation I'd overheard earlier in the Chronic Inc. office. "Ever heard of a group called Motel Crypto or Four-Fifty-Seven?" I asked, remembering those names from Alexa's e-mails.

"Crypto Four-Fifty-Seven is a rap group that just left Lethal Force," Chooch said. "Everybody's leaving the Malugas because they're still a Compton-style gangsta rap company. Now that Maluga is out of jail, he's back to threatening everybody, trying to get his old acts back and hanging on to the ones he still has like Floor Score." He looked closer at me. "I thought you hated this kinda music. Why are you interested in all this?"

"Just am," I said. "I'll call and check in every couple of hours. I'm sorry I can't be in there with you."

He smiled. "I'll watch over Mom. You go find out who killed David Slade."

"Deal."

He started to get out of the car, but I had one last thought and stopped him by saying, "Hey, Chooch, you still got your laptop in here?"

He nodded, opened the back, rummaged under his seat, then pulled it out and handed it to me. "You might have to use the lighter plug. I don't know how much charge is left."

"Thanks," I said, and hugged him.

I sat in the Jeep and watched him walk back into the hospital. Then I headed back to the Valley. I'd stupidly left Alexa's computer in the Acura and I needed to retrieve it.

All the way over the hill, I kept turning this new information over in my mind.

There were still a few things that didn't fit, but in my mind the accounting had just changed, and a few things were finally beginning to add up. There had been a mistake in my original tabulation. I should have known to trust in Alexa no matter what. The error my mistrust had produced was hiding a larger truth, and that truth just might exonerate her.

CHAPTER THIRTY-THREE

I was parked in Dupar's lot with Alexa's computer resting on my lap. I left the material on her computer, but made a DVD copy and transferred the information to a blind file on Chooch's laptop. After I finished, I picked up my cell phone and scrolled through the contacts to find Figueroa's number. It was almost midnight, but I dialed him anyway.

"Yeah?" his sleepy voice mumbled after the second ring.

"It's Shane."

There was a long pause before he said, "Okay."

"I need to see you and Tommy tonight."

"Meet you at our office on the fifth floor of the Police Administration Building," he said. "We can be there in an hour."

"All good, except for the part about meeting at the PAB."

"Shane, we're not meeting you any place but Parker Center."

"I've got Alexa's computer. There's some interesting stuff on it you might wanta hear about."

The mouthpiece of the phone was suddenly covered by his hand and I heard his muffled voice say, "Go back to sleep, Rachel. I got it."

When he came back on the line he said, "Just a minute." Then I was on hold. A few seconds later, he was back. "Hadda change phones, sorry."

"Rafie, I can't take a chance, going down to Parker Center. I might not walk out of there. If you guys want this computer, meet me at the Greek Theatre in an hour."

"The Greek? You're kidding me."

"You remember Sergeant Loveboy from Valley Vice?"

"Big fat guy. Retired."

"That's him. He's the plastic badge at the Greek now. He'll let you in."

"What's going on, Shane?"

"Tell ya when I see ya." Then I hung up. I left my Acura at Dupar's and put the Jeep in gear, pulling out of the parking lot.

The Greek Theatre sits in a small canyon off North Vermont Avenue in Griffith Park. Once, about three years ago, in an attempt to add culture to my life, Alexa had dragged me to a summer concert of Classics. While the rest of the audience was listening to Tchaikovsky and Mozart, my mind wandered and I found myself studying the layout. The amphitheater was nestled in the hills, surrounded on all sides by forest. I realized it would be possible to get in and out of this place by coming down from the fire road on the hillside above the canyon. I put the amphitheater on my list of possible spots for a clandestine meet. This location became even more attractive two years ago when my old Valley Watch Commander pulled the pin and became a night security guard at the amphitheater. Sgt. Dorsey Loveboy was a fat, loose-jointed guy who looked as if his shirt was always untucked even when he was standing a dress inspection. But we'd had a good relationship, which I was now planning to take advantage of.

I pulled up North Vermont Avenue and stopped about fifty feet back from his post. I blinked my lights twice to wake him if he was dozing, then I pulled up and watched as he stood up from the swivel chair in the guard shack and looked out at me. He was wearing an oversized Romark Security uniform designed to resemble LAPD blue. He leaned down and looked into the driver's side window of the Cherokee. I saw a slight smile cross his lips.

"Scully. Still on the right side of the dirt, I see. Musta got a lot quicker than before."

"How you been, Sarge?"

He leaned in closer and said, "I'm real sorry about your old lady, Shane. Never really knew the lieutenant, but the word I got is she's good people."

"Thanks."

There was a pause, then he said, "From what I've been hearing on TV, this can't be a social call."

I nodded and said, "I need to use this place tonight. Can you pop the back lock on E-gate for me, leave this gate open for some friends of mine?"

"I don't need any trouble."

"I'm just meeting two cops from Homicide Special. Since they're undercovers, we didn't want to use the PAB. This seemed like a good, quiet place," trying to smooth it out.

"Just don't screw me up, Shane." He knew he wasn't getting the full story.

"I promise. I'm going to come in from the back. These guys may be a little hinky, but they're good cops. Just let 'em in."

He gave it a long moment of thought before he turned and walked away from the car to open the gate.

I turned the Jeep around and pulled back down the drive. Then I made a right and headed up Vermont toward an unmarked fire road, which ran along a ridge above the dense growth of trees that surround the Greek. I stopped on the hill above the theater, parking on the shoulder, leaving the car pointing downhill. Then I made my way back down through the dense foliage toward the back of the concrete amphitheater. I didn't think Rafie and Tommy would try and hook me up, but if they did, I could make a break out the back of the stadium and climb the hill to the Jeep. If they followed me, they'd be a mile away from their cars.

It took only five minutes to reach the back of the amphitheater. I found the E Stair gate, which Sgt. Loveboy had unlocked for me, swung it open, and entered the theater.

The Greek is one of the most beautiful open-air concert venues in Los Angeles. It can seat thousands on wood benches attached to concrete risers. A row of pink-white security lights illuminated the place, casting a rosy glow on the thousands of empty wood seats. I placed Alexa's computer under one of the benches down front, memorized the seat number, then moved away from it and sat in the last row, as high up as I could go. From this vantage point, I could see the whole layout stretched below me under the stars.

I waited for half an hour.

Then I saw them coming into the amphitheater through the main entrance. Both wore jeans, tennis shoes, windbreakers, and frowns as they moved forward and stood looking around. They appeared to be alone. I was easy to spot sitting up in the last row, and Rafie pointed me out to Tommy.

"This is fun," Tommy yelled.

"You guys alone?" I yelled back.

"Yeah," Rafie called out, adding sarcastically, "Request permission to approach, Oh Fucked One?"

I waved them up and watched as they climbed almost a hundred steps and finally stopped at the eighty-fifth row, where I was seated. They were both winded when they arrived.

"Okay," Rafie said, "where's the computer?"

"Not so fast. I need you guys to help me first."

"Yeah," Tommy said. "What kinda help? You can't need career advice 'cause you ain't got a career."

I didn't need any more of that, so I launched right into it.

"I talked to Sergeant Rosencamp, who's the new president of OJB. He told me that a while back David Slade made a nine-one-one call and got the Malibu sheriffs to send a car up to Stacy's mansion to bust an intruder that turned out to be him. Do you guys remember that?"

"How could anybody forget? When it happened, it was all over the department," Rafie said.

"Do you guys remember when that was?"

"I don't know," Tommy said. "Mid to late nineties."

"Which was it, mid or late?"

"I don't know."

"You know anybody you could call who was in IAD back then, somebody who could pin the date for us? I'd do it, but right now I don't have any friends down there."

"Why you need the date?" Rafie said.

"Sergeant Rosencamp told me one of our people at I.A. called the Sheriff's Department with the suggestion they make a voice print to find out if it was Slade who called in the original complaint. That voice print was what busted him. I want to know which one of our people in I.A. had the idea to do that, and when, exactly, it was."

Rafie looked at Tommy, who shrugged. Then Figueroa contributed a name. "I think Fred Duma was an advocate at I.A. in the nineties."

"Call him," I said.

"I don't even know how to get Duma's number."

"Lou Spinetta, maybe," Tommy said. "They were partners in South Bureau before Duma went to I.A."

After a few minutes, Rafie had Fred Duma on the phone.

"I got him," Rafie said. "He says he was a defense rep at I.A. off and on in the nineties."

"Ask him," I said.

So Rafie asked Duma my two questions and then paused and listened. "Are you sure about that?" he finally said. "Okay . . . okay. Sorry I woke you, man. Thanks."

He disconnected, then turned to face us. "That's funny," he said.

"It was 'ninety-eight, right?" I said.

Rafie nodded.

"Alexa was in I.A. back then. It was her idea to call the sheriffs and tip them, wasn't it?"

"I don't get it," Tommy said. "If she was in a relationship with this guy and was friends with him since the Academy, why would she blow him in to the sheriff?"

"Damn good question," I said softly.

CHAPTER THIRTY-FOUR

What the hell's going on?" Tommy said. He sat down on the amphitheater bench beside me.

"I've been wondering how an LAPD sergeant, like Slade, can pull guns on civilians and then walk out from under the I.A. complaints with just some days off and a departmental reprimand," I said. "Why didn't any of the civilians this guy was pulling down on go to the District Attorney and get him to file a criminal complaint?"

"If Alexa was involved with him, maybe she kicked those charges loose and made peace for him with the D.A.," Tommy said.

"And then she calls up the County Sheriffs and tips them to the voice print idea on the nine-one-one call in Malibu? How's that fit?" I said. "She helps him beat the road-rage beefs but turns him in on the nine-one-one thing?"

"Shane's right," Tommy said. "Doesn't make much sense."

They exchanged looks, so I went on. "Since I'm on everybody's shit list, I was hoping to get you guys to check with PSB tomorrow. Get somebody down there to pull those old road-rage incidents. See exactly who the original complainants were. I need full background checks on them. I'm going to give you guys Alexa's computer; you'll find a file marked OVERTIME DE-PLOYMENT SCHEDULES. It opens with the password 'lacey.' Scroll down a few pages and you'll find a lot of e-mails between Slade and Alexa. They're from the last two months. On the surface, they look like love letters, and at the end there's some kinda blackmail threat on Alexa from Slade. But I don't think that's what they are anymore. They talk about having a floor score, which I originally thought was sex, but it's not. It's—"

"A rap group," Rafie finished. "Curtis Clark. I just got his new CD, *Savage Bitch.*"

I nodded. "The e-mails contain the names of rap groups and music management companies in messages written to sound like love letters. One e-mail mentions the Biltmore Hotel on Pico. There's no Biltmore on Pico. They talk about having a meeting at the Crypto Motel in room four-fifty-seven. No such place. But my son tells me there's a rap group called Crypto Four-Fifty-Seven. I think the whole thing is code. You need to take the computer to Secure Documents and get somebody you trust down there to decode it. But you guys need to keep this to yourselves. I think when we get the cheese, it will blow the top off this murder case and it might not make the guys on the sixth floor happy."

"It still doesn't lay down for me," Rafie said. "Why is she passing e-mails back and forth with Slade, who was dirty?"

"Yeah," Tommy said, "the guy was a shitcake."

I didn't want to lay it all out yet, but Rafie read my expression. "You got a theory, don't you?" he said, then added, "If you want us in this, we need all of it."

"There's only one way it makes sense," I finally said. "The reason the road rage incidents didn't go to a full Board of Rights or a criminal justice proceeding is because I think they were all setups. Those motorists didn't pursue their cases after I.A. gave Slade those wrist slaps, because they were all in on it. Maybe they were the families of cops helping the department dirty up Slade so he could go undercover. That's what I want you to find out."

They nodded, knew there was more, and waited.

"I think Alexa tipped the sheriffs to the voice print idea for the same reason," I continued. "The department was cementing David Slade's cover as a rogue cop, so he could infiltrate Maluga's music business, start by working security, and then worm his way up. Before Lou went to prison, he and Stacy got separated. But they didn't get divorced. I think the reason for that is Stacy's the brains behind Lethal Force. Lou supplies the street cred and keeps the acts in line. They stayed married because they needed each other. When Lou went to the Q, they were already living in separate houses. Nobody was in Stacy's bed. Slade was a notorious ladies' man, so he hit that. What better way to get info than in the bedroom?"

They looked like they were buying it, so I went on. "Add to that a few more facts. Slade was already a Crip from the same hood in Compton and knew Stacy and Lou from Compton High, making him a good undercover choice. Alexa wouldn't have been his friend at the Academy unless he'd made a complete life change." I looked at them and said, "I don't think David Slade was a rat. I think he was a hero who gave up his life on the job."

"So where's the computer?" Tommy finally asked.

"Under seat B-twenty-three. Call me when you know anything."

I stood to go, and they stood with me.

"You're saying this sting started with Alexa and Slade back in 'ninety-eight?" Rafie said.

I nodded. "Alexa and Slade weren't shot because of a busted relationship or a blackmail attempt. They were shot because Slade's cover got blown."

CHAPTER THIRTY-FIVE

I left the Greek Theatre by the back exit and headed back down the hill toward the 134 Freeway.

I liked my theory about David Slade being Alexa's undercover a lot better than I liked the idea of him being her lover, but there were still a few pieces that, no matter which way I tried to put them in the puzzle, wouldn't fit.

One was Tony Filosiani. If Alexa had placed Slade into deep cover, there was no way that she would have been able to hide it from the chief. If Tony knew about all this, why didn't he tell Mike Ramsey or me? Why had he let it turn into such a PR mess?

The second piece was the arrest warrant they'd put out on me. If this thing started in Internal Affairs in the late nineties, why were those guys running around with a charge sheet accusing me of murder? Somebody—some commander at PSB—had to know about it.

By the time I arrived at USC Medical, it was two o'clock in the morning. My head was throbbing from lack of sleep, so I went to the cafeteria first and got a cup of black coffee. I was just about to leave with my plastic cup, when I saw the young ER doc who had treated Jonathan Bodine, making her way toward me. She had a worried look on her face, and I knew instantly, that the Crown Prince of Bassaland was in trouble.

"Detective, I've been calling you on that number you left. It goes straight to voice mail. Why didn't you answer?"

"Problems?" I said.

"Mr. Bodine is insane."

"Oh, come on, not really insane. Deluded maybe, probably disillusioned on occasion, but surely not insane."

"He started a fire out of bedspreads in the men's room of the ward I transferred him to. He was doing an African fire dance or some damn thing. He set off the sprinklers. I'm transferring him to the mental ward first thing in the morning."

I really didn't want Bodine transferred to a psych ward. That was the last thing my shaky alibi needed.

"You're his admitting doctor," I said. "If you'll prepare release forms, I'll take him home with me when I leave and you'll be done with him."

"It's the middle of the night."

"I won't tell, if you won't."

She thought about it, but not for long. "Anything to get him out of here."

"Bring him back to ER and I'll grab him on my way out."

So much for that.

I took my coffee to the elevator and went up to the coronary care unit. The place was quiet. I knew the nurses on duty would stop me if I went by the main desk, so I waited until they were involved with patients who needed middle-of-the-night meds, then snuck past the vacant nurse's station and into Tony's room, closing the door.

Tony was sleeping. A drip trolley full of goodies was feeding solutions into him and a catheter tube was draining it all away. I moved to a chair beside his bed.

"Chief?" I said softly, as I touched his arm.

After a few seconds Tony opened his eyes.

"Huh?"

"Hi," I said and held his weak gaze.

"What time is it?" he whispered, his voice still more or less a croak.

"I need to talk to you," I said.

"I did the TV interview. It's gonna be on the *Today* show. Supposed to air tomorrow," he said.

"Good." I decided I'd better get into this before I was discovered and thrown out. "I've been out doing what you said."

"What's that?" He sounded tired. His eyelids drooped.

"I've been out trying to prove that Alexa didn't shoot Slade."

"Good," he said weakly. "That's the ticket."

"Chief, you said you had an I.A. file on your desk about Slade."

"Right."

"I think all that stuff in the file is made up. The road-rage stuff, the nine-one-one call. I think it was all done to make him look like a rogue cop so the department could set him up for a deep cover assignment."

"Where did you get that?" he asked. He looked trapped and tried to rise up.

"Doesn't matter where I got it." All of a sudden, I wasn't sure how much I could trust this guy. "If Slade was a deep cover, then all those light reprimands he got at I.A. were the direct doing of the Chief of Police. Back then, I.A. had a provision that let the chief review all sentences. He couldn't make a sentence heavier, but he could make it lighter. I think that's what Chief Brewer did. At first I thought it was because Brewer was corrupt and had something going with Slade, but now I think it was because he really wanted to plant Slade inside the Maluga organization. When you took command, I.A. would definitely have filled you in on that kind of deep cover op. So you had to know Slade was a UC when I talked to you yesterday."

Tony looked at me carefully before finally saying, "This is not something I will discuss with you."

"You're not gonna discuss it? You're the one who told me there are times when I should risk everything to find the truth. I thought you were one of the good guys."

"You don't have the whole truth."

"They're tattooing Alexa and me in the media. Don't you think the department owes *us* some truth?"

"Sometimes command is about priorities, Shane. Sometimes it's a balancing act where you pick the lesser of two problems. Alexa is in a coma. Word I'm getting is she's not going to get any better. They're operating Monday morning, but it's just window dressing. She's already slipped away from us."

"She's not dying," I said, my voice rising in anger.

"I think she is, and *if* she's gone, then what they're saying about her on TV can't hurt her. I'm betting in the end this won't stick to you."

"I thought you cared about her. You're just like the other guy."

"I do care about her," Tony said softly. "In fact, I love Alexa like a daughter. But there are things you don't know about, and they demand this course of action."

The door behind me opened and a nurse was standing there.

"What are you doing? His heart monitor on our station is going crazy. Get out of here this minute!"

I stood and moved to the door, but Tony stopped me. "There's department rationale guiding this, Shane."

"There may be department rationale," I said. "But the reasoning sucks."

"There's still people at risk. I'm supposed to be the chief of the entire department. That includes everyone, not just you and Alexa. I have to evaluate each situation, examine risks, and play no favorites."

I turned and walked out of the room without answering.

As I left the hospital I picked up John Bodine. He was still wearing Chooch's bloody sweatshirt and his head had tape all over it.

"Here we go again, John," I told him. "Don't try to be quite so original this time."

He looked at me and shook his head. Then he started right in. "In California, ain't no originals. Out here, everybody so busy bein' original, they all be 'zackly the same."

I grabbed his wheelchair and pushed him out of the ER. Once we were outside, I stood him up.

"Don't be yank-slammin' me around. Lookit this what you done." He pulled up the sweatshirt to reveal a pound of tape and gauze wrapped around his chest, stomach, and abdomen. "This here tape an' shit's all that's holding my dick on. So don't be pushin' and shovin'."

I got him out to Chooch's Jeep.

"Where you gonna dump me now?" he said.

"I'll make you a deal," I said. "If you shut up, you can sleep in the back. I'll sleep in the front."

"Thought you was gonna let me bunk in that sweet garage room you got. Now you sayin' I gotta sleep in this Detroit coffin."

"Shut up, John."

"Man, you ain't nothin' but some drives-too-fast, run-a-man-down, gutter scum."

A classification that seemed to fit.

CHAPTER THIRTY-SIX

*A*lexa and I were in Antigua. We had gone swimming and were a mile up the beach from the hotel, lying naked on sand that had not yet cooled in the night heat. I could feel its warmth on my back and hear the gentle lapping of the waves against the shore. The scent of lush, sweet flora overwhelmed my senses. I held my beautiful wife, stroking her lustrous, black hair. Then she rose up and looked down at me while soft moonlight fell across her breasts. Somewhere, in the shallow lagoon beyond, a fish jumped, then splashed back into the water and zipped away in a streak of green fluorescence.

Alexa laughed, smiled at me, then whispered, "I love having you inside me. I love your hands. The way you touch me."

I was hard and pushed deeper into her. Her breast brushed my lips and I kissed it.

"Muthafucka," she said as I held her tighter.

What a strange thing for her to say, I thought.

"Hey, muthafucka!"

I opened my eyes. It was Jonathan Bodine in the backseat.

"You awake?" he asked.

"No."

"You talking, means you awake. I ain't some head case, no

matter what them piss-in-a-bottle white coats at the Mental Health say."

"Let's try and get some sleep, John."

We were parked in the upper lot behind the Greek. Dorsey Loveboy had opened the gate and told me we could park here for the night, but had to be gone before the maintenance crew arrived at seven. I was stretched out across the console and front seats of the Jeep Cherokee and my legs were cramping. I glanced at my watch. Four-thirty A.M. The sun would be up in another hour; we'd have to be rolling in two.

"Them alphabet docs at the Mental Health called me insane. Called me a paranoid schizophrenic. Pissants wouldn't know a paranoid schizophrenic if he shit in their lunchboxes."

"I've got a big day tomorrow, I need to sleep."

"It's a cheap diagnosis anyway, 'cause half them dirtbags down on the Nickel is either running on ether, heroin, or Mystic Glue. The way I see it, if a man hears voices and there ain't no voices, then he's a whack-job pure and simple, right?"

"Yep."

"But if he hears voices and they really *is* voices, and them voices 'splains stuff to him, tells him what's gonna happen, then he's a visionary. Big damn difference."

I didn't answer, hoping he'd just shut up. My cell phone was on vibrate and it had fallen off my belt, so I picked it up and checked for messages. I was worried that if something had changed and Chooch tried to call from the hospital, I might have missed it. Nothing. John kept up an endless litany.

"If you think people are plotting against ya, and the half-steppers really are, then you ain't paranoid, you just accurately informed. Them dickwads at the Mental Health don't understand that."

"Shut up, John."

"You're just a skeezy nickel slick who plows over po folks who's just minding their business, crossing with a light." He'd miraculously added a traffic light to our accident. "But 'side from that, and 'side from you gettin' me gizmoed for walking around with too much a your green in my jeans, I gotta tell you, for a po-lice, you ain't half-bad. You gimme food and ya don't just throw me away, like most a the shit birds I meet."

"Maybe if you didn't steal their stuff, that wouldn't happen quite so often."

John ignored that and kept going.

"I ain't insane neither. Was Edgar Allan Poe insane 'cause he drank himself to death? Was Van Gogh? That crazy Dutchman cut off his ear and today folks pay millions for one a his silly-ass, don't-even-know-what-it-is charcoal sketches. What is insanity? I challenge anybody ta give me a definition. Can't be done."

"Insanity is when you keep repeating the same behavior while expecting a different result." A definition that fit him perfectly, but it didn't slow him down. He just changed subjects.

"I hear dead people's voices. Okay? So big deal. But my voices tell me stuff. Like, Chief O. Half-stepper died in the African plague of oh-six, but he told me your old lady's lyin' in a coma. All the time we spent together since ya ran me over, and you ain't once told me that your old lady was about to catch the bus. I hadda hear it from a crazy old African chief been dead a hundred years. See what I'm sayin'?"

"You saw it on the TV in the ER like everyone else."

"Them docs clockin' your old lady at the hospital got no faith and less vision. You want a definition of insanity, how 'bout a bunch a bozos tryin' to change what's written in the big book? Tryin' to change what can't never be changed while all the time thinkin' it's their *job* to change it. That's insanity!"

"Can we please go back to sleep?"

"When you got princely powers, you get a library card, lets you see in the Big Guy's book. Some of it be hard to understand, but I got my dead peeps like Chief O whisperin' down, explainin'. When he tells me your old lady ain't supposed ta go, then you can bet it ain't her time."

"John, please."

"I ain't kiddin', Shane."

I sat up to look over the seat at him. It was the first time in two days that he'd actually called me Shane.

Then, without missing a beat, he segued again. "L.A. ain't my home, anyway. This just a place where I been sent for a few years to learn some lessons. I been learning the natural order a the universe so I can guide dumb shits like you around. I already know some of the Big Guy's secrets. Like check this one out. When someone dies, their soul gets handed off to some random dude in the afterlife, and he flings the soul as far as he can. It sails over an endless sea and awakens in another time and place. The weight of the soul and strength of the toss determines how close to the center of heaven the spirit lands."

"Sort of like a game of celestial lawn darts," I deadpanned.

"When you get to the crossroads and them God wannabes at UCLA puts it to you about yer ole lady, you remember what the Crown Prince from Cameroon just tole ya."

"Okay, John. I'll remember. Can we go back to sleep now?"

"I gotta take a dump, first."

With that, my personal guide to the universe threw open the Jeep's passenger door and blundered up into the trees to do his business.

CHAPTER THIRTY-SEVEN

It was six-forty-five in the morning and I was driving down the hill, away from the Greek Theatre. John had refused to get out of the Jeep and was asleep in the backseat.

"The hell you doing?" he growled, waking up momentarily as I braked too hard.

I stopped at a Micky D's and picked us both up some coffee and Egg McMuffins, then got on the 134 heading west. It was early and the Sunday morning traffic was light. I got off the freeway at Malibu Canyon Road and headed into the mountains, up the twisting two-lane highway toward the ocean. By seven-forty-five I was again parked across from the Maluga estate, half a block down from the ornate gate, safely tucked back in the trees out of sight. With the Jeep stopped and the windows up, the smell of our breakfast started to permeate the interior, popping Bodine out of his princely slumber.

"Man, that smells better than teenaged pussy," he said, sitting up and looking over the seat at the McDonald's bags on the passenger seat beside me. I handed him one, along with a cup of coffee.

"Breakfast in bed, your highness."

"More like it," he yawned.

As he bit into a McMuffin and sipped the hot coffee, he

looked around at his surroundings and spotted the wrought-iron fence that fronted the Maluga estate with its acres of rolling lawn beyond.

"Pricey digs," he said, fumbling his sandwich. It dropped on the backseat, but he picked it up and ate it anyway.

"Don't make a mess back there. This is my son's car."

I reached into my glove box and took out my Sony miniature tape recorder. I hooked it up to the VXT radio receiver to again record conversations from Stacy's bug. I activated the system and listened through my earpiece. Nothing yet, just a low hiss. Stacy obviously wasn't near the equipment.

"Okay, John," I said. "This could end up getting dangerous. I can't be responsible for you. It's only about a mile walk down the road to the Coast Highway. I want you to get out. You can relocate at the beach. Since nobody knows you down there, maybe they won't kill you. Or if you want, I'll give you enough cash to call a cab and get you wherever you want to go."

"I thought you told that ER doc you'd take care of me."

"I just said that to keep you out of the mental ward. We're not gonna be roommates, so get out."

"I got a six-inch hole in my gizzard. I can't be walkin' a mile to the beach," he whined.

"I'm on police business. I don't want you back there. Don't make me throw you out."

Then a crafty look came into his eyes. "You ain't gonna be doing no such thing," he said.

"Why not?"

"'Cause any fool can see you up here spying on these poor rich folks. Got yer little tape and all. Maybe I just rings their bell and gives them the four-one-one. Bet there'd be a big thank-you check in that." Then, without pausing, "You gonna eat that last McFuckit?"

"As long as we're on it, I'm getting real tired of this endless stream of profanity. I like a good four-letter word just like the next guy, but man, you need to clean up your act. It's hardly any way for the Crown Prince from Bassaland to talk."

"How the fuck do you know? You ever been to the Bassaland? You even know where Cameroon is, you ignorant sack-

a-shit?" After that we both sat in silence for a long moment.
Then he said, "I ain't getting out a this car. You throw me out,
I'll get all up in yer bidness here."

This really wasn't working, but I didn't trust John not to
blow my cover in search of a reward, so I decided to wait and
ditch him once we were safely away from the estate.

"Suit yourself," I said. "But if this gets strange, you're on
your own."

"Don't you go worrying 'bout Prince Samik Mampuna," he
pouted. "I be on the scene with my gangsta lean."

I'd never be rid of him. This guy would be at my funeral.

So we waited as the sun made a slow climb up into the east-
ern sky, cooking the top of the black Jeep. It was going to be a
hot day. John repositioned himself to the front seat and I put
down both windows. We had an argument over the radio. He
wanted some progressive jazz station so high up on the dial
only dogs could hear it. There was no compromising with him,
so I left the radio off.

At eleven-thirty-eight exactly, I heard voices over the VXT
earpiece. The conversation was muffled because the pager was
probably still in Stacy's purse. I got ready to move.

Twenty minutes later, I heard the servo-mechanisms on the
gate start to click, then heard the wrought-iron monster begin to
creak open. I was determined not to repeat my mistake from before. Most people have a favorite route when they're going to
town. I was betting Stacy would take the same one as yesterday,
unless she was heading to the Valley, in which case, she'd drive
right past where I was parked. At least I was in a different car
this morning. Over the earpiece, I could faintly hear gangsta
rap playing and wondered if she was in the Rolls. When the rap
music started to fade, I put the Cherokee in gear and pulled out,
heading toward the Coast Highway.

I accelerated to catch up, came around a sharp bend, and saw
the big tan Phantom at a stop sign a hundred yards ahead. I
slowed abruptly, throwing John into the dash.

"The fuck you doing?" he complained.

"Police work."

He leaned forward to peer into the car, which was only a few yards ahead. "Some dangerous job you got here. Nothing but one itty-bitty little platinum fox drivin' that thing."

I stayed several cars back as I again followed Stacy into Hollywood. She made her way to Wilshire Boulevard and headed toward the Miracle Mile District, a very expensive section of commercial real estate between Fairfax and La Brea Avenue. The high-priced developments are near the L.A. County Museum of Art and many are architectural statements, earning that stretch of real estate the moniker of Museum Row. Several huge talent agencies and television production companies had moved their offices out of Hollywood into this glittering business center.

Finally, Stacy pulled into a lot a few blocks past Hauser Boulevard and parked. I slid in just seconds behind her and found a place two lanes over. She got out of the Rolls, locked it, and walked up to the sidewalk on Wilshire. She was dressed in a tank top and skin-tight black jeans with heels. Her platinum-blond hair shimmered in the bright sunlight. I watched as she entered an office tower in the middle of the block, then I looked over at John.

"Will you get out now?" I asked.

"Since I don't got no self-instruction, I ain't bringin' no self-destruction."

"I assume that's a no," I said. "Okay. Then at least make yourself useful and keep an eye on that Rolls. If I get ditched inside and it leaves before I get back, give me a heads-up. Use Chooch's car phone and call me at this number." I wrote down my cell and gave it to him.

Then I got one of Chooch's ball caps out of the backseat and put on my dark glasses.

"Good disguise," John sneered. "That oughta fool 'em."

"If you steal the phone, radio, or airbags outta this car, I will hunt you to the end of the earth and break your legs," I promised. He fixed a worried frown on me but seemed to get the message.

I got out of the Cherokee and walked along the sidewalk to the front of the huge brick-and-glass structure that went up thirty floors. I passed through inch-thick glass double doors fronting the lobby and walked into a cavernous reception area that had no sign of Stacy Maluga. A security guard watched me warily from behind a fortress-sized marble desk as I studied the building directory.

Halfway down, under L, I saw Lethal Force, Inc. Their offices took up two entire floors, twenty-six and twenty-seven.

I headed to the elevator and the cop on the desk called out, "Gotta sign in, sir."

I turned and walked over to him, pulled out my tin and flashed it. "How's this working?" I said.

He held both palms out in a gesture of surrender and I took the elevator to twenty-eight. I got out into a brokerage firm's lobby, then found the fire stairs and went down one flight. I stopped just outside the twenty-seventh floor, then put the earpiece in and listened. Either I was too far away from the bug or the poured concrete walls were too thick, because all I heard was the soft hissing. I went down one more flight, paused behind the door on twenty-six, and listened again.

Now I could faintly hear Stacy Maluga's voice, tinny and far away in my ear. I rotated the receiver, trying to tune her in.

"I still got all my mad skills, baby," she was saying. "You gotta trust me." I turned the unit again and finally got slightly better reception. Then I hit record on the tape. "This ain't gonna go away 'less we fix it," she continued.

"Yeah, but you talkin' about doggin' out Curtis and Lionel. Lotta heat gonna come down on that play," Louis Maluga answered. "You a good milk shake, baby, and nobody says you can't bring boys ta the yard, but we go up on those niggas and the cops gonna be in my face. I'm still pullin' a tail." Talking about being on parole.

"Curtis went and got hisself some white boy accountants an' lawyers," she persisted. "They going after all those back royalties and performance payments and such. The fool's even talkin' about enforcing his key man escape clause over Dante Watts. I'm tellin' ya that Boon Johnny about ta raise up on us. If he can force an audit, them books won't hold. Fraud is a felony too, Louis. They file on that, you gonna get violated and be back in Q just the same."

"Shit," Lou said.

"Look, sugar, we ain't got much time. Once Curtis files a lawsuit, we can't do nothin' but watch that boy pick us clean 'cause if we move on him then, we'll look guilty. That means we gotta do this tonight. These two niggas ain't in no choir. Lionel may wear them nice white vines now, but he still just a street G went to city college. He still got that buncha nose-bleeds on Sixtieth to deal with. We set this up right, it won't hit us. Hear me out, baby. Let me run it for you."

"I don't wanta talk about this here. These offices ain't water-tight. I got Rawson sweepin' 'em twice a week now. You wouldn't believe what we find in the walls."

Then there was more muffled talk that I couldn't understand and a door slammed. I ran back up to twenty-eight, exited the fire stairs, and was back on the brokerage floor. I pushed the down button, but stood there for almost three minutes before the elevator arrived.

When I got back to the lobby, there was no sign of the Malugas. I thought I had beaten them to the entrance, but I didn't want to get busted standing here, so I sprinted for the parking lot. When I got to the car, I was relieved to see the tan Rolls still in its parking space. I jumped into the Jeep. Bodine was slumped down in the passenger seat with his eyes closed.

"Stay down, I don't want 'em to see us," I cautioned.

"If you talking about that little blond spinner we followed over here, she's gone."

I looked over and he nodded.

"She and some brown-frown the size of a dump truck dipped outta here in a yellow Ferrari two minutes ago."

CHAPTER THIRTY-EIGHT

We sat in the parking lot for a couple of minutes while I tried to figure out a profitable course of action. For some reason, Bodine was now ranting about the African slave trade in the eighteen hundreds, which he called the Black Holocaust. I tuned him out and tried to piece together a plan. The tape I just made sounded like a plot against Curtis Clark and Lionel Wright set to go down tonight. The problem was, if I tried to book it into evidence and get a case number, I'd be signing up for a boatload of trouble with the department. Nothing on the tape was admissible because it had all been illegally acquired. With no warrant or even correct paperwork from Sally to get the bug installed at ESD, we would both get hammered. As John's voice continued to drone on about slave traders in 1820, I tried to come up with a solution that wouldn't land me and Sally Quinn in a jackpot.

My tape was worthless in the criminal justice system, but it had to be worth something to Curtis Clark and Lionel Wright. Maybe it would buy me a place at the table. If I was going to clear Alexa's name, I had to find a way to somehow get to the inside. Chooch told me that it was common knowledge that Maluga had been feuding with Curtis Clark, but he didn't know why. From what I'd just overheard, it seemed the feud was over stolen royalties and back performance pay.

John kept ranting.

"African slavers was kidnappin' our tribal warriors an' hiding them in the jungle in this old abandoned French village— my great-great-grandfather, Chief O, chased 'em there. That village was a Dantean nightmare."

Dantean nightmare? Where did he get this stuff? Had he actually read both Thomas Mann's *Tonio Kröger* and Dante's *Inferno*?

I dialed 411 and the exchange operator said, "City and state, please."

I told her what I wanted and she gave me the number, which I dialed into my phone. John kept trying to get my attention.

"Hey," he said, but I ignored him. "Hey, I'm talkin' at you."

"WYD Productions," a woman's lilting voice answered after two rings.

"Lionel Wright's office, please."

"I'll connect you to his assistant, Miss McKenzie."

As I was being transferred, Bodine got frustrated and slipped into one of his high-volume rants.

"This here be my legacy," he shouted. "It's what my life is about. I'm talkin' about a criminal catastrophe—the fuckin' Black Holocaust and all you can to do is blab on yer phone!"

"Shut up, John," I shouted back. "I've got a situation here!"

He fell silent and began to pout.

"Lionel Wright's office," a woman with a clipped British accent said.

"This is Detective Shane Scully with Homicide Special at the LAPD. I need to speak with Lionel Wright or Curtis Clark."

"I'm sorry, Mr. Wright is not available and Mr. Clark doesn't record for us. Try Lethal Force, Inc. They can give you a number."

"Lady, this is a police emergency. Your boss is about to get murdered tonight. I have a surveillance tape he should listen to. If you want him and Curtis Clark to see the end of the week, you'll put me through."

There was a long pause. "I'm sorry, what?"

"You heard me. If you'd rather let them get assassinated, I guess that's your call."

I was putting some stress into her day. Her cool efficiency disappeared. "I c-can't promise anything," she stuttered. "Mr. Wright doesn't—"

"You call him. Tell him what I just said. I'll meet him anywhere. House, office, street corner. He can pick."

"Where can we reach you?"

"I'll call back in ten minutes."

I hung up without saying good-bye. John Bodine was staring at me wide-eyed.

"Bust A Cap is slammin'!" The Black Holocaust seemed lost in the wake of Lionel Wright's celebrity. "You know him? That half-stepper is pure cheddar, man! You really know him?"

"Not yet, but I think he's in my future."

Since the WYD phone number had an 818 area code, I put the Jeep in gear and headed toward the 818 section of the city, which was generally the Valley. Bodine stayed strangely quiet as I drove.

Ten minutes later, I dialed WYD. I was again put through to Lionel Wright's assistant, Miss McKenzie, who sounded anxious now.

"Mr. Wright will meet you at his office. Go to our underground parking garage on Sunnyslope off Ventura and ask for the private elevator. One of his security assistants will meet you there."

"What about Curtis Clark?"

"We're trying to contact him."

"Give me an address."

"It's Wright Plaza on Ventura Boulevard between Greenbush and Sunnyslope. We're the whole block. Call me from the garage."

"See you in ten," I said.

"We gonna go see Bust A Cap?" John gushed. "I love that half-stepper."

"John, pick a corner you like, 'cause you and I have finally reached the end of our time together."

"This is one nigga don't get his ass peeled like no black banana. I got some mojo workin' here."

"Okay, then I'll pick one for you. Ah, yes, how about this one?"

I pulled over and put the Jeep in park. Then I went around, opened the passenger door, and dragged him out of the car by his collar. I yanked too hard and he stumbled and fell, landing on his hip. He grabbed his wound and screamed in theatrical pain.

"I'm gonna sue!"

"Have your guys call my guys."

I got back into the car and for the second time since yesterday, left him in the street.

Even as I drove away, something told me I hadn't seen the last of him.

CHAPTER THIRTY-NINE

When I go to potentially dangerous meetings with people I don't trust, I always scope out the location in advance and try to arrive late. Sometimes that shakes up the equation and you get a better look at what you're heading into.

I was parked across from Wright Plaza, watching to see if any unusual activity was taking place in preparation for my arrival. The plaza was intended to be an architectural statement piece with twin glass towers connected by a granite mezzanine bridge. There were too many subtle but pretentious rainbow arches incorporated into the design for my taste.

While I waited I called Sally Quinn in the Valley Division and got her just as she was heading out to lunch.

"Sally, I need a background check on Lionel Wright," I told her.

"You gotta cool your jets, buddy. Being in your posse is career poison. This has become very political."

"The minute they found Slade in Alexa's car, it was political. Mike Ramsey has been scrambling around like a cat burying turds on linoleum. He'll do anything to stay out of this jackpot. Alexa and I are just a convenient way out."

"And how does that bring us to Lionel Wright?"

"I need his jacket. Especially anything pertaining to old

scores he's got out against him down on Sixtieth Street. That's a Blood neighborhood, so check the gang book or call Organized Crime. I can't remember his name, but I think they have a sergeant down there solely working hip-hop music crimes."

After a short pause she said, "I oughta have the air in my head changed for even considering this." Then I heard her take a deep breath. "Okay. Call me in an hour."

"Sally, thanks for hanging with me." But she had already hung up. After that call, I tried to fit these new pieces into my expanding puzzle. If Lionel Wright had started on Sixtieth Street in South Central, it probably made him a Blood or at least Blood friendly. The Malugas and their whole bunch were Compton Crips. It was certainly possible Lionel Wright had financed his early success in the music business through street crime. I was parked across from twenty million dollars' worth of real estate with Lionel Wright's name on it. So let's not hear any more of *that* argument. Crime definitely pays.

While I watched and waited, I called Chooch on his cell phone. His battery must have been fried because I went straight to voice mail. I left a message that I would be there in time for Alexa's surgery at ten A.M. tomorrow. Even though I was pretty sure the rat squad would be there waiting to pick me up, I'd find a way to deal with them. No way was I going to let Alexa go through that surgery without me.

Then I saw a long, white, stretch limo pull into the underground garage at Wright Plaza. Bust A Cap had arrived. I waited another ten minutes and no threatening gangsters were slinking around, so I put the Jeep in gear and drove down Sunnyslope into the underground garage at Wright Plaza. There was a security stand on the A-level in the middle of the drive near the elevators. I pulled up and a large brother with cornrows, wearing a starched short-sleeved Wright Plaza security uniform, looked in at me.

"I'm here to see Lionel Wright at WYD Records," I said.

The guard was a big muscular guy with gang tats peeking out from under the stretched short sleeves of his uniform.

"Name?" he said, as if he were checking in guests at a leper colony.

"Shane Scully."

He looked at his clipboard and pointed to a visitor parking place nearby. There was no sign of the white limo that had arrived only a few seconds before me. It had probably gone down to some secure parking space below. I pulled in where instructed, got out of the car, and chirped the lock. The guard waved me over, motioning with the index finger of his right hand. A demeaning come-hither gesture.

"I'm supposed to meet somebody from security," I called across the thirty feet that separated us, not about to be beckoned like a naughty child.

"'At's right, and security is on its way. You gonna wait for the man right here," he ordered.

I reluctantly crossed the pavement toward him and stood next to the booth.

"You po-lice?" he asked.

"Is that gonna be a problem for us?"

"You got a strap, you best give it to me."

"Back at ya."

We stood there and stared daggers at each other.

At that moment, the elevator opened and two mastodons with shiny, shaved bullet heads exited. Both were about the same size and shape of KZ and Wayne from Stacy Maluga's house. Narrow waists, corded necks, and bulging thighs. Dimensions hard to obtain without steroids. They wore expensive tailored black suits with banded collars. When they reached the security guard, one of them said:

"We got him, Kaz."

"He's packin', Vonnie. Wouldn't give it up."

"It's okay. He's the law," Vonnie replied, showing executive potential. As we walked to the elevator, he said, "I'm Vondell Richmond. This is Taylor Hays," indicating the other security guard who looked at me with undisguised contempt.

Vondell used a key card, which hung from a chain around his neck, to activate the elevator door sensor. As it opened, he said, "If you'll please follow us?" Polite but cold.

The east tower of the building was only five stories, and Lionel Wright's suite of executive offices took up the entire fifth floor. When the elevator opened, we walked out into a snow-white reception area: white furniture, white carpet, white drapes. The only color came from several giant abstract canvases, which must have been done exclusively for this space, because aside from bold slashes of red and blue inside their ornate frames, they were all painted on the same stark, white background. The effect was surreal and startling.

The receptionist was a ten-point-five on a scale of ten with coffee-colored skin and features so delicately sculpted, it was hard not to stare.

"Mr. Scully?" she said with her beautiful British accent. "I'm Patch McKenzie. I believe we spoke. Is there anything you'd like to drink?" No stuttering now. She'd recovered her composure since we'd talked.

"I'm fine," I said softly.

"I'll tell Mr. Wright you've arrived." She then spoke quietly into a tiny microphone headset that was barely visible at the side of her face.

I was standing on two-inch-thick white plush pile carpet while classical music played softly over an expensive Muzak system. The environment was serene and restful. It felt like God's waiting room. Hardly what I'd been expecting. A moment later, Patch McKenzie smiled up at me.

"Mr. Wright will see you now," she lilted.

CHAPTER FORTY

The inner office occupied half the top floor in the East Tower and had one full wall of tinted plate glass that looked out across the valley toward the purple San Gabriel Mountains. The white-on-white color scheme continued in here but there was now a distinct commercial flair. One interior wall featured lighted glass nooks showcasing Bust A Cap merchandise—everything from clothing, hair products and street warrior videos, to a line of male cosmetics called Bust A Move For Men. There were several prominently displayed, framed concert posters of Lionel Wright in various performance poses as Bust A Cap. In each he was stripped to the waist, chiseled chest and arm muscles glistening, sweat flying as he flipped his head, screaming into cordless microphones.

Slouched in a club chair across from a large partner's desk was a classic street banger; ebony black complexion, hair in beads and braids. He wore designer warm-ups and had multiple diamond-encrusted medals hanging from gold chains around his muscled neck. Completing the look were four-hundred-dollar basketball shoes. As I entered, he started clocking me with an unfriendly stare.

Standing by the window was a tall African American about thirty. Handsome, with a classic profile, he was dressed casually in jeans and a white tux shirt, talking into a Bluetooth phone headset that flashed maniacally at his left ear.

"That would all be fine, Andre, except I found out this morning that you forgot to let the Nation of Islam contract," he said. "I've been scrambling to hire fifty Fruit of Islam event guards on extremely short notice. They're gouging me. I also just learned that despite our contract, your merchandise manager isn't staffing the lobby or manning our event display racks, so I'm also faced with that."

He listened for a moment, and then waved a hand in my direction motioning me to hang on.

"That's not gonna happen because your hall fees need to come way down. All these screw-ups are killing my take-home. I never let event overhead eat up more than twenty percent of gross."

"Fucking-A," the banger seated at the desk muttered.

Now I recognized the deep bass voice. I had it on the mini-tape in my pocket from yesterday. Curtis Clark.

"It's too late for me to change venues, and you know it, so don't even start with that. Life is long and there's lots of business for us to do in the future. If you wanta see me down the road, you gotta leave a little something on the table, my brotha."

He listened for a moment and said, "Done. I'll have Jared send you an e-mail confirmation. Peace out, babe." He pushed the little button on his earpiece, took off the Bluetooth, and folded it up.

"Event coordinators. Buncha pirates. Sorry." He crossed to me and stood a few feet away. I could smell his cologne—pleasant musk tinged with pine. Not at all bad. Maybe I'd have to check out Bust A Move products for men. "I'm Lionel Wright," he said.

"Shane Scully." We shook hands. His grip was firm and dry.

"I understand you have a badge. Want to show me?"

I fished my credentials out of my pocket and handed them to him. He took his time studying them.

"On the job almost twenty years," he observed.

I've been tinning people since '86 and he was the first one

who'd actually read my date of issuance. It told me something
about him.

"This is Curtis Clark," he said. "I understand your business
also concerns him."

I looked over at Clark, who didn't acknowledge the intro-
duction, but continued to glare, gangsta-style, looking through
me like a pane of glass.

"Okay, Detective, this just happens to be a pretty busy day.
I'm producing a big awards show tonight. I wouldn't have made
room for you, but you frightened my assistant, Miss McKenzie,
and she insisted. So if we could get to it?"

"Maybe you should just hear what I've got."

I pulled out the tape recorder. I'd already cued it up, so I hit
Play and put it on his mahogany desk. The first recording was
of Stacy and Curtis in his office on Sunset. Curtis shifted un-
easily, as Stacy gave him classified information about the accounting and performance royalty thefts at Lethal Force Inc. I
stopped the tape before we got to the blow job.

Lionel looked at me for a moment when the tape stopped,
then said, "Okay, well, that's Louis and Stacy for you. Lou
never got the memo sayin' we're leaving our weapons at home
now. He still thinks it's cool to negotiate over gun sights. It's a
good thing Curtis made a friend outta Stacy, or he never would
a known how much they were stealing from him."

Lionel's voice was soft velvet. He had a very cultured pre-
sentation. I knew he was a record mogul and a rap star, but I
was having trouble reconciling this handsome businessman
with the posters of him on the walls screaming and flinging
sweat around.

"Back in the day, Louis once hung the lead singer from
Brothers With Voices over a balcony at the Sunset Marquis and
threatened to drop the poor bastard unless BWV jumped labels
to Lethal Force," he continued. "That's the day he earned the
nickname Luna. But that kind of behavior is strictly yesterday.
Like Stacy said, it's a different business now. The big corporate
labels won't stand for that. Hip-hop's gone mainstream."

"Maybe, maybe not."

I recued the tape, pushed the Play button again and let them

listen to the second recording, the one I'd made just an hour before. It was hard to hear through the slight hiss, and both Curtis
and Lionel instinctively leaned forward. Curtis glanced over at
Lionel when Stacy mentioned wanting to take out both of them
tonight. It wasn't exactly what he'd been expecting to hear from
a woman who gave him sex and inside information. The tape
played on as the talk turned to the key man clause and Dante
Watts. Curtis frowned again when Stacy said that Lionel still
had big trouble down on Sixtieth Street.

When the tape concluded I stood there and waited. Silence
can be a great tool in an interview. A subject often gets nervous
and attempts to fill the lull by blurting something useful. Curtis
was agitated and angry. He felt betrayed. But Lionel only nodded his head and gave me a sleepy smile.

"No comment?" I finally said.

"The man is painfully consistent," he purred.

"Seems like Stacy is a pretty manipulative woman," I said.
"Playing a dangerous game. Kind of the Lady Macbeth of hip-
hop. You're not worried."

"Somebody got to finally close the brotha and this cave bitch
down," Curtis said, suddenly exploding to his feet.

Lionel raised a hand and silenced him. "'Course I'm worried. Who wouldn't be? Lou's a homicidal maniac and Stacy's a
lying, scheming whore. But Curtis and I are equipped to deal
with them."

"Do you really trust the Fruit of Islam to protect you on a
long-term basis?" I asked. "If I had a head case like Maluga
coming after me, I'd want my own people."

"I'm only using FOI for my event tonight. They're concert
specialists, not a bodyguard service. My personal security is all
taken care of, but thanks for your concern."

We locked gazes so I moved on.

"What was all that about Dante Watts and the key man
clause?" I asked.

He took a moment to decide if he wanted to confide anything in me. But then, because I'd just brought him some useful
information, he gave a small shrug and said, "This is already on
the vine, so what the hell." He leaned on the edge of his desk.

"In the late nineties Dante Watts was a label exec and A&R man for Lethal Force. He discovered a lot of new acts. But he had his own way a doing things, and that pissed the Malugas off. Two years ago, Dante discovered Curtis and Floor Score on an underground label."

Curtis Clark again shifted slightly.

"Dante hooked Curtis up with Lethal Force and got an outside attorney to cut his first two-album deal. Watts picked a good lawyer, and without telling Curtis, he had a clever escape paragraph written into the contract. The language was good and the Malugas' business affairs guys completely missed it; so did Curtis. The key man clause stated that if Dante Watts ever left Lethal Force or died, Curtis could walk out of his deal. Dante had a sweet cut of Curtis's coin and he put that clause in to protect his ass from Lou in case Lou tried to fire him or kill him. Last year he got into a big row with the Malugas over missing royalties and performance fees on Floor Score's concert appearances. He thought the Malugas were skimming net profits and holding back prepayment guarantees. In the middle of this beef, Dante Watts just disappeared. That's Lou's way of making problems go away. He disappears you. He musta whacked poor Dante before he could tell him about the clause. Stacy was the one who finally told Curtis. Apparently, she reads all the contracts and found the clause. We've been doing a forensic audit and we're still trying to get to the bottom of it. Looks like somebody over there illegally pocketed about ten million dollars. The bottom line is when Dante went missing, it gave a multi-million-dollar act his right to walk. Now Curtis is gonna record for me, but that's not gonna be a headline until we file our lawsuit."

"You guys are missing a piece," I said once he finished. "She helps Curtis break his contract and then goes to Lou and uses that knowledge to get him to commit a murder. You got a few dots that aren't connecting." The room fell silent. Then I asked, "How about your problems down on Sixtieth Street?"

"Everybody has a past, my friend, even you."

Then Lionel's desk phone rang. He picked up a headset off his desk and spoke into it. "Hang on a minute, Patch. I'm almost done here." He watched as I retrieved my tape recorder.

"Why don't you take me on as temporary security?" I said. "With all this intrigue, it might be nice to have a badge-carrying cop on hand."

He smiled. "I run my security team under strict State of California guidelines to eliminate any hassles with your buddies down at Parker Center. So unless you've already been to the Bureau of Security and Investigative Services and have your PPO license, I can't use you."

Without my noticing, Vondell Richmond and his partner, Taylor Hays, had quietly reentered the room, and were standing just inside the door, summoned mysteriously at exactly the right moment.

"You're making a mistake," I said.

"Then you're invited to my funeral," he said without an ounce of sarcasm or irony.

Vonnie and Taylor escorted me out of the room while Curtis Clark practiced his Murder One stare.

The outer office was momentarily unoccupied. Patch McKenzie was off beautifying some other part of the building. I glanced down and noticed some backstage passes in envelopes lying on her blotter. While Vonnie and Taylor moved ahead of me to the elevator, I palmed one off her desk.

"You guys better strap up," I said to them as we all stepped into the elevator. "I think your boss is gonna need you tonight."

"That's why we come to work every morning," Vondell said pleasantly.

The doors closed on this plush-pile wonderland and we zipped down to the ugly realities of the street below.

CHAPTER FORTY-ONE

It was a little past two by the time I left Wright Plaza. I got into Chooch's Jeep, opened the envelope I'd just lifted, and extracted the backstage pass. The awards show was something called the Tip-Top Hip-Hop Oasis Awards. The performance segment was called: STAR WARS. Given what I knew, probably an unfortunate choice of words. A separate printed sheet said that the show started at eight P.M., but instructed all of the performing acts and their visitors to be in the El Rey Theater by seven P.M., when the backstage doors would be locked. Sound checks were from seven to seven-forty-five. The El Rey was in the Mid-Wilshire district.

If somebody wanted to kill Lionel or Curtis, what better place to do it than a music awards show where there was a long history of past gang violence and where members of rival Crip and Blood gangs would be in attendance? There'd be enough beef jerky standing around to fill Dodger Stadium and half of them would be strapped. For the shit to jump off, all that needed to happen was one insult from a guy wearing the wrong colors. Once the guns came out, confusion would reign and people could easily die. Even though there would be hundreds of people, there'd be no witnesses because everybody from the hood is gunshot-blind.

There was nothing else I could do before seven o'clock, but I wanted to visit Alexa. I needed to hold her hand and tell her how much I loved her. I knew she wouldn't be conscious, and if the cops from PSB were there, I might get busted. But still. . . .

I headed down Ventura and turned onto Coldwater. Half an hour later I arrived at UCLA Medical Center where I parked in the main structure, went through the double glass doors to the elevators, and rode up to Neurosurgery. No cops, no trouble. So far, so good.

As I walked down the corridor, it occurred to me that this was exactly the kind of dumb-ass move I'd been making my entire life. Break the rules, ignore the consequences, go down in flames. Repeating the same behavior while expecting a different result—my own definition of insanity.

I spotted Chooch in the partially filled waiting room studying his USC playbook. I cleared my throat and when he looked up, a concerned expression passed over his face. I indicated I needed to use the bathroom, then headed toward the men's room down the hall. A few seconds later Chooch arrived.

"Dad, what are you doing here? They're gonna see you."

"I needed to come."

We hugged each other, and then he reported that Alexa's condition still had not changed. The doctors were keeping her in a drug-induced coma that would continue until just before the operation, when the anesthesiologist would take over. "They won't let anyone but her doctors and Luther see her," Chooch concluded.

"I know, but I'm gonna try, anyway."

"Dad—"

"I've got to, son." He looked at me for a long moment. "You know all this stuff on TV where they're saying your mom was in a relationship with Slade?"

"That's a total lie," he said, hotly.

"I know, but for a few hours yesterday, I was buying into that. I had some time when I didn't believe in her. Now I feel horrible about it."

"Dad, if you go back there and they catch you, they'll call security. You know where you're gonna end up."

"Just go to the front desk and keep the head nurse occupied. I'm going to find out where they keep the gowns and masks. Nobody will recognize me."

"Don't do this, Dad."

"If this goes bad tomorrow, I've got to at least tell her I'm sorry and how much I love her. It may be my only chance." He held my gaze. "What room is she in?"

"Six-ten."

I found a supply closet down the hall and grabbed a set of green surgical scrubs, a cap, mask, and paper slippers. I returned to the men's room and gowned up, then walked back toward the waiting room and nodded at Chooch.

While my son went over to the nurse's station and started an animated conversation, I crossed to a side door, opened it, and quietly slipped inside.

Alexa looked much smaller than before, like she was slowly wasting away under her surgical dressings. Her head was wrapped in gauze and she was attached to a mile of plastic tubing. Stuff was gurgling and hissing all over the room. Pumps and machines were keeping her alive. I found a chair and sat next to her bed, then took her hand in mine. I could hear my own steady breathing through the mask, feel her delicate pulse under my fingertips.

I remembered how it had started for us just five short years ago. I had hated her on sight back then. She'd been prosecuting me at Internal Affairs for a crime I'd been falsely accused of. She was I.A.'s number one advocate prosecutor with a stellar record of convicting dirty cops. Beautiful and self-assured, she was determined to get my badge. As things turned out, she got my heart instead.

Now I watched her lungs slowly filling with air, her chest rising and falling slightly with each mechanical breath. I marveled at the soft texture of her subtle beauty.

What would I do if I lost her? Even though I had doubted her, I'd never stopped loving her. That had to be worth something.

"I'll always love you," I whispered softly.

The machines gurgled and hissed, while her heart monitor kept the rhythm. It was ugly, foreboding music. A concert of despair.

CHAPTER FORTY-TWO

I met Sally Quinn at a restaurant called The Turf House, in the Valley. She chose the place because it had a history of health department violations and the food was so lousy it was cresting on dangerous. Cops, who are notorious chow hounds, never ate there, so we had a good chance of not being seen. We sat in a booth in the back, nursing lukewarm coffee in chipped mugs.

"This place is as bad as advertised," Sally frowned. "Can you believe it? There's a fly in this coffee." She showed me the insect. It was listlessly swimming in a circle in the lukewarm sludge, trying to find a way out. I waved at a waitress to try and get Sally a new cup, but the woman studiously ignored me.

"You're not gonna tell me what this is all about, right?" Sally said. She started fishing unsuccessfully for the fly with her butter knife.

"Hard to testify to things you don't know about."

She nodded, then dropped the knife and pushed a folder across the chipped wood table toward me. The smell of burning grease wafted in from the kitchen. Sally leaned forward and lowered her voice.

"It's all in that file, but to save you time, I'll hit the highlights. As you suggested, most of this background came from the gang book downtown and from a sergeant in street intel named Donavan Knight who works the hip-hop gang scene."

She took a breath and launched in. "Lionel Wright was born in March of seventy-two. Only his name isn't Lionel Wright."

"Don't tell me, it's Bust A Cap."

"Orlee Lemon," she said. "Broken home. Mother was a crack whore. Father unknown."

"I've heard this story."

"Pretty typical, except Orlee was really smart. A's at Jefferson High. Did two years at City College, then transferred to Cal State. Graduated with a major in business and a minor in music."

"Where's the *but*?"

"Orlee Lemon was a smart kid *but* in his youth he was also very wild. Back when he was still in elementary school, he was doing street corners around Sixtieth for a shot caller named Mister Smith." She looked up at me and smiled. "No kidding. That was his given name, Mister."

I found his mug shot, a fat guy in his late twenties with two or three chins.

"Mister's gang handle was Crocodile Smith because even as a kid he always wore really colorful, expensive crocodile shoes. Nothing good in that folder about him. Lots of ag-assaults. One second-degree murder. Did a long bit in the SHU at Pelican Bay. Got paroled in ninety-seven."

"So how does Lionel Wright fit?"

"Turns out, while Croc Smith is away at the Bay pounding sand, Orlee Lemon went to college, then graduated and became Lionel Wright, started rapping. The Croc gets out of the joint, sees his baby G Buddy is now all grown up and cutting underground sides in a garage. Decides to go into business with him."

"This was a voluntary partnership?"

"Who knows? I did a little extra checking before I drove over here and there's a neat story that goes with Lionel's first recording contract."

"Let's hear."

"Croc had big bucks from drugs, guns, and street crime, but the gun-dealing beefs had the Feds sniffing him and they put the IRS on his tail. With Big Brother watching, Crocodile couldn't spend his money without risking a federal tax case, so he's cash rich and money poor. He needs to find a way to put his dough to work where there's no IRS paper trail. He and Lionel get a CD ready, and they target a rap impresario named Ajax Matson. Ajax is what they call a "raptrepreneur." He owns a label called Walkie-Talkie Records, which has a big worldwide distribution deal with Atlantic. Guys like Ajax are inundated with CDs from wannabe artists, so getting a mega-producer like him to play your song is like next to impossible. But Smith and Lionel think up a way around this problem. They button-hole Matson at this dance club in Hollywood and Croc hands Lionel's CD to the man, along with ten thousand dollars in crisp bills and tells him, 'You play this while we watch. Whether you like the CD or not, you keep the ten large.' "

"Not bad," I said. "So Ajax listened to it?"

Sally nodded. "And it's good."

"So then Lionel records for Ajax, right?"

"Right," Sally said. "Two albums. Ajax came up with his hip-hop name Bust A Cap. Both albums went gold. Then Lionel leaves Walkie-Talkie and starts WYD records and becomes a raptrepreneur himself. He's his label's first big star." She glanced across the restaurant. "Man, you think we could get some coffee that's at least hot enough so this fly can't do the backstroke in it?"

I waved at the waitress again, but she did an exemplary job of ignoring me.

"Anyway," Sally sighed, "our background on Lionel Wright says that from there on, it was a new life. Great big house in Bel Air, cars with lots of vowels in their names."

"But the problem was?"

"The problem was that Lionel Wright was about ten times smarter than Crocodile Smith, who looked fine in his gang drapes down on Sixtieth, but looked like terminal cancer in the offices of trendy Westside media companies. Lionel had started integrating with Hollywood movers and shakers. He was deal-ing with big media conglomerates and filmmakers, writing soundtracks for motion pictures. He turns out to be great at marketing and puts out Bust A Cap clothing, which is a smash in Wal-Mart, Target, and on the Internet. Then all the other stuff happens, the hair products, video games, the whole schmeer. But he's still got this three-hundred-and-fifty-pound slobbering street G standing behind him pissing people off. Two years ago Lionel made his break. It ended up being something called the Shootout at the Barn."

"I remember that. In Compton. The Barn was some titty shake. A lot of guys left on stretchers."

"You got it. Lionel does the termination meeting there 'cause it's his homeboys' club. Croc Smith sees it coming and everybody comes strapped and with backup. Six guys end up dead. Among them was Smith's younger brother, Junior Smith—gang handle, Roundwheel. Lotta anger still simmering over that. It became a straight-up revenge issue for The Croc. He started trying for some payback on Lionel. But Lionel has big money and he employs top-shelf security. Smith is a street villain whose idea of a smooth hit is to blow up your car. So to date there have been three attempts. All failures."

I picked up the folder and started to process this, thinking Lionel Wright had a lot of trouble heading his way. The old payback hit from his first partner on Sixtieth Street and now the Malugas. I was starting to see what Stacy Maluga might have in mind. All she had to do was set up Lionel Wright and Curtis Clark for Crocodile Smith and his posse and let the Sixtieth Street shot-caller do the wet work. Because of Smith's past history with Lionel, the Malugas would be way down on the suspect list.

I looked up at Sally and said, "Thanks."

"These are not nice people, Shane."

"Apparently."

"David Slade was still living up at Stacy Maluga's when he died," Sally said. "So this whole thing with Alexa has a gangsta-rap connection?"

"If you want, I'll spill the whole deal, but trust me, you don't want to get mixed up in it."

"I didn't like you using me to get ESD to plant that bug, but you're a cop who gets results, and I want a partner who's not afraid to kick a door, now and then. I've been working with a wuss for two years, so if you need some backup, I guess I'm volunteering."

"Even I wouldn't do that to you," I said. "But thanks for offering."

We reached out and slapped palms.

"Good hunting, partner," she said.

CHAPTER FORTY-THREE

The El Rey Theatre is an art deco building and registered historical landmark in the Miracle Mile district of Wilshire Boulevard. Throughout the years, its rococo frescos and thirties-style marquee have been completely restored and the theater has now become a trendy, live concert venue. Most of the big acts from pop to hip-hop have played there. Aside from the facility's new, state-of-the-art sound system and lighting board, there is a grand ballroom and a nine-hundred-seat theater, with an upstairs VIP lounge and full-service kitchen.

I pulled into a red zone on Burnside Street which was diagonally across from the theater where I could see both the front on Wilshire and the back parking entrance on Burnside. I was twenty minutes early, but the place was already hopping. There were half-a-dozen TV trucks lined up and a red carpet was laid from the front entrance to the curb. Fans thronged the sidewalk in front of the theater, trying to get photos of arriving rap stars. They spilled over into the curbside lane on Wilshire, which had been blocked off to accommodate the overflow. Half a dozen uniformed LAPD officers diverted traffic and were attending to crowd control while reporters from *Access Hollywood* and *Extra* jockeyed for prime position on the camera line.

I watched as Ferraris, Lamborghinis, and stretch limos ran a

gauntlet of reporters and fans on Burnside. They were waved
into artist parking in the rear of the theater by two uniformed
guards under the supervision of an imposing brother wearing a
tan suit, white shirt, bowtie, and an African Kufi hat. Fruit of Islam security was becoming commonplace at big hip-hop
events. Gleaming car doors opened to discharge men wearing
fur coats or designer warm-ups. Fans screamed from behind the
chrome rail barricades shielding the parking lot as the rappers
moved to the backstage entrance, trailing hot-looking women
like knots in a kite's tail. The white stretch limo I had followed
into Wright Plaza was parked in a VIP spot next to the back
door, so I knew Lionel was already inside.

I didn't want to use my backstage pass until just minutes before the doors closed, because as one of the few non-blacks in
attendance, once inside, I was not going to blend in. For the
next twenty minutes I kept my eyes on the parking lot. I was
looking for Stacy or Lou Maluga and the three possible hitters
from Sixtieth Street who were in The Croc's known associates
file. Their pictures, tucked in a manila envelope Sally had given
me, were on the seat beside me.

I opened the file and again glanced at the first mug shot on
the top of the pile. Mister Smith, aka Crocodile Smith. Lousy
teeth and a sumo wrestler's build. He looked fat, greasy, and
unhealthy. His yellow sheet revealed him to be a Martin Luther
King High School dropout, but with a graduate degree in violence from Pelican Bay State Prison. His teens were a litany of
gun and drug busts that grew in later years, to assault felonies.
Reading his charge sheet was like taking a slow ride through a
bad neighborhood.

His known associates file, clipped to the top sheet, identified
a thug named Little Poison, Smith's number one tight. His real
name was DeShawn Brodie. The two had ended up in the same
squad car a total of three times. His mug shot revealed a tall guy
with an undershot jaw who was missing half his left ear. His
height and weight were six-foot-three, two hundred ten pounds.
The next known associate was a hitter from Sixty-third Street
named Jordan Kendal whose street handle was Krunk. A drug
dealer with an attitude who regularly beat up his customers or

anybody else who was handy. The yellow sheet chronicled a pile of felony ag-assaults, most for no apparent reason. Apparently something would piss him off and he'd just snap and throw down. His picture showed a surprisingly good-looking guy with a weight lifter's sloping traps. If he was popping Arnies to get those shoulders, roid-rage might explain the multiple assault beefs. Krunk and Crocodile Smith were cousins by marriage. I closed the file and placed it on the seat beside me.

I was pretty sure the Malugas would make an appearance. Because of the size of the event, and the fact that Lethal Force still had big acts under contract, a guy like Maluga would be expected to attend. My guess was if they did show, they'd stay well out of the way, probably buddy-up with somebody influential who could vouch for their innocence when the play went down.

Ever since Slade was found dead in Alexa's car, I'd been trying to figure out the time line and affix a motive that would pull all of this into sharper focus. I'd been accumulating little bits and pieces of information and now thought I had enough to finally sketch out a rough picture. While I waited and watched the theater, I took out a notebook and started writing down each fact, theory, or guess in chronological order. I started by listing things I was more or less certain of, even though much of it was not provable.

My theory was that six or eight years ago, in the late 1990s, Chief of Police Burleigh Brewer had used the trumped-up road rage and 911 incidents to dirty David Slade's reputation so he could be placed undercover inside the increasingly violent and murderous world of hip-hop music. David Slade and Louis Maluga both went to Compton High School and were in the same Crip street gang, so it would have been easy for the department to plant him.

Although each circumstance varied when deep cover agents were used, the department usually limited the number of people with knowledge of the assignment to just a few command rank officers in order to protect the UC. When Alexa took over the Detective Services Group after Chief Brewer's ouster, she was undoubtedly briefed on Slade's assignment by the new, incoming chief, Tony Filosiani. Alexa knew Slade from the Academy and my guess was because of the rumor that they had dated back then, Alexa and Slade cooked up the love letter e-mail idea as a way to communicate.

Once the initial contact was made, Slade probably started out by working event security for the Malugas, then slowly established himself as a member of their inner circle, and under that guise had most likely been gathering information on the criminal operations at Lethal Force, Inc., detailing a variety of crimes from accounting fraud to assault and murder.

Following this line of thought, it seemed reasonable to speculate that after Lou went to prison and Stacy was estranged from him, Slade used the opportunity to move in with her. From the even more privileged position of her bedroom, he continued to funnel information to Alexa either through clandestine meetings or disguised as intimate e-mails. He was undoubtedly the source of much of the music industry gang intel for the past six or seven years. That was where my more or less reliable guesswork ran out.

Next, I made a calculated assumption. The Malugas, or someone inside their organization, may have discovered Slade going through records or planting bugs—something. Realizing he might be an LAPD undercover, they started following him.

Alexa told me when I left her at Parker Center on Thursday that she had one errand to run and would be home in an hour and a half. If she met up with Slade and the Malugas were tailing him, then they could have waited until Alexa drove to some secluded spot like the top of Mulholland and taken care of business. They killed Slade and kidnapped Alexa, holding her hostage until the race card was played in the press. They used her cell to call our home phone until the machine picked up, then they forced her to confess to killing Slade on tape. Alexa must have known she was as good as dead. Knowing her, if the Malugas had threatened my life or Chooch's, she would have confessed to Slade's murder to buy our safety.

I closed my eyes for a moment as the painful memory of my own shallow behavior tormented me. How could I not have trusted her when she had been willing to die for me?

More shiny imports and limos pulled into the parking lot as I sat blinking back tears, trying to reconstruct the rest of it.

As far as the Malugas were concerned, Alexa and Slade were now finished business. But Curtis Clark and Lionel Wright were still a big problem. If I had reasoned all this correctly, maybe I could bust the Malugas for the attempted murder of Lionel or Curtis. Stacy was hard and savvy, but she had never done any prison time. She might trade her estranged husband, Louis, to avoid a prison stretch.

Just then a black late-model Chevy Impala SS with tinted windows pulled into a bus stop up the street from me. When it passed by the Jeep, I heard the loud sound of rap pounding against its tinted windows. Pimped-out Chevy SS sedans were big show cars and popular rides for gangstas and G-wannabes in L.A. The black Impala was hunched low over expensive blades on low-profile tires. The four-door sedan was big enough to hold seven. Instinct told me it was a wrong car. I dialed Sally Quinn at Valley Homicide.

"I need you to run a plate for me," I told her. "I don't want a record of this request logged at the Communications Division."

"Go," she said.

"Ida-Mae-Victor three-five-six," I said. "If the tag's legit it should come back as a late-model black Impala SS."

A few seconds later the car pulled away from the bus zone and headed up the street, slowing as it rolled past the crowd near the artist and VIP parking. Then it sped up and hurried to the corner at the end of the block.

"Registered to a Jordan Kendal, aka Krunk," Sally said, coming back on the line. "Twenty-three West Sixtieth, Los Angeles. He's in the known associates file I gave you on Smith."

"I know. Listen, Sal—I need help. I'm at the El Rey Theatre on Wilshire. There's about six or eight blues already out front working crowd control for a rap awards show Lionel Wright is throwing. The shit's about to jump off. Fruit of Islam is working hall security. Put out a hotshot dispatch and get me some backup."

"I'll put out the call but I'm on my way, partner."

Of course, by the time she got here from the Valley, this would be over, but I loved her for trying.

I waited until the Impala turned right at the corner. Then I started the Jeep and headed after them. I tried to stay half a block back and followed as the car made another right and headed slowly down an alley that ran along the back of the theater. The Chevy pulled up and parked next to a chain-link fence.

I nosed the Jeep in behind an overflowing Dumpster, got out, and moved to a spot where I could maintain my surveillance. The passenger door on the Chevy opened and after a minute, a huge brother exited the Impala. Crocodile Smith was an immense blob of a guy, dressed in all black, wearing oversized chrome shades. Even from where I was hiding I could see big, yellow crocodile shoes on his feet. He moved around the car, opening doors like a valet. Then the serious talent got out. I saw two of the characters that Sally had included in the K.A. file. DeShawn Brodie, aka Little Poison, and the roid-raging Jordan Kendal, aka Krunk. They were joined by two other guys I didn't recognize who looked implausibly young, just teenagers.

The hitters all wore baggy jeans, expensive basketball shoes, and had black MAC-10 machine pistols hanging under their arms from nylon slings. While these four calmly started checking clips and tromboning rounds, The Croc handed out loose-fitting windbreakers. With oversized jackets now concealing their ordnance, Smith gave out final instructions. Then he watched as his wet team headed for the chain-link fence. All four went easily up and over, dropping gracefully on the other side.

They sprinted to the back wall of the theater, where Krunk pounded on a metal door with the heel of his hand. It was immediately opened by someone with white-blond hair. I couldn't see the face, but that dye job definitely belonged to Stacy. The four shooters quickly disappeared inside. Smith walked to the driver's side of the car and eased his gelatinous body behind the wheel. The Impala started rolling as rap pounded on the smoked windows. It turned at the intersecting alley and headed away from the El Rey.

I knew I didn't have much time. I put the Jeep in reverse and floored it, turned around in the alley, then swung back into the VIP lot and skidded to a stop. The FOI guard and his security troops were no longer there. Even the fans behind the barricade had left, seeking better vantage points. I threw the gearshift into Park, jumped out, and ran to the stage door. It was now closed and locked. I pounded hard on the metal. No one answered. I checked my watch. It was seven-ten. I'd missed the damned cutoff.

I pounded hard again. "Open up!" I yelled. I was about to turn away and look for another way in when the door suddenly opened and Vondell Richmond peered out at me.

"What you want?" he said.

"Lionel gave this to me," I lied, flashing my backstage pass.

"No, he didn't," Vondell growled. "I made out the guest list and ran all the security checks. You ain't on it."

"Hey, Vonnie, you got uninvited guests. Four hitters from Sixtieth Street just jumped the fence in the back. Somebody let them in here through the side door. It looked like Stacy Maluga."

He didn't answer.

"I know you don't need my help, but I saw the shooters. I can point these guys out for you. I'm not trying to bitch up your show, man. I'm trying to save Lionel's life."

Then he made another good executive decision and let me inside the theater.

CHAPTER FORTY-FOUR

A pounding rap song was being performed on stage for a sound check as I stepped inside the theater.

"Follow me. Stairs are faster," Vondell said, and started climbing up a narrow back staircase. We arrived at a door displaying a sign handwritten in Magic Marker that read VIP LOUNGE—PASSES REQUIRED. Vondell opened the door with a special key card and we entered a large room filled with guests. The lounge featured red and gold decor and was dominated by a long, dark oak bar being worked by two beautiful, coffee-colored twins in strapless evening gowns. The area was populated by hip-hop celebrities and beautiful women turned out in trendy, body-baring creations. The vibe was electric. Everybody engaged in animated conversation.

Vondell pushed me firmly up against a side wall and said, "Okay. Listen to me. This is a strained situation in here. Some of these brothers got bloody histories. Only thing keeping this in line is most a these people is hopin' to take home some brass for their trophy cases. See if you can stand here without starting a riot. I'm gonna round up my posse."

Then almost as if he'd been beamed down from the crystal chandelier, Taylor Hays appeared and hovered at my elbow.

"Stay with him," Vonnie instructed. "You seen Lionel?"

"Sound booth," Taylor said.

"Scully, fill my man in," Vonnie said and hurried off.

"Four uninvited guests, all packin' MAC-tens." I pulled the police mug shots from my back pocket and showed him the grainy faces of DeShawn Brodie and Jordan Kendal. "These are two of them."

"I know these niggas. Bloods, off Sixtieth," Taylor said.

"They're all wearing baggy jeans and loose black wind-breakers."

A minute later, Vonnie reappeared with two other guys and a brother in a tan suit who was introduced to me as Elijah Mustafa, head of FOI security. He was a large, no-nonsense-looking brother holding a small Handie-Talkie radio to communicate with his FOI guards, who were all wearing NSA-style earpieces.

Vondell motioned us to follow him. I fell in behind Taylor, who flexed through the crowd rolling his shoulders. We exited through a side door in the VIP lounge and walked along a glass-lined corridor that overlooked the empty theater below. It was getting close to eight o'clock. The doors to the theater would open soon. There were rows of center aisle seats marked off with ribbon for VIPs and their guests. One entire side section was set up for the press. On stage, a female rapper and her backup singers were pounding out a hip-hop number while the sound engineer adjusted levels from the booth.

We passed through another door and climbed a set of metal stairs backstage, finally arriving at the sound control room, high up in the rear of the theater. The door to the booth was open, revealing a cramped space outfitted with a state-of-the-art digital mixing board. Three video screens hung from ceiling brackets overhead, allowing the director, producer, and sound tech to monitor what was happening on stage.

Lionel Wright was leaning over the board with an engineer, finessing the pots, adjusting levels. He was in stage makeup and had rejected his own Bust A Cap running gear in favor of a Sean John warm-up suit with diamond earrings and gold rope chains.

"Man, Twista Sista got a slammin' cut here. We shoulda

opened with this," he said and leaned down into the microphone. "Okay, that's tight, Latisha. We gotta wrap it up now.
You guys sound great."

On the overhead screen I saw the stage manager escort the
act offstage.

Lionel turned to me, and I handed him the two mug shots.
"These guys and two others showed up here ten, fifteen minutes
ago. Your old shot caller, Crocodile Smith dropped 'em off."

"Sounds like you been doin' peeps at my past, Scully." Then
Lionel turned to Vondell. "That old-school G is probably down
here tryin' t' mess up the bang."

"Forget the show," I said. "They're here to put a bullet in
you."

"I've survived this asshole for two years. Tonight's not going
to be any different."

"This isn't good," Mustafa said. "This place is a maze of
basements, corridors, and rooms. They could be anywhere.
Come out when the lights dim and go to work. Gonna be hard
to stop 'em."

"We need to sweep the building," I said.

"I agree," Vondell chipped in.

Then in the damnedest display of criminal audacity I've ever
witnessed, everyone in the room, except me, pulled out a hunk
of German iron and started checking clips and chambering
rounds.

"Hey, hey, hey," I said, taking a step back. "You can't do
that."

"Whatta you want us to do," Lionel said. "Hit these G's with
pepper spray?"

He turned to Mustafa. "Find your guys. Give them a heads-
up and get a sweep going." He pointed up at a monitor that
showed the doors were open and the audience was now stream-
ing into the concert hall. "I got audience already moving in
downstairs. We gotta try and sift through all these armed people
without starting a riot."

"I'm on it," Elijah Mustafa said and took off. I heard him
clamber down the metal staircase as the rest of us trooped out
of the booth and back along the corridor overlooking the the-

ater. The audience milled below looking for seats as we descended the stairs to the lobby. Taylor peeled off and moved in
the direction of the open theater. Lionel followed, and I grabbed
his arm and stopped him.

"You can't go in there," I warned. "There's too many sight-
lines. You're the target."

"I'm not gonna hide from these bustas," he said, showing
good street cred.

The lobby was now packed to overflowing as guests with
tickets were herded in from the street and squeezed against the
large lobby bar where five more female bartenders, who
looked like models, were serving drinks to rap stars, music execs, and flashy-looking wannabes. I surveyed the teeming mass
of human flesh and counted several members of the Fruit of Islam positioned among the partygoers. Their tan suits and Kufi
hats made them easy to spot. People began to recognize Lionel. As they surged forward, we were pushed even tighter
against the bar.

"What up, family?" one guy said in greeting, pushing close.
It felt dangerous. Out of control. We were trapped, unable to
move.

Lionel grinned, waved, and shouted greetings to rival record
execs and rap stars. "There's a secure room in the basement,"
Vondell said. "Let's hole up there till Mustafa gets this locked
down."

I nodded my approval.

"I can't hide in the basement. I got a show to produce," Lionel said.

Vondell and I ignored him. He took Lionel's arm and, with
me out front clearing a path, we tried to make our way toward
the basement doors at the side of the room. It was tough going.
I was pushing people right and left. Vondell propelled Lionel
along behind me. As we approached the double doors at the
back of the lobby, more people jammed in around Lionel, im-
peding our progress. Some had deals they wanted to discuss,
others wanted their pictures taken with him, a few tried to give
him CDs. Then he was pulled away from me by a big guy
dressed in purple.

"Hey, cuz . . . I want ya t' peep my new act," the man said. I got blocked and in seconds was separated.

Vondell stayed with Lionel. I tried to follow, but a vise-like grip clamped down on my arm and I was spun around. I found myself looking directly into the round, basketball-sized face of Louis Maluga. He was dressed in a black suit. His huge arms bulged the sleeves of his jacket. Around his neck was a gold rope chain displaying one ornate, diamond-encrusted word: KILLER.

"You seem to get around," he growled at me.

"How you doing, Lou?" I pointed to the necklace. "Advertising?"

"Go sell your wolf tickets to somebody who gives a shit," he said ominously.

"I'm not selling wolf tickets. I'm here 'cause I love music that threatens your life in four-four time." I looked over and saw a very hot-looking woman in a low-cut gown. It had slits going up to her hips and down to her navel.

"Is this the lovely Sable Miller?" I said. "She's beautiful. Nice goin', Lou."

"You best pump your brakes, Chuck. You lookin' to get served, keep it up."

"A guy on parole shouldn't engage in verbal assault on a police officer," I said.

Then somebody grabbed Louis by the shoulders and gave him a hug.

"What up, cuz?" the man said. "We gotta jam."

Lou held my gaze a second longer. Just before he was pulled away, he said, "You been warned, asshole."

I watched him disappear into the milling crowd. He was so huge, I didn't lose sight of him until he was halfway across the lobby.

I turned to look for Lionel, but now the lights were flashing and people surged more energetically toward the theater. I was swept along with them. I finally spotted Lionel and Taylor Hays moving toward the elevator heading back up to the production booth on the second floor. Lionel was flanked on both sides by Fruit of Islam security, who were warding off approaching guests.

They were almost at the elevator when the doors opened and I saw Krunk and one of the other teenage shooters standing inside. Their windbreakers were closed and the Fruit of Islam guards, not realizing the danger, reached in to yank them out of the elevator.

"Look out! It's them!" I shouted, plunging toward the elevator. Krunk and the punk next to him pulled back their coats exposing MAC-10 machine pistols. As they swung the guns up, I lunged forward. Lionel was seconds from death. I was only a few feet away, so I reached out and jerked him aside. Then I dove past the two FOI guards and crashed into the elevator, hitting Krunk chest-high with a sort of half-assed flying tackle. I managed to knock him sideways, throwing off his aim and bringing him down just as he squeezed off a burst from the machine pistol in his right hand. Then the other G started firing.

Bullets whizzed around in the crowded lobby and people began screaming. From the staircase area, another gun opened up. I couldn't see it because by then I was on the floor of the elevator on top of Krunk while people were punching, screaming, and kicking my head.

Another burst of gunfire erupted, but I didn't see what happened since I was rolling around, trying to dodge the kicks while getting the stuffing pounded out of me. I rolled right, then left. Finally, I got my feet under me and pushed up. When I was vertical, I couldn't see Lionel, Taylor, or the FOI security. But Krunk and the other G were still on the floor of the elevator with their guns out fighting for their lives.

I heard someone scream, "Freeze! Police!"

Two more guns started firing.

I've been in some pretty amped-out situations, but nothing that ever came close to this. I caught a glimpse of the action in the lobby and saw what looked like a hundred men whirling and throwing punches. Crips, Bloods, civilians, and cops were all locked in a senseless free-for-all. Out of the corner of my eye I saw Krunk and the other shooter being dragged out of the elevator.

Then I took a shot to the jaw and dropped to one knee. I

managed to struggle up again. But this time I was facing a uniformed cop.

"Thank God," I said, just before I caught his swinging night-
stick to the side of my head.

That was the last thing I remembered about the Oasis
Awards show.

CHAPTER FORTY-FIVE

I opened my eyes to red lights flashing against a shiny white wall. I saw medical supplies and heard the distant chatter of half a dozen police radios. Then a blurry-looking young man in an EMT uniform leaned over and peered into my eyes.

"Welcome back," he said. But he kept splitting into two people, then slowly merging back into one. It was beginning to make me nauseous.

"Can you remember your name and why you're here?" he said.

"Don't ask any police questions until his division commander arrives," a gruff voice said. I strained to look in the direction of the second man. It was then I realized I was on a metal gurney in the back of a rescue ambulance. Next to the open back door of the R.A. sat a big, blurry, blue blob. His uniform and fuzzy chevrons identified him as an LAPD sergeant. He was also splitting and merging. I was close to vomiting on myself, so I started breathing deeply in an attempt to avoid that humiliation.

"Can you remember where you are?" the EMT asked.

"Ambulance?" I said. But beyond that, I was lost. My recent past was a snowstorm that made no sense. Except for an overriding sense of panic, which I couldn't account for, my memory was a mess.

"You're at the El Rey Theatre on Wilshire," the sergeant prompted. "That help any?"

I nodded. It seemed vaguely familiar. I thought maybe I'd once gone to a music awards show there, but that was all I could dredge up.

"What's your name?" the EMT asked.

"I'm . . . I'm Scully. I'm Shane Scully," I said, pretty sure I got it right.

Then he held up some fingers on his right hand and asked, "How many do you see?"

"Too many," I groaned.

The EMT turned to the sergeant. "He's got a fairly severe concussion and memory loss, which in most cases is temporary and intermittent. It should start coming back. When we get him to MCJ make sure the infirmary there keeps a close eye on him. His left pupil is dilated. I don't like the look of it. I'll flag everything on my field treatment report."

"MCJ?" I said. "I don't wanta go there." That was the Men's Central Jail on the ground floor of Parker Center. *Why were they taking me to jail?*

"We're not taking him there," the sergeant said to the paramedic. "The acting chief wants him to get his MT on the thirteenth floor. He wants to keep him away from the media. According to my watch commander, it's a nightmare at Parker Center."

I lay there trying to get my head to clear. I couldn't quite remember what the thirteenth floor was, but felt pretty sure it was not a good place for me to go. Then my thoughts started to stabilize and I suddenly knew the thirteenth floor was the jail ward at County-USC hospital.

"Whoa, whoa," I said. "I don't want to go there, either!"

"Ain't your call, sport," the uniformed sergeant said. My vision was beginning to come into sharper focus now and I saw that he had a big Irish face and the red, bloated potato nose of a heavy drinker. His nametag read: E. Riley.

Then my heart froze, as a big ugly piece of memory came crashing back, burying me under an avalanche of pain and sadness. Alexa was near death in a coma. She'd been shot in the head and was being operated on at ten A.M. tomorrow at UCLA. The memory, when it hit me, was so devastating it was like coming to grips with it for the first time. I took several minutes to get my heart and emotions recentered. I tried to sit up on the stretcher but was unable to because my left wrist was handcuffed to the metal rail of the gurney. My ribs on that side were sore.

"What the hell is this?" I said hotly, looking dumbfounded at my handcuffed wrist. Once I was vertical, my head started to throb and a horrible pain suddenly seared behind my eyes. "Am I under arrest? What's the charge?"

"Don't know yet. That's gonna be up to the homicide dicks at RHD."

"RHD? I didn't kill anybody." But to be perfectly honest, I couldn't remember whether I did or didn't. I yanked my left hand violently against the restraint.

The sergeant leaned toward me. "Calm yourself down, bud. You're in custody. My partner and I are gonna be with you till your division commander or the acting chief decides what they want to do. Now lie back down." The EMT helped me back down on the metal gurney.

Slowly, a few vague thoughts started to wander around in my head, looking for their correct place in time. I waited until they fell into some kind of recognizable order. David Slade had been found dead in Alexa's car. Alexa had been found shot in the head in a house in Compton. The e-mails I'd found that broke my heart. I remembered I had some kind of a new theory, which might exonerate her, but I couldn't remember what it was. All of this came drifting slowly back to me. Little bits and pieces of confusion. When assembled in the correct order, they formed an ugly mosaic. But everything that had happened inside the El Rey Theatre was still a deep, black hole.

Then I remembered the mini tape recorder with the Malugas' recorded conversation threatening the lives of Curtis Clark and Lionel Wright. I didn't want to explain to detectives how I got that without a warrant, so I snuck my left hand under me and felt for the unit, which was still in my back pocket. By moving to my left I could just get my handcuffed wrist to the strap hanging off the tape recorder. I had to find a way to get rid of it before I was admitted and searched at the thirteenth floor. I worked the recorder slowly out of my pocket by pulling the strap, then pushed it between the pad of the gurney and the wall of the truck. I lay listening to the cacophony of police radios outside and tried to tighten and refine the chronology of the last two days. Little by little, details sharpened. But my memory only extended to the moment where I followed the five g-sters in the black Impala SS into the alley behind the theater. After that, nothing.

Then Sally Quinn appeared at the back of the ambulance and showed the sergeant her badge.

"I'm his partner," she said, looking past him at me.

"You can't talk to the suspect," Riley said. "Step back. The sixth floor is all over this, so we're gonna do it exactly right."

At that moment, his shoulder radio squawked his name and he pushed the transmit button and said, "Whatta you got, Kyle?"

"Deputy Chief Ramsey is sending two fifth-floor guys over to County-USC to interview Scully. Ramsey wants him transported pronto," Kyle's voice buzzed through the speaker. Then he added, "Deputy Chief says don't let anybody near him. Strict isolation."

"Shane, I'm coming with you," Sally said, moving forward.

"The hell you are. Step away, Detective," Sgt. Riley barked, blocking her with a beefy arm. He already knew he'd caught a potential career-ending red ball and that any slight deviation from orders would get him body-slammed with a reprimand and, depending on sixth-floor politics, even a possible mandatory retirement.

Sally stepped back as the sergeant triggered his mike. "Get your ass back here, Kyle. We both gotta ride with this guy during transport."

What the hell happened inside that theater? I wondered. The whole thing was white noise in my head. I couldn't even come up with a half-assed story to save myself.

In less than a minute, the second cop, Kyle, pushed past Sally Quinn, climbed into the ambulance, and pulled the door shut, taking my worried partner from view. He was tall and slight of build with a narrow chin. The two chevrons on the sleeve of Kyle's uniform identified him as a Police Officer Two.

"Let's roll," Riley said.

The EMT knocked on the panel between the truck and the cab and in a second we were in motion, heading toward the county jail with my future in serious doubt.

CHAPTER FORTY-SIX

The thirteenth floor jail ward at USC Medical is a county facility policed entirely by the Los Angeles Sheriff's Department. My experience over the years has been that the
deputies there seemed to delight in making their brother LAPD
officers wait with their prisoners for as long as humanly possible before checking them in and providing treatment. I figured I
was in for a long, frustrating night.

Attempting a clandestine arrival, my police guards instructed the ambulance driver to swing around to the rear of the
hospital where we could pull up to a long, poured-concrete
loading dock with a wide setback that allowed forklifts to move
medical supplies back and forth to the freight elevators. I was
being whisked in the back way to avoid media contact.

During the short trip over here, I'd learned that Sgt. Emmet
Riley worked out of the Central Traffic Bureau. He had already
begun to treat me with unpleasant disdain. I had already pegged
him as a department loser. If you're a fifty-year-old sergeant
and still working traffic, something is pretty wrong. He looked
like a drinker just clocking time until he got in his thirty.

When we pulled up to the loading dock and the back doors
opened, two deputy sheriffs and a watch commander were already standing there with a wheelchair. It looked like there

would be no waiting around tonight. A cop in custody is a big deal and I could already tell that the anxiety level surrounding my bust was amping up. Everybody was determined that this was not going to cost them career momentum or days off.

I'd been around this kind of thing before. Once over in Rampart, I was in the stationhouse when a patrol cop charged with rape was brought in for booking. As soon as he was escorted inside the station, the energy in that shop started arcing off the walls, threatening to zap anybody who got it wrong. Now it was happening to me.

The EMT got ready to pull out the stretcher. I looked back and saw that my little mini tape recorder had fallen on the floor and was clearly visible up against the wall. I sat up, swung my legs down over the gurney, and managed to kick the unit out of sight under an equipment rack in the back of the truck.

"Get the wheelchair," the sheriff's watch commander ordered one of his deputies, while the other one recuffed me, this time with my hands behind my back. The watch commander pointed to the wheelchair and I stood carefully, fighting a dizzy spell as I got into it.

"I'm Sergeant Armando Padilla," he informed me. His dark, Hispanic features were stern and showed no concern for my plight. "You're being transferred into Sheriff's Department custody. The LAPD arresting officers will stay with you, but while you're in my custody, we do things my way." He looked at me, then over at Riley and Kyle. "Everybody Jake on that?"

"Listen," I said. "I didn't—"

"Shut up," he ordered. "I don't want to hear anything from you. I don't care what your sad story is. I just wanta know you're on board with this and aren't gonna cause problems. Are we Jake?"

"We're Jake." I couldn't remember the last time I had heard that expression.

"Your division commander and two guys from Homicide Special named Sepulveda and Figueroa are on their way over. They'll do the initial field interview. Until then, I'm going to get you checked in and looked at by the docs on thirteen. You will be isolated for the moment. No calls or visitors. Do exactly as I tell you and we'll get along."

He was so tense, I could see no advantage in putting up an argument. This guy just wanted me in and out of his custody without incident as fast as possible. As far as all of these cops were concerned, I was little more than a career problem with feet.

"Okay," I said.

Padilla looked over at Sergeant Riley. "Gimme the transfer documents. You can sign him over and I'll take custody down here."

I waited for a minute while they both signed papers on a clipboard. Padilla took the MT log from the paramedic and looked at his two deputies.

"Okay, let's move him."

One of them took wheelchair handles and pushed me across the loading dock into an empty freight elevator. The wooden door rolled down and we began to ascend to the first-floor lobby.

On the way, Padilla addressed his two deputies. "When we get up to the lobby, I want you guys to clear the first floor from the admitting desk to the elevator. Nobody gets into that hallway while we're transferring him to the jail elevator. Call upstairs to thirteen and get everyone who doesn't need to be in admitting out of there."

"Right," one of the deputies said.

"Any press here yet?" Sergeant Riley asked.

"Right now, just a photo stringer who hangs out hoping Nick Nolte or some other Hollywood notable gets led in here in handcuffs. But that's about to change, 'cause two RAs just called base. They're bringing in a couple a rappers who got shot at the El Rey. One's critical. This place is gonna turn into media central. Our job is to make sure Scully stays off the news."

"We'll throw a blanket over it," Riley said. But there was a distinct lack of confidence in his voice.

"What rappers got shot?" I asked, wondering again, *What had I done inside that theater?* Nobody answered my question.

While the deputies stood guard, I was quickly wheeled through an empty hospital lobby and transferred to the jail ward elevator. We rode up in silence. When the doors opened on thirteen, I saw that the admitting room had been cleared and was almost empty. I was a disgraced and handcuffed media star being moved through a cloud of negative expectations.

I'd been to this floor to get arrestees treated countless times before, but now it was very different. This time there would be no hanging around, or waiting to get processed. Two white coats were waiting as I rolled off the elevator. The doctor in charge had a strong chin, blue eyes, and gray-black hair the color of lead.

"I'm Doctor Larimore," he said, with no trace of courtesy. He turned to Padilla's deputy and said, "Put him in Ob Two, Larry. The last one in the back."

As quickly as that, I was wheeled through a metal door to the accompanying sound of a buzzing lock. Then I was whisked down a white corridor toward the rear of the facility where the lone isolation treatment cell was located. I could smell fresh paint mixed with the odor of antiseptic. We rolled past a series of closed doors where the feral eyes of injured prisoners peered out from behind wire glass windows, watching my progress. There were half a dozen deputies in attendance, called in, I assumed, for my benefit.

I was wheeled inside the small treatment room and parked. Sergeants Riley and Padilla came in, followed by Doctor Larimore and his white-coated colleague. The room had one window, facing west, toward the ocean. The view was protected by heavy chain link affixed to the outside wall of the building.

"How's your head?" Doctor Larimore asked, perfunctorily.

I contemplated a suitable response, but all I could come up with was, "It's had better nights."

"Okay, Detective, I need to do a quick neurological exam. If I determine that we need an MRI or Sonic Imaging, we'll do that next. Hopefully, it's just a standard concussion with no important or lasting aftereffects."

"Hopefully," I said, wondering when the rest of my memory would return.

He took out a penlight and shined it into my eyes.

"The EMT's radio call said his pupils were dilated. You have the paramedic's FTR?"

"Right here," Padilla said, and handed the Field Treatment Report to the doctor.

He glanced it over, then said, "Okay. This is promising. The dilation is way down now, almost normal." Then he looked at me. "How's your vision?"

"I was having some double vision a while back, but it's stopped now."

"Good."

He held up three fingers and thankfully, I saw three and told him so.

"Can you remember where you live?"

"Venice."

"The complete address, if you can."

"Three thousand Grand Canal Court."

"Any gaps? Stuff you can't remember, specifically around the time of the trauma? Often with this kind of thing, there'll be some temporary memory loss surrounding the incident."

"I remember everything," I lied.

I already knew this case of amnesia was going to be a big problem. For the time being, I had to at least act as if I had a memory of what had happened. If the cops knew I had no recollection, and one of those rappers actually died, then the District Attorney could put any case he wanted on me—including murder. Nobody would alibi me and with no memory, I had no way to dispute anything.

"I think he's stabilized, but we'll keep him in isolation until tomorrow, just to be safe," Doctor Larimore said.

"I guess me and Kyle can split," Sergeant Riley said, wanting to be rid of me.

"You better stay until his division commander and those two homicide dicks get here," Padilla said, then looked at the doctor. "Is it gonna be okay for them to interview him?"

"Yeah, sure," Doctor Larimore said. Then he turned to me. "If you have any nausea or light-headedness, I want you to ring that buzzer next to the bed. We'll check in with you every forty minutes or so."

I thanked him, and he and the other doc, who had been silent the entire time, turned and left the room. Riley and Padilla remained behind for a minute.

"Okay, Scully," Padilla said. "I'm sure you've been up here and done this a bunch yourself, but for the record, here's the drill. As I already told you, you're in Sheriff's Department custody. I don't expect you'll be here long, but while you are, I want your continued cooperation. Your people can talk to you, but any decision that affects custody is mine. Are we Jake on that?"

"Jake," I nodded.

Then, without saying another word, Sergeants Riley and Padilla stepped out of the room. The door buzzed and I was locked up and alone.

The next half-hour was filled with tests. Nobody bothered to tell me the results. All I could think about was Alexa. I had to find a way to get out of here before they operated on her at ten A.M. I knew I couldn't do anything but sit in the waiting room at UCLA and pray. I knew my presence wouldn't change anything, but I had an overpowering need to be there just the same. It was as if missing Alexa's operation would spill over everything and guarantee a bad result. Unfortunately, the more I thought about it, the more I realized it would be next to impossible to make bail and get my arraignment set in time.

Once I was returned to the isolation cell a wave of depression-produced fatigue overcame me so suddenly that I could not keep my eyes open. I just couldn't take one more blow or disappointment. All I wanted to do was run and hide. In a surge of either self-pity or self-preservation, I started to shut down. I lay back on the bed, closed my eyes, and mercifully fell asleep.

My dream took me back to Antigua. Alexa was in my arms and my heart ached with love and longing. We knew we had the whole world to play in. Our future stretched out before us like a ribbon of adventure and opportunity. We laughed as we walked into the glittering surf, splashing the water as we went, marveling at how lucky we were. Our bodies were washed by the surf and kissed by the sun. There was nothing but good times and blue skies ahead.

CHAPTER FORTY-SEVEN

Somebody was shaking me awake. I looked up into the scowling face of my division commander, Jeb Calloway. Cal's shaved bullet head glowed in the cold fluorescent lights of the observation cell.

"Sit up," he ordered. No "How you feelin'? How's the head?" All business.

It took me a minute to orient myself. I swung my legs off the bed and sat up, rubbing my eyes. A quick inventory of my memory made me realize I still couldn't pin down much of what had happened inside the El Rey. I had a fleeting memory of walking down a glass-walled corridor with Lionel Wright. Empty theater seats stretched out below us. That was it. My headache was worse than ever.

"Can you get these guys to give me some aspirin?" I asked.

"Hey, Deputy, find a doc. He needs something for his head," Cal said to one of the sheriffs.

Rafie and Tommy were standing across the hall opposite the open door. After a minute, an intern brought in some pills, which I took with a cup of water.

"You're in a world of hurt," Cal said when the intern left. "You got one chance in all this, and that's to come one hundred percent clean. Rafie and Tommy are gonna do a preliminary field interview and offer you a deal Chief Ramsey managed to strike with the D.A. It was tough getting this kicked down, so if you're smart, I suggest you take it."

"Captain, I'm . . . I didn't do anything. This is a big mistake."

"You didn't do anything? Are you nuts? You ignored a direct order from the acting chief and withheld evidence. You screwed up Slade's murder investigation by illegally entering his house without a warrant. You also searched a rap producer's house without paper. You're a person of interest in the Slade hit, and now you're also the prime suspect in a homicide at this rap awards show—all in twenty-four hours."

"What murder?"

"Singer named Diamond Simonette. Performs under the name Diamond Back. The guy was pronounced at this facility an hour ago."

"I never heard of him. Why would I kill him?"

"Rafie, get in here and card this guy."

I knew Cal liked me but his abrupt tone told me he was getting frustrated.

Figueroa came in and pulled a Miranda card out of his wallet. He stood next to the bed and read the familiar warning in a flat voice that echoed in the hard walled room. When he finished he said, "You understand these rights I have read to you?"

"Yeah."

Captain Calloway stood. "Okay, you guys do the F.I." He checked his watch. "It's almost midnight. I gotta go back to hold Ramsey's hand and deal with the chain of command. After you're through here, get the docs to clear him and transport him over to the Men's Central Jail. We'll do the probable cause declaration and booking there. And watch out for news crews. We don't want them to know where Scully is or have to make a statement till tomorrow morning's press conference."

"You're really gonna book me for murdering some rapper I've never heard of? Where's my gun? Who has it? Sergeant Riley? Was he the arresting officer? Check my piece. Ballistics won't get a match."

He didn't respond to any of this. Instead, he said, "We got

witnesses and a security camera that both say you attacked two
black guys in an elevator without provocation. Started the
whole ruckus."

As he said it, I remembered diving into an elevator, going
down hard and getting kicked. I touched my right side again.
The dull, aching pain was still there, confirming the memory.
The problem was that I didn't know *why* I dove in that elevator,
or what happened next.

Cal stood and said, "I'm really sorry about this, Shane. But
everybody's been telling you to go home and sit down. Because
you wouldn't listen, this happened." He turned and walked out
of the room.

Tommy closed the door. Rafie set his tape recorder on the
bed between us, then turned it on and verbally slated it. Tommy
crossed and sat on the edge of the bed.

"How'm I good for this Diamond Back guy's murder?" I
asked them, hoping that when they answered, more of what
went on inside the El Rey would come back to me.

"You perpetrated a felonious assault, which ended up causing a riot. Guns were fired and Diamond Simonette died. The
chief wants you booked for homicide under the Felony Murder
Rule."

The Felony Murder Rule is a California law that, without exception, everybody in law enforcement dearly loves. Simply
put, it states that if someone dies during the commission of a
felony, all of the perpetrators involved with the crime could be
charged with murder whether they pulled the trigger or not.

My favorite application of this rule occurred when I was in
Valley Patrol. Two white trash rednecks from Stinky Creek,
Arkansas, tried to take down a liquor store. They grabbed fifty-
eight dollars and forty-five cents in cash and while they were running out the door, the store owner grabbed his counter gun and
killed one of the fleeing suspects. We caught the other hillbilly
two blocks away and the D.A. eventually charged him with the
death of his buddy. Under the Felony Murder Rule, if they could
prove I started that riot and someone died, I was technically
guilty of murder. But it was a discretionary charge and it seemed
pretty flaky for the department to be laying it on one of their own.

"You guys are really gonna try and put this murder on me?"

"Orders from on high," Tommy answered. "How many times did me and Rafie ask you to stand down?"

He was right. But what would he have done if it were his wife lying in a coma? "Did you get Forensic Documents to scan Alexa's computer and decode any more of those e-mails?" I finally asked, trying to change the subject.

"Hey, Shane, we're through answering those kinds of questions. You're not a colleague. You're the suspect. Get used to it." He cleared his throat, then looked at Rafie. "We need some answers. Let's start with what were you doing at the Oasis Awards. What piece of brain-dead thinking led you to go down there and attack a building full of gang-bangers?"

Of course, there wasn't much I could tell him. I still couldn't get my head around the idea that the department wanted to charge me with this rapper's murder. I was thinking Chief Ramsey was probably just trying to jack me up and take me off the street until this whole, sad, Alexa-Slade media circus settled down.

But Rafie surprised me. "We've been given permission by the D.A. to make you Queen for a Day on the Slade hit."

What he was talking about was something called a proffer of immunity. Cops called it Queen for a Day because it allowed a suspect to confess to a crime and at the same time get immunity from the very crime he was confessing to. In return, he had to put the hat on somebody else—an accomplice. I didn't see how it fit. I had no accomplice to roll over on.

"That last e-mail on the computer reads like a blackmail attempt by Slade on Alexa," Rafie said, sensing my confusion. "Here's how we think it went down. Slade says to Alexa, gimme money, or a promotion, or whatever it was he was looking for. The e-mail says 'If I don't get what I want, I go to the Old Man.' Which is you! But rather than get shaken down by a piece of shit like Slade, Alexa decides to go to you and see if she can beg forgiveness. The two of you find a way to come to grips with her adultery and finally decide to dust him off to keep him quiet so he doesn't embarrass you and ruin Alexa." The room was quiet after he finished. Tommy scuffed his feet.

"You guys need to get over to CAA and see if you can find an agent to represent this," I said angrily.

Rafie went on, "The department is getting mauled by all these black activists in the media. Ramsey really wants it to go away. So here's the deal: You roll over and put the hat on Alexa for the Slade hit and the D.A. will give you immunity on that murder and kick this rap awards thing down to involuntary manslaughter. You end up doing a nickel in the State Pen and come out in time for your forty-fifth birthday."

I couldn't believe what I was hearing. I just sat there staring at him.

"Shane, we're just trying to find an easy way out of this for everybody," Rafie continued. "Alexa isn't gonna make it. I called the hospital and talked to a doc on the neurosurgery ward. She's scheduled for an operation in a few hours but they don't have much hope she's gonna make it. So if you want this deal, I suggest you make it before she checks out. Once she's gone, everything comes off the table. Not even this asshole we got for a D.A. will grant you immunity against a dead accomplice."

"Get out of here, Rafie," I said softly. "You too, Tommy."

As Rafie turned off the tape, Tommy looked over at him. "I told you he wouldn't go for it." Then he turned to me. "We didn't want to make that pitch any more than you liked hearing it. We were ordered to by . . . by people."

"Right. The Powers That Be."

He nodded, and turned to Rafie. "Let's get out of here. I need a shower."

The door lock buzzed and they left. I sat on the bed feeling lower than I ever had in my life. There was nobody to turn to. Nobody.

Who cared? Only Chooch, and he was just an eighteen-year-old kid who had more than he could deal with already. He was outside and I was in. I could only talk to him through bullet-proof Lucite.

I sat in the stark, white room and wondered how I would get out of this, knowing all the while that I probably wouldn't.

CHAPTER FORTY-EIGHT

They woke me again at two A.M.

Rafie and Tommy were back inside my cell with two sheriff's deputies, everybody in a big hurry to get moving.

"Come on, we're going for a ride," they said, as I started rubbing my eyes.

"Where?"

"You've been cleared by the docs here. You're getting booked at MCJ."

Ten minutes later I was back in cuffs, rolling down the corridor in the wheelchair, heading toward the elevator.

Rafie told me the thirteenth floor had booked fifteen people from the El Rey riot tonight. The rest were over at the Men's Central Jail. Because of all the celebrities involved, there was press roaming everywhere. In the lobby, on the first floor. They were even sharking around in the parking lot, writing down license plate numbers. To defeat them, the deputies had cleared the fire stairs and locked the interior doors for the three minutes it would take to transport me to the loading dock. I was pulled out of the wheelchair by Tommy Sepulveda and stood up next to the fire door on thirteen. I felt ten feet tall and a foot wide as I wobbled there light-headed and confused. Tommy looked tired and frustrated as he studied me.

"You okay?" he asked.

"You really care?"

"Yep, I do. I feel terrible about this, Shane. We both do. Tell us how to play it differently and still keep our jobs, and that's what we'll do."

"How was *I* supposed to play it, Tom? My wife is shot and maybe dying."

"I know," he said sadly. "It all sucks."

Rafie came up the stairs after checking the eleventh-floor door, and motioned us forward. "Okay, let's go."

We walked down thirteen flights and took a supply corridor out of the hospital to the rear loading dock, where their Crown Vic was parked. A light rain was falling. Rafie led me across the dock, down the steps. He pushed me into the back of the car and then climbed in beside me. The handcuffs were rubbing my wrists raw, but I decided not to complain. I just wanted to get this over with. Tommy got behind the wheel, and with the windshield wipers clacking, off we went, zipping quietly around the side of the hospital, tires humming on the wet pavement. The parking lot at the front of the hospital was full of TV trucks. All seven local news channels and some cable and wire services were camped out waiting for a glimpse of me in handcuffs. My life had gone from bad to worse.

The drive across town was quick because there was no traffic at this hour in the morning. We got up on the freeway where the tires sang loudly in the rain cuts on the pavement as we flew along. The downtown horizon glowed a dull orange in the distance, the strange coloring caused by low clouds over L.A. that were up-lit by powerful yellow street lights. As we rolled down Sixth Street, the Police Administration Building loomed ahead.

"Turn right on San Pedro," Rafie instructed from the backseat. "Let's not go past the front of PAB. The press is still all over out there."

Tommy turned onto San Pedro and made a radio call to the jail, telling them we were seconds away. Then we pulled up to the rear of Parker Center and stopped outside the chain-link fence at the back entrance to the MCJ.

While the windshield wipers metronomed, Tommy blinked

his lights for security, and after a second the electric gate opened. The car passed through the narrow driveway and pulled into an empty metal-caged area where the gray jail buses were staged each morning to transport prisoners to court. A trustee wearing a purple jumpsuit pulled the gate closed behind us and locked it, securing us inside the chain-link box. There was an opening to the right of the car that led up ten steps to a sally port. The wire-enclosed pathway bent left and led to the booking area at the back of the jail. I'd been here hundreds of times, but it looked different to me now. Foreboding and dangerous.

Rafie again triggered his radio mike. "This is D-Nine to MCJ Central. We're in the pen with the prisoner. Send out some custodial officers and make sure the booking area is clear."

"Roger that," a voice answered.

Minutes later, two police custodial officers in blue LAPD-like uniforms came out of the cement block booking shed and approached inside the wire-enclosed walkway.

Jail custodians were not sworn police officers, but were trained at the Police Academy in jail tactics only. They carried no weapons and had spent no time on the street. They were strictly custodial specialists. Both men descended the stairs and opened the back door of the car. Everyone wore the same cut-from-granite expression. No one engaged my eyes.

"Hang in there," Rafie said, as I was pulled out of the back of the car.

I looked back at Figueroa and Sepulveda. We had shared space on the fifth floor of this building for almost a year, their desks only a few feet from mine. Now a cavern of distrust loomed between us. But I wasn't mad at them. They were as compromised as I was.

"Would you guys call Glen Gustafson and tell him I need his help fast? If he can come down here tonight it would really help."

Rafie and Tommy exchanged a look. "You really gonna use that liar?" Tommy said, surprised. "Even for a lawyer, he's roadkill."

"That's why I want him."

"Can't do it, Shane," Rafie said. "We're on this side now, you're over there." That pretty much covered it.

The custody officers removed my cuffs and gave them back to Rafie. Then I was led down the chain-link corridor into the jail area.

The booking shed was painted in ugly, contrasting colors, creamy yellow with a bilious green trim. In front of me were five booking windows that looked a lot like teller stations at a bank, complete with bullet-resistant acrylic glass. I was led up to the first station and the lone booking officer inside nodded at me.

"Empty your pockets and take off your belt and shoelaces. Leave all your money and personal effects on the counter, comb included."

I did as instructed, then asked through the scratched glass, "When is my bail being set, and when am I being arraigned?"

"No bail. Not tonight."

"Bail gets set automatically when you're booked," I reminded him.

"Except when the D.A. puts a hold on you. He's going before a judge on a bail deviation hearing at your arraignment, which, right now, is scheduled for Tuesday at nine A.M."

He put my possessions, including my badge, wallet, and both empty clip-on holsters, into a cellophane bag and counted my money, laying it on the counter, getting ready for me to sign off on it.

I started to panic. If my arraignment was Tuesday, I was stuck here until then. I needed to get out, now. I needed to be at UCLA by ten A.M. I couldn't remember what I had done in the El Rey Theatre, but since they were charging me under the Felony Murder Rule, the witnesses and videotapes obviously couldn't get me for shooting that rapper straight off. The standard bail cap for all homicides is one million dollars. More than I had. But I had a plan on how to get it knocked down. I'd been hoping to hire a criminal defense attorney named Glen "Gunner" Gustafson. Twice I'd testified against clients of his whom I'd arrested. Both times during the cross Gunner had shredded me on the stand, attacking my choice of words and recollections, creating the impression I was impeaching myself even though I wasn't. He was brutal but damned effective. I was hoping Gustafson could get the charge knocked down to involuntary manslaughter or even wrongful death. That would depress the bail to a figure I could handle. Bail on lower weight felonies was usually in the hundred-thousand-dollar range.

Bondsmen will traditionally take 10 percent of the bond in cash and a guaranteed appraisal on your house or other personal property as collateral for the rest. I had about ten grand in the bank that would cover the lower bond. There was no way I could see to get our house appraised before eight A.M.

I signed for my possessions and was moved back over to the booking area where I was instructed to sit at a small wooden desk with a night-shift WC named Patrick Collins. I watched Collins fill out the booking sheet, charging me with first degree 187, which was a joke. Then he led me to the fingerprinting area to be photographed and printed. Just as on the thirteenth floor, all the sleeping drunks and bystanders had been cleared out of the downstairs holding cells. The rooms were empty as they rolled my prints electronically and shot the mugs.

"I need to talk to my attorney," I said.

"It's pretty late," Collins said. "Let's get you settled, then we'll see if anybody's up to take your call."

He led me to the first-floor elevator. "We're putting you on the Walk of Fame," referring to A-block, which was a corridor of single occupancy cells where celebs like OJ, Robert Blake, and Robert Downey were all held in isolation before their arraignments. Afterwards they were transferred to the Iso unit in the main jail at the Twin Towers two blocks away. A-block at Men's Central Jail contained ten cells, and unlike the large dormitories situated on the second floor, none of these cells had pay phones inside.

We took the elevator up and I was led down the hall past the sleeping figures of men locked in large, twenty-man barred rooms. As I passed one dormitory, I noticed a man dressed in a silk shirt and shiny leather pants. His scowling face looked familiar.

"I smell bacon burnin'," the man said malevolently as I passed.

I was closed inside my isolation cell before I realized who he was. Stacy Maluga's bodyguard, Insane Wayne Watkins. He was locked up in his Oasis Awards glitter clothes, looking like he wanted to tear my head off. Worse still, he was only twenty feet away.

Almost close enough to do it.

CHAPTER FORTY-NINE

I was in cell A-5. It was small and contained only a bed, a sink, and a steel toilet. The bars were painted the same cream color as the floor. I sat on the thinly padded, red vinyl mattress and tried to sort this out. I knew I had to recapture my memory of what happened inside the El Rey Theatre, so I started with my last recollection. I pictured myself back inside Chooch's Jeep, parked on the street outside, and tried to walk myself through it a step at a time.

I remembered watching the black Chevy Impala SS slide by my parking place, its darkened windows vibrating gangsta rap. I tracked my progress, as I followed the black four-door Chevy down the alley behind the theater. This time, my memory continued on beyond where it had stopped before and I remembered the fat gangster dressed in black, wearing chrome shades. Mister something . . . Smith. With the gaudy yellow crocs. Crocodile Smith. I remembered Krunk and the other one—Little Poison and the two younger bangers. In my mind's eye I watched as those four scaled the fence and knocked on the back door. I remembered Stacy, or someone who looked a lot like her, letting them inside. A lot of pieces were starting to return. The VIP room. Walking down the glass-walled corridor to meet Lionel Wright in the sound booth. A big guy in a tan Kufi hat.

Elijah Mustafa from the Fruit of Islam. Then I recalled Louis
Maluga bracing me in the crowded lobby, threatening my life
while the gorgeous woman I assumed was Sable Miller stood
nearby and watched, waiting to see what would happen. But
there the memories abruptly ended. I still couldn't fathom what
I had done that led to the riot.

I needed to get the custodial officer so I could make a phone
call. I stood and started tapping on the bars with my wedding
ring—the only piece of jewelry the booking sergeant let me
keep.

"Stop that racket or I come down there an' put a foot up yer
ass," a sleepy voice from another cell growled.

After a minute, Sgt. Patrick Collins arrived and looked in at
me. "Shhh!" he hissed. "One riot a night oughta be enough for
anybody."

"There's no phone inside this cell."

"It's three A.M. No attorney's gonna talk to you until morning."

"Hey, Patrick, that's just not your decision to make. I got a
right to phone calls twenty-four hours a day, no exceptions.
Read the jail manual."

"It's great havin' a cop in here, so we don't forget the real
important stuff," he complained.

But he took out his keys, opened the cell, and led me down
the hall. The big holding dorm that housed twenty sleeping
prisoners was dimly lit by night-lights, but even in the faint
glow, I saw Insane Wayne standing at the bars glaring, dressed
to thrill in silk and leather.

"You best look out, motherfucker," he growled as I passed.
"Bad shit be coming."

"Don't talk to him," Sgt. Collins ordered.

"That's a threat," I said. "Aren't you going to do something
about it?"

Collins didn't respond and pulled me farther down the corridor to a large shower room with a wire mesh door. He opened
the door, pushed me inside, then shut and locked me in. There
was a phone on the wall outside with a cord that was just long
enough to reach through a metal porthole that had been cut in

the chain link. The way it worked, I could stand in the locked shower stall and by pulling the receiver in with me, I could then reach through and dial the phone attached to the wall outside. I retrieved the handset while Sergeant Collins watched me.

"You mind?" I asked.

He finally turned and walked out of earshot. I could just make out the corner of Insane Wayne Watkins's cell a few feet beyond the intersecting corridor. It was so dim over there, I couldn't quite see him, but I could feel his insolent glare coming out of the darkness, vibing me.

I reached through the narrow port, dialed information and asked for Gustafson Law Associates. Once the operator gave me the number, I called it collect and got a woman on his answering service who was polite, but seemed tired of dealing with dirtbags calling collect from jail in the middle of the night. I told her what I wanted.

"He makes jail visits after court in the morning. If you got booked tonight, you won't be arraigned until Tuesday or Wednesday, anyway."

"I need to talk with him now."

"Honey, it's three A.M."

"Wake him up. I'm the cop accused of killing David Slade and that rapper, Diamond Back, at the Oasis Awards. My case is gonna be worth a million in free national publicity. You tell Gustafson to call me in the next ten minutes or I'm moving to Thomas Mesereau, who happens to be the next celebrity guy on my list."

She hesitated, so I said, "I'm in a shower cell. I'm holding a phone through a porthole. This is not a good situation down here. Don't keep me waiting." I gave her the pay-phone number and hung up.

Three minutes later, the wall phone rang. I reached through the hole and picked it up.

"Shane Scully?" a rough voice said.

"Yeah," I replied, keeping my own voice low so I wouldn't be overheard by Wayne Watkins.

"Gunner Gustafson."

"Didn't take you long," I said.

"Knock it off. Let's go, cowboy, it's late so gimme your story."

His voice was raspy, like a fighter who'd been hit in the windpipe too many times. But it fit him. I remembered he was only five-foot-six, but the guy was definitely street product. When I'd testified against his dirtbag clients, both were found not guilty. It had angered me at the time, but now it warmed my heart.

"Start at the top and don't leave anything out," he said.

I filled him in on all of the facts I could remember. I told him I had amnesia surrounding the immediate event, but my memory was slowly coming back.

"You didn't tell the cops you couldn't remember what happened," he said, sounding worried.

"I may be stupid enough to be in jail, but I'm not *that* stupid."

I explained where I was being held and about Alexa and why I needed to get out on bail by ten A.M. When I finished, I heard him breathing slowly on the other end of the line.

"And you said the D.A.'s going after a bail deviance on the first degree murder?" he asked.

"That's what the booking sergeant told me. I don't have a million. I guess my house is worth maybe three-quarters of that and I only have about one hundred grand in equity. But none of it matter because I can't wait until Tuesday. I need out fast."

"You don't make it easy, friend. You've left me no time to put together a bail package. And if you can't make the million bond, we're gonna need to file our own bail deviation request, which means I'll need to put together the standard choir of angels who can hallelujah and amen all my arguments as to your saintliness. We need people who are beyond reproach—your son, your division commander, if he'll stick his neck out, your priest if he's still talking to you—anybody else you can think of. But I can't do any of that by ten A.M. I also need to get an appraisal on your house and have a bondsman qualify you. Again, no time. Put this off until Tuesday, you'll at least be giving me a fighting chance."

"My wife is undergoing surgery. Didn't you hear what I told you?" I was getting angry with him.

"Okay, okay, hold your water. I'll call the guy who books Division Thirty arraignments first thing in the morning and have your name put on Monday's court appointment sheet. But I won't promise anything. If I screw this up, it's one hundred percent on you." The recent story of my life.

"Thanks," I said.

I hung up the phone and whistled for the custodian.

"Hey, fish! I got somethin' for you," I heard Wayne Watkins growl from across the hall. "You about to get fronted. There's people in here 'bout to buck down on yer ass."

He was threatening me right in the men's jail. Something wasn't right. How would he pull it off? I was a high-profile, isolated prisoner.

Sergeant Collins arrived. The door to the shower was unlocked and I was led outside. Collins walked ahead of me, leading me back to my cell.

"I got yo four-one-one right here," Wayne growled, holding something out through the bars—a rag or a torn sheet.

I swerved slightly, putting myself between Sgt. Collins and Insane Wayne, blocking the custodian's view. Then as I passed by his cell I snatched a torn cloth out of his hand and wadded it into a ball inside my fist.

After I was locked back in my cell, I held the cloth up to the dull corridor light. It was a torn piece of bed sheet. On it, Wayne had written something in blood. I strained to read it.

Trustees. Maluga rules. Fire.

I looked at the message again, trying to figure out what it meant. I sat down on the bed and then lay back, turning the problem over.

I took the three sections of the note one at a time.

Trustees.

I knew from past experiences with the jail that trustees more or less ran the place. Most of them were first-timers in on low-weight drug dealing beefs. They swept up and delivered the food trays to isolation cells, made minor repairs, and kept the jail buses washed and cleaned. The majority of the trustees were gang-bangers, both black and Hispanic, but without seri-

ous violent crimes in their jackets. That still didn't mean one or
two weren't monsters in training.

Maluga rules.

I thought about that for a while as I wondered how far a
trustee might go to please a rich thug and rap mogul like Louis
Maluga. I suspected fifty thousand in cash or a promised rap
contract would buy a lot of cooperation. Could he corrupt a
trustee with money or a promise of fame or glory? Probably.

Fire.

How did that make any sense? This was a concrete and steel
facility. Hard to find much that would burn. I wrestled with this
and then found myself thinking back to the buses in the parking
area and that African-American trustee who had the key to the
drive-in cage. It suddenly occurred to me that there was gasoline in those buses. How hard would it be for a trustee to slip
underneath and siphon some out? How hard to smuggle a book
of matches in here?

I sat up and pulled the mattress off the bed and studied it. It
was thin, but with a hard, red plastic cover. It might make a
good shield. I put it on the floor beside the bed and lay back
down on the cold metal shelf. How long I waited, I don't know.
There were no clocks. The sound of men snoring punctuated
the silence. I gripped the edge of the mattress and thought
about the next morning and how long it would take me to get
bailed out, if I could even arrange it. I wondered where Chooch
was and if I should get the sergeant to take me back to the
shower so I could call him. I couldn't bear to tell him I was in
jail for murder. After struggling with this for a while, I decided
to wait until I knew more. He had enough to deal with just looking out for Alexa, and since he hadn't called the jail, I could
only hope he'd been asleep when I was arrested and hadn't seen
anything about it on TV yet.

Finally, I drifted off. My mind was looking for comfort
somewhere else. But this time I didn't find it in a dream. I slept
fitfully. I thrashed and rolled, fighting demons that came at me
in shadowy forms. In most cases I was running, trying to get
away from faceless enemies I could sense but couldn't quite see.

Then I heard someone outside the bars of my cell and my eyes snapped open. I couldn't see who it was, but I caught a glimpse of purple.

Trustee.

Something wet splashed on my arm. I smelled gasoline. I snatched up the mattress and held it out in front of me as more gasoline from a plastic water bottle sprayed into the cell. Most of it hit the hard mattress, then splattered onto the floor. A lighted match followed and the room exploded.

"Fire!" I yelled, and danced back into the far corner of the small cell shielding myself with the mattress. I could barely get away from the heat and spreading flames. I was trapped and starting to catch fire.

My sleeve was burning as well as some of my hair. I slammed my burning arm against the wall in an attempt to extinguish it, then clawed at my head to put out the fire. I don't know how long I was inside fighting to stay alive. I was choking on smoke, and fire was beginning to get on my clothing. The gasoline-soaked floor was ablaze and spreading quickly. The billowing smoke triggered a fire alarm and the sprinkler system in A-block turned on. Water rained down. Suddenly, three custodial officers flung open my cell door and began spraying me with fire extinguishers. I dropped the mattress and dove through the door, rolling on my shoulder in the hallway to extinguish the fire that was now burning my shirt. They shot the fire out with CO_2 cannisters.

For the next few minutes the custodial officers beat down the flames in my cell as the sprinklers in A-block continued to drench us. The entire floor was thick with smoke. Prisoners were coughing and screaming in fear all around the block.

It took twenty or thirty minutes until most of the prisoners were moved out of the dorm cells on two and taken down to the staging cells on the first floor. I was led to the jail medical ward for treatment.

Sergeant Collins was shaken as he sat to fill out an incident report. I had seen nothing. A purple uniform. I couldn't identify my attacker. Collins promised that all of the trustees would be interviewed by detectives and polygraphed. Wishful thinking.

Nobody was going to agree to a plea bargain or make a voluntary statement on a polygraph.

My burns were mostly superficial. Some of my hair and eyebrows had been singed off and there was one bad place on my left arm. The MT greased and wrapped it, then gave me pills for the pain.

Two arson detectives from upstairs pulled me into an I-room. I knew this would go on for the rest of the night.

"You think we should send him back to the thirteenth floor?" one of the arson dicks asked the young doctor working the jail ward. Like everybody else, he was in a big hurry to hot-potato me off to somebody else.

"I think he's okay," the doctor answered.

"Lucky you had that mattress handy," the arson detective said.

I had a jail breakfast at six o'clock and as I was finishing, Sergeant Collins came over, holding a sheet of paper.

"The list just came over from Division Thirty and your guy worked a miracle. You're on it."

I thanked him and watched as he walked back to his desk.

Through it all, I couldn't shake one question.

Why had Insane Wayne Watkins saved my life?

CHAPTER FIFTY

Division Thirty is in a massive, no frills, stone building, with linoleum floors and security checks at every door. The place smells of sweat, and, for some reason I can never fathom, tobacco. The arraignment court is on the second floor and occupies most of the north side of the building. The courtroom itself is a huge, square space that has a closed-off glass area where next-in-line arrestees wait. It's a criminal conveyor belt. Prisoners are walked in, their charges are read, they're asked how they plead, then bail is determined and a date for the preliminary hearing is set. Bing-bang-boom-next. When it's over, you're either taken to the bond clerk downstairs, or transported over to the big Twin Towers jail where you are held over until trial.

Handcuffed, I followed an LAPD court cop to the second floor and into a small attorney's room. When the door opened, I saw Gunner Gustafson. He was a fifty-year-old lunchbox-shaped guy with wide shoulders and longer-than-normal arms, all of which contributed to a slightly ape-like appearance. His curly brown hair was cut close and he had the fighting chin of a Nordic thug. His suit was wrinkled and nondescript.

He stood when I entered, but on his feet or in the chair, he was about the same height, his lower torso being abnormally compact. Still, there was nothing even remotely funny about him. He was small, but on home turf. In this arena, he was dangerous.

"Get those restraints off. I won't have my client paraded in front of the judge wearing chains," he snapped at the police guard.

"I'm sorry," the cop said. "Can't do it."

"Make this an issue, Sonny, and I'll find a way to give you some grief. Scully ain't going nowhere. Put a guy outside this door, or walk with us to court if you're so worried, but for the love of God, stop arguing 'cause you're gonna lose."

The officer knew Gustafson, and since he didn't want trouble, he reluctantly unchained me.

"Now get the hell out. This is an attorney-client conference," my gunslinger snapped. The uniform backed out of the room and shut the door. Then, Gunner Gustafson put out his hand. "Shake it like you mean it," he smiled. It was a little like shaking hands with a stone carving.

"I called a guy I know who's in Venice real estate to zip over and give me a legal appraisal of your digs," Gunner said. "Got him out of bed at four A.M. Since he couldn't walk the inside and doesn't know what condition it's in, he'll only guarantee me an appraised value of six hundred thou. That's probably about twenty-five percent under what it's really worth. But once the bondsman accepts his appraisal, if it turns out to be too high, he could get sued for the difference if you skip. Traditionally, bail appraisals are low. It's a bad deal, but it's the best I can do on such short notice."

"How'll I get out?" I asked.

"Okay. You've got equity of around one hundred K. Discount that by twenty percent, which is a bond standard, and that leaves you with around seventy-five thou. You said you have ten grand in cash at the bank?"

I nodded.

"To get you out by ten we gotta get bail lowered to around seven hundred and fifty thousand. On Murder One, that's gonna be tough."

I told him about the attempt on my life in jail and he snatched up his phone and started making calls. He wanted a

copy of the attempted homicide report sent over right away by
messenger. He wanted a list of custodial officers who were on
duty last night called and set up to testify if necessary. He
wanted all the arson and IO reports. The guy was impressive
shouting orders to subordinates and jail employees. When he
was finished, he hung up and looked over at me.

"We got one thing going for us," he said. "We didn't draw
one of those numb-nut pussies from the normal judge's rotation. Apparently, because of sickness, vacations, and brain mal-
functions, they're short on graybeards this morning. We were
assigned a civil commissioner, just appointed, name of Andre
Easton. I went before him last week. He's a cherry. Guy's so
new he still thinks he's actually supposed to make decisions instead of just rubber stamp the District Attorney's charge sheet.
That's the good news. The bad news is we got the D.A. himself
trying this sucker. Because it's you and he likes to get his picture taken, Chase Beal is in the docket for the people. I hate that
guy worse than country music. I'd purely love to kick his
skinny prep-school ass."

At ten till eight, we were being led into an empty court
room. I'd been transferred by police car half an hour early because my case was being heard half an hour before court nor-
mally opened. As a result, there was no press and the only
people in attendance were the cops guarding the door, the
bailiff, the court reporter, and the clerk. The regular jail buses
hadn't even arrived yet.

At the prosecutor's table sat Chase Beal. Up until now, I had
only seen him on the *Six O'Clock News*. He was smaller in
stature than I'd thought. He also looked like one of those guys
who spent at least an hour a day in some Beverly Hills gym
running the treads and trying to put a move on the Pilates instructor. He had narrow shoulders, a trim waist and movie-star
hair. His eyes had been described once in the press as being
fiercely blue, but I suspected contacts. Sitting behind the bench
and at the extreme other end of the fitness scale was Commissioner Andre Easton. A big, round-shouldered, flabby-looking
guy in judge's robes with a shock of sandy, longish hair. We

took our place behind the yellow, distressed glass and remained standing.

"Division Thirty, State of California, is in order," the bailiff said loudly. "Commissioner Andre Easton presiding." No gavel, no nonsense. We were off and running.

"This is case number three-four-zero-zero-six, *People* versus *Shane Scully*," the court clerk said. "Charge being filed against the defendant is one-eighty-seven, murder in the first degree."

"Who's here on behalf of the people?" Commissioner Andre Easton droned. Because everybody in the room knew the District Attorney was trying this himself, the question was just for the court record.

"Chase Beal for the people," the D.A. caroled in a loud tenor appropriate for church.

"Glen Gustafson for the defense," my street fighter rasped.

"How do you plead?" Easton asked, looking at me.

"Not guilty," I said.

"Okay, I have a motion before me, by the District Attorney requesting a bail deviation. Let's hear about that," the commissioner said.

Chase Beal cleared his throat. "Commissioner Easton, this man, Shane Scully, is a suspect in the prior high-profile murder of Police Officer David Slade. He's also now being charged with the first-degree murder of Diamond Simonette. The people don't think a one-million-dollar bond is anywhere near sufficient. Further and to the point, this is an officer who has recently displayed a blatant lack of self-control. He has made two unlawful searches without warrants as well as being unlawfully involved in numerous other cases in the past. We've filed several documents in support of all this. I think you have them in your file up there along with his past Internal Affairs charge sheets." He shuffled his papers. "We'd like to . . ."

"Hold on a minute, Mr. Beal. Let me read this stuff. I'm not from Yale, like you. Went to little old Glendale City College. Gonna take me a minute." I liked the sound of that. We had a class war going. Then Commissioner Easton looked up. "Says here the I.A. charges were all dropped in oh-two." He was frowning.

"Your Honor, the people contend those charges were dropped for dubious reasons. Detective Scully's record shows a longstanding slipshod approach to the law. We believe past behavior strikes to character, regardless of whether I.A. filed its charges. It's our contention that, when taken as a whole, this officer's record supports the people's case that he is a rogue cop and, as such, is also a flight risk." Beal took a breath, then continued. "As a police officer and notorious rule-bender, he also has access to weapons. He knows the street and could easily obtain a forged passport. Our feeling is he needs to be held with sufficient bail to guarantee incarceration."

"And what would that figure be?" Easton asked, raising bushy eyebrows.

"Five million dollars," Beal said.

"Is he kidding?" I blurted. Gunner was looking down into his briefcase and failed to stop my outburst. "I can't even afford a million," I raged at the commissioner.

"Shut up, asshole. Let me do this," Gunner growled under his breath.

"Mr. Gustafson?" Commissioner Easton said. "Any response?"

Now my guy went to work.

"We City College guys probably just don't get it," he began. "As his reasons for this ungodly bail, the District Attorney documents I.A. charges that have been dropped but says we should acknowledge them anyway, while ignoring a distinguished twenty-plus-year career in law enforcement, where Detective Scully has risked his life numerous times protecting the public." Gunner shook his head in disbelief. "Further, in response to Mr. Beal's first point, the incomplete Slade murder investigation, let me say, if the people have an actual case against my client on that, then I suggest they file it. If not, then stop talking about it, 'cause it's just not relevant. Further, let me add that my client is a double Medal of Valor winner, who currently is assigned to Homicide Special, arguably the most elite murder squad in the entire country. I would also like to point out that his wife, the acting head of the Detective Bureau, is undergoing brain surgery at UCLA Medical at ten o'clock this morning. As a loving husband, Detective Scully should be allowed to make reasonable bail so he can be there to help make decisions on her behalf. I'd further point out that since this one-eighty-seven is being filed under the Felony Homicide Rule, nobody—it seems—is claiming he actually killed anybody. It's pretty obvious that my client is being grossly overcharged with Murder One in a transparent attempt to keep him from making bail. At best, this is Involuntary Manslaughter, or Negligent Homicide or maybe nothing at all."

"Except, as you know, the Arraignment Court doesn't determine the filing, Mr. Gustafson; the District Attorney does," Easton said. "Mr. Beal can charge him here with whatever he wants. A trial will eventually determine if he's been overcharged."

"I know, but trying for unreasonable bail under a bogus Murder One indictment is certainly something we can discuss in relation to the District Attorney's bail deviance request."

Easton nodded. "Fair enough."

"Third, I sent you an arson report of an incident that occurred at the Men's Central Jail at three A.M. this morning," Gunner continued. "You should have the report by now. If necessary, in less than an hour I can fill this court with witnesses to the event. In essence, somebody tried to kill Detective Scully by squirting gasoline into his isolation cell at MCJ and throwing in a match in an attempt to immolate him. You can plainly see his hair and arm are burned. Unless Mr. Beal can guarantee that the jail will do a better job of keeping this man alive, I don't think we should further risk his life by forcing his incarceration in an unsafe facility under overreaching and unfair bail requirements."

The commissioner turned to his clerk, who was just returning from chambers and handed Easton the arson report. He quickly scanned it, and then looked up.

"Anything to say, Mr. Beal?"

"Commissioner, what happened in that jail or why, has no effect on this hearing. Should we now let everybody out because one attempt was partially successful down there? That's ridiculous. The incident, such as it was, is being investigated. If a crime was committed, charges will be filed."

"Okay. Proceed, Mr. Gustafson," the commissioner said.

"We have also filed a bail deviance request of our own," Gunner said. "My client can't make the million-dollar bond. We want the bail lowered to five hundred thousand dollars, which is in keeping with the facts surrounding the charge. Detective Scully needs to be at his wife's side. Further, in attesting to Detective Scully's stability, the court should note that he has a son enrolled at USC and a house in Venice, California, that is almost half paid for. This man is not going to cut and run, Commissioner. He'll be here for trial."

Commissioner Easton was in a tough place. Whatever he did, his decision was going to be second-guessed. I could see the frown stretch across his craggy face. Finally, he looked down at us and pronounced his decision.

"Bail will be left at one million dollars," he said, playing it safe.

"Your Honor, I don't have a million dollars," I blurted.

"Then you're remanded to custody at the county jail until trial. Preliminary hearing is on October twelfth. Clear the court," he said and the bailiff turned and waved at the COs to come get me. As this was happening, Gunner Gustafson was reaching for his vibrating cell phone.

"Man, not even eight-thirty and this thing is already giving me a rubdown." He flipped it open and answered it. "Yeah . . . yeah . . . sure. I guess." He turned at looked at me.

"You switching lawyers already?" he frowned. "I'm a better kisser than that, aren't I?"

"What are you talking about?"

"Pryce Patterson for you." I must have looked confused, because he added, "Senior partner at some white-shoe Beverly Hills law firm. He's their big muckety-muck." Gunner handed the phone over. "Knock yourself out."

"Hello?" I said.

"Is this Shane Scully?" a cultured, nasal voice said.

"Yes."

"Has your bail been determined yet?"

"A million dollars, why?"

"I'm right downstairs in the lobby with an open cashier's check. If you'll meet me at the bail clerk's desk, we'll do the paperwork and you'll be out of here in a jiff."

"A cashier's check? How come?"

"My client, Lionel Wright, has taken an interest in your case," the nasal voice replied.

CHAPTER FIFTY-ONE

Pryce Patterson looked like his name. All that was missing was the tennis racket and the Alpaca sweater tied around his neck. His suit was a custom Brioni, and he had one of those ninety-day wonder attitudes that allowed him to look through rimless glasses and down his nose at the world. Not exactly my kind of guy. I wondered why a street guy like Lionel Wright would hire such a vanilla pastry.

"I'm not a criminal attorney," he intoned needlessly. "My specialty is estate planning and wills." Answering that question. When it came to managing money, a vibrant personality is not a prerequisite.

We were standing in the bond clerk's cluttered office on the first floor of the courthouse. It was a little after nine A.M. Gunner Gustafson appeared with the release papers and as soon as he showed up, Pryce Patterson began casting glances at my legal assassin, wondering, no doubt, how this bellicose midget had ever managed to pass the bar. Like a French poodle that suddenly finds a coyote in his backyard, he was unsettled and slightly appalled.

I signed the bail slip. Because Lionel Wright had posted the entire million, I didn't need to involve a bondsman. I was notified that when I showed up for my October twelfth scheduled court appearance, the bond would be returned, minus a few hundred dollars for processing.

Patterson handed me a business card with a phone number written on the back and said, "Mr. Wright requests that you give him a call once you have a chance." All very polite, as if we were buying art instead of freedom.

We all walked out of the courthouse at nine-fifteen, right into the teeth of ten reporters, all of them pissed because they'd been juked by the half-hour time change, causing them to miss the colorful news event in Division Thirty. There were lots of shouted questions.

"Detective Scully! Any comment on your arrest for murder?"

Yeah, right. Good luck on that one.

Tucking my tail, I again ran from those jackals like the media fugitive I had recently become. All I wanted to do was get over to UCLA. Gunner offered me a ride back to the El Rey Theatre to pick up Chooch's Jeep, which I prayed hadn't been towed. I desperately needed his laptop. If I hustled and the Jeep was there, I could still make it to the hospital in time. It was a miracle that I had pulled this off.

We got into Gunner's new gray Mercedes S-55, which was the last car I would have expected him to own. He seemed more like a Ford truck type of guy. He put the expensive car in gear and powered away while TV crews raced to the sidewalk to photograph our exit.

"Don't talk to those guys," Gunner said, jerking a thumb over his shoulder at the scrambling pack of reporters. "Contact with the media will only fuck us in the ass."

I love a plain-talking lawyer.

"We need to set up a meeting," he went on, "I'll start filing my discovery motions this afternoon. We'll see how much real ammo the D.A. has. Then sometime in the next two days we have to sit down and go through it."

"Good. That's fine." I waved a vague hand at him, not paying much attention.

"Are you even listening to me?" he said, picking up on my distraction.

"No." I looked over at him. His fighter's chin was pointed defiantly out the window at the morning traffic. "I'm sorry. With my wife going into surgery, I can't focus on this right now, but I will call you."

When we pulled around behind the El Rey, wonder of wonders, the Cherokee was still in the alley. Gunner dug into his wallet and handed me a cheap card that looked like it had been printed at Kinko's. I thanked him for all he'd done on such short notice. Then I headed to the car and took off.

At ten-fifteen I finally arrived back at UCLA. There were several news crews holding down this location as well. I noticed that a stage had been built in the parking lot for a press conference. Crews were setting up a sound system. A banner declared: BLACK JUSTICE. BLIND FAITH.

My beautiful wife could be dying while politicians and activists were getting set to dance on her grave. At least I didn't have to hide anymore. I was out on bail. I could go where I wanted.

As I made my way up to Neurosurgery, I was stopped twice by hospital security and had to show an ID that corresponded to a patient's name to get in. When I finally got there, I found Chooch sitting alone in the small waiting room. As I came through the door, he jumped to his feet and embraced me.

"Dad . . . Dad . . . thank God you got here," he said, holding on to me as if afraid to let go.

"It's okay, son," I said, trying to calm us both, but having no effect.

"You got arrested. I knew you wouldn't want me to leave Mom. I tried calling the jail, but they wouldn't put me through."

I didn't tell him about the fire at MCJ and being held and questioned all night. Then he was focusing on my burned hair.

"It's okay," I said. "Little accident. Here's my parental tip for the day. Never play with fire." I smiled. He didn't. "No real damage. Once it grows out, it'll be fine."

"Thank God you're here," he said. "It was such a madhouse; Luther finally made the hospital throw the press out. It's been horrible."

We sat together in the empty room. Then Chooch said,

"Luther says it's gonna be hours till we know anything. If you want, we could get some coffee."

"I want to stay here. You don't know how hard it was for me just to make it in the first place."

So we sat in the small lounge and waited. Around eleven a newspaper guy and his photographer found a way past security and came through the door asking questions and snapping pictures. I got up and advanced on them, not sure if I was in complete control of myself, but I'd had it. I snatched the camera out of the photographer's hand. It was a digital and I can never figure those things out. I wanted to rip out a roll of film and theatrically expose it, like some hero in a '40s movie. But after battling with the camera for a few seconds, I pitched it over to Chooch, who removed the memory card and tossed the camera back to the man.

"You can't do that," the reporter protested.

"Get the hell out of here, asshole." I got right in his face and he took a frightened step back. It felt good to finally take charge of at least one moment in my life. He took two more hesitant steps, and then he and the photographer turned and quickly left.

We sat and again waited. Time ticked off the clock in slow motion. Five minutes seemed like an hour. The only sounds were the hushed voices of the hospital staff behind the glass enclosure. No cops showed up to support Alexa. She had been pilloried in the press, tried, and found guilty. At the Glass House, careers were in jeopardy. The rank and file knew when things were too hot to touch. It's an instinct that develops quickly in political environments.

Then I smelled the musty odor of unwashed clothes and sweat. When I looked up, Jonathan Bodine was standing in the doorway ten feet away. His chopped-off hair was almost as ridiculous as mine. He was still wearing Chooch's bloodstained sweatshirt, but it was now covered with a layer of grime.

John nodded at me and said, "Howdy do, half-stepper."

"What are you doing here, John?"

I was surprised and quite touched to see him. Of all the people in Los Angeles, the only one who came to support us was this half-crazy homeless person. But then he ruined the moment when he said:

"Ain't ate in almost a day. You're the only muthafucka I can ever get ta feed me."

CHAPTER FIFTY-TWO

e had a few hairy moments, but she made it," Luther said. His face was drawn. Etched with stress. It was just a few minutes past noon.

Chooch, Luther, and I were standing just inside the surgical staff area near a sliding, frosted-glass partition that was above a reception desk and separated us from the waiting room.

"Time is our ally now. The longer we keep her alive post-op, the better our survival chances are."

"What's this crazy Jim Crow nigga talking 'bout?" an unmistakable voice blurted.

I turned to see that Bodine had moved up to the counter and was looking in through the open partition. His wretched appearance was causing Luther some concern.

Our neurosurgeon glanced at a passing surgical floor nurse. "Can you get someone to help this gentleman?"

The nurse went off in search of security.

"Go fuck yourself," Bodine said. "The Crown Prince of Bassaland ain't gonna be going nowhere."

Luther frowned at me.

"He's with us," I said. "Sorta . . ."

Luther snapped a look back at John with his chopped-off dreads. Then he glanced at my freshly burned hair and eye-

brows. I saw indecision flash. He was probably thinking he'd
just thrown in with a bunch of crazies.

"What do you mean, the longer we keep her alive post-op,
the better our *survival* chances are?" I said.

"I won't lie, Shane. There was a lot of damage. Once I got in
there, I did what cleanup I could. I restored some blood flow.
Enervated and repaired some veins and arteries. I recovered
half-a-dozen bullet fragments and some more bone chips, but
there's some in there I couldn't safely get to. We left the skull
patch open, so if there's swelling, the pressure won't build. In a
few days, if things go well, I'll replace the bone flap and reat-
tach the scalp. Till then, we pray."

"Jesus," I whispered.

"I never promised you a perfect result," Luther said.

"Samik Mampuna promises perfect results every damn time.
I know what's in the future. I got peeps up there lookin', talkin'
to me."

John waved his left hand, which was still clutching a half-
full cup of soda from the cafeteria. " 'Member what I told ya
'bout these God wannabes who think it's up to them what happens t'folks." He motioned to Luther. "This ass-wipe here don't
have any damn way t'change nothin'."

With that, Luther walked over and slammed the sliding glass
partition on the counter shut, cutting off John's tirade and turning him into a ghostly apparition waving his arms and ranting
on the other side of the frosted glass.

Bodine turned up the volume. " 'Member what I be sayin'!"
he shouted through the glass. "I get this direct from the boss.
From Chief O. Your old lady ain't on the ark till Chief O
punches her ticket."

Through the closed frosted partition it looked as if someone
in a blue uniform walked up, collared him, and roughly pulled
him away.

"I've got to make rounds now," Luther said. "Check with me
in two hours, and we'll talk again at six tonight."

After he left, Chooch and I made a quick search of the floor,
looking for Bodine, but didn't find him. I couldn't worry about

him any longer. I'd fed him a cafeteria breakfast and for now, that's all I could contribute.

Chooch and I returned to the waiting room and talked. Mostly, we shared old memories of Alexa. After about an hour, he said, "Dad, I've got to get out of here for a while. I'm fragged."

I could imagine. I told him I would take the next shift until the meeting with Luther at six. Then we walked down to his Jeep and I retrieved his laptop, which contained the cloned disk from Alexa's computer. I hugged him. We stood in the parking lot, clutching each other, both afraid to let go.

When I walked back up to Neurosurgery, there were tears in my eyes. *Time was our ally,* that's what Luther had said. But as it crept off the clock, time felt like my worst enemy. I still had the jail property bag with all my possessions, so to keep busy, I started to unload it and put things back into my pockets. I finally recovered my cell phone at the bottom of the bag and when I flipped it open, there was an urgent message to call Tommy Sepulveda's cell.

I dialed and waited for him to answer.

"Sepulveda," he said in a hushed voice.

"It's me."

"Just a minute. I'm in the hall up on five. I'm going outside."

I waited for two minutes, hearing his footsteps as he left the building. Once outside, he came back on the line.

"Shane?"

"Still here."

"I heard you got out. I'm glad. How's Alexa?"

"I don't know. The doc says time is our ally—whatever that means. Thanks a bunch for showing up and supporting her."

There was a long silence while he dealt with the cheap shot. Then he pushed on. "Listen, you asked me about Alexa's computer last night. Me and Rafie talked. We know how jammed up you are, and frankly, man, I'm not sure what I would do if Frannie was laying where Alexa is."

I waited, while it sounded like he was walking again. Then he said, "Just a minute. I'm in the parking lot. It's a mess out here. Lotta TV people. Gotta find a better spot." There was more walking and his breathing got louder. Then, the walking stopped and he spoke again. "Rafie and I figure you probably made a copy disk of the files on Alexa's computer before you gave it to us. You don't have to say yes, or no, but when we went back to get the computer from Documents, we found out that operations Nazi, Commander Summers, already took the computer out of there. It's up on the sixth floor in Ramsey's office along with the report. Rafie and me don't even know what's on it. But we chatted up one of the guys over in Documents. He didn't know we were being screened off by the sixth floor and let something drop."

"I'm listening."

"The code they were using is fairly simple. It's just every other sentence."

"Really?"

"Yeah. You erase the first, the third, the fifth, et cetera. What's left is the message."

"What is it that you want from me?" I was feeling like this was some kind of setup, but I wasn't sure. I'd screwed with them so much, I couldn't read those two anymore.

"If you've got a copy of those e-mails, and you can decode the damn things, Rafie and me could use a call."

"Why should I trust you guys?"

There was a long moment before he said, "Because Ramsey is starting to panic. This isn't like with Tony Filosiani. Everything on the sixth floor is about containment now. But me and my bow-legged Mexican partner still want to clear this damn murder case."

CHAPTER FIFTY-THREE

Dark Angel,
My thoughts are always on you. We must meet tomorrow
night. I can't go another day without holding you. You need to
give me another floor score. I ache to see you. How about
Crypto 457?

Love—Hambone

When I erased the first, third and fifth sentences, it read:

Dark Angel,
We must meet tomorrow night. You need to give me another
floor score. How about Crypto 457.

Hambone

The next one read:

Dear Hambone,
Time away from you is agony. This time Watts is the key. I can't
be away from my Queen. It's all about lost performance and
royalty. Don't make me wait, darling. I've got WYD and plenty
of ammo. I'm in the cut, waiting.

Edited, it read:

Dear Hambone,
This time Watts is the key. It's all about lost performance and
royalty. I've got WYD and plenty of ammo.

Originally, I thought Slade was talking about a love nest
meeting in Watts, which is in South Central. Now I knew he
was talking about Dante Watts and the missing performance
fees and royalties.

As I sat in the hospital waiting room, scrolling the e-mails on
Chooch's computer, I realized that every communiqué was
carefully worded to look like a love letter that cleverly disguised its true content. They detailed what Slade had learned in
Stacy Maluga's bedroom and at Lethal Force, Inc.

I reached into my pocket and pulled out Pryce Patterson's
business card, with Lionel Wright's phone number written on
the back. I dialed and waited.

"Residence," a soft female voice answered. I recognized
Patch McKenzie's cultured English accent. I wondered what
she was doing at his house. She was certainly beautiful enough
to interest a hip-hop mogul. "It's Shane Scully," I said.

"Oh, we're so glad to finally hear from you. I'll pop off and
get Lionel. I know he wants to talk to you." And I was on hold.

She called him Lionel, not Mr. Wright. I suspected my guess
was correct. After a moment, Lionel came on the line.

"What up, dog?"

"Thanks for bailing me out. You didn't have to do that."

"You didn't have to save my life in that theater."

"We need to meet."

"Solid."

"You're still in a lot of danger. I can't talk over this phone. I
don't trust it. I have a six o'clock meeting I can't miss, then I'll
be over. What's your address?"

"Thirty-four-fifty Bel Air Drive."

"I'll see you around seven, maybe a few minutes before."

After I disconnected I sat on the couch outside Neurosurgery and waited. It was only four o'clock. I had time to leave messages for Rosey Rosencamp and Dario Chikaleckio. I also called Tommy Sepulveda.

"I'm making progress," I told him. "Keep your cell phone on."

Then I sat back and closed my eyes. I knew that my current blessings finally outweighed all my early disappointments. The dark, lonely past had been erased by a family full of love and, more important, optimism for my future. But now I was teetering again on the edge of desperation.

These last few days, I'd been having two visions of Alexa. In one, she was my beautiful wife, loving and smart. The person with whom I'd be blessed to spend the rest of my days. She was always entertaining, because even though she lived by a strict moral code, she was extremely creative, and inside that code was often able to surprise me. In this first vision, I was a grinning, dopey, lottery winner who couldn't comprehend the depth of my good fortune.

Then there was the second, darker vision. Alexa was lying inert on an operating table with half of her skull open, her scalp unattached, breathing through tubes attached to hissing pumps and machines. In this vision, she was lost in the vagaries of a vicious head trauma, asleep in a sea of anesthesia from which she might never be rescued. Worse still, there was nothing I could do but sit here with this damn computer on my lap and fight for her reputation, which, if things went wrong, she would never need again.

I kept bouncing back and forth between these two visions, unable to find a good place to stand, knowing the first vision was just a memory, while the latter was a tragic reality. I could deal with neither and was spinning uselessly in my own grease.

Chooch returned a little before six and Luther showed up exactly on time. The meeting was short.

"She's still stable," Luther said. "Her heart and respiratory system are normal, but she is still on the respirator. Right now, I'm afraid to disconnect any of her life support, so we have to wait and see. You guys should get out of here. Sleeping in this room doesn't help Alexa. Eventually, the press is gonna find a way past hospital security and you don't need any more negative press. I'll call you if anything changes."

"I'm not leaving," Chooch said quickly.

I didn't want to leave either, but knew I had to.

"Suit yourself," Luther said to Chooch. There was a distinct chill coming off him.

"Luther, thanks for everything you're doing," I said, trying to make peace.

"Yeah," he said softly, but the next thing he uttered told me his anger was directed at himself and not at me. He suddenly looked down at his hands. "God's tools, I used to call these." He shoved them deep into his pockets. "Maybe your friend is right. Maybe I'm just a crazy Jim Crow nigga after all."

CHAPTER FIFTY-FOUR

I drove up Sunset Boulevard into an orange sun, then turned onto Bellagio Road and followed it up into the hills past the Bel Air Country Club until I hit Bel Air Road. The houses here are among the most expensive in Los Angeles—large mansions, some with fairway views. Lionel Wright's house was not visible from the street, concealed behind an exotic seven-foot hedge that was full of thorns and stickers, which ran for half a block before ending at a massive gate. There were no initials, just twenty or more golden-tipped wrought-iron spears that pointed skyward and looked impossible to scale without risking castration. I rang the buzzer and announced myself. Then, feeling like Goofy entering the Magic Kingdom, I watched while the magnificent gates swung wide allowing me to proceed.

The drive wound into a beautiful property surrounding an elegant, white wood-framed Georgian mansion, atop two tiers of rolling lawns. The residence looked to be around twenty thousand square feet with a sloping, cantilevered roof that shaded a large, Southern-style front porch. I pulled up under a porte cochere at the side of the house and got out, carrying my briefcase. Apparently, Lionel had reconsidered and was using the Fruit of Islam for personal security after all, because stone-faced Elijah Mustafa was waiting for me, still sporting a tan Kufi hat and a fifty-yard stare. He checked me for weapons, found I was unarmed, then looked inside my briefcase, which contained Chooch's laptop.

"Hey, dog, what it be like?" I said as he rummaged, trying to see which way he'd bounce.

"This way, please." Nothing.

He closed the case, handed it back, and turned, showing me his broad back. Then he led me toward the house. We went up some stairs and through the side door into a huge reception area. The sun was low on the horizon, and a high cloud cover had turned the light in the entry red-gold as it slanted through garden windows.

A very pleasant-looking, slightly plump, sixty-year-old African-American woman wearing a simple dress, expensive jewelry, and a red-brown shoulder-length wig was waiting for us in the massive, Tara-like entry hall. She offered me a wide smile and warm greeting.

"I'm Justine Lemon," she said, extending her hand. "God bless you, son. You saved Orlee's life."

"Lionel's mother?" I asked. The guy had so many names, it was hard to know which one to use when addressing her.

She smiled at me and nodded. "Finally back from my addictions and demons, thanks to our Lord Jesus."

"Amen," Elijah Mustafa said softly. It seemed a strange thing for a Muslim to say.

"Come in, please. Come in. Let's not just stand here in this drafty entryway. Orlee is in his office."

She led me to a sweeping circular staircase and we began to climb to the second floor. When we reached the landing, I saw a glass door that led to another wing on the west side of the house. The door was etched with the white letters WYD.

Unlike his sterile white-on-white office on Ventura, Lionel Wright's home was done in rich, antebellum colors. The interior design was classic and magnificent, as warm and textured as the office was cold and austere. Expensive turn-of-the-century paintings hung in lighted, recessed alcoves all along the upstairs hallway.

I guess I was gawking because Justine Lemon said, "She's a peach, ain't she?" smiling at my reaction, then added proudly, "The writer Sidney Sheldon used to live here." She pointed to the glass doors. "Wrote his novels in that wing where Orlee does his music now."

She opened the glass door, and with Mustafa trailing us like a cold, dark planet we entered Lionel Wright's inner sanctum. The long corridor leading to the music suite was festooned with gold and platinum records and music-industry awards. We reached an office the size of a basketball half-court. Vondell Richmond and Taylor Hays were waiting near the door and Vonnie nodded at me in a semi-friendly greeting. Whatever I had done at the El Rey Theatre seemed to have earned their respect.

"'Sup, homes," Vondell said.

"How you doing, Vonnie?" I replied, as if we were buds.

I looked at Taylor Hays, who now smiled thinly in return. It was the first actual sign of recognition he'd ever shown me.

Across the room, talking on the phone, sat Lionel Wright. He was in jeans and a wife-beater tank, showing off a cut physique and arm muscles that bulged. He stood, took off his headset and handed it to Patch, who was looking especially good this afternoon in a short, cropped top and skintight jeans. I definitely preferred these people in this less formal environment.

"Come on in, Shane," Lionel said graciously, crossing to me. He reached out and gave me a dap.

I'm not good at soul grips because I'm so used to shaking hands the old-fashioned way. I always get it wrong and it comes off awkward. After fumbling the handshake, we stood there smiling.

"That was righteous, what you did for me last night," Lionel said.

Since I couldn't remember exactly what I'd done, I explained that problem and ended by saying, "I only remember diving into the elevator and getting stomped."

Lionel filled me in on what happened, explaining that I'd jerked him to the floor and saved his life before I dove at the

two Sixtieth Street G's, knocking them backward and foiling
their assassination attempt. As he spoke, flashes of that event
filled my head, completing most of the lost memory. He explained that the two bangers had managed to get away in the
midst of the riot, but something told me that was B.S. It seemed
more likely that they were taking a dirt nap somewhere.

Then Lionel turned to Vondell, Taylor, and Mustafa. "Could
you guys help Mama hang those new paintings? I've got some
business here with the detective." Not wanting, I guess, to expose his mother to the grittier aspects of the hip-hop music
business.

Mrs. Lemon smiled at me and again said, "God bless." Then
she, Mustafa, and the two leg-breakers exited the room, leaving
only Patch to witness what came next.

Once they were gone I said, "Thanks for the bail. It meant a
lot. I needed to be at UCLA, and without that cash, I wouldn't
have made it."

"Your wife?" Lionel said. "How's she doing?"

"I'm not sure."

He gave that a moment's thought, then turned and moved
back toward his desk, which sat near a wall of windows. The
house sat on a hill with a gorgeous view overlooking much of
West L.A.

"You said something about me being in danger. I appreciate
the concern, but in my work you usually either end up kissing
somebody or dissing somebody. Right now it seems I got some
twelve-gauges bustin', but I'm used to it 'cause I been at risk
since I was fifteen. Best way to stop my shine is to get police involved."

Patch shifted slightly. She finally moved over and sat on the
sofa where she began to study me closely.

"There were some e-mails on my wife's computer," I began.
"They were disguised to look like love letters." I then pro-
ceeded to tell him about David Slade being planted inside
Lethal Force by the LAPD, and how he'd been sending information to Alexa via computer. I ended by saying, "I think that's
what got him murdered."

"That still doesn't answer how the Malugas found out Curtis

was switching labels," Lionel said. "Nobody but me, Curtis, Patch, and now you know about that."

"Somebody from Floor Score may have let it slip," Patch said. "Curtis is a blowhard. He's got no street smarts, despite his upbringing. I never felt good about him keeping quiet." Then she added, "If Maluga knows, then those twenty songs are gonna be a problem."

"What twenty songs?" I asked.

"Floor Score has recorded twenty songs that nobody knows about except the Malugas, and now me," Lionel said. "They're unreleased. That's enough for two new Curtis Clark albums. The way the copyright laws are written, the songs belong to the publishing house that holds the artist's contract at the time of his death. That means if Curtis dies before he switches labels, Lethal Force has the copyright on two posthumous platinum albums worth at least thirty million in sales, plus they'll never end up paying Curtis his disputed fees and royalties."

Nobody had to express what we all were thinking. Thirty million dollars and a label defection was certainly a good enough murder motive for a pair of psychopaths like the Malugas.

"Since he went to prison, Lou and Stacy have been marginalized," Lionel said. "Now that he's out, he's trying to rehabilitate his ghetto rep. The man's focused on all the wrong things—one week he's throwing charity banquets in Malibu, tryin' to make nice with L.A.'s movers and shakers, next week he's in some dust-up at a concert, threatening somebody's life. Worse still, he took his eyeballs off his arts."

I raised my eyebrows and Patch explained, "Artists."

"Right. And the acts don't like it," Lionel added.

"For instance, Curtis is annoyed because Lethal Force's marketing is bad and he's not getting big movie deals like Fifty Cent and Ice Cube," Patch continued. "Hip-hop has become one big casting couch where everybody's trying to get a role in a movie. The Malugas fell behind that curve. WYD already has two film projects set up for Curtis in the fourth quarter of next year."

"You said you needed to show me something," Lionel said, cutting this off and changing the subject.

I opened my briefcase, removed the laptop and pulled up the last e-mail Slade had sent to Alexa. Lionel leaned over my shoulder to read it aloud.

" 'Dear Hambone: I guess it's over. If you don't come through by Sunday night, floor score is gonna RIP. Sorry you can't see the big issues, but that was always a problem for us. S.M. will be laying in the cut flippin' switches. Play it my way or I'll mess you up. It'll be an Oasis Award beat down with no-body left standing, especially the dude. We reap what we sow. Dark Angel.' "

Lionel finished reading and said, "What is this?"

I explained the code to him and read it aloud for them again.

" 'If you don't come through by Sunday night, floor score is gonna RIP.' Rest in peace," I added. " 'S.M. will be laying in the cut flippin' switches.' S.M. is Stacy Maluga."

Lionel nodded. "And 'flippin' switches' is street slang for shot-calling, running a criminal operation."

I read the rest aloud.

" 'It'll be an Oasis Award beat down with nobody left standing, especially the dude.' "

"I'm The Dude," Lionel said. "It was my baby G street handle. I hated it. Took me five years, but I finally plowed that under."

"They missed at the Oasis, but I don't think they're through trying," I said. "If they were going to try again, where would it be?"

It didn't take him long to answer.

"This Tuesday night at Mandalay Bay in Vegas," he said. "It's a WBO title fight between Lenny 'Lights Out' Moore and Austin Sugar. WYD Fight Management is promoting it. World press will be there, international news coverage. That's where Curtis Clark and I are gonna announce that Floor Score is leaving Lethal Force and switching labels."

"If I was you, I'd change my plans," I told him.

"I'm not running from the Malugas," he said, getting angry. "Rap's gotta be more than just niggas wearing fresh Bally kicks and gold chains getting their heads shot off. Rap is a street corner conversation, which right now represents fifteen percent of the entire music market. That's billions. So if the Malugas wanta step up and work it, then my message to them is bring it on, baby. I'm out here every day."

CHAPTER FIFTY-FIVE

We met in my backyard in Venice. It was three o'clock the following afternoon. Rafie and Tommy both reread the last e-mail from Alexa's computer, while Rosey and Dario stood in the afternoon heat contemplating the sunlight reflecting silver-white off the mirror-flat water in the still Venice canals. Sally Quinn sat in a lawn chair, fanning herself with a handful of gang intel reports. She had been very quiet since arriving ten minutes ago. I had a strong feeling she was busy reevaluating our potential partnership. I had already run all of my theories by everyone here and I wasn't getting much in the way of positive feedback.

"Tell me again, what we're supposed to do about all this?" Tommy finally asked, after he finished reading the edited messages for the second time.

"Shane is looking for backup," Rosencamp interjected. "He thinks we're gonna be his posse." He was showing me a game face that I couldn't read at all.

"Except these rappers all have their own private security," he continued. "We ain't gonna get close 'cause cops make these dirtbags nervous. 'Less they're dirty cops. Which we ain't."

"The whole thing comes down to street cred," I countered. "Lionel doesn't want to look weak to his own people, so despite the threat, he won't cancel this event. He intends to go to Vegas and make the announcement tonight as planned. I'm pretty sure the Malugas are gonna do everything they can to stop it. Lethal Force can't take another big defection like Floor Score. It would signal weakness; other acts would bolt. Everything is on the line for them. That's why I think they have to make a careless, violent statement. They have a financial motive as well."

Then I told everyone about the twenty songs that Curtis had already recorded and how much money was at stake. When I finished, they were all quiet.

"Who handles Lionel Wright's security?" Rafie asked.

"He's got some personal bodyguards and he's contracted Fruit of Islam. They're good, but the event is at the Mandalay Bay and that makes it tougher. According to Elijah Mustafa at FOI, most Vegas casinos don't allow any firearms inside. They make all of their patrons go through metal detectors. But Mandalay Bay is an exception. They don't use metal detectors or wands. They're on the honor system, so it's safe to assume that all the principal players in Lionel's party, plus any hitters the Malugas send are gonna be packing."

"Are you actually asking us to show up in Vegas and join a parade of armed street G's so we can save some rap asshole's life?" Dario asked.

It was the first thing he'd said since he'd shown up here half an hour ago. He was in off-duty clothes and his blue golf shirt was stretched tight against his impressive weight lifter's body. "Slade was a bad cop. How can we trust anything that dirtbag wrote in these e-mails?"

"David Slade wasn't who any of us thought he was." I filled them in on what I'd learned—about Slade's dangerous UC assignment and how the department had set up all the road-rage complaints and the 911 call. I knew that OJB had been concerned about him and the effect he had on all their reputations. I speculated that when this information clearing his name was made public, it would be good for all of us.

"He was risking his life reporting back to Alexa," I concluded. "Slade worked UC for over two years. The guy sacrificed his reputation, his promotions, and ultimately his life. He was a hero, but Chief Filosiani's got his own game working. Alexa's in a coma and can't vouch for him, and I can't prove he wrote those Dark Angel e-mails, so unless we come through, I will never be able to prove she didn't kill him or that he spent two years risking his life to bust the Malugas."

The silence following that soliloquy hung in the afternoon heat like rotting fruit.

Rafie was still studying the e-mail. Finally, he closed the computer and looked at me.

"Forgetting for a minute that we don't have an ounce of jurisdiction in Nevada, and forgetting that if we go proactive out there, this could spark up into the mother of all gang wars, tell me again how we're supposed to protect Lionel Wright and Curtis Clark." Rafie leaned back and continued. "'Cause I agree with Rosencamp. If Lionel or Curtis start traveling around with a bunch of off-duty cops, they look like pussies. That's why those guys all use FOI Security. It's perfect for them because they get good protection, but Fruit of Islam is outside the system. It fits with the gangsta image and flips off the straights. Those two won't let us anywhere near this."

"I can get us in," I said. "The guy owes me. I can make us part of his entourage."

They all looked at me like I was smoking something.

Then Rosey looked at his watch. "It's three now. If we was actually gonna do this dumb-ass job, how long do we have to get our act together?"

"Lionel is flying to Vegas on his private jet at five this afternoon. They're having a security meeting in the hangar before take-off in an hour. I want us to be there."

As they all continued staring at me, I realized that everybody was thinking it was just this kind of behavior that had filled up my 181 file at PSB and got me in so much trouble over the years.

Rosey finally spoke. "I can't expose the other OJB members to something like this."

"You guys are my only hope," I said and then turned to Tommy. "I thought you said you and Rafie wanted to solve this case. I guess what you meant was you were looking for a safe way to solve it."

"That's not fair, Shane," Tommy said. I could tell I'd hurt his feelings.

Then Sally Quinn stood, and my heart sank. She was my partner and if she turned on me, they all would. Her freckled schoolgirl face looked solemnly toward us. "Who ever promised police work was gonna be all neat and tidy?" she said. "I love this department. We're all members of an exclusive club that is totally getting pissed on right now. Extraordinary times demand extraordinary measures. I think we should do what Shane suggested and take a flyer here. What's one trip to Vegas, more or less? At least this time, you guys won't lose any money or get the clap."

I could have kissed her.

Rafie stood next. "I'll go," he said.

"Okay," Rosey said. "But only me and Dario, if he agrees."

Dario took a moment, but then shook his head. "My dad told me to go into the grocery business 'cause people always gotta eat. I chose police work 'cause people also gotta have protectors who enforce the rules. I live by the rules. I believe in them. I can't do this, man. I won't blow ya in, but I can't go along either."

I told him I understood. Then we all watched in silence as he got to his feet and left my yard by the back gate. He walked slowly down the canal path and around the corner to where his squad car was parked.

"I guess that means all the rest of us are in," Tommy said, and one by one they all nodded. I walked inside and grabbed my last back-up piece. It was an S&W Airlight revolver which I kept locked up in my gun safe in the living room. The rest of them followed me into the house and watched as I clipped the fifteen-ounce round-wheel onto my belt.

"Thanks," I said, feeling a wave of gratitude.

"I'm not doing it for you," Rosey said. "I'm doing it for my friend, Alexa." Then, because that sounded so sentimental, he pointed at the small thirty-eight riding my hip and quickly added, "If that's your version of firepower, we're gonna be seriously outgunned. I hate gettin' in a face down with a Crip crew that's packin' choppers. All we got is department-issue iron and a pocket full of light loads."

"I know where we can pick up some heavy firepower," I said.

We left Venice in four cars with red lights flashing, sped down the 405 Freeway and made a quick run through Compton, where I shimmied through the broken back window of the house on Cypress. Once inside, I retrieved David Slade's fully automatic AR-70 from the deep recesses of his bedroom closet.

CHAPTER FIFTY-SIX

On the way to Van Nuys Airport I called Chooch at the hospital. He told me that Alexa's condition was unchanged and that Luther still wanted to keep her on life support, which didn't sound to me like a very good sign. I told Chooch where I was going and what I was trying to do.

"Dad, be careful," he warned. "I can't lose you both."

"Don't worry. You won't lose either of us," I said, knowing that promise would be out of my hands as soon as I hit Las Vegas.

"Mom's gonna make it, isn't she?" Chooch sounded lost. It was as if he'd become a little kid again, holding on to a desperate hope. Hearing him like that almost broke my heart. I told him I didn't know, that it was in God's hands. Then I said I loved him and, after a few empty promises, hung up. It was hard for Chooch being caught in limbo like this. Hard for both of us not to know what was waiting for us in the weeks ahead. So much depended on Alexa's survival. I tried to get my mind off these troubling thoughts and focus on the danger that lay only hours ahead in Vegas.

When I glanced in my rearview mirror, I could see Rafie and Tommy's maroon Crown Vic in the diamond lane, tracking behind me followed by Rosey's blue Toyota and Sally Quinn in a brown department plain wrap.

Several times during the last few days, I'd been wondering about Insane Wayne Watkins and the note he had written in blood that had saved my life. Rafie had told me outside of Stacy's mansion that he didn't know where Watkins came from. That he was new. Maybe it was time to find out. I radioed dispatch and ran him. He came back empty.

"Maybe Wayne Watkins is an alias," I said to the RTO. "Run me a deep cover check and get in touch with gang intel. Maybe he's in the gang book under his street handle, Insane Wayne."

I gave the operator my cell call-back number and hung up, looking for my off ramp. Lionel had given me specific directions to the airport, instructing me to exit the freeway at Roscoe Boulevard and go to Aviation. I was to look for a Syncro Aircraft Interiors sign and turn left toward the field. From there he told me to proceed to the Syncro facility located at the end of the drive next to the runway. FOI security would check me through. I had informed Lionel earlier that I might bring a few people with me. He hadn't told me the size of his plane, or how many people he was bringing. The only information I had was the tail number: November-25-Lima. I hoped he would have enough room for all of us.

I spotted the Syncro sign and turned as directed, pulling up to a field gate. After giving an airport guard our names and the tail number, he opened up and waved all four cars through.

We pulled up in front of Syncro, which was housed in a series of factory-style, bow-truss buildings that looked like they'd been built during World War II. Elijah Mustafa and two of his tan-suited, hat-wearing brothers were waiting. They glared impassively, as always. I wondered if they had classes at FOI where they practiced that look in front of a mirror.

I waved at Mustafa, who ignored my greeting, so I parked, pulled the case containing the Beretta AR-70 out of my trunk, and walked toward the building. He grabbed my arm as I passed and pulled me back.

"Whoa, whoa, whoa," he said. "Where you going? Whatta ya got there?"

Sally, Rosey, Tommy, and Rafie were out of their cars and in a similar face-down with his other two stone-faced guards.

"This guy doesn't really think he's gonna pat me down," Rosey said, looking at the man in front of him. At six-foot-four, weighing at least two-fifty, Rosencamp towered over the FOI guard. "You best step off, little brother."

"We've got strict orders to check people we don't know for guns," Mustafa said softly. "Open that case."

"Let's not go down this road," I said. "These guys are all LAPD. We're not gonna get shook down like a bunch a street G's at a concert. Make an exception."

It was a tense situation until Mustafa reconsidered. He nodded to his two guys and they stepped away from us.

"Let's go," I said, and we headed into the building.

Once inside, I could see why Elijah Mustafa chose this place. There was a large, narrow hallway that led to an airplane hangar in the back. One way in, one way out—a perfect layout to control security. The walls were lined with photographs of plush airplane interiors that Syncro had installed. Through an open door I saw long upholstery tables where airplane seats were waiting to be covered in fire-retardant, FAA-approved fabric that someone once told me cost thousands of dollars per yard. The building had been cleared of all employees, so no one was working.

We entered a vast enclosed hangar. The floor space was painted shiny white and the building interior was as sterile as an operating room. In the center of the hangar sat a huge, snow-white Boeing Business Jet, a corporate 737. It had been foolish to wonder about passenger accommodations because the plane was large enough to carry a college marching band. Painted on the jet's tail in gold letters trimmed in black was N-25-L.

Rosey came up behind me and whispered in my ear. "Nobody but an asshole would pick a jail sentence for a tail number."

He was right—25 with an L was known throughout the criminal justice system as a twenty-five-year-to-life sentence. The lunacy of that was underlined by the fact that the rapper Snoop Dogg had been the first one to coin the phrase.

A group of about twenty well-dressed men and women were clustered under the wing of the jet. The mostly African-

American men were all done up in Melrose fashions. The women were of various shades and sizes. Beautiful and sexy, they all looked straight from the Victoria's Secret catalog. White seemed to be the color of the day. Aside from the jet, Lionel Wright was dressed in a white tux. Holding his arm and looking spectacular in a glittering, white sequined mini-dress was Patch McKenzie. Lionel spotted me and broke away from her, his heels echoing on the hard shiny floor as he approached.

"That's some posse you got, brother," he said, looking at Rosey, Tommy, and Rafie. "Gonna have t' bag you boys some bitches." Right now he hardly sounded like a guy with a business school degree. He was in his Bust A Cap persona, talking street. I introduced him to everybody. When I got to Sally Quinn he said, "Okay, this is working." Grinning at her, using a wide, bad boy smile. Getting some swerve on.

As he reached for her hand, Sally took it and said, "Watch where you try and put that, 'cause I'm packin'."

"I like this girl," Lionel laughed.

Just then, Elijah Mustafa called for attention.

Everyone fell quiet. When Elijah spoke, people seemed to listen. He never cursed or used slang. That was part of his quiet force.

"I'm Elijah Mustafa, with Fruit of Islam Security," he began. "We've been hired by Mr. Wright to guarantee your safety at this event tonight." Everyone stayed very quiet to hear him because he had barely raised his voice. "We believe that Mr. Clark and Mr. Wright may be in some danger. I know that some of you are aware of this fact and have brought weapons. I won't embarrass us all and attempt to take them away from you, but I'm asking you to please, leave them behind in your vehicles and let us take care of your safety. The flight to Las Vegas is approximately forty-five minutes. We will land at McCarran International at the executive jet terminal. After we deplane, ground transportation will be provided by the Fruit of Islam and will consist of twelve well-trained men and a caravan of ten Navigators—enough for all of us. Once we are in the hotel parking structure we want everyone to stay in the SUVs until my team can clear a secure path into the pre-party being held at the Mandalay Bay Hotel, in the Foundation Room of the House of Blues.

"Fruit of Islam security personnel will all be wearing hats similar to mine." He pointed at his African Kufi. "Please bring any concerns or observations regarding security to our attention and do not attempt to deal with them yourself. Anything you want to add, Mr. Wright?"

Lionel smiled and then announced loudly, "Everybody, we're here to have a party. So like Elijah said, leave your pistols and choppers in your cars and let's all go to the bang." This was followed by cheers and a smattering of applause. It wasn't lost on me that nobody went back to his car to ditch a weapon.

I spotted Curtis Clark standing with a small group of admirers over by the boarding stairs to the plane. He was scowling, his normal expression.

Lionel turned to me. "Listen, cuz, despite all the drama here, I'm askin' you not to bag up on any half-loads tonight."

"Do what?" I said, wondering what he was getting at.

"The man is telling us there's gonna be drugs," Rosey clarified. "He don't wanta face no twelve-ten prosecutions."

"Don't worry," I said. "I've got priorities here. Besides, once we get out of California, my badge doesn't work anyway."

He slapped me on the shoulder and everyone began to board the plane.

The BBJ comfortably accommodated thirty. The jet was divided into three main seating groups and there was a separate owner's suite in the tail, complete with a queen-sized bed and a bathroom with a stand-up shower. Two caterers were busy working in the forward galley, serving food and drinks. The interior decor was lush. The cabin was outfitted with gray, dove leather club chairs, long, tufted sofas, and mahogany and gold tray tables that lifted effortlessly out of wall pockets. As the plane filled, laughter and conversation surrounded me.

I found myself somewhere in the middle of the cabin in a seating group of club chairs with Rosey and Sally. I'd lost sight of Rafie and Tommy when we boarded, but then saw them sitting with four exotic-looking women near the front of the plane.

"Anything to drink before takeoff?" a beautiful Asian flight attendant asked, leaning down and favoring me with a whiff of designer perfume.

"Beer," I said. "Heineken, if you have it."

"We have a full bar menu." Then, hoping to upgrade my tragically blue collar order, she added, "We have a fresh supply of Alizé I could recommend. It's a French beverage that Mr. Wright stocks. It's quite an expensive aperitif made from passion fruit and cognac."

"As much as I love passion fruit, I think I'll stick with the Heineken."

The flight attendant frowned and hurried away to get my order. "I think you ruined her perfect day," Sally said.

The plane was pulled from the hangar by a tug. Once we were out of the building, the engines fired and five minutes later we were thundering down the runway and lifting up into a smoggy, late afternoon sky. People all around me chatted and laughed. They sipped exotic drinks made with passion fruit and cognac. Sally, Rosey, and I sat quietly, contemplating the trip we were embarking on, pondering the insanity that had brought us here. The black case containing David Slade's AR-70 rested ominously at my feet.

CHAPTER FIFTY-SEVEN

My little guy is just starting T-ball," Sally Quinn was saying. Rosey had gone to the head, and my partner's freckled face lit up by degrees as our conversation segued to her youngest son. "The Valley homicide unit was great for a soccer mom, because it's a light division and the rotation is slow, so I could swap out hours and still drive carpools."

I saw where this was heading. "You want, we can stay flexible—as long as you don't stick me with all the autopsies," I said.

She smiled and patted my hand. "I wasn't looking for that, Shane. Just worried about missing games. I'll handle my end. You don't have to worry." She turned and looked out the window of the expensive jet. "I gotta hand you this much," she said. "This is a much sexier gig. Sure beats working dust-buster beatdowns in the Valley."

Then a shadow fell over me. I looked up and saw Elijah Mustafa standing in the aisle.

"You got a minute for me, Mister Scully?" His voice was soft and his expression stoic as always.

"Sure." I stood and followed him into the empty bedroom suite in the rear of the plane. He closed the door and turned to face me.

"What's in the black case?" he said without preamble.

"Jammies."

"What caliber jammies?" Not smiling.

"Look, Elijah, I'm not here to cause trouble. I'm here to prevent it. I hope you'll realize soon that we're on the same side."

"Mister Scully—"

"Detective Scully," I corrected, trying for some status.

"This trip is a big problem," he went on. "Most of the men on this flight are street G's. Mister Wright tells me they're his friends, and since I'm his temporary employee, I must take him at his word. I've done my best to check them out, but he has instructed me to walk lightly because as you know, insults to honor can turn deadly."

"You're in a tough business," I said.

"Yes, I am." He favored me with another of his long, penetrating stares before adding, "So I ask you again, what kind of fire stick are you lugging around in that bag?"

"Beretta-seventy with two thirty-round clips."

"Not exactly a close combat piece. Kinda hard to open fire with a full machine gun inside a populated casino. That gun is at best useless, at worst dangerous. You look smarter than that to me."

"I'll make you a deal. We'll leave it in the Navigator after we get to the Mandalay Bay. However, if something happens out on city streets, you may be glad we have it."

He gave it some thought, then finally nodded. "Can you hit anything with it?" he asked.

"Let's hope we don't have to find out." Then, to get his mind off it, I said, "Why don't you tell me which of these people you're worried about and I'll put a call in to the department from one of these air phones and see what comes back."

"I'm worried about all of them," he said. "Given what happened at the Oasis Awards, I'm looking for anybody who has an affiliation with those Sixtieth Street G's. Here's the passenger manifest." He reached into his pocket and handed me a sheet of paper. "How long will it take?" he asked.

"Ten, fifteen minutes."

Then he said, "That was good work at the El Rey Theatre.

My people missed those two in the elevator. We almost walked into it."

"Thank you for the compliment, Mister Mustafa."

"It was only an observation," he said softly, but a smile so slight it was barely there, bent the edges of his stony expression.

I split the list with Rosey. Mustafa cleared two separate phones and we adjourned to the bedroom suite and closed the door to start running names. All fifteen men on the flight checked out—mostly they were old homies of Lionel along with some music biz types and one or two poser wannabes, but no Sixtieth Street G's. I reported this to Mustafa, who nodded but said nothing.

We touched down at McCarran, and with the engines roaring in retrograde, the plane slowed quickly, then made a turn toward the east end of the tarmac where the small corporate jet center was located. The BBJ taxied to a stop at the end of a line of executive jets and the engines shut down. While our party of gun-toting, jewelry-encrusted fight fans waited, Mustafa hurried down the boarding stairs and walked the short distance to the flight center.

A few minutes later, I watched from the window as a line of ten black Navigators drove onto the field and pulled to a stop on the left side of the plane.

After we walked down the exit stairs, I found myself standing with Lionel and Patch near one of the vehicles.

"Why don't you ride with us?" Lionel said. "Mustafa tells me you've got a street sweeper in that bag there. Never hurts to come prepared."

We got into the first SUV with Lionel. Elijah Mustafa was behind the wheel with another FOI security man in the far back. Curtis Clark and two attractive women I didn't know got in last, filling seven of the eight seats in the lead car. I had met with my group and we had agreed to split up and spread out. I watched out the back window as Rosey and Sally got in an SUV in the middle of the caravan and Rafie and Tommy boarded the last one in line. Once everyone was inside, the ten vehicles drove slowly off the tarmac, a metallic centipede of shiny black Navigators. Then we passed through the side gate of the executive jet terminal and out onto the city streets of Las Vegas.

"The pre-party starts in ten minutes," Lionel announced from the passenger side of the front seat. "Mustafa wants to come in the back way for security, so we're taking Paradise Road, then doubling back to the Las Vegas Strip."

Curtis Clark had settled in the second row and was glowering insolently. "If that busta and his white mama try doggin' me out, I'm gonna buck down on his ass. Them two is gonna curl up like bitches."

I glanced at him, but I didn't see any danger in his opaque eyes. He was just scared and talking trash.

We rolled past the shiny new Wynn Las Vegas, a fifty-story sliver of glass, and Mustafa turned the lead vehicle onto the strip leading our motorcade toward the Mandalay Bay Hotel. A skyline of memorable building profiles passed outside our smoked glass windows: Harrah's, the MGM Grand, the Luxor, with its Sphinx and Egyptian pyramid motif. We were hardly sneaking into town. Our showy procession was turning heads all up and down the glittering strip.

Then the glass-fronted, forty-three-story Mandalay Bay Hotel appeared out the front windshield half a block away. We turned into the underground parking structure and started down the ramp to the sub-basement where there was a secure entrance, which Mustafa had chosen in advance. Our line of black Navigators pulled up in front of four new Kufi hat–wearing security men.

Mustafa turned to look in at us. "Local brothers," he said, pointing at the men who, true to form, were all wearing NSA-style earpieces. "Stay here until I check the downstairs corridor." Then he exited the vehicle as Curtis Clark took off his blue Floor Score baseball cap and stuffed it in the seat pocket.

The tension in the car grew. Everybody knew that once we got out and headed into the hotel, there would be a million sight lines and no turning back. Several minutes later, Mustafa returned with a Las Vegas police sergeant.

"Okay," he said. "All clear. This is Sergeant Bowman with

the Las Vegas Metropolitan Police. He's in charge of the law enforcement contingent."

As promised, I left the street sweeper under the backseat of the Navigator and followed Lionel and the rest of his party into the Mandalay Bay Hotel.

CHAPTER FIFTY-EIGHT

The fluorescent lights lit the basement corridor as the footsteps of thirty people echoed against its hard, cold surfaces. We passed extra chairs and stage flats stacked in alcoves. It felt gray and claustrophobic down here. Everybody, even the hardened street G's, had stopped talking. After walking for almost two hundred yards under the mammoth hotel, we stopped at a freight elevator and Elijah Mustafa turned to face the crowd.

"This leads up to the main level," he said. "Then we will have to make a short trip through the kitchen and across the casino floor to another elevator that leads to the Foundation Room at the House of Blues. I don't expect trouble and our people have been screening upstairs, but it's a large casino and it's impossible to check everyone. If something goes down, one of us will yell 'Ragtime.' If you hear that word, scatter. Make your way back down to this place. There will be security positioned here to help you."

"I'm sorry about all this," Lionel said. "But after what happened at the Oasis Awards, I don't want to lose anybody. Just stick close together."

"It's cool," a street G called out. "I got this savage life down, brotha." Nervous laughter followed.

There were about fifteen tan hats standing around, and when the elevator arrived and the door opened, it was easy to see it wasn't going to be large enough to handle all of us at one time. The first glitch in Mustafa's plan.

"We're going to have to make two trips," he said, unfazed. "Half will stay behind with Mohammed Sayid."

A tall, muscular FOI security guard raised his hand and people started to divide up into two groups. Mustafa put his hand on my arm and pulled me into the first elevator.

"Stick with us," he said. Maybe I was beginning to grow on the guy.

Sally Quinn and Rafie also made the first group. We were wedged in there with Lionel and Patch, Vonnie, and ten party guests.

Then the wood slat door was pulled down and the elevator started up.

As we approached the first floor, I could hear pans banging and people talking. We got out into a large pantry area where a dozen men, mostly Hispanics, wearing red coats, were filling food trays. Mustafa sent the elevator back down for the second group.

I looked into the kitchen at a dozen more people working on food orders. I wondered if Mustafa's people had checked them all.

"I don't like this," I said to Sally, who had moved up next to me. She nodded and clutched her handbag, which I knew had her thirty-eight police special inside.

Then Rafie whispered in my ear. "I'm gonna stay toward the back, cover us from behind."

I nodded at him and he separated from Sally and me. Our four remaining FOI security guards stood on the perimeter of the group watching everything, their eyes on the kitchen workers. The elevator returned with the second group.

The rest of the party joined us and started milling around in the busy food-staging area. Everyone seemed to sense the danger and was wearing different versions of the same tight smile.

Then our group of thirty, with ten guards herding us, headed out of the kitchen and into the casino's main area for the short trip across the casino gaming floor to the Foundation Room elevator. This was the most dangerous section of the journey. Once we got upstairs, we would have better control.

I could see Mustafa in front, talking quietly into a small lapel mike. Rosey, Rafie, Tommy, Sally, and I had split up again and were spread out as we moved along, trying to provide as much perimeter security as possible. Slots rang loudly, and occasional winners shrieked in joy. All of us, hardened street G's included, snapped our heads with each shrill noise. Then the gamblers on the first floor started to notice the strange procession making its way across the casino. A few shouted, "It's Bust A Cap!" or "There goes Curtis Clark from Floor Score!" People started surging toward us. I hoped they were just autograph seekers.

Halfway across the floor, somebody caught my eye. He was tall with light black skin and braided cornrows. As we neared, he spun away from the slot machine he was playing, and I could then see an under-shot jaw. Half of his left ear was missing. It was DeShawn Brodie, aka Little Poison, from Croc Smith's crew. He lunged toward us, pulling something out of his coat. I couldn't see what it was, but wasn't about to take chances.

"Gun!" I shouted, and all hell broke loose. People started screaming and immediately, the Fruit of Islam closed ranks, grabbing Lionel and Curtis, shielding them from danger. Two other FOI guards dove forward and grabbed Little Poison, throwing him to the floor. The room was a spinning mass of confusion. Some in our group were trying for the exits, others were starting to pull weapons.

Mustafa yelled, "Ragtime!" as they hustled Lionel and Curtis across the casino. I left Sally and Rafie, bolting after. All the while, I kept thinking something about this was wrong. The attempt by Brodie was clumsy. I began to wonder if DeShawn was only there to turn Lionel and Curtis, to get us heading back toward the kitchen where the real danger was. I hurried to catch up, pulling my Airlight revolver as I ran. By then, Mustafa and five of his security had already reached the pantry.

"Listen, something isn't right. Slow down a minute," I shouted. But Elijah Mustafa was too busy herding everybody into the freight elevator. I managed to push in with them. He got the door closed and we were heading down into the basement.

"We need to slow down," I said again.

"Bring up the car," Mustafa called into his radio mike to one of his drivers. "Pull it up at the entrance. We're coming out."

The elevator door opened and we were again moving fast, running back through the two-hundred-yard cement tunnel in a desperate flight toward the garage. Even though I thought we were making a mistake, I couldn't get Elijah's attention.

We arrived in the parking structure just as one of the black Navigators screeched to a stop nearby. There were two tan-suited Kufi hats in the front seats. Curtis piled in and I dove into the back seat next to Lionel. Just then I heard a rash of gunfire echo in the garage a few feet behind me.

I turned to see the obese shape of Crocodile Smith standing close, holding a MAC-10, still wearing his cool chrome shades, black wardrobe, and yellow crocs. As I turned, he knocked the Airlight revolver from my grasp using the barrel of his weapon. The gun flew from my hand. Then Smith fired again. Elijah Mustafa went down, his chest riddled with red.

"Go! Go! Go!" Lionel yelled at the driver, but the Navigator didn't move. Croc Smith jumped into the car and pulled the door shut.

"Git rollin'," he yelled, and only then did the SUV lurch away from the basement entrance.

When I looked toward the front seat, I saw that the FOI security guard on the passenger side was pointing an automatic weapon back at us.

"Once we're out, go right," Crocodile Smith ordered.

The Suburban powered up the one flight. It was then that I focused enough to realize that the gun-wielding FOI guard was KZ, one of Stacy Maluga's steroid twins from Malibu. The other one, Insane Wayne, was driving. They all threw their Kufi hats on the floor as the SUV shot out of the garage onto the street.

The Croc pointed his gun at Lionel and Curtis.

"You a couple a dead niggas," he said, angrily. For a moment, I was the only one in the car who didn't have a gun pointed at me. I was about to try something stupid when I felt cold steel touch the back of my skull. Somebody had risen up in the seat behind me and pushed what felt like a double-barrel shotgun against my head.

"Don't be a hero," the White Sister said.

CHAPTER FIFTY-NINE

The navigator turned right and headed out of town. I couldn't believe how brazen this kidnapping had been, and yet somehow, they'd pulled it off.

"You can't be serious with this," I said impotently. "It's never gonna work."

But something told me it would.

I saw Lionel out of the corner of my eye watching Croc Smith, who hadn't stopped glowering at him. His corpulent jowls were quivering with rage, finally ready to get even for the shooting at the Barn where his brother had died. He was seconds away from dropping us when Curtis started up.

"What's goin' on here?" he said, hysteria creeping into his voice. "This ain't right, mama." He was looking at Stacy, pleading with her.

"You best shut your punk-ass mouth, Curtis," Croc said. "Ain't about you. You just a pay down. It's about Orlee here." He glowered at Lionel. "Yours is finally comin', my brotha."

Despite his girth, I was surprised that Smith's voice was high-pitched, almost feminine. Even so, he was hard to ignore, holding a MAC-10, still dripping red with Elijah Mustafa's blow-back.

Curtis cranked around further in his seat toward Stacy.

"Mama, whatchu doin'? I thought we was pumpin' fresh."

"Croc, shut this fool up," she snapped.

Without warning, Smith backhanded Curtis, knocking him sideways into me.

"This ain't right," he whined.

I could see dismay and disbelief on his face. It had finally replaced his insolent glare. He couldn't believe Stacy was doing this to him.

"Come on," pleading now. "This shit ain't right. I didn't do nothing but what you told me. How come I get caught up in this?"

"You think I'd really cross Lou? I was setting you up, nigga. You and Lionel. Me and Lou played ya. Lotta shit gets settled tonight."

I looked into her savage blue eyes and I knew she was lying. I had too many pieces of the puzzle, I'd overheard too much on her pager. She was telling a different story to everyone. But I still couldn't see what her game was, so I kept quiet.

Curtis was starting to panic. I looked over at Lionel, who had a ghetto dead expression on his face, showing nothing.

"Mama, you can't be doing me this way," Curtis whined.

"Shut the fuck up, Curtis," Stacy hissed.

"Mama, your nigga had went to jail when we dropped the *Savage Bitch* album. When that went platinum, he kept taking his forty percent. The brotha was off doing his bit and still taking his ducats. You the one told me that wasn't right. You the one told me he was holding back my payments and such. Now you throw me under the bus? I don't get this. Whatchu be doin'?"

Stacy discharged one of her shotgun barrels into the back of the Navigator seat where Curtis was sitting. The seat ate up most of the bird shot, but some of the pellets got through and he screamed in pain as half a dozen riddled him. Blood started seeping out of the back of his shirt. I couldn't help but wonder why she had bird shot instead of double buckshot in the weapon. It had probably saved Curtis's life.

"Mama, come on. Mama, don't be doing me this way," he sputtered.

"Shut up, Curtis," she yelled. "I can't listen to no more a your whinin'."

I looked over at Lionel and saw that while he was as frightened as I was, he wasn't panicked. He caught my eye and raised an eyebrow in a "can you believe this?" expression.

The car rolled steadily out of Vegas, breaking no laws, moving with the flow of traffic. The Croc stayed hunkered in the well by the door with his gun trained on Curtis, who had finally been frightened into silence. Stacy stayed behind us in the back and reloaded the right barrel of her shotgun. This time I saw that she thumbed buckshot into the cut-down 12-gauge, known on the street as a ghetto stick. As we drove down the strip, the smoked windows on the black Navigator gave our kidnappers visual protection. People strolled the sidewalks in groups, going from one casino to another, completely unaware that a few feet away, three people were being held at gunpoint on their way to certain death.

I knew that sooner or later, I had to make a play. Then I looked at the seatback in front of me and spotted Curtis Clark's Floor Score baseball cap that he'd stuffed into that seat pocket before entering the Mandalay Bay. I suddenly realized this was the same car we'd ridden in on the drive from the airport.

I looked over at Lionel. His eyes were still on Crocodile Smith, but he felt my gaze and shot a look in my direction. I glanced down at the floor where I knew David Slade's Beretta AR-70 was wedged under the seat. I made a surreptitious gesture, miming a gun with my index finger, cocking my thumb back and forth. I glanced down again at the floor and then he nodded slightly.

Message received.

One of us had to get to that Beretta before Stacy, Wayne, KZ, or The Croc blew us to shreds.

Ten minutes later we were clear of downtown Vegas and heading up onto U.S. 95. There wasn't much I could do to get ready. Too much depended on geography and circumstances. I'd have to read the layout once we got there and make up my plan on the fly.

I knew it would be a long shot if I ever survived this, so I sat there and tried to prepare to die. I reasoned that if Alexa didn't make it, then at least I would be joining her. I told myself that Chooch could survive on his own now. He had his values in place. I tried to get comfortable with the idea that at least I could go to my death knowing that I had reclaimed myself—that I was finally a better person than I had started out to be. I told myself all of this, but underneath the logic, my survival instincts were churning. I just didn't want to die.

As we headed into the desert, I tried to fill in the rest of the pieces that had led to this. I had been right when I guessed Little Poison had just been in the casino as a diversion to send us all running toward the garage. Stacy, KZ, and Wayne had jumped the two FOI security guards who were watching the cars. They had relieved them of their tan hats and radios, then stolen the Navigator and pulled up as we ran out. Mustafa was shot in the chest and looked dead as he fell, so it seemed safe to assume that with him out of action, our FOI backup was trashed. If we were going to survive, it was up to Lionel and me. Curtis might lend a hand, but he looked pretty shaky.

Now we were speeding out of the city into the desert. The moon was high over the highway, glinting off the hood of the Navigator. Wayne continued driving at exactly the correct speed limit, obeying all traffic laws. After we passed a small shopping center, Stacy told him to make a right turn. We swung off the highway onto a narrow, two-lane desert road and Insane Wayne slowed the Navigator so he wouldn't overdrive the headlights.

We continued on for almost fifteen minutes, then lights flashed ahead of us in the dark, and Stacy motioned with her shotgun.

"Out there," she said. "See 'em? That's Lou. He's gonna follow us to the spot where I had the graves dug."

"Got it," Wayne said.

The SUV slowed and a black, four-wheel-drive Humvee pulled out and followed close behind us along the highway, its headlights illuminating the back of our heads.

After traveling for another ten minutes, Stacy pointed to a small desert road.

"Out there," she said.

Wayne turned the Navigator, and the Hummer followed. After about a mile the road ended and Stacy directed us to a spot in the desert where our headlights picked up three freshly dug graves.

Two armed Crips wearing blue do rags were waiting, still holding shovels. Their Hertz rental was parked a few feet away with its high beams illuminating the scene. We pulled to a stop and Smith opened the side door. When Lionel and I climbed out I saw Lou Maluga exit the Humvee holding his big Desert Eagle.

Curtis didn't want to leave the Navigator.

"This ain't my doin'," he said to the Croc, who was trying to get him out of the car. "That shit at the Barn didn't have nothin' t'do with me, brotha. I'm just a singer, man. I don't put no smack down."

"Get your crybaby ass outta there," Smith screamed, pulling back the slide on his automatic and shoving the gun into Curtis's face. "This be Louis's play, so it gonna happen."

"I was never really gonna change labels. He's gotta believe that!"

I saw insanity flash in Smith's eyes and thought Curtis was going to die right there. Then Lou Maluga arrived at the Navigator side door and put a hand on Crocodile Smith's shoulder, pulling him aside.

"Come out, Curtis," he said softly. Then without warning, Lou reached inside and with one quick powerful jerk, yanked Curtis out of the SUV. He rolled onto the sand at Maluga's feet. Then KZ yanked him upright.

"Stand over there," Stacy ordered.

The three holes had been dug next to a stand of Joshua trees. We were led over and each of us was forced to stand next to one of the graves. I looked down into a sandy, three-foot-deep hole in the ground and wondered if this was where my precious remains were going to rot for eternity. I'd planned on something a little more formal.

Curtis started begging again; this time he seemed close to tears. "Louis, I can make this right, brotha. I didn't want any a them old performance payments. I never would a known about any a that if it weren't for Stacy. She told me everything." Then he turned to the White Sister. "Why'd you put me up to this, then back down on me? I don't get none a this."

"Shut up!" Louis said. "You gotta pay what you owe, nigga."

I was getting ready to add my testimony, tell everything I'd picked up on the VXT, when Louis raised the Desert Eagle and thumbed back the hammer, freezing me in mid-thought.

"You think you can kill me and Curtis and just walk away?" Lionel said softly. "This ain't like Dante Watts, where nobody gave a shit. This is *L.A. Times* front page, Lou. This is network, baby. You gonna be watching this every night on CBS till they hook you up and star you in the broadcast."

Something in that sentence jogged my brain. I needed to come up with something usable fast and it needed to be something I could prove. Lou wouldn't believe what I'd overheard on the pager because I didn't have the tape with me to play as evidence. As I stood looking at the three holes in the ground, something started buzzing around in my thick head. They had set this up to kill Lionel and Curtis. Stacy sent her two Crip grave diggers out here this afternoon, but nobody knew I was going to stumble into the mess.

"Listen up, cuz. I got a play here. This gonna ring solid." Curtis was pleading again. "I got two albums' worth of songs already cut. I give them all to you, baby. Okay, I give all that wax away. Do ya feel me? I'm tryin' hard t'make this right."

Louis Maluga was street gristle who couldn't take much more of Curtis. I saw the same murderous look in his eyes that I'd seen in Malibu when we'd faced off in his African print living room. He was ready to throw down. I knew once the shooting started, it wouldn't stop until all three of us were dead. Stacy had way too many stories. I had to knock one down. It was now or never.

"Hey, Louis," I said. "When's the big day? You and Sable pick a date yet?"

He looked over at me with a dumb look on his round face. Under the circumstances, it was probably the last thing he thought anybody would ask.

"What?" he said, trying to understand why, seconds from death, I would ask that question.

"You and Sable." I tried to smile, but my jack-o-lantern grin was stretched thin across dry teeth and felt phony. I pressed on. "I put a bug in your ride, man. I been listening to you and her snuggle. Good stuff there."

I turned to Stacy. "You gonna be the matron of honor? Carry some flowers? Maybe wish the bride well with a nice toast at the reception?"

Stacy looked at me with such a strange, angry frown that I knew I was in fertile territory.

"Shut the hell up," she growled. "Whatta you bringin' this up for?"

" 'Course with a wedding on the horizon, that means you and Stacy gotta get a divorce," I said. "Couple a things here don't quite add up, Lou. For instance, how're you two gonna divide up your company in divorce court without going broke? California is a community property state. Once you get through paying your long-term capital gains, most of your assets are gonna go to pay for the war in Iraq."

"There ain't gonna be no divorce and no wedding," Louis shouted. "Where'd you get this shit?" He was pressing, leaning too far into it. His body language screamed lie.

"She knows, Lou," I said. "She knows you're getting set to dump her. That's why we got one too many graves out here."

I was flying half-blind, clawing at loose ends hoping to un-ravel this knot. I could see from their expressions that I'd started something. Stacy fumed while Louis frowned. He was working on it. He had survived in a brutal, deadly street world by trusting his instincts. Stacy glowered at me, still holding the shotgun in her delicate hands, but in her anger, it seemed almost forgotten.

"What're you talking about?" she yelled.

"One hole for Lionel, one for Curtis. But who's this third one for?" I asked.

"It's for you, motherfucker!" she was screaming now.

"I don't think so. You didn't know I was gonna be here. I was a last-minute add." I pointed to the Crips with shovels. "These guys were out here digging hours ago."

"Lou, I'm gonna put this guy down!" Stacy growled and raised the shotgun until it was pointing at my stomach.

"No," Louis said. "I want to hear him out. Let him talk."

It was hard to focus on Lou while Stacy was twenty feet away, pointing a cocked shotgun at me. But I forced myself to turn and face him.

"This third hole is for you, Louis," I said soberly.

"You're outta your mind!" Stacy screamed.

Her reaction said I wasn't. I figured I was dead anyway, so I just plowed on. I looked at Stacy.

"What's he good for anyway? Lou's a record company disaster. A dinosaur. No acts want to record for him anymore. You built this label, Stacy. You're not gonna watch it go down in a divorce so this guy can marry some silicone Barbie from the Valley. You got this beat down started. You riled up Curtis, leakin' stuff till he got so upset he decided to change labels. That sets up Lou's motive for Curtis's murder. But Lou, it only works for her if you also die in the shoot-out. That way, she inherits 'cause you're still married." I turned to Crocodile Smith. "You're the designated shooter, Croc. You've got a motive and you're gonna die with the murder weapon in your hand. You all die and leave the cops to sort it out. God knows there's enough bad blood between you all to justify it."

"He's lyin', Lou."

Louis wheeled on her, his face contorted with rage. "You been leakin' our accounting to Curtis to force all this?"

Suddenly, Crocodile Smith pointed his gun at Lou. But Lou was ready, and spun and fired, blowing him backwards into the sand. Lou and Stacy were now faced off with guns drawn on each other, about to execute a street divorce. It was a moment that lasted no longer than a heartbeat but seemed frozen in time.

Nobody was paying attention to Lionel, who moved slightly to his left, closing the distance between Lou and himself.

Then without warning, Lionel dove at Louis, and knocked him backward into the nearest grave. Lou rolled up into a sitting position, poking his head over the top of the hole. As he did, Stacy fired both barrels at him and blew his head clean off his shoulders.

I turned and started a zigzag run back to the Navigator as weapons started discharging all around me. I heard Stacy slam the double barrel closed.

A reload.

The shotgun fired again and a double-load of heavy buck-shot flew by my ear, its wind ruffling my hair. In front of me, the side window of the Navigator turned to crystal as the pat-tern hit.

I yanked open the door, rolled into the backseat, and grabbed the Beretta AR-70. The case fell open and I pulled the heavy weapon out, jammed in a clip, threw myself to the ground, and rolled under the car. I heard guns firing and people screaming. I jacked a round into the tube and started spraying lead. For an instant Insane Wayne was in my sights, but I remembered the note that he'd passed that saved my life, and I held my fire. He ducked down as more guns barked in the dark. Barrel flashes il-luminated everybody's positions. I fired the Beretta until both clips were dry.

Then I heard the 12-gauge bark again and Lionel Wright screamed. Seconds later, I caught sight of Stacy, lit by moon-light, running across the sand carrying her shotgun. I got up and ran after her, passing the carnage at the gravesite on my way. I couldn't see Insane Wayne but glanced again at Louis Maluga, flat on his back in one of the graves, his head blown from his shoulders. Smith was on his back. He'd died like he lived, with his yellow crocs on. The two grave diggers were both wounded and trying to crawl away, leaving red trails in the sand. Lionel lay in one of the holes clutching his leg, which was pumping blood from a hole in his thigh.

"Put a pressure compress on that," I yelled. "Use your belt and tux jacket. I'll be right back."

Then I took off after the White Sister, chasing her across the desert in the dark. She had set this all up and I was determined she wouldn't get away. I didn't know where Curtis Clark or KZ were, but I kept running in the deep sand until my legs and thighs burned. I finally stopped near several rock formations and listened for any sound, trying to decide which way to go.

That was when I heard the click of both shotgun hammers directly behind me.

I was toast.

"It's still gonna work out," she said. "Smith still goes down for all of this. You got enough baggage to fit the frame. Motive. Method. Opportunity." Her voice was high and manic. She was in a state of agitated panic, overdosing on adrenaline.

I turned slowly and then I saw her standing beside a large rock outcropping about ten feet away, holding the shotgun. It was perfect spacing. Far enough away so I couldn't get to her, but close enough so she couldn't possibly miss with a double load of buckshot.

As we faced each other I glimpsed a shadow move in the rocks beyond her.

"Any last words?" she said, my imminent death glittering in her pale, blue eyes.

"Just four."

"Say 'em."

"Look out behind you."

A dark figure was silhouetted against the rock formation, ten feet from her. I could just make out a man holding a MAC-10.

She panicked as she spun, pulling the triggers. Both barrels on her ghetto stick barked. The man behind her fired simultaneously.

Her pattern just missed.

His didn't.

Stacy's left leg blossomed red and she screamed, pitching forward into the sand. She flopped back and forth, screaming profanities.

The figure stepped away from the cover of the rocks, and I saw it was Wayne Watkins. It was the second time in two days that he'd saved my life. I wondered why.

"Los Angeles Sheriff's Department," he said.

CHAPTER SIXTY

After we used my cell to call 911, he told me his name wasn't Wayne Watkins; it was Sgt. Wallace Wayne and he had been a Sheriff's Department gang squad undercover for almost two years. He'd been put in the hip-hop music business by the county sheriff for the same reason David Slade had.

When I asked what he knew about Slade's killing, all he would say was, "Slade helped duke me in. We knew each other back at Compton High. The rest is classified. It's gotta wait till my supervisor clears it."

It took less than ten minutes for the first Highway Patrol unit to arrive. The officers took one look at the mess and started screaming for more help over their radio.

Later, Sgt. Wayne and I were standing next to the Navigator watching as a dozen Highway Patrol officers and paramedics began to mop up. By then, Lionel Wright was unconscious from loss of blood and was loaded into the first rescue ambulance. It sped off to the hospital with its roof lights and siren strobing, passing another incoming RA as it left. Earlier, Sgt. Wayne and I had tried to stem the bleeding on Stacy Maluga's leg by wrapping it with our jackets and tying it off with my belt, but she had also lost a lot of blood and was in shock by the time the second paramedic truck arrived. The EMTs did a quick field triage, then loaded her into the back.

We watched the ambulance fishtail through the deep sand until it also reached the two-lane road and sped away. When it was gone, Sergeant Wayne and I went looking for Curtis Clark. We found him a quarter of a mile away, hiding in a rock out-cropping.

"Man," Curtis said. "That cave bitch sure know how to take it to the street." Whatever that meant.

"Time to man up, Curtis," Wayne said. "You gotta make a statement and own some of this." We pulled him out of his hiding place and led him back to the crime scene.

The Nevada Highway Patrol called Vegas Metro Homicide, and then began walking around the carnage, stringing yellow ribbon and shaking their heads in disbelief. They hadn't seen this kind of a bloodbath since Bugsy Siegel left town.

In accordance with crime scene protocol, they separated Sgt. Wayne and me until the Homicide dicks arrived. I ended up in the back of a Highway Patrol Chevy Impala. The patrolman confiscated my cell phone and wallet and all I was left with as I sat there were ugly thoughts and a deepening sense of doom. I didn't know if Sgt. Wayne could finally put David Slade's murder on the Malugas. If he couldn't, and Stacy died from her wound without talking, then the only thing I'd managed to accomplish was to kill all the available witnesses who could clear Alexa.

I saw a blue LVPD minivan pull up and park a few feet away. Two crusty old guys in rumpled suits with gray hair and cop stares got out. Vegas Homicide had arrived. I watched as they talked to the lead deputy on the scene. The Highway Patrol had called for Condor lights, and while I was watching the new arrivals, a generator started up and blue-white halogen spilled out from the top of a Condor crane, illuminating the gruesome scene.

After quickly surveying the scene, one of the Homicide dicks grabbed a patrol officer and headed to the car where Sgt. Wayne sat. The other homicide cop collected a deputy and came over to talk to me. He opened the door and sat in the back as the deputy got in front. Standard protocol. The deputy was there to witness my preliminary field interview and watched in silence through the wire mesh that separated us from the front seat. My homicide guy was in his late fifties with silver brushed-back hair and a sun-ravaged complexion. He had a long face and eyes that had seen too much to be surprised by anything, but I could tell this quadruple killing had captured his interest.

"I'm Lieutenant Barry Bush," he said. "My partner over there with your friend is Steve Goodstein. The Highway Patrol tells me you guys are both cops from L.A."

"Yeah, I'm LAPD. The guy with your partner says he's an L.A. County sheriff, but you should check that out 'cause all I got is his word on that."

"I used to work L.A. Homicide," Lt. Bush said, sounding relaxed and friendly. "When I remarried, I retired out here. But I'm not a casino guy and I got bored, so I re-upped and caught on with LV Metro."

He was filling time with chit-chat while he took out his mini-recorder, found a fresh tape, inserted it, and turned on the unit. Then he said, "Okay, I'm gonna skip the Miranda for now. I'm not arresting you. Let's call this a voluntary statement. Fair enough?"

"Sure," I said.

"Gimme the background particulars, starting with your full name."

I gave him my name and rank and told him I worked out of Homicide Special at Parker Center.

"Who's your C.O.? Back when I was in L.A. there was no Homicide Special. The top murder teams were all part of the Major Crimes Unit."

I knew Bush was just filling the car with B.S. to get a loose feeling going. He wanted to set up a friendly atmosphere so I wouldn't guard my responses. I've pulled the same routine on hundreds of guys. It told me that even though I was a cop, he still didn't trust me.

"My C.O. is Captain Jeb Calloway," I answered.

"Little muscle-bound character who looks like he could break stones with his hands?"

"That's him."

"Wasn't he with SWAT or CRASH, one of those high-octane, kick-ass units?"

"This is good kitsch, Loo, but I'm onto it. Can't we just get this over with? I'm having a really bad night."

He studied me and finally nodded. "Okay, then how do two L.A. cops end up in the middle of *my* desert with all these dead black people?"

"It's a long story."

"That's why I carry two-hour tapes," he drawled.

I started at the beginning and told him the incredible tale of my last week, ending with the chartered flight full of hip-hop music people to the Mandalay Bay Casino, including the garage kidnapping, the shooting of Elijah Mustafa, and our subsequent trip into the desert to be murdered by the president of Lethal Force, Inc. and his estranged wife.

When I was finished, he sat there and looked at me with skeptical, unblinking eyes. "All that story needs is a main title and some end credits," he said.

I nodded.

Then he spoke into the recorder for the record. "This preliminary declaration was given voluntarily in the presence of Highway Patrol Officer Duane Lewis and Lieutenant Barry Bush. The tape has not been shut off or edited and has been running for twenty continuous minutes. It is eleven-seventeen P.M. on July sixteenth, a Tuesday night." Everything exactly by the book.

Sgt. Wayne and I were transported to the police station in separate cars. I met Lt. Bush's captain, who said he was formerly with Chicago PD. I found out that most of the cops on Vegas Homicide were transplants from other departments. Finally, after our statements had been signed and witnessed, Sgt. Wayne and I were allowed to speak to each other again. We got some vending machine coffee and sat in the empty lunchroom.

"After high school, I joined the Compton PD," he said.

"Compton had a corrupt department with bad city government. Lotta cash payoffs. About ten city councilmen and our chief eventually got indicted. When the new mayor decided to close down Compton PD, the job got contracted out to the L.A. Sheriff's Department. I switched badges and stayed on."

Even though he'd been instructed by his gang intel commander to say nothing about his two years undercover, he took pity on me and finally conceded that on the night David Slade was killed, he'd been left behind at the Maluga estate by Stacy. She told him to go down to Lou's Malibu Colony house to work security for a party Lou was having. He told me he couldn't help me with Slade's murder. In fact, he was Lou's alibi for the time of the homicide. I hadn't figured Lou for an innocent bystander, but there it was.

"Something heavy was going down with Stacy that night," he said. "She was all riled up, screaming at people. But she only took KZ with her. He was her main guy when it came to street actions. They knew each other from back in the day. When they got home later that night, KZ was spooked, but he wouldn't tell me what happened. By then, he was scared to death of Stacy. She was willing to do anything. I think she's a sociopath." He then looked at me. "I know that doesn't help clear your wife," he said. "But that's what went down."

So I still didn't have enough. It was the way my luck had been running all week.

At about two A.M. the Las Vegas cops cut us loose with a reminder not to leave Las Vegas without checking in first.

We drove over to the Las Vegas Sunrise Hospital where Rosey, Sally, and my LAPD posse were waiting. When I got there, I found out Lionel Wright had survived two hours of emergency surgery and was in recovery. His condition was listed as guarded. The press hadn't found out he was there yet because the hospital had admitted him under the name on his driver's license, Orlee Lemon. Stacy came out of surgery at five A.M. She'd lost so much blood she'd had a cardiac arrest on the table and was now in critical condition.

At ten the following morning a search helicopter found KZ wandering lost in the desert. He'd been hit in the arm but the wound was minor and required no stitches. He refused to talk to police and demanded an attorney.

Under the circumstances, his arrest seemed like a hollow victory.

CHAPTER SIXTY-ONE

I got back to Los Angeles on Thursday morning and went straight to the UCLA hospital to continue the vigil with Chooch. Nothing changed over the weekend, and by Monday Luther wanted us all to meet.

"I'm not saying that things can't change," he said. "But usually, within three or four days, we see some reflex, some movement—something. I've tried to wean her off the life support system, but the minute I do, she stops breathing."

We were in the ICU waiting room. Chooch and I tried to absorb what he was saying.

"She's not coming back?" I finally asked.

"I told you at the beginning that these things are impossible to fully predict. Right now this looks pretty grim. I think you and Chooch need to start evaluating options."

"I'm not unplugging her," I said defiantly.

"In that case, you need to find some kind of extended care facility. I hear this one's pretty good." He took out a pad and pen and wrote down a name. Then he handed it to me.

"Bright Horizons?" I was incredulous. "Who are they kidding?"

"Most extended care facilities have names like that. Bright Horizons, Eternal Hope, Happy Endings."

I folded the paper and looked over at Chooch. His face was drained of color. We left Luther and went down to the cafeteria where we sat with mugs of coffee on the table between us, but we couldn't drink them on sour stomachs.

"What do we do, Dad?" he asked.

"I don't know. I can't let her go. I just can't. I'll put her in one of those hospices and I'll keep her alive and I'll . . ."

Then the tears started coming and Chooch put his arm around me. In moments, his own tears were mixed with mine.

I tried several times to reach Alexa's brother, Buddy. He and I had never gotten along and I dreaded making the call. But I couldn't reach him. His office said he was on a vacation trip up the Amazon River and would call when he returned at the end of the month.

The following week, I sat with Alexa's attorney, a pretty, pale-skinned woman with bird-like movements and honey-brown hair. I'd never met her before. Her name was Lydia Cunningham and her law firm was on the twenty-fifth floor of a Century City high-rise. We sat in a book-lined conference room and she studied Alexa's last will and testament while I looked out the windows at the glass towers all around us, wondering if I would be able to get through this meeting full of questions about what to do with Alexa's jewelry, her stock portfolio, her faltering life.

"It's right here," Lydia said, thumbing through the thick document. "I thought I remembered putting that in. We drew this up six years ago."

Six years ago, Alexa and I hadn't met yet. It seemed like a lifetime.

"Her heroic measures codicil states that if for any reason she becomes vegetative, she doesn't want life support or any other heroic means of prolonging a hopeless existence."

"But what if in a little while she . . . ?" I couldn't finish. I just turned to look out the window again. *Could they force this on me?* I wondered. "I was going to move her to an extended care facility," I said, looking back at Lydia. "I mean, she could wake up. Miracles happen." I was desperate.

"That's right, and none of us knows what the future will

bring. But you don't want this to turn into a Terri Schiavo situation. Alexa's wishes are clearly stated here. I'm bound as her attorney to turn this over to her doctors and the insurance company."

"And we can't keep her alive?" I pleaded.

"Is she really alive?" Lydia said. She kept her voice soft, but even so, the words tore holes in me. "Shane, you could fight this in court, but it will cost you a fortune and you'll lose. Her wishes are clearly stated here and eventually will prevail."

I heard back from Buddy. He listened while I explained Alexa's desperate condition. He sounded sad, but said he had just received a huge promotion and was now heading regional sales. He wouldn't be able to come to L.A. until things changed for Alexa one way or the other, which was a polite way of saying he'd come to her funeral. He managed to weigh in on the heroic measures debate before hanging up. He didn't think we should keep her on life support. I, on the other hand, didn't think he should stay in Philadelphia. We ended up the conversation not feeling very good about each other.

I moved Alexa to Bright Horizons and started looking for an attorney to fight the provision in her will. The facility was in Santa Monica and it was expensive, almost two hundred fifty dollars a day, which, because of her heroic measures codicil, was not going to be covered by insurance. I'd have to write the checks myself. But if I had to sell the house in Venice to support this, I'd do it. At least for as long as I could afford it. After the house was gone, I'd figure out something else.

Bright Horizons was an old one-story building on Lincoln Boulevard, five blocks from the ocean. It was clean, but it wasn't bright and there were no horizons. The place had a death-row vibe, a no-man's-land where its residents hovered between disparate states of existence.

Alexa's room was small, with one window that looked out onto a small, empty patio. I bought a flowering fig tree and donated it to the courtyard. I had it placed right outside her window, so she would have something to look at. I knew it was silly because she was in a coma, but it didn't matter because it made me feel better.

The room was equipped with portable life support machines, which were very small, considering the huge task they were being expected to perform. They sat atop tables or were attached to the rolling bed where Alexa lay. She looked small and thin under the sheets, her black hair growing in tangles out of a shrinking death mask.

I would brush her hair and then sit for hours looking at her, trying to see the woman she had once been. But Alexa had already begun to transform. The most beautiful person I'd ever known was lost somewhere, wandering vacantly inside her own head. I would hold her hand, feel her mechanically induced pulse, and wonder, despite all this equipment keeping her alive: Was she even in there? Or was I clinging to a fantasy while I ignored her own stated wishes? Was this to be my final act of love—to keep her trapped inside a dead vessel, so that I could nourish some faint selfish hope of my own?

I began slowly to contemplate the monstrous act of unplugging her and letting her go.

Chooch applied for a medical red shirt from the USC football team, then dropped out of fall semester and came home.

Gunner took me to dinner. My compact courtroom brawler extended his condolences with sad eyes, then explained the deal he had made with the District Attorney. I could see him light up as he told the tale. He gloried in reliving how he had threatened Chase Beal with a media blitz and how he would prove that the city had used Alexa and me as scapegoats. The D.A. had dropped all charges against us in return for our not filing a civil suit. Gunner told me that he had finally kicked Chase Beal's skinny prep-school ass.

Meanwhile, Stacy Maluga recovered, and Alexa got weaker. Stacy had lost partial use of her right leg, and she was being held in the Las Vegas jail, charged with quadruple homicide. If convicted, she would most likely end up on death row.

Lionel Wright had returned to L.A. and was recovering at his Bellagio Road estate. He wanted me to come and have lunch, and we picked a date for the following week.

Curtis Clark appeared on several entertainment news shows. In his retelling of the shootout in the desert, he'd been wearing a mask and a cape, and had almost single-handedly brought the evil Malugas to justice. He decided not to sign with Lionel Wright and announced he was joining the team at Sony Music. What a guy.

I followed the case in the newspaper and on TV. Occasionally Rafie or Tommy would call with updates. One afternoon Rafie told me that KZ was finally beginning to comprehend that he would be convicted of David Slade's murder and began negotiations with the L.A. prosecutors. Rafie said the D.A. was using Alexa's condition as a lever. If she was unplugged and died, KZ would feel the full weight of the law as an accomplice in a double police homicide. He finally took a kick down to one count of manslaughter and in return, put the hat on Stacy Maluga for David Slade's murder and Alexa's shooting. He confessed that after executing Slade, he and Stacy took Alexa to the house on Cypress and forced her to admit to the murder on our answering machine. Then Stacy shot her. It was pretty much what I figured.

Alexa had finally been cleared.

Of course by then she was in a death coma and it was no longer a news story. Reverend Vespars and Roxanne Sharp were off to more profitable racial injustices and weren't around to comment on the fact that they'd all been wrong and had destroyed her reputation with insinuation.

The days dragged on, but Alexa didn't get any better. I requested a leave of absence from the department and took daily trips out to Bright Horizons to sit by my wife's bed.

One day I came out of the house and got in my car for my daily trek to Santa Monica. Jonathan Bodine suddenly sat up, scaring the hell out of me. He'd been sleeping in the backseat of my car.

"You can't just crash in other people's cars," I gasped.

"Crown Prince lays his head down in some shiny Jap coffin and you're getting all baked 'cause you ain't been asked first," he retorted. "This pile a junk's gonna end up in the Smithsonian. Everybody payin' money comin' t'see 'cause Prince Samik Mampuna gone an' slept here. Be like with Jesus, or Elvis or some such shit."

I needed to change the subject before I strangled him. "I suppose, as usual, you haven't eaten," I said.

"Yep. Always hungry. Don't get enough carbs. My insides is growlin' like a grizzly with its balls on fire."

Nice simile. "I'm going out to see Alexa," I told him. "There's a McDonald's down the street. You wanta come, I'll buy you lunch."

"Then let's get this bus rollin'. His Royal Highness needs a McFuckit," he said.

An hour later I was in Alexa's room. John Bodine was fed and standing beside me. He had McNugget particles still clinging to his beard as he looked down at her.

"Man, she be illin'."

"Don't breathe germs on her, John." I was becoming more and more worried about her catching something in her frail condition.

"Whata ya gonna do?" he finally asked.

"She doesn't want to be kept alive like this," I said. "I'm thinking about unplugging her."

"Ain't her choice. You don't get no vote, neither."

I told him about the codicil in Alexa's will, explaining that the court was going to unplug her if I didn't. He didn't seem to hear any of it.

"I told ya about my great-great-grandfather Chief Ossawanga. In the Bassaland he was a famous muthafucka. Chief O is up in the Big Guy's house. I tole ya, he's like some Last Ride kinda ticket-taker. He's the one you gotta see, you gonna get a place on the ark. He got the passenger list and such."

"John, this really isn't helping."

He pointed at Alexa and shouted, "This one here ain't supposed ta go, you dumb half-stepper! She ain't on the list. Can't you get nothin' through yer shit-fer-brains head?"

"John, I don't want to argue with you about this. It's a legal thing."

"Lawyers and doctors. When you gonna learn these posers ain't got no vision? They just got better cards in their wallets."

"John . . ."

"Your wife ain't ready, man. This here ain't up for discussion." He was starting to get agitated and raised his voice. "I get all this straight from Chief O. All day long I gotta hear that old fart yammerin' at me from some cloud. Put up with his nonsense month after month, year after year. Ain't no way to shut him up 'less you do what he says. But you just a drives-too-fast-plow-a-muthafucka-down, asshole who don't never listen!"

Now he was screaming and his dusky complexion had turned bright red with anger. There was no doubt he was crazy. The question was, would he get violent? I tried to get him out of the room.

"Come on, John. Time to go." I took his skinny arm.

"Get your hands off a me!" he shouted and broke away. "She ain't ready! She ain't supposed to go! When you gonna start payin' attention?" Then he turned and ran down the hall.

I could hear him ranting all the way out of the building and into the street.

CHAPTER SIXTY-TWO

If we unplug her, will she feel it?" Chooch asked, tears welling in his black eyes.

We were having dinner at Mama's Fish House up on the Malibu coast. It was one of Alexa's favorite places. We sat in a small booth next to a plate-glass window overlooking the Pacific Ocean.

"I've been thinking a lot about that, Chooch. What if they got it right and she's already gone? By keeping her body alive, are we cursing her to stay on earth when she should be free to go to heaven?"

"Do you believe that?"

"I don't know what I believe. I know I don't have the answers." I looked out at the gray Pacific, which was rolling endless, greasy swells toward us, exploding, grenades of white foam under the window. The sun hung low on the horizon, lighting a pewter sea.

"I keep thinking she's gonna wake up. She's gonna come back to us," Chooch said.

"It's been a month and a half," I said. "And it was her stated wish not to employ heroic measures. I want desperately to do right by her."

After that, we sat in silence for a while.

"You need to go back to school, son. Classes start in a week. I think they'll readmit you for this semester. Maybe you could even rejoin the team. Your red shirt year won't help you if you don't practice."

"And what will you do?"

"I'll figure that out. I'm not sure I can do anything quite yet. I need to reevaluate a lot of things."

"So, you've made up your mind on Mom regardless of what I think?"

"At first I thought this should be a shared decision, but then I realized it wasn't fair to put something this big on you. I'm her legal guardian. So, yeah, I've made up my mind. Tomorrow I'm gonna tell the people at Bright Horizons it's okay to let her go. I'll just need an hour or so to say good-bye."

The next morning I returned to the hospice. I knew it was going to be the hardest thing I would ever do. Since Chooch didn't agree with my decision, he decided not to come. I didn't force him. I knew it was something each of us felt deeply in our hearts. When I arrived, I found the administrator. He was a skinny old man with slicked-back hair and a pasty complexion. His name was Clark something, and I told him that I had decided to honor Alexa's legal wish.

"I think it's for the best," he said.

"I'll need some time with her first."

We walked down the corridor to her room and went inside.

Alexa wasn't there.

In fact, nothing was there. Not the bed, not the heart-lung machine, not the respirator. Nothing. The entire room had been stripped.

What followed next was a frantic search. Nurses, interns, and Bright Horizons clerical people started running up and down hallways, flinging open doors, startling patients, checking rooms. We couldn't find her anywhere.

"She's got to be here somewhere," Clark said, his now-pale complexion shining with blue-white panic in the harsh fluorescents.

More searching. More frantic looks. Alexa could not be located.

"I've never had anything like this happen before," Clark fretted.

Just then, the fire alarm went off.

"What the hell?" Clark said, and ran from his office with me on his heels.

The fire alarm panel was in the entry closet and when we looked, the LCD screen indicated that there was smoke in the basement storage area. We headed downstairs taking the concrete steps two at a time. When we got to the lower landing, there was smoke billowing from the storage room at the end of the hallway.

Then I heard a voice chanting. "*Ayyeee-yeee-bammba-bass-mantu-tu. Ayyeee-Ayyeee-bobas bot-y-kon-amakayos.*"

Bodine.

I barged through the door into a large storage area where old broken nightstands and three-legged tables were stacked. In the corner of the room sat Alexa's hospital bed. The Sunday *L.A. Times* was engulfed in a raging fire, burning inside an upside-down trashcan lid. As the fire alarm brayed, John Bodine danced around the two-foot-high flame. He was stripped to the waist, his skinny body glistening with sweat. He chanted and danced, spinning and jumping, giving his chopped-off dreads a ride.

"What's this bum doing down here?" Clark yelled.

I ran to Alexa's bed. John had already unplugged the heart monitor and respirator with its life-saving tubes. She lay prone, with her eyes shut, dead. John continued to sing and dance around the fire.

Clark started stomping out the blaze in the trash-can lid, the sound of his heels ringing the metal like a giant gong.

"The fuck you doin'?" John brayed, trying to push Clark away.

"Who is this idiot?" Clark screamed. "Get him off me!"

"Eat my dick!" Bodine screamed back.

I grabbed him. "John, what are you doing? Why did you steal Alexa?"

"Chief O always in my ear. Do this. Do that. You try livin' with some two-hundred-year-old African bag-a-wind yammerin' inside your head all day long." That was his explanation.

"You unplugged her?" Clark was trying to catch up.

"All that junk weren't doin' no good," John brayed. "Souls ain't gonna fly 'less they're marked ready, and this one here ain't ready. This be all down in Chief O's book."

I looked down at Alexa again. She was lying inert, but as I watched her, something, some shadow moved behind her eyelids. Then after almost a minute, her chest rose and she took a faltering breath of smoky basement air.

"Look at this!" I shouted. "She's breathing!"

"Ain't you been listenin'?" John said. "'Course she's breathin'. She ain't done here yet."

We all watched as her chest slowly began to rise and fall, breathing without life support. I touched her hand and then the most wonderful thing happened.

She opened her eyes and looked at me.

CHAPTER SIXTY-THREE

Like the Lone Ranger, John Bodine didn't stick around to be thanked. He snuck away before he could be arrested for starting a fire in the hospice basement.

The correspondents on the *Six O'Clock News* called it a miracle.

Chooch and I could barely believe she was back. It was too good to comprehend. We immediately transferred her back to UCLA, where she was again placed under Luther's care and began a long, torturous recovery. Weeks went by with little progress, but then suddenly, she'd take a small baby step forward. After a month she began to say words. At first, they didn't come in recognizable sentences, but as she looked up at me in frustration, it was clear she had thoughts she was trying to communicate.

Delfina came back a week early from her summer in Mexico. She'd been in a small mountain village near Cuernavaca with no phones, so she and Chooch had only talked three times. When she heard about Alexa, she wanted to come home early and did. Immediately, she started pitching in. She sat for hours after school helping with Alexa's speech and physical therapy.

I learned that head trauma wasn't at all like it was portrayed on television or in the movies. The recovery process was lengthy and tedious. Luther met with Chooch, Delfina, and me one afternoon in late October and gave us some long-awaited good news. He had just completed a battery of neurological and spinal column tests that indicated all the lobes of Alexa's brain were functioning and her nervous system was slowly regenerating.

"I'm not promising a full recovery yet, but that's definitely something we can start to anticipate," Luther said, smiling. "Right now our prognosis is wait and see."

He was proud of his skill as a surgeon, proud of his patient. "I think that last surgery was pivotal," he said. "We restored blood flow, debrided the dead tissue. Got the intracranial pressure up."

"I can't thank you enough," I said. But underneath, I suspected that it wasn't so much Luther as it was John Bodine, or Chief O, or some crazy African mojo that was responsible for waking her up and bringing her back.

Later that week I met with Tony Filosiani in his office at Parker Center. Great White Mike had cleared his things out and retreated, to the routine and safety of the Operations Division. Tony looked thin. The weight loss didn't agree with him. He was one of those guys who needed to be cherubic.

"When you coming back on the job full time?" he asked.

"I'm bringing Alexa home in a few weeks. Maybe once she can do things for herself, I'll think about it."

"Her doctor says she should make a full recovery." He smiled. "Her job is waiting, too."

"Right now I'm just happy to have her back." Inside, I was still numb. I couldn't escape the terror of how close it had been.

"I know you think I let you down," Tony said, "but I couldn't talk about Slade being an undercover. I had a deal with the sheriff to protect Sergeant Wayne."

"I understand. No hard feelings."

But even as I said it, I knew things would probably never be the same between us. When he thought Alexa was dead, or dying, he had been willing to let her reputation and her memory be destroyed. There should have been better options. On the other hand, I never understood how things got done in the political environs above the fifth floor, so I tried hard not to judge him.

Football season was almost over. Chooch had returned to school and ended up quarterbacking the scout team as a red shirt. He seemed bigger and stronger. Delfina was halfway through her senior year, getting A's and narrowing down her college application list.

We brought Alexa home the second week of December. She moved carefully around our Venice house, a little rickety, with headaches and fingertip numbness. Big parts of her memory were gone. She seemed solemn and distant much of the time, as if the universe had shifted and she was having trouble fitting it all back together.

One night, just before Christmas, we sat in our backyard, holding hands. Franco, our cat, sat right at Alexa's feet, looking up, watching, guarding her from harm. It was chilly, so I went inside and returned with a blanket to put around her knees. She had wanted to be outside because a family of ducks had arrived and she enjoyed watching them swim with their babies.

"I feel so bad about David Slade," she finally said. She spoke very slowly, forming her words one at a time, laying them out methodically, as if each one was hooked carefully to the one before. In the past month, this slow speech had been worrisome to me, but Luther told me to give it time.

"What about David Slade?" I asked as Franco finally jumped up into her lap, turned around three times, and then plopped down.

She looked over at me and said, "I used to date him."

"I know."

"It was never really serious. He was . . . he was fun and he had so much potential. He had come so far from where he started. He was a remarkable man."

"It's okay," I said. "You don't have to go through it. I had relationships before I met you." I didn't want to hear any of this.

"It wasn't like that," she persisted. "We went out. And we were friends, not lovers. But Shane, I feel so responsible for what happened to him."

"You didn't put him undercover," I reminded her.

"But I knew it was getting dangerous. I should have pulled

him out. I got greedy. I wanted what he was bringing. I gambled with his life, and lost."

"It's not an easy job you've got," I told her. It was the same thing I'd said to Elijah Mustafa.

She squeezed my hand. The ducks swam into view. A mother, a father, and four ducklings. Alexa tore a piece of bread she had brought out with her and tossed it into the canal. The mother duck swerved and grabbed it, never slowing her progress. If you're going to survive in L.A., it's a fast-lane experience, even for ducks.

I changed the subject and somehow we got to talking about the horrible month when she was in the coma.

I told her about Jonathan Bodine. How I'd hit him with the car that night after the training day, and how he stole her computer with the e-mails. I also told her how I thought he had saved her life by stealing her bed and doing a fire dance in the basement of the hospice. I hadn't gone into too much of this before, because I still didn't know how much of his crazy mojo I was ready to buy into.

"You believe all that?" she finally asked, when I had finished. "You think he talks to dead people?"

She was watching me carefully and her face glowed in the moonlight. I could now begin to see her again the way she'd been six months ago, before all of this had happened. I knew one day soon she would be completely restored. It was a miracle.

"I don't know what I believe," I finally said, but then I suddenly changed my mind. "Yes, yes I do," I corrected myself. "I think John had something to do with it. I know this is nuts, but I think God sent him to us. Maybe it was not an accident that I ran him over. Maybe it was God's will."

She sat quietly, petting Franco.

"On cold nights like this, I worry about John," I continued. "He's out there alone. Nobody on the Nickel likes him. He's not very healthy. No meat on him. Street people beat him up because he steals their stuff."

"You want to see if we can find him?" Alexa asked.

That was one of the things I loved about her. She knew how to indulge me without ridiculing me.

"Yes. I want to find him. He's probably hungry. He never eats a regular meal unless I buy it."

"Then let's go," she said, standing up.

We got into the Acura and I bundled the blanket around her. Then I went back into the house and pulled my new thick parka with the fur collar and pair of sweatpants out of the closet. Both presents for John Bodine if I could find him. Last, I grabbed some fifty-dollar bills.

We set off looking. I drove to the Nickel and talked to Horizontal Joe.

"That guy?" the sleeping man grumbled. "If he ain't already dead, somebody oughta kill the prick."

I talked to a hooker with brown teeth who shot heroin and turned her tricks inside the Alices. Her street name was Connect-the-Dots because of all the needle scabs on her arms.

"Nobody keeps track a that nigga," she said.

I checked the Weingart Center and most of the SRO hotels. Nobody had seen him recently, nor really wanted to. I even drove over to the Pacific Electric tunnel and asked some old men who were walking out.

"Man's a sorry waste a skin and groceries," one of them grumbled.

It was getting late, and I saw that Alexa was getting cold and tired. So I put the car in gear and headed home. On our way, I happened to drive past the L.A. Library on Fifth Street. It's an imposing architectural structure that bears Byzantine, Roman, and Egyptian influences with some Spanish and modern themes. The building has survived earthquakes, fire, and one ill-advised attempt at civic improvement. It has been beautifully restored and now houses millions of volumes. I'd always been amazed that John had quoted *Tonio Kröger*. It had surprised me when he'd mentioned a Dantean nightmare. When I'd hit him, all those months ago, we were just one block from here.

I pulled the car to the curb and told Alexa that I would be

right back. Then I ran up the steps of the library and went inside.

"Do you have a guy who comes in here, got a terrible haircut with chopped off dreads? Skinny, homeless black guy who smells bad?"

"Classic literature, second floor," the librarian said without even looking up.

That's where I found him. He was still wearing Chooch's sweatshirt. The blood had been washed off, but the knife holes were still there.

"John?" I said.

He turned, a book of Shakespearian plays in his grimy hands.

"How ya doin', half-stepper?" More or less his standard greeting.

"I've been looking all over for you. It's cold outside. I was thinkin' you could come home with me, get a hot meal, stay a few days till this cold snap passes."

"You wanna invite me to stay in your dumb-ass garage, then throw me out 'fore I can even get a good night's sleep? I'm onto you. I got your ways. You won't be foolin' no more with the Crown Prince of Cameroon. On the Nickel I may not be popular, but at least they understand me."

"John, I'm pretty sure you saved Alexa's life," I finally admitted. "I don't know how to square that. It's the greatest gift anybody has ever given me."

He closed the book and set it on the shelf, then pulled another down. He didn't seem to care.

"She wants to meet you. She's outside waiting. I brought some warm clothes for you. A new parka and some warm sweatpants, some money for a hot meal."

His eyes got bright with mischief. "Now you finally talkin'."

We left the library, but not before one of the security guards thoroughly searched John. Apparently he'd been caught stealing books and pawning them at Jungle Jack's.

"I ain't never coming back here. Gonna go to another city," he promised the guard. "This town don't know how ta treat a royal personage."

I led him to the Acura and Alexa rolled down the window and looked at my scruffy friend.

"You're John Bodine?" she said, smiling up at him.

"I'm Samik Mampuna, Crown Prince of the Bassaland," he corrected her.

"Shane tells me you saved my life. I wanted to thank you."

He seemed embarrassed, then said, "I didn't do shit." He turned to me. "Is zat enough? Do I gotta say any more? How 'bout them warm clothes and what-alls?"

I went to the trunk, got them out, and handed them to him along with four fifties. I watched as he put the clothes on over what he was wearing.

"Things are way too big. Whyn't cha get me stuff that fits?" he complained. "You a complete piece a shit, you know that? You ain't worth yer weight in vomit. Still gonna go get me a smart street lawyer. Your junk's all gonna be mine 'fore long."

"I'll be here if you ever need me, John," I told him gently.

"Who needs some run-me-down-lie-like-a-junkie popcorn fart like you?"

He turned and, shaking his head in disgust, started up the street wearing my new parka with the fur collar turned up. He didn't have his shopping cart tonight. Somebody had probably taken it from him. He looked small and alone, and I was still worried for his safety.

I got behind the wheel, but before I could start the engine, John came back and knocked on Alexa's window. She rolled it down and he looked in at her for a long time. His expression was puzzled, as if he couldn't remember what he wanted to say.

"Yes?" she finally asked.

Then he held up one of the fifties and showed it to her.

"This the only muthafucka ever feeds me," he told her solemnly. Then he turned and walked slowly up the street, finally disappearing in the dark.

It was the last time I ever saw him.

ACKNOWLEDGMENTS

No book gets written without a lot of help from experts. This one was no exception. High on the list of thanks is Jonathan Hiatt, M.D., professor and chief of the Division of Surgery at UCLA. John went through all my brain injury material, straightened me out, and made suggestions. If there are any brain docs out there who find problems with the information noted here, please know they are mine alone. Christopher Chaney, a Pasadena defense attorney, was a great help to me with all the legal stuff. LAPD Sgt. Lamont Jarrett, who is also a novelist, was a big help with the criminal justice material.

I received a lot of help at the LAPD and the Men's Central Jail, especially from Sgt. Kenneth Santolla of the Jail Division and Bond Clerk LaDona Moore.

342   *Acknowledgments*

Thanks to Steven Greener for all of his insight into the world of rap and to Detective III Skip Bachman of the LAPD, an old friend from years back who saw me sitting in the waiting area at the Men's Central Jail one day and said, "What the hell are you doing here, man?" We went to lunch, and as always, Skip was a wealth of information.

Thanks to Joe Kaczorowski, president of the House of Blues, and his assistant, Mary Lou Antkoviak, both old friends who used to be with Cannell Studios. They hooked me up with HOB VP of Operations, John Van Zeebroek, who in turn walked me through the Las Vegas material.

At St. Martin's Press, I am blessed by my publisher, Sally Richardson, and my editor, Charles Spicer. These two friends have never failed to support me. My thanks to Matthew Shear, my St. Martin's publishing guru on the paperback side, also to Joseph Cleeman, my associate editor and all-around good guy, and to Matt Baldacci, friend and marketing genius.

Thanks to my agent, Robert Gottlieb at Trident Media Group, for guiding and shaping my novel-writing career and for being a great coach and friend.

A little closer to home in L.A. are the troops in my office. Jane Whitney, who works tirelessly on the manuscripts, inputting, catching goofs, and adding comments. My right hand and troubleshooter, Kathy Ezso, is a bulletproof editor in her own right. Without her, I'd be stuck in traffic somewhere on the Pasadena Freeway. Thanks to Jo Swerling for advice and criticism.

Most important, thanks to my family. My three children, Tawnia, Chelsea, and Cody, who light the fire in my heart, and to my beautiful wife, Marcia, who received the dedication in this book by being my soul mate and partner for life. I met Marcia in the seventh grade and married her right after college. Forty-two years later we're still in love. Shane has Alexa and she's great, but Marcia is perfect.